W9-CLV-243

BERSERKER'S STAR

Tor Books by Fred Saberhagen

THE BERSERKER® SERIES

The Berserker Wars
Berserker Base (with Poul Anderson, Ed Bryant, Stephen
    Donaldson, Larry Niven, Connie Willis, and Roger Zelazny)
Berserker: Blue Death
The Berserker Throne
Berserker's Planet
Berserker Kill
Berserker Fury
Berserker's Star
Berserker Prime (forthcoming)

THE DRACULA SERIES

The Dracula Tapes
The Holmes-Dracula Files
Dominion
A Matter of Taste
A Question of Time
Séance for a Vampire
A Sharpness on the Neck
A Coldness in the Blood

THE SWORDS SERIES

The First Book of Swords
The Second Book of Swords
The Third Book of Swords
The First Book of Lost Swords: Woundhealer's Story
The Second Book of Lost Swords: Sightblinder's Story
The Third Book of Lost Swords: Stonecutter's Story
The Fourth Book of Lost Swords: Farslayer's Story
The Fifth Book of Lost Swords: Coinspinner's Story
The Sixth Book of Lost Swords: Mindsword's Story
The Seventh Book of Lost Swords: Wayfinder's Story
The Last Book of Swords: Shieldbreaker's Story
An Armory of Swords (editor)

THE BOOKS OF THE GODS

The Face of Apollo
Ariadne's Web
The Arms of Hercules
God of the Golden Fleece
Gods of Fire and Thunder

OTHER BOOKS

A Century of Progress
Coils (with Roger Zelazny)
Dancing Bears
Earth Descended
The Mask of the Sun
Merlin's Bones
The Veils of Azlaroc
The Water of Thought
Gene Roddenberry's Earth: Final Conflict—The Arrival

FRED SABERHAGEN

BERSERKER'S STAR

TOR®

A TOM DOHERTY ASSOCIATES BOOK

NEW YORK

East Baton Rouge Parish Library
Baton Rouge, Louisiana

This is a work of fiction. All the characters and events portrayed in this novel are either fictitious or are used fictitiously.

BERSERKER'S STAR

Copyright © 2003 by Fred Saberhagen

All rights reserved, including the right to reproduce this book, or portions thereof in any form.

This book is printed on acid-free paper.

A Tor Book
Published by Tom Doherty Associates, LLC
175 Fifth Avenue
New York, NY 10010

www.tor.com

Tor® is a registered trademark of Tom Doherty Associates, LLC.

Library of Congress Cataloging-in-Publication Data

Saberhagen, Fred, 1930–
    Berserker's star / Fred Saberhagen.—1st ed.
        p. cm.
    "A Tom Doherty Associates book."
    ISBN: 0-765-30423-6 (alk. paper)
    1. Space warfare—Fiction. I. Title.

  PS3569.A215B476 2003
  813'.54—dc21

                                                          2003041016

First Edition: June 2003

Printed in the United States of America

0 9 8 7 6 5 4 3 2 1

BERSERKER'S STAR

O N E

If the Templar colonel hadn't warned Harry Silver not to transport anyone from Hong's World to Maracanda—hadn't told Mr. Silver he'd better not even think of moving his ship in that direction—Harry might have managed to ignore the young woman and her heartbreaking story. And if Harry had ignored her, he certainly would not have listened to the two men who also claimed a pressing need to get to the same place.

And if the Space Force captain, bustling along worriedly half an hour after the Templar, hadn't made a point of looking Harry up to repeat the colonel's warning almost word for word, Harry might still have turned down his three potential passengers. But as matters stood, with two separate and eminently respectable authorities practically commanding him to stay away from a certain world, he found the temptation to go there all but irresistible.

That was even before he took into account the chance to make a good amount of money on what amounted to a private charter.

"I will pay you very well, Mr. Silver, to carry me to Maracanda," the young woman was saying now. Her voice was small and intense, a good match for her body. So far she had told Harry very little about herself, beyond the fact that her name was Lily Gunnlod, and she was trying to catch up with her husband, who was named Alan, and who seemed to have abandoned her and flown away to get himself into some kind of trouble in a distant solar system.

Lily was actually claiming that her dear Alan had been kidnapped, carried away by religious fanatics, but Harry had his doubts about that.

Meanwhile the two men, who had introduced themselves as Mr. Redpath and Mr. Dietrich, claimed to have vital business on Maracanda, and an urgent need to get there quickly. The four people were gathered outdoors on a pleasant evening, while around them the evacuation of Hong's World moved steadily along, a more orderly process than Harry had expected it to be. Getting a million or so people, the whole population of a sparsely settled planet, onto ships and into space was a sizable job—though, of course, if the population had been a billion or more, it would have been a whole lot worse.

All four people in Harry's little group had recently been traveling, and all were wearing slightly different versions of a practical garment, the more-or-less standard coveralls that a lot of people liked to wear on long space flights.

"It is a matter of life and death to me, Mr. Silver. I tell you my husband has practically been kidnapped." Over the past several hours Lily Gunnlod had repeated virtually the same words so many times that Harry had lost track. She hadn't really filled in any details yet, but then he hadn't asked for any.

This time she was leaning a little closer, directing her dark and burning gaze right into Harry's eyes, as if to hypnotize him. He had been stared at before, but not very often as fiercely as this. Somehow he had the impression that all the fine muscles in Lily's little body must be thrumming like taut wires. The world she wanted to go to was one that Harry didn't know, had never heard of as far as he could remember. A place called Maracanda, where she was convinced she was going to find her husband.

Gradually she was filling in a few more details. It didn't sound like the people she accused of kidnapping her dear Alan had actually tied him up and carried him off. No, the implication seemed to be that her once-faithful husband had been seduced by some strange religious doctrine, his mind warped by the fantastic stories and promises of dangerous cultists. To Harry it sounded like a good bet that one of the dangerous cultists would turn out to be a woman, though, so far, Lily hadn't suggested anything along that line.

The home that Lily and her husband had once shared was in a solar system a long way from Hong's World, on whose surface she and Harry were standing now. Even farther than Maracanda, and in the opposite direction.

She seemed genuinely young, partly because of her fierce demeanor, and if she hadn't kept going on about how much she wanted to find her deranged husband, Harry might have allowed himself to find her distractingly attractive.

Harry, a man of indeterminate age, average height, and wiry build, was standing up straight with his arms folded. He wore lightweight flight boots and his own slightly modified version of simple coveralls. The look of his hands and hairy forearms suggested superior physical strength. His nose had once been pushed slightly sideways and never perfectly repaired. His eyes were dark, his hair moderately short and darkish.

With thousands of occupied planets in the portion of the Galaxy now settled by Earth-descended humans, some of the planets known to different people by different names, it wasn't strange that someone could name a world that Harry had never heard of. Or maybe he had heard of it and just couldn't recall the details. But he had a hazy impression that there was something truly extraordinary about the place.

He asked the woman now: "Just where the hell is Maracanda?"

Redpath, one of the eager businessmen who had been waiting their turn to plead, answered for her. "It is in the Aleph Sector." Evidently Mr. Redpath's own need to get to Maracanda was so urgent that it had caused him to develop a nervous tic, which kept his eyebrows moving erratically. In general, he had a lean and hungry look.

Dietrich, the other businessman, was a solidly built fellow now standing behind Lily on her left. From time to time Dietrich nodded his head, as if to assure Harry that the arguments his colleague and Lily were putting up were valid. Mr. Dietrich did not seem nervous at all. What his hard stare seemed to indicate was meanness, though he had hardly opened his mouth since Harry met him. Redpath and Dietrich were wearing modest backpacks strapped over their coveralls, and a similar pack rested at the lady's feet.

The four of them were standing on the edge of a broad esplanade leading to the local spaceport, under a pleasant, starlit evening sky in which traces of sunset still lingered. They had formed a compact group because of the pressure of traffic, foot and vehicular, moving steadily round them. Now and then the group shuffled a little this way or that, its members doing what they could to keep out of the busy flow in two directions of people and slow-moving machines. So far the whole process of evacuation was not nearly as noisy as it might have been.

Harry wanted to make sure that his prospective passengers understood the situation. "I hope you people realize that you don't need to hire me, or anyone, just to get away safely. The Space Force and Templars have both sworn they'll get everybody off world in time. In a case like this, I'd be inclined to believe 'em."

"I understand the position," said Lily Gunnlod. She spoke the common language with an accent that Harry could not quite place. "Both the Templars and the Space Force have strongly urged us to take passage aboard one of the rescue vessels they have so gallantly provided. But the problem is that both organizations insist on carrying us in the wrong direction, farther from Maracanda."

"That is our case also," said Mr. Redpath, lean and nervous.

Harry still addressed himself to Lily. "That's because they think it's dangerous to go where you want to go. They're probably right. You know, I've been warned, twice in the last couple of standard hours, not to take you people there."

The three received that news with no surprise at all. The woman surprised Harry, though, when she said: "But I have seen you, Mr. Silver, in a vision. And I know that you are going to help me find my Alan."

"Yeah?" That made him pause for a moment. "Visions don't gain you any points with me, lady. Mystic prophecies have a strong tendency to be wrong."

The woman only looked at him, while the twilight wind of Hong's World blew at her curly hair, under the slowly darkening, perpetually moonless sky. She was being patient, but she seemed to have the attitude that all of Harry's objections were irrelevant.

He was almost sure, now, that he was going to try to please little Lily by doing what she wanted. And of course if he was going to Maracanda, he might as well take the two men, too. But experience cautioned that he should first try for more information.

He said to Lily: "I don't want to charge you lots of money for a wild goose chase. Tell me more about this missing husband, and what makes you so damned sure that he's on Maracanda."

"I know my dear Alan must be there because I know who his

kidnappers are, and what they intended when they lured him away." Lily's voice was strong and sure, but with those words, emotion came surging up behind her eyes. It did not seem to be the kind of feeling that brought forth tears. Desperate action would be more likely.

"Why do you doubt the woman?" asked Redpath, sounding nervous.

Harry looked at him. "I thought you didn't know her, or her husband?"

The lean man blinked. "That is correct. As I have told you, my partner and I encountered the lady for the first time here, only a few hours ago. But I am convinced she tells the truth."

On the other side of Lily, Dietrich nodded.

"If it's really kidnapping, it sounds like a police matter," Harry observed.

Lily was shaking her head. "You don't know what the police are like on my home world."

Harry had to admit that that was true.

She added: "Besides, even if they were fully competent, they can't help me here and now."

Also true, Harry supposed. Still looking his potential passengers over, he said: "You understand *why* the Templars and the Space Force are warning me not to take my ship in the direction the three of you want me to go? You do know something about berserkers?" It was hardly possible to be a human in the Galaxy and not know that, but Harry wanted to make the point.

"I know enough," the woman answered quickly. Her attitude kept insisting *let's get on with it*. The two men nodded.

Harry wasn't finished. "Then you understand it's quite possible that the bad machines have somehow caught wind of the fact that this whole system is being evacuated. So a berserker force might be deploying this way." The robotic killers could have high expectations of catching a large swarm of human craft, many with little or no armament, only second- or third-rate defensive shields, in disorderly flight.

The deadly danger posed by a nova sun, the threat that sent all the humans of Hong's World flying for their lives, would mean nothing but opportunity to berserker machines. They had been created, as an ultimate weapon, by a race about whom little else was known. A race now called the Builders, who had been engaged in a desperate war, at a time when humanity on Earth still lived in caves and fought with clubs.

Programmed to destroy everything that lived, berserkers were agents and engines of death. Ages ago, these superb weapons had turned on their living creators and reduced the Builders to little more than interstellar dust. But still the weapons themselves raged on and on across the Galaxy, endlessly repairing and reproducing themselves, improving their own design and refining their killing capabilities.

No death machine had ever been deterred by the prospect of its own annihilation. The only value a berserker's calculations assigned to its own existence lay in its killing power. The only real loss it perceived in its own destruction was the subtraction of that measure of power from the total available to the cause of death.

While the four people stood conversing, the businesslike evacuation kept going on around them. So far, the sounds and sights and smells of fear and chaotic confusion were present only in potential. Thanks to the Space Force and the Templars, the two separate organizations for once cooperating smoothly, there were nerves and there was grumbling, but no screaming panic.

"In this case, Mr. Silver," said Redpath, "we cannot allow even berserkers to stop us."

And Dietrich finally opened his mouth to challenge Harry: "Do they terrify you, Mr. Silver?"

Harry squinted at the fellow. "They have, in the past. They

probably will again. But not when the chance of meeting 'em's no greater than it seems to be in this situation. I can accept a reasonable amount of danger—for a reasonable price."

It was the first time he had raised the question of payment. The woman promptly named a figure. Redpath and Dietrich exchanged glances, and the lean man said: "We will match that sum."

Harry raised his eyebrows. "You're all willing to pay that much, I guess you're really serious about it."

"I am serious indeed." Lily prodded: "You have been recommended to us, Mr. Silver. We hear you are a very good pilot."

"I am."

"And willing to take chances."

Harry nodded. "That's sometimes true as well."

Redpath put in: "We have even heard that you are wanted by the Space Force, in a certain other sector of the Galaxy, for stealing a c-plus cannon." The lean man smiled at Harry when that got a reaction. "Oh, not that we object! If the story is true, it shows a degree of—well, of enterprise—on your part that we in our present situation find very attractive."

The Space Force captain a little while ago, when warning Harry against accepting this job, hadn't brought up the matter of the cannon, doubtlessly because she hadn't yet been told about it. But it was no idle rumor. In another sector of the Galaxy, not enormously far away by fast starship, certain Space Force officers were much interested in finding Harry Silver, were trying very seriously to charge him with that spectacular theft.

All three of Harry's prospective clients were eyeing him fiercely, with varying degrees of what seemed a near impossible mixture of fear, respect, hope, disapproval, and secret admiration. There might have been a hint of blackmail in Redpath's remark: *Do what we ask, or we turn you in to the local authorities.* If so, the blackmailer had miscalculated. Whatever authorities might currently remain on Hong's World had all they could handle just trying to get everyone evacuated, and they were not about to start any kind of legal proceedings in a courtroom that would soon be vaporized.

Mr. Dietrich seemed to have been the most impressed by the story. "A c-plus cannon," he marveled quietly, shaking his head. He sounded shocked, not so much by the idea of a crime as by the spectacular magnitude of Harry's daring.

Harry stared grimly back at the solidly built man. "It's a long story, based on a misunderstanding. Explanations never catch up with rumors, but maybe I should give one anyway. Actually, it was the Space Force who installed the cannon on my ship—there was some berserker trouble at the time. When that was over, of course, they wanted the damned thing back. Well, there were reasons why I couldn't find a good convenient time and place to hand it over."

Evidently none of the three before him cared much about his explanation, not even enough to listen to it carefully.

"You've simply got to take us," the young woman was saying to Harry now, while on either side of her her escort stood nodding their heads earnestly in agreement.

Meanwhile, all around them the good citizens of Hong's World, nervous and busy, some with tear-streaked faces but not yet frantic, were still coming and going, on foot and in a variety of slow-moving vehicles. Some were carrying bags and boxes, odd household items, a strange assortment of objects that they hoped to save if there turned out to be room on the evacuation ships. Now Harry thought the people might be stepping up the pace a bit. Many of those who passed kept taking quick glances up at the twilight sky.

Hong's World had never possessed any noticeable moons, and where Harry was standing, the local sun had sunk below the horizon half an hour ago. But the sky contained an impressive array of stars.

There was one very bright star in particular, a white dwarf informally known to the inhabitants of Hong's World as Twinkler, and actually a distant binary partner of Hong's Sun. The people who were getting on as fast as they could with their evacuation kept casting nervous glances up at Twinkler's cheerful little image. Not that there could be anything remarkable to see in that bright dancing spark—not for several hours yet.

But everyone knew that peaceful presence was a horrible illusion. Something extraordinary indeed was on its way from Twinkler toward Hong's World, a vast change sweeping on to engulf this pleasant planet, to end the life of anyone who might still be on it at the time.

Twinkler had recently undergone a sudden and surprising metamorphosis. The consequences of that change were approaching Hong's World, the wavefront of a stellar explosion, a deadly eruption of radiation and particles, moving as rapidly as light, more inevitable than sunrise. What was coming would put an end to all sunrises and sunsets when it arrived. But hours would pass before the Twinkler's soft and mellow image swelled rapidly into a glaring blast of light and other radiation, a blinding, destroying, angel of death. Thanks to the Templars and the Space Force, there was every reason to hope that when it did, there would be no living eyes remaining on this world to register the impact.

There had better not be. Humans could fight berserkers, and could sometimes even win against them. But no one could fight a nearby sun gone supernova.

The little star just winked at Harry slightly as he glanced up at it. He knew the twinkle was innocent, simply a common effect of planetary atmosphere, but still Harry's nerves gave a little nervous twitch each time it happened. Twinkler seemed such a cheerful, bright companion, pure and simple, ready to offer a reliable beacon through this planet's perpetually moonless nights. Fully deserving of the place it had held in local children's stories, through the generations since this world was colonized.

Meanwhile, an intermittent stream of ships kept dribbling up into the sky, from this spaceport and others scattered around the planet. The warning had come in time, because it had been carried by a robotic courier traveling much faster than the blast. If all went smoothly, the great withdrawal would be accomplished in good time.

Fortunately, a robotic observatory had been in orbit around Twinkler, and signs of the explosion had been detected early, in the form of a veritable avalanche of precursor neutrinos. Particles with virtually no mass, traveling as fast as light, had been picked up within minutes by automatic sensors, while the blast front of the explosion itself was still fulminating within the outer layers of a star suddenly gone berserk; neutrinos passed through that barrier, as they did through almost everything else, as if it were not there at all. The warning, rushed on by superluminal robot courier, had reached Hong's World in time to allow for evacuation.

Fortunately, as it had turned out, the population of the single habitable planet in Hong's system had never been much higher than one million people. And within a matter of days more than a thousand ships, summoned by swift couriers from other relatively nearby systems, had been mobilized for the job of getting them away. Between the Space Force and the Templars, there was every reason to believe that the job of evacuation was going to be successfully accomplished.

All of which was a notable relief to Harry Silver. He shuddered inwardly at the thought of having to pack his *Witch of Endor* with refugees, like fish in a freezer. He would like to get off the planet before the authorities changed their collective mind and decided they had better pack his ship with people after all.

Packing his ship to maximum capacity with people would have meant dumping his expensive cargo of freight right here on the ramp, just abandoning it to be stolen or destroyed, accepting dead economic loss. As matters stood, he could still nurse hopes of being able to sell the specialized machinery on some other world.

Harry was beginning to wonder whether the authorities might have overshot the mark a bit in their effort to prevent panic. The likelihood of everyone being safely evacuated was so well established that it even left some people room for argument as to whether the whole thing was necessary.

One of these, a fellow actually carrying a placard, had stopped to confront the little group of four—probably because everyone else in sight was obviously too busy to listen to him.

At the moment the fibers in the smart material of his sign were showing bold black letters on a white background, reading: WE ALL BELONG TO HONG. Even as Harry watched, the message changed, translating itself into another language. Maybe, Harry thought, the protester believed this lovely planet harbored similar feelings of loyalty toward him.

In keeping with an ancient tradition having to do with prophecies and prophets, the placard-carrying man had wrapped himself in a white cloth sheet that was seemingly his only garment, except for a pair of sandals that had a handmade look. The prophet's voice was melodious, loud, and commanding. Maybe, thought Harry, what had decided the fellow to take up this line of work was just the opportunity to show off his voice and bearing. The volume of his voice was boosted, and the tones rendered rich and full, by an invisible amplifier that Harry thought must be buried somewhere in his beard.

His physical presence was not as commanding as he evidently thought it was. But whatever impression he might have made on people in ordinary times, at the moment few were paying him any attention.

The burden of the prophet's argument seemed to be that there were, after all, deep shelters, dug out early in the settlement process, in anticipation of a berserker attack that had never materialized.

"They are deep indeed, a thousand kilometers down in living rock. We should be down there now, letting Mother Hong shield and protect her children."

Glad to see that he had the attention of Harry and his group, the protester pointed with a full extension of his arm, a winning, dramatic gesture. "The stars look all right to me. Twinkler looks the same as ever."

Lily and the two men flanking her were still awaiting Harry's answer, but he kept being distracted by the show going on behind them. Now another had appeared, a contrarian demonstrator who stopped to complain about the way the evacuation was being handled. This fellow had chosen white for his prophetic garment also, in the form of a long coat formally buttoned.

The burden of the message urged by Prophet Number Two was that everything would be all right if only the problem could be managed in accordance with the precepts and techniques of science. In fact, he had calculated that everyone on the side of the world away from Twinkler could survive.

"I have developed overwhelming proof on my computer. Also, if the Great Light was really coming, it would be here now."

Glad of an audience, if only a small one and annoyed, Prophet Two pressed on. And if, he was saying, for safety's sake, it really might be better to get everyone off this planet, then the matter should be approached scientifically. And if some group really insisted on staying, well, it would improve the gene pool of the race to let them have their way.

Harry wondered if uniformed caretakers were going to show

up at the last moment and drag the white-clad pair away to some hospital ship for their own good. But that was quite unlikely. All of this world's caretakers were on their way out, along with everybody else.

One and Two now seemed to have reached some measure of agreement. One chimed in: "Well, I mean it might be possible to leave some kind of sensors, to measure and record how great an effect the explosion actually does have when it reaches this planet. Then when it's all over, and people come back, we can see just how much of a danger it actually represented."

Harry put on a thoughtful expression and looked around. "You know, that never occurred to me. And you know what else? I'd say there's been a sharp drop in the price of local real estate. There must be some terrific bargains waiting to be snapped up."

Prophet Two seemed ready to take him seriously. "I wouldn't be surprised," he answered. "You know, I wouldn't be surprised if someone has been doing just that. This whole panic could have been started for that very purpose."

Two drew a deep breath, having built what seemed an excellent foundation from which to launch a speech. After all, everything, everything in the human universe, came down to a matter of money. The whole business of evacuation was a hoax, a scheme, set in motion by certain corporations interested in real estate.

Prophet One chimed in, disputing details. The argument between them was degenerating into a haggling over costs. And taxes, especially taxes. There was no understanding a government that forced rich people to pay them. This had something to do with the fact that the evacuation was all a government plot, hatched by socialists who intended to seize the people's property.

Meanwhile, Harry had some business to conclude. Loudly he broke in, "But that's a lovely idea, about recording the explosion." He might almost have been sincere. His voice dropped to an undertone, as if he were speaking to himself: "I wonder I

didn't think of it—there are days when I have ideas like that."
More loudly: "Where will you mount your recording devices and
sensors?"

Prophet Number Two was ready to carry the argument forward—maybe it was worthwhile having your world destroyed if
that gave you grounds for such a delicious protest. He looked
about him at the solid paving of the esplanade, the sprawling
hectares of the spaceport, almost empty, on one side. "Would it
matter that much where you put them? Some of them on the surface, of course. How about right here? And bury the others deep."

Harry appeared to find that an impressive insight. "Hey,
you're right. It wouldn't matter. Could put 'em right here, or over
there. Or even bring all the sensors down in your deep shelter
with you."

"No, you couldn't—"

"How deep is this wonderful shelter? Maybe twenty thousand kilometers?"

Prophet Two looked at him almost pityingly; he thought
Harry had his numbers all scrambled, just didn't understand. "Sir,
the planet is only twelve thousand kilometers in diameter. The
deep shelters, the ones that are available right now, and have room
to save us all, are a full thousand kilometers underground."

"And no berserker is going to dig that deep—you hope. But
one thousand klicks is too shallow to do us any good today, and
twelve thousand would be no better. Because a few hours from
now, when Twinkler's blast front hits this world, it'll turn every
centimeter of that to flying atoms."

Harry took a step closer, as if the argument had turned personal. "You clodpate, we're talking about *a Type Three supernova*,
less than a full light-month from where we're standing. Maybe
you should put your sensors on the surface of Hong's Sun. It'll be
the only thing in this system that survives, and it'll be seriously
roughed up."

One of Harry's potential customers was applauding. Lily's cute little face had lit up with something like enthusiasm. The two businessmen just stood there looking sour, waiting for this babble to be over.

Prophets One and Two, united at last, were regarding the four of them as if they were all entirely crazy.

. . . .

T W O

. . . .

Later, Harry could never remember the exact words with which the fateful contract had been concluded, but at some point he had found himself agreeing to carry Lily where she wished to go. Then, having committed himself, he thought he might as well bring the businessmen along. Now all four of them were walking briskly toward Harry's ship.

Calm-voiced messages, meant to be reassuring, were being broadcast almost continuously over the public communication system. There were plenty of ships available, and so forth. Few people seemed to be paying much attention. One of the details being casually mentioned in passing, though certainly not emphasized, was the fact that berserkers were known to be in an adjoining sector of the Galaxy. No problem. The evacuation ships would be taking everyone in the opposite direction.

Both Templars and Space Force were doing more than simply commanding and enforcing evacuation, carrying refugees away. Several billion kilometers from here, they were also deploying fighting ships to try to intercept the anticipated berserker attack.

Even as Harry and his new clients trudged along, they could watch one of the big evacuation vessels lifting off, looking huge though it was kilometers away. It was packed, Harry was certain, with hundreds, perhaps thousands, of human beings, and whatever personal belongings they were being allowed to take.

At that moment, some anonymous Templar with an imperious voice, made all the more commanding by amplifiers in a passing groundcar, was ordering all owners of private ships to stand by, delaying liftoff until further notice. All cargo space aboard ships still on the ground was being commandeered for priority freight salvage.

Harry's arm snapped up in a crisp salute, acknowledging the order, the suggestion of instant obedience somewhat spoiled by the gesture's being delivered left-handed. Otherwise he kept moving without breaking stride, shepherding his three clients with him.

"How much of a problem is that going to be?" Dietrich asked, looking back over his shoulder at the groundcar as it slowly cruised away.

Harry kept going. "None at all, as long as we ignore it."

Prophets One and Two, once more arguing fiercely with each other, had vanished in the passing throng. Everywhere heads were bobbing up and down as people kept looking up at the gradually darkening sky, as if they might be able to see the great doom coming before it got here. Pointless, of course, but Harry caught himself repeatedly doing the same thing.

Here on the balmy surface of Hong's World, it was still a

warm, clear evening. A well-dressed woman, trudging along with her children in the same direction, was trying to explain to her young teenager that yes, all the stars would continue to look just fine, until the star in question started to look a little strange, about an hour before the arrival of the blast front.

The children all nodded, wide-eyed. They were ready to be taken care of, as they had been for all of their short lives.

Then abruptly the young girl turned to Harry, who happened to be walking beside her, because, he supposed, his boots and coveralls might make him look like some kind of an authority. He hoped it wasn't simply the way he walked that would give people that impression.

The girl asked: "Are the berserkers doing it?" Her voice, her look, held a hint of fear.

Harry needed a couple of seconds to decide that the question wasn't really all that crazy. "Even berserkers can't fire up a nova at will. Though they're probably working on it."

The mother was looking at him now. "But other people say the Twinkler is actually going to explode."

"Not 'going to,' lady, it already has." Let someone like the recent demonstrator get to this woman, and she might refuse to leave. Her choice, but the threat to the children bothered Harry.

He said: "What you now see in the sky is like a recording of Twinkler's last few hours of peaceful life. Get your kids on that ship. Don't let any of these loonies talk you into staying."

Over the next few years, here in this relatively crowded stellar neighborhood, the blast wave of Twinkler's nova was going to totally wipe out several solar systems, purge them not only of existing life but also of seedbed planets that could conceivably produce new generations. All of their orbiting rock would go, everything that was smaller than the stars themselves. When the coming wavefront really hit, planets as massive as Jupiter would disappear, like seeds blown off a thistle in a gale.

That thought brought lines of poetry popping into mind. When Harry had first heard of the disaster, he'd talked to his ship about it, and the *Witch,* as she sometimes did, had come up with an appropriate quotation:

> *When shall the stars be blown about the sky,*
> *Like the sparks blown out of a smithy, and die?*
> *Surely thine hour has come, thy great wind blows,*
> *Far-off, most secret, and inviolate Rose?*

It was supposedly from some ancient work called "The Secret Rose," by one William Butler Yeats. Harry wasn't sure just what a "smithy" was supposed to be.

His thoughts jumped back to the protester's plan of somehow recording the disaster. Humanity, of course, enjoyed the advantage of having ships and robotic couriers that could effectively move much faster than light, were capable of jumping out of harm's way in a small fraction of a second. Still, it would be very hard to record the advancing wavefront, or even look at it, this close to its source, so soon after the explosion. There were only a few premonitory signals. The thing propagated so fast that there was no seeing it until it had arrived. Only later, months or years later, would it be possible to stand off and watch from a safe distance.

Even though no human eye had yet beheld it, the wavefront of destruction was rushing on at the speed of light, engulfing every second a vaster volume of space. With the advantages of superluminal travel, people would still be able, for years to come, to see those ruined stars and planets as they had been, when life swarmed in their systems.

The trick, thought Harry, would be to have your robot ship emerge from flightspace immediately behind the blast front, in an area of normal space through which the front had just passed—

except that, when things got as bad as it seemed they were going to get, the continuous outpouring in that region of several kinds of radiation would quickly overwhelm even the most heavily shielded ships, first smothering the sensors and then vaporizing them, so that little or nothing could be seen or recorded. But still it was likely that someone would send a robot ship to try.

Running an eye over his new customers, as they all kept moving on, Harry once more took note of their small packs. "You people have any additional baggage you want to bring?"

Redpath and Dietrich shook their heads no. Lily said, "I have everything I need, thank you, Mr. Silver. How long will the flight to Maracanda take?"

"Can't say until I consult with my ship's data bank. But with a little luck, I'll get you where you want to go."

"Actually," Lily observed, "Alan would tell you that what you call luck will have little to do with our prospects of success."

"Oh?"

"No, he'd say that our fates are in the hands of great Malakó." She walked in silence for a few strides. "Alan's been looking all his life for something—something real and permanent. Maybe he's found it at last."

Harry looked at her sideways. "A great truth provided by his kidnappers."

Lily shook her head. "Every system of belief has its fanatics, people who carry things too far. I'm hoping that most of the people in this Malakó thing will be comparatively sane."

"You can always hope." Harry kept walking, but turned his head. "Haven't heard of the great Malakó. Is she—or he—the one in charge of seeing that the stars burn steadily?"

"If I were already a believer, Mr. Silver, I would find your flippancy offensive. If my husband were here, I don't know what would happen."

Harry blinked at her mildly. "I'm not trying to be offensive. It just comes naturally."

She gave him a brief and thin-lipped smile. "In any case, the answer to your question is actually yes. My husband, according to the note he left me, is now solemnly convinced that Malakó is in charge, as you put it, of all the stars and all the worlds and all the life within the Galaxy." She paused. "Maybe I will come to believe also."

In fact, Harry had heard the name of Malakó before. About all he knew about it was that there was a cult, or religion, whose members deified and worshiped the Galaxy—just as, in olden times, there had been those who found Earth's little sun to be god enough, and more than enough, for them.

Whether any god could be blamed for it or not, Twinkler's great explosion had already happened, there could be no argument about that.

Now another huge ship was lifting off from the nearby field, and shortly after it yet one more. Harry was thinking that most of the towns, the settlements, isolated estates, all across Hong's World, would be deserted now. A lot of work and planning gone for nothing.

" 'All that calm Sunday, that goes on and on,' " said Harry in a musing voice.

Lily was crisp. "That sounds like some kind of quotation, Mr. Silver."

"Blame my ship. She likes quoting poetry at me. I've heard so much of it, I'm starting to do the same thing."

He could feel his clients all looking at him, trying to decide whether the man about to take them on his ship just might be crazy as a loon.

*   *   *

Harry found himself beginning to be intrigued by the woman and her quest. He asked her: "Does your Alan have more than one name?"

"Alan Gunnlod."

"He took your name when you married? Or—"

"Does it matter? Actually, I took his."

According to this young woman who evidently doted on him, Alan was also young, and just about his only flaw seemed to be that he was dangerously impressionable.

"He tends to become—very enthusiastic about things. And then he frequently becomes disillusioned, months or years later, and changes his mind. But when he does, sometimes it's too late."

Her manner did not soften when she talked about her husband, and Harry began to wonder if Alan would get a spanking when she caught up with him. It began to seem more probable that anyone married to this lady might earnestly consider the idea of going on an extended vacation from her, or getting away entirely. Of course, if you really had been grabbed by kidnappers, Lily could be a good one to have in charge of rescue operations. She might not be the smartest or the strongest one around, but she wasn't easily discouraged.

"I'll show you what he looks like," she was saying now. "I've got a holo of him here." And she brought a little cube, about a centimeter on a side, out of a pocket and twisted it to turn it on. "I'll set the image for life size," she added.

Lily retained the recording device on her small palm, but the glowing, life-sized image of a man, wearing what might have been the uniform of some athletic team, and carrying a wooden stick or bat, sprang out of it and kept pace with her as she walked. The image didn't walk, but just glided ghostlike beside her, tracking the cube still held in Lily's hand. Alan Gunnlod was making a fifth member of their group. Alan had a pale face, and a small black mustache.

Redpath and Dietrich looked on stolidly as they kept walking, a captive audience. None of this mattered to them, as long as they could get where they were going. When Harry had asked them casually what their business was, he'd got a two-word answer. "Mineral rights."

Evidently he was not going to be invited in on the ground floor of a new business opportunity that absolutely could not miss. That was something of a relief.

Alan wasn't saying anything, so it seemed that this was not his goodbye note to his wife. Harry supposed that might have been too personal to be exhibited to strangers.

Lily was looking at the object her husband's image was swinging gently back and forth, a specially shaped wooden club that Harry supposed might be used to hit some kind of ball. She said: "There was a time when he was all excited about sport rituals."

Harry grunted. He wasn't sure just what Alan's sport rituals might be, and he thought he could contentedly live out the rest of his life without finding out.

It was often very hard to tell the true age of anyone who was determined to look young, in this era when health and strength could often be prolonged for centuries, new teeth grown in as needed, and living skin preserved unwrinkled. Listening to Lily and looking at the holograph, Harry got the impression that Alan must be young indeed. And the more he looked at Lily, and listened to her, the younger she got, too.

"This was taken a few years ago," she admitted. "But he hasn't changed that much."

Harry nodded. "How long since you've actually seen him?

"It's been months. I'm beginning to lose track."

"But you say he left you some kind of message when he took off."

She sighed. "One thing that worries me is, I don't know if

he's eagerly expecting me to follow him or not. Maybe I've lost him. But I don't give up easily. I couldn't tell."

After a pause she went on simply: "The message he left wasn't about us, at all—it was just about Malakó, and how he had finally found what he'd been seeking all his life, and how wonderful it was."

Fiercely she squeezed the little message cube between her fingers, and Alan's ghost, still holding his game bat, obediently flew back into it.

Harry and his three paying passengers had turned off the main thoroughfare onto a side road, where they joined the steady flow of people to the landing field through one of the regular gates, which this evening was standing permanently open. The guard booth at the gate was deserted, and from a speaker on top of it a robotic voice was endlessly repeating some inane command having to do with the proper places to deposit surplus personal property. As far as Harry could tell, no one was paying the voice the least attention. In a few hours, all the depositories and all the property on this planet were going to be turned into a sleet of atoms.

These recorded orders were interlarded with warnings that the field was closed, and that people wanting to use it should make alternate arrangements. Harry supposed that the robots were doing the best they could when abandoned by all human supervision. He tried to derive what comfort he could from the thought that Twinkler was at least going to wipe out all this residue of recorded orders and advice.

Now the four people were walking a plain, narrow road across the field itself, passing one broad, empty landing pad after another, each with various connections, and all for fairly small craft, like Harry's. The big ships were normally assigned to another portion of the field.

There were notably fewer ships of any kind on the ground than there had been the last time Harry had passed this way, only a few hours ago. Those remaining were widely scattered, separated by hundreds of vacant berths. Some had queues of people standing before entrance hatches, in the process of an unhurried loading.

Slow-paced music, tuneful and familiar to the population of Hong's World, seemed to drift down out of the perishable sky itself. The robots again, doing what they could.

All in all, things seemed to be going as well as could be expected. Security in the usual sense was clearly at a minimum. Harry and his party were a couple of hundred meters into the field, almost at his ship, when a speeding groundcar stopped beside them and disgorged a Templar officer in battle dress—not the same one who had earlier tried to tell Harry where not to go.

He looked anxiously at Harry and his companions. Then he said: "I heard someone here was trying to complete a religious pilgrimage to Maracanda."

Lily stopped and turned. "My husband's gone there on pilgrimage, and I'm trying to catch up with him."

Harry had known a fair number of Templars over the years, and over various sectors of the settled Galaxy, and he had a lot of respect for some of them. In theory, and often in practice, they were a tightly run organization of dedicated people who devoted their lives and fortunes to battling berserkers. Sometimes the reality came close to the ideal. On occasion the Templars took the offensive. Other times, as now, they concentrated on protecting pilgrims and other travelers from the death machines. In practice this often meant trying to keep open certain lanes of space travel, organizing convoys and conducting evacuations.

Lily was telling the officer: "I don't know much about Templars."

Harry said: "All Templars I've ever met have been religious, in one way or another. Probably some are devotees of Malakó. All of them tend to view berserkers as an actual disease infecting the Galactic body—and themselves as cells of the immune system.

"I've told the lady that I'll take her there," Harry reassured the officer. He had to raise his voice because the noise level had gone up sharply, with the passage of a caravan of groundcars conveying more refugees to another of the remaining ships. Some more or less organized group was loud in the background, singing, chanting as they marched to their evacuation ship.

"I'll come with you," the Templar promised, "to make sure there's no trouble about you getting off."

All around them the great retreat was going on. Even as Harry watched, another ship, smaller than the previous leviathan, went up, buoyed by invisible force in undramatic silence, only a couple of hundred meters away. And now there went another.

The four reached Harry's ship. She was built in the shape of a somewhat elongated football, about eight meters wide where her beam was widest. She was sitting on her stern, ready for liftoff.

Harry Silver had owned this ship for some years—actually, for more years than he liked to think about. She wasn't new by any means, but he had done what he could to keep her equipment up to date.

The Templar observer frowned at some faint markings on one side of the hull. The letters were in an antique script, and difficult to read.

"What's your ship called?" the Templar asked.

"*Witch of Endor.*"

" 'Witch?' " The man seemed unfavorably impressed.

"It's just a name," Harry assured him.

Still, the officer gave Harry a long look. "Berserkers are reported out that way," the Templar observed at last.

"We know," said Harry. He was thinking that the next official who told him where to go or not to go would stand in some danger of being punched.

Instead, this officer rejoiced that Harry was going to take his coreligionist to join her husband on what amounted to a holy pilgrimage. He gave Lily Gunnlod a kind of benediction. "Blessings of Malakó upon you!"

The physical sign of the blessing followed. Raising both hands, fingers curved, to one eye, as if miming the use of a small handheld telescope.

When it seemed that the benediction was being widened to include him, Harry said: "Thanks very much, I'll take all the blessings I can get." He saw the faces of the two businessmen turn slightly, looking at him.

As the Templar moved away, Harry turned to Lily. "Benedictions are welcome, but I still want half payment in advance. Bank credits are okay, hard coin as usual is best."

"Of course." She opened a seam on her coveralls and reached into an inner pocket.

Dietrich and Redpath were doing the same thing, digging into pockets and coming up with their shares. This was the kind of sacred ceremony they obviously understood.

Harry got his payment—hard coin, in a material virtually impossible to counterfeit. In another moment he and his clients were moving on, right up to the flank of Harry's ship, the *Witch of Endor*. He laid his hand on the main hatch, for identification purposes, and began to subvocalize the code that would let them enter.

In another minute, the four of them and their modest baggage were aboard the *Witch*, hatches snugly closed. Since the local port authority had disappeared, there would be no formalities to delay their lifting off and departing from the Hong's World system.

His ship's data bank had no problem at all in coming up with a fairly direct route to Maracanda, which was indeed in the sector where Harry's passengers had placed it.

Then, with Lily Gunnlod and the two businessmen secure in chairs, just to be on the safe side, they were in readiness.

Harry was giving his full attention to the job, melding his mind with the thoughtware that controlled the ship. The artificial gravity eased itself on, almost imperceptibly taking over the business of determining up and down, light and heavy, the whole management of mass and inertia in the ship's interior. When Harry gave his *Witch* the mental command for liftoff, the peaceful-looking surface of Hong's World seemed to drop away from beneath them like a released bomb, but no one inside felt even a tug of acceleration.

Visible directly through cleared statglass ports, the Twinkler's pretty image, ceasing to twinkle now that the air was nearly all below them, still gave no hint of the blast of death it had spawned. A couple of hours of gentle, charming starlight still remained, no more than a fragile curtain over onrushing disaster.

Before Harry kicked his ship into flightspace, it was possible to look out directly one last time through his statglass ports. Still there was nothing to be seen but the swiftly diminishing bulk of the planet they had left, and the seemingly unchanged stars. Soon Hong's System would be gone from view.

Of course, if you were to retreat a few light-years and unlimber your telescope, you might watch a replay of its last few pleasant years, growing eternally more and more remote.

After making sure the autopilot was on the job, Harry had eased off his pilot's helmet. He continued to be curious, in a professional way, about his clients. "So, anybody know any good stories?"

Redpath and Dietrich remained glumly silent. Lily said: "The only story I can think of is my own and Alan's. And I've already bored you quite enough with that."

Harry thought she looked almost as grim as his two male passengers. He told her: "You can still hope for a happy ending. So, you've been traveling for a while. How'd you get this far?"

Lily told him that she had taken advantage of some kind of Templar shuttle service that ran through zones of the Galaxy where berserkers were perceived as being active. Not, of course, that

Templars were likely to carry travelers where the threat was *really* dangerous—humans, even Templars, generally stayed out of those zones altogether, unless some governmental power amassed enough ships and weapons to send in a task force, hunting.

Redpath and Dietrich listened without comment. They gave no sign of becoming more talkative or of relaxing their grim outlook on the world. About all they let Harry know was that they had been prospecting for some kind of minerals on Maracanda, until some other urgent business, unspecified, had called them away.

"We had to go off world to make some arrangements for transportation." Redpath's face twitched again, as if uttering that many words in a string had made him nervous. Of course, space travel in itself made some people edgy.

Lily Gunnlod asked the businessman: "And was your trip successful?"

He looked at her as if suspicious of her motives. "Oh yeah. Yes, I think it was."

"Right now," added Dietrich, "it's looking pretty good." His hard face almost smiled.

Conversation showed no signs of picking up, the three passengers having little to say to Harry or to each other. Maybe they were all just tired. Harry's announcement that his little ship could afford them each a small private cabin was greeted with a kind of dull satisfaction, as if they had expected nothing less. The impression they gave was rather that of people resting between rounds of an exhausting contest.

Still curious about his destination, Harry slipped his pilot's helmet on again. He had no trouble calling up more details about Maracanda from his comprehensive data bank. But when he had studied the symbols and the images for a bit, he just sat there staring at the holostage.

Their destination had turned out to be an oddity indeed.

There ought to be no trouble about getting there, but some extraordinary maneuvers might be required on the approach to landing.

Presently Harry swiveled his chair to confront his passengers. "You people sure you've got the right name for where you want to go? The name is listed, all right, but the object's not even credited with planetary status."

Redpath frowned. "I tell you, we've lived there. It's shown as habitable, isn't it?"

"Well, yeah."

Lily gave him her chill, determined look. "Maracanda is the right name."

"It is not surprising," said Mr. Redpath with nervous dignity, "if your catalogue does not call it merely a planet. It is by no means an ordinary world."

"But a good place to do business, hey?"

Dietrich nodded gloomily and managed to get out a few words. "We understand that mediocre pilots sometimes have difficulty with the approach and landing. But we assumed that you, given your reputation, certainly would not."

Harry frowned. "Actually, I don't see any real problems looming in my part of the job. I've already set a course. According to this, there's a reasonable spaceport on Maracanda, which strongly implies regular travel to and from the place. Though I would say the approach instructions are unique." It seemed that if he wanted to get away from people giving him warnings, he was going to the wrong destination.

Soon Harry had the *Witch* plowing through flightspace in the direction that his passengers wanted her to take. The Space Force and Templars would both be sore at him for setting such a course, assuming any of them bothered to detect his trail, but it wasn't the first time he'd rubbed them the wrong way.

"Is everybody ready for a little dinner? Room and board are included in the price of the tickets."

Making practical decisions regarding food and drink occupied everyone for a time. None of Harry's passengers had so far shown any gourmet sensibilities, but all of them admitted to being hungry. Orders were taken, and the serving machines went to work. Those that actually brought the food were basically moving boxes, with odd numbers of inhuman legs and arms. In keeping with general practice in this berserker-haunted Galaxy, none of Harry's servants was in the least anthropomorphic. Some berserkers were fashioned in the general form of their most stubborn enemy, because that made it more convenient for them to operate equipment designed to be operated by humans.

Eventually, Harry returned to the subject of what he had found in his data bank. "Interesting. It says your destination is an azlaroc-type system."

Redpath: "That is correct."

"What does that mean, exactly?" Lily asked. "I mean, every time Maracanda is mentioned, it's described as something really out of the ordinary. But so far I haven't been able to understand just what it is." She looked at her two fellow passengers. "You two say you've been there. What's it like?"

The pair continued to resist interrogation. At last Redpath shrugged and said: "It's a place, a lot like other places."

"Really?"

"From the business point of view, that is. I mean, some people get rich, others go broke."

Dietrich grudgingly put in: "And yeah, one thing that makes it special is that the shrine is there. What they call the Portal. That Malakó thing, like you say. Some people are into shrines."

Harry said: "I had to look up Maracanda, to check if what I thought I hazily remembered was correct. Basically I had it right. Means it's like one in a hundred billion, for screwiness."

According to the data bank, maybe half a dozen bodies—technically they were not planets—of the type were known to exist among the several hundred billion stellar systems in the great Galaxy. Besides the "habitable body" from which it took its name, the system's chief components were a neutron star and a black hole. These three principal bodies moved in a peculiar orbital dance, tracing the form of a figure eight, each passing at times between the other two. This strongly implied that Maracanda must be much more massive than any Earth-like planet, heavier than Jupiter, in a class with objects huge enough to count as suns.

How any object in space could weigh in with that kind of mass and still be classed as habitable was more than Harry could figure out on the spur of the moment, yet there it was, snugly occupying a niche in his data bank, being passed off with a few comments about zones of gravity inversion.

Whatever the peculiarities, Harry could discover no reason not to visit the place; the existence of a spaceport showed that a lot of other people made the journey and survived.

Recalling his orphaned cargo, he asked his passengers if they thought there would be much of a market on Maracanda for six large boxes, said to contain food-processing machinery. But none of them seemed to know or care.

Dietrich and Redpath had their heads together on the far side of the control room, deep into one of their private conversations. But this one seemed more intense than usual, as if they were discussing, then agreeing on, some matter of considerable urgency.

Lily spoke up, berating the men for not being more social. "We're going to be shipmates for—how long? A whole standard day?"

"Somewhat longer," Harry put in.

"And so we might as well be socially comfortable. What do you say?"

They didn't say much, only stood there side by side. Now and then one of them would shoot a speculative glance at Harry. It reminded him of the way some people acted when they were about to play some practical joke.

The business became more and more obvious, until Lily finally reacted openly.

"What are you two doing? Is there some problem?" Suddenly there was a hint in her voice that she might be accustomed to giving orders and having them obeyed.

Dietrich was looking at the young woman coldly. "No problem that's any of your business, lady." The tone of his voice had also changed.

Redpath was giving Harry a look with something of triumph in it. He chimed in: "No need for the pilot to worry about anything either. Right? Mr. Silver, your time of worrying is just about over."

Harry looked up with interest. "Really?"

Dietrich had pulled out from somewhere an object that could only be described as a small pistol. "We like your little ship here, Mr. Silver. Or should I call you Captain Silver? Ex-captain. We like your ship so much that it now belongs to us. Got that?"

Harry didn't answer. He made no move to do anything. He just sat there, looking interested but not appearing to be much worried, waiting to see what was going to happen next.

Lily still protested. "The pair of you must be out of your minds!" She got up from her chair and took a nervous turn about the deck. There wasn't much room to pace in the small control room with its four big chairs. "What can I say to you? We have our passage all set, going to Maracanda! Isn't that what we all wanted? What do you think you want? Is this some kind of joke?"

"You ask too many questions, lady." That came from Redpath; Dietrich had retreated into silence. All three passengers were now out of their chairs.

When Harry spoke, he still sounded almost calm. "The lady had a point, asking what you think you want. I've got a better question for you, though: What do you think you're going to get?"

Dietrich casually waved his weapon, as if just making sure that everyone had seen it. "I'm a qualified pilot, Silver, so you should remember that we don't really need you at all. All we need is your ship. And, of course, as the new owners, we should get a rebate on our fares." His grin showed slightly crooked teeth. "Just try to fight us, just give us a little bit of an argument, and your personal troubles will quickly be all over."

Lily was still on her feet, standing with fists clenched. She shot a fierce look at Harry, as if she expected him to jump out of his chair and put these mutineers in their place. But mostly she was staring at her fellow passengers. With every passing moment she looked more outraged, as if only now had she grasped the full import of what was happening. She could not believe her eyes. At last she almost screamed: "You imbecile! Put that gun away!"

Mr. Dietrich ignored her. Still keeping a very close watch on Harry, he motioned slightly with the muzzle of the little gun. "All right, ex-captain, time to get down to business. Just stand up and step away from your chair. Hands away from all the manual controls—I'm a pretty good pilot, and I know where they are. Then you're going to walk over here, just a little closer to me, and put your hands up on the wall."

Harry still had not moved a muscle, except that his eyebrows had gone up. His hands, fingers laced, were clasped over his trim midsection. His voice was dangerously quiet. "No refund on your fare. I ought to tack on an extra charge."

Lily let out a wordless noise. She sounded more angry, outraged, than terrified.

The man with the gun kept it pointed right at Harry, while he turned his eyes toward Lily. "I told you before, sit down and shut up."

Instead of shutting up, she got even louder, turning to Redpath in a kind of desperate appeal. But he was watching the gunman with approval; it was plain that the two were in full agreement.

Harry's eyes were flaring dangerously. He was sitting up straight now, but otherwise had made no move.

Dietrich barked: "Silver, out of the chair! You've got ten seconds!"

Lily said: "Mr. Silver, you'd better move." She was looking from one of her fellow passengers to the other. "You unutterable fools!"

The gunman's expression as he looked at her had morphed from anger to something like contempt. He only shook his head, and once more treated Harry to his steely glare. "Five seconds, Silver."

Harry stayed where he was. "Any other orders you'd like to give? Might as well spout 'em all at once, while you've still got my attention."

Dietrich seemed about to add something else, but before he could get out the words, the expression on his face had changed. He swallowed, blinked, and then glanced down at his own right hand, looking surprised to discover it empty. His weapon had just fallen to the deck, sliding free from fingers that could no longer hold it.

He tried to clutch with both hands at the bulkhead beside him, and with his palms got just enough pressure on the smooth surface to keep himself from falling hard, but by the time his slithering body had reached the floor, he had begun to snore.

On the other side of the control room, Dietrich's colleague was no longer offering him encouragement. Mr. Redpath was now sitting on the deck with his back propped against a console, eyes half closed, drooling a little. Nearby, Lily's slender body had lost its grace, along with the ability to stand upright. She was flat on her back, her dark eyes rolling, lips moving slightly, as if she might still be trying to protest.

For perhaps half a minute, the interior of the ship was very quiet.

The interval of silence ended when the *Witch*, somewhere in her randomizing circuits, chose that moment to project a little soft background music.

When it had finished, it let a few more moments of silence pass before inquiring, in a calm and gentle voice: "Any further instructions?"

"No," said Harry, still in his chair. He was shaking his head, expressing thoughtful disapproval, like the director of a play whose cast had failed him miserably. "No, no, no. Nothing more just now, thank you." He understood perfectly well that it was crazy to be thanking a machine, but sometimes, usually when he was upset, the words slipped out.

After treating himself to a couple of deep breaths, Harry eased himself out of his chair. Going unhurriedly to a small locker nearby, he extracted from it a roll of strong tape. Moving first to Dietrich, then to Redpath, he taped each man's hands securely behind his back. They were no more than half conscious, and could only watch helplessly as Harry picked up Dietrich's fallen pistol, then in the course of a quick, efficient body search, gathered a similar weapon from inside Redpath's coveralls. He also relieved each man of a receipt showing how much cash he had paid Harry Silver for transportation.

Next Harry dragged the men one at a time to a capacious locker opening at deck level. When he had shoved them both inside the storage space, he slammed the door and locked it.

Then he turned back toward the fallen woman.

· · · · · · · ·
F O U R
· · · · · · · ·

Pleased at not having to look at
the pair of incompetent pirates any longer, Harry could relax a little. He was breathing somewhat faster than normal, more with
anger than exertion, as he bent over Lily's fallen form, treating
her nose and mouth to a few sprays from a small flask he took
from his pocket.

While she gradually regained the power of movement, he
went through Redpath's and Dietrich's backpacks, finding very
little in them but what might be expected from men traveling light.

Redpath's pack did contain a smartpaper book that Harry
found mildly interesting. The text that showed when he opened it
amounted to a Malakó religious tract, but when Harry's fingers
found the small switch on the spine, the print changed swiftly
before his eyes, and he was holding a treatise on interstellar cus-

toms law. One more touch on the switch produced a porn manual with moving pictures.

Restoring the book to its place, Harry stowed both packs neatly in another locker. Shortly he was back in his pilot's chair, where he got busy checking in with the autopilot, making sure the *Witch* was still chugging along smoothly on her course to mysterious Maracanda, and that no other problems had come up while his attention was elsewhere.

Less than a minute after inhaling Harry's spray, Lily was up on her feet, leaning on the bulkhead. At first she did not try to talk. On slightly unsteady legs she made her way toward the elaborate combat chair adjacent to Harry's. When she saw that he did not object, she let herself sink down into it. Harry, hands again folded over his middle, shot her a glance, but his attention stayed mainly with the information coming through his helmet.

"You must believe me, Mr. Silver," the young woman offered at last. Her voice was slow and subdued, and her expression somewhere between seasickness and tragedy. "When first I met those—those two—they seemed quite reasonable. I had no idea they were going to make such a . . . that they would attempt anything like that. No idea at all." She was shaking her head slowly, as if in intense pain.

Harry grunted. His voice was neutral. "Not your fault. When I take on strangers as passengers, I can't be sure what they're going to do. So I've got a system worked out, lets me deal with 'em when they make bad choices. As soon as your pal Dietrich said he—"

"He has never been my pal." Lily had stopped shaking her head. Her voice was getting stronger, and her eyes were bright again. "I tell you I met him, both of them, for the first time only a few hours ago. Oh, they could be very *plausible*! Not that they had much to say about anything, even their cursed *business*." The last word sounded like a curse.

"All right, he's no pal of yours. Just a traveling salesman. Soon as the salesmen announced that they were taking over, I gave the ship a certain command, never mind just how. Life support began to put some fancy goodies into the air. Colorless and odorless stuff, very reliable."

For a moment she regarded him in silence. Then: "You also breathe. Or maybe you don't."

"I've been breathing for some time, lady, and I intend to keep on. The antidote is also very effective, as you can now testify. I dosed myself before we lifted off. Just a routine precaution for someone in my line of work."

The woman slumped a trifle in the big chair. Certainly not despair, but maybe the beginning of discouragement. "Mr. Silver, I really had no idea they meant to steal your ship."

"You said that before. All right, I guess I can believe you without too much effort."

But Lily wasn't through. "And when I saw that Dietrich had actually pulled a gun, I screamed at him, I pleaded with them both to stop acting like idiots! You heard me."

"I did. That's the reason you're not in the locker, too."

She cast a glance in that direction and her anger flared. "Back on Hong's World, when we—when the three of us decided to join forces, seeking transportation—I had no reason to think they would turn out to be idiots. Criminal idiots. But they have. So, what happens to them is not important."

Facing Harry again, Lily leaned forward, stretching between their chairs to put a small hand timidly on his arm. "I still say what I said before. The only thing that matters is Alan. We must find him, so I can bring him home."

Harry grunted. "Your husband may be all that matters to you, but now I've got some other problems to deal with. I can't just ignore attempted piracy." He was thinking that if he didn't have a live witness present, he'd be greatly tempted to simply shove the pair out of the airlock in deep space. If later it turned out that somebody cared about their disappearance, there would be no record anywhere of their ever being on his ship.

It wasn't a possibility he wanted to discuss out loud. Neither did the woman, apparently. Or maybe it just hadn't occurred to her yet.

Lily said: "When you tell the authorities on Maracanda what those two tried to do—"

Harry cut in: "I don't like to rely on authorities for anything."

"Ah. Perhaps you hesitate because of the matter of the c-plus cannon?"

"That does reinforce my natural tendency. What are your natural tendencies?"

She sighed. "Right now my only tendency, if you want to call it that, is to find my husband and bring him home. Haven't I made that clear already?"

Harry grunted. He found himself leaning more and more to the idea that Alan had simply taken off with some other woman. This one was cute enough, and probably bright enough, but he could see already that she might quickly become wearing on the nerves.

She was once more staring at the door of the big locker. "I really don't care what happens to these two fools, but it would be wrong of you to make other people suffer for their insanity. I mean by keeping me and Alan apart any longer than necessary."

"Lady, we're going to get along better if you stop telling me how to distinguish right from wrong."

"Oh. I am sorry."

"Look, I've contracted to transport you to Maracanda, and I will. But before I can concentrate on that job, I've got to decide what to do with those two clowns."

While speaking, Harry put his pilot's helmet on again and

studied his passenger through the faceplate as he began a mental consultation with his astrogational data banks.

Lily's anger at her former traveling companions seemed to be cooling a bit. "I do ask you to spare their lives." She paused. "Honestly, I do not think they would have killed you."

"No? They wanted my ship, and I wasn't about to sign it over. When they'd finished me, they wouldn't want to leave you hanging around as a witness. You might think about that. Would have kept you and Alan apart for a good long time."

Lily closed her eyes. "You are right, of course." She opened them again. "And I must thank you for saving my life. Still, I do ask you to spare theirs, as a matter of humanity. Then, if you want me to forget the incident, just leave it unreported when we get to Maracanda, that's fine. As long as—"

"You're not delayed in getting on with your big goal in life. All right, I try to please the paying customer. The traveling salesmen don't go out the airlock until we're parked some place where they can breathe. But finding such a location may involve a detour. It could delay your search."

That, it seemed, could make a difference. Lily raised her fine eyebrows and took thought. Then she asked: "How much of a delay?"

With folded hands, Harry riffled mentally through the thoughtware connecting to the data bank. "Actually, they're in luck. And you are too. There seem to be a couple of choices, at less than average interstellar distances. Maybe I'll let 'em pick the one they want . . . then dump 'em on the other. No, that would just be wasting time. I'll make the choice. Should cost us no more than three or four extra hours—if you think your husband will keep that long."

Lily drew a deep breath. "I think you are wise to spare their lives, and I fully appreciate how angry you must be. Only please, whatever you do, let it be quick. We must press on and rescue Alan."

"Oh yeah, glad you reminded me, I had almost forgotten about him. He's some relative of yours, right?"

Harry had already decided, privately, that hauling the two dissatisfied customers on to Maracanda was out of the question. He had only a vague idea of the legal complications he might face in pressing charges against them there, but that wasn't the real problem. The real trouble was that he couldn't see himself voluntarily appearing before some Space Force magistrate, the venue he'd most likely get on a marginally habitable world, as Maracanda appeared to be.

And there was yet another difficulty. Harry said: "There's just one more thing. When I went through their pockets, I didn't find much money. Nothing to suggest they would have been able to pay me the remainder of my fee, not that I feel entitled to it, under the circumstances. But it looks like they were planning a hijacking from the start."

"You didn't search me." Lily sounded almost cheerful.

That wasn't precisely true; Harry had administered a quick patdown, checking for obvious weapons, before giving his paying passenger the spray. But if she hadn't noticed, that was fine. "No, I've been a real gentleman, so far."

"That too is appreciated, but it is not essential." Lily offered him a small, speculative smile. "Be assured, I am carrying sufficient coin to pay my own full fee." Then something changed in her eyes, changed subtly in the position of her body. "I believe you are a man of honor, Mr. Silver."

Harry grinned, without any joy or humor in it. "Did you see that in a vision, too? I wouldn't count on it."

"I see it in your behavior. No, let me confess, there was no vision. Back there on Hong's World, I just made it up. I hadn't begun to know you then. Many men would have been impressed."

"Did you make it up about the kidnapping?"

A frown creased Lily's pretty forehead. "Not really. Alan was—he said he was—ready to go with the people who took him away. But I know that was only because they had already brainwashed him. Those people frightened me. I may need help, he may need help, when it becomes a matter of my trying to see him."

"You mean the Malakós will have him locked up somewhere? Where he can't have visitors? That would be illegal in most places."

"But you don't know what they're like. It would be very good to have someone like you, Mr. Silver, at my side when that time comes, if it does."

Harry took a little while before he answered. "You think you've begun to know me now?"

"Yes. I do." That was definite.

Lily soon got around to asking where her cabin was. Declining the pilot's offer of a snack and a drink before retiring, she retreated there, saying she intended to get some rest. The *Witch* was big enough, though just barely, to offer several private staterooms, spaced round a central common room, one deck lower than the bridge where Harry sat in his pilot's chair. Cargo was stowed, and fuel and engines housed, on levels closer to the tail, lower as defined by the artificial gravity. Fuel was crystallized hydrogen, to feed the massive fusion lamps of the main drive— not that any ship or machine could carry fuel enough to propel its mass across many light-years at transluminal velocities. That could only be accomplished by catching and riding the galactic currents through the domain humanity called flightspace. But just tuning in to those currents burned a lot of power.

*   *   *

Harry's remaining first-class passenger favored him with something of a thoughtful look when she said good night, leaving Harry not totally convinced that she intended to lock her cabin door. But he wasn't going to check it out, or even ask the *Witch* whether Lily had done so.

Instead, as he often did on flights of medium length, like this one, he ordered up a sandwich and a double scotch. Then he dozed in his comfortable pilot's chair. In the background, the *Witch* was playing muted music for her master, today's selection ancient and Chinese. Yes, he *liked* his ship. Not only as a smoothly running way to get around, but just as living quarters, a place to spend his time. The amount of room aboard was sufficient to keep him from feeling cramped, but still it was conveniently compact, with many of life's good things within easy reach.

Too bad that despite her good cooking, smooth voice, and pleasant conversation, the *Witch* was only a chunk of hardware and a pattern of software, unable to do more than go through the motions of liking him. Of course, there were a lot of people in the same condition.

Several times there sounded a muffled banging from inside the big storage locker. Harry thought it rather harmonized with the Chinese music, which still came on at intervals. Harry smiled slightly in his sleep.

Six standard hours later, the *Witch* emerged from flight-space, and within minutes Harry was directing her into an approach for a docking, with a recently abandoned object in orbit round a deserted rock. The system's primary, a reddish sun, was dim and distant.

As if she had heard Harry up and moving about, Lily presently appeared, walking daintily on small bare feet, at the head of the companionway leading down to the cabin deck below. Her hair was damp, as if from showering, and her coveralls looked fresher—probably she had requested a new one from the automated housekeeping service.

"I slept soundly," she announced, "knowing that the ship was in good hands—and assuming we were making good time."

"I appreciate your confidence. Yes, we've done all right, timewise."

"Where are we?"

"Just came out of flightspace, right about on the rim of a system called Thisworld."

"That's an odd name."

Harry grunted. "Not the oddest I've ever heard. A few years ago there was a scientific research station here, but it's been abandoned. Now it's about to become a vacation resort."

"Oh?" She looked in faint puzzlement at the holostage, mounted on its flat-topped pedestal near the center of the cabin. At the moment the stage was bare, nothing but a small, blank tabletop.

"I meant it will be a kind of spa for two people you might just happen to know, even though they're not and never have been your associates. How about some breakfast?"

"Just tea, thank you. That was a delicious dinner."

"Thank the *Witch*. She's a good cook."

"She is also your favorite companion?"

"In some ways." Chewing on a fresh-baked breakfast roll, Harry thought over the details of what he wanted to accomplish, sighed, and decided that even should the station still be holding a normal atmosphere, he had better put his full armor on before he went clumping around through rooms of unfamiliar hardware. He disliked wearing the armor, but sometimes there was no reasonable alternative.

He had the derelict facility in sight now, its image coming up clearly on the stage. What readings he could get indicated there was still good, breathable air inside. The servo-powered arms of the armored suit would make it easy to handle any objections he might get from the two people about to start their vacation.

He thought there was no need to go as far as putting on heavy combat armor, one suit of which he kept in storage for emergencies. Not for the likes of Redpath and Dietrich. Instead he got one of the lighter, everyday outfits out of its handy locker and began reluctantly to get himself into it; suiting up was one of the necessary chores that he did not enjoy. Meanwhile he tersely explained the essentials of his plan to Lily. She only nodded, obviously wishing that this delay was over.

Harry said to his passenger: "Before I get them out of the locker, I want to take a quick look aboard the station, just to make sure there won't be any surprises—abandoned weapons, a functioning lifeboat. Things like that could mean I'd have to do some heavy rethinking about this project."

"I understand." Lily wasn't going to offer any advice this morning.

The abandoned research station was several times the size of Harry's ship, built in the shape of a thick-rimmed wheel about fifty meters across. It hung in what was approximately a twelve-hour orbit, circling a planet once considered marginally habitable, but whose settlements had been abandoned within a few decades of their establishment. The planet called Thisworld certainly looked uninviting hanging in nearby space like an unhealthy orange. Harry's perfunctory attempt to raise any inhabitants on the radio was met only with silence.

While easing the *Witch* closer and closer on manual control, he could see that the equipment left behind by the departing researchers included a small enclosed repair dock, with a partially disassembled lifeboat resting in it, as if it might have been scavenged for spare parts. No other small craft were in sight, nor were there any large visible hatches that might conceal one or more.

"Why was this station abandoned?" Lily wanted to know.

"I expect because of the increased berserker presence in this sector. To make it defensible, you'd have to add practically a whole colony, lots of hardware, at least a couple of hundred people. It probably just didn't seem worth the effort."

"Oh."

He looked at her. "Well, there might have been some other reason. This was a private operation, so who knows why the owners may have changed their minds."

Still nudging the *Witch* along on manual, Harry brought her to a gentle docking at an airlock only a few meters from the lifeboat. To Harry the setup seemed very well adapted to his purposes. He sure as hell wasn't going to deprive himself and the *Witch* of a useful boat, not simply to provide two pirates with a place to breathe.

He said: "I'm going to just take a quick look around over there. Be right back."

Lily nodded her agreement.

Having docked, Harry entered the airlock and carefully stepped through the mated doorways into the abandoned station. As he stepped aboard, a few automatic lights came on, which was reassuring. Berserkers did sometimes set booby traps, but this seemed an unlikely site for the enemy to take such trouble. If they had been here, it was far more likely that they would have sterilized the place of microscopic life, and there was no sign that such a cleansing had taken place.

The station's artificial gravity was turned off, permanently, Harry assumed, but the slowly decaying spin of the wheel-shaped body provided a little something in the way of up and down. According to Harry's suit gauge, the air was adequately thick and breathable.

Before returning to his ship to collect the prospective cast-aways, Harry went to the lifeboat and took a look inside, observing a satisfactory state of disrepair. Awakening the small craft's robot brain, he got it to answer some questions. The answers assured him that the boat in its present condition was incapable of carrying anybody anywhere, except on a suicidal jaunt into nearby space. Well, if Dietrich and Redpath chose to take that kind of gamble, that would be up to them.

A minute later, Harry was back in his own control room.

When he yanked open the door of the big locker and the men lying on the floor saw him wearing a space suit, Redpath immediately began to squawk.

"We can't be at Maracanda yet!"

"That's a shrewd insight." Harry clamped an armored fist on one ankle of each man and tugged them out, squirming. "We're not. Couldn't manage to get each other's tape off, hey? Must be something really sticky."

"Where are you taking us?" screamed Dietrich. "We don't have suits!"

"Won't need 'em where you're going," Harry's suit's airspeakers told his victims. "If you're lucky. Or if Malakó has kept up the air in your new home. Maybe you prefer to look at it that way."

Then Harry tsk-tsked. "Look at that, you've made a mess." Nervous Redpath had peed in his pants during imprisonment. One of the ship's small housekeeping devices, no doubt alerted by its keen sense of smell, had come out of its nest in a bulkhead, plunged into the open locker, and was already cleaning the deck.

When the men saw Lily on her feet and free, they began crying out for her help, wanting to get her to intercede for them. Redpath yelled: "Ms. Gunnlod! Don't let him do this!"

And Dietrich chimed in: "Lady, will you tell this crazy man

to stop? Tell him we were only trying to speed things up? Only wanted to get where we were going as soon as possible?"

"How could anyone believe such utter nonsense? He'd think I was in your insane scheme with you!" Standing with arms folded, Lily answered them in a low and savage voice.

"Anyway, I have pleaded for your lousy lives. You are not going to die today, which is better treatment than you deserve." For good measure, she added what seemed to be a curse of her own, in some language Harry couldn't understand.

Switching back to the common tongue, she said to him: "In truth, we are both lucky to be rid of them with no more trouble than this. My only worry now is—you know what."

"Yeah, dear Alan's next on our list of things to be done. Maracanda sounds like an interesting place. I might never have seen it, if Alan hadn't been kidnapped, and you hadn't come along."

In another moment Harry was dragging the pair roughly, a collar of each squirming body gripped in one armored fist, into the main airlock. He also had hooked each of his own arms through the straps of one of their backpacks.

When the outer door of the lock opened, it wasn't into vacuum, and one man puffed out the breath he had been unconsciously trying to hold.

One of the men was cursing Harry now, spouting some exotic language that sounded like nothing Harry had ever heard before. He nodded and smiled in appreciation, liking the sound, which was rather musical, while still managing to convey the sense.

Now they were both demanding to be told just where they were.

Harry smiled inside his statglass helmet. "Why, you are here, gentlemen. Right here. Just look around, and you can see that for yourselves. If you have any complaints, you know where you can file them."

Set in the station's outer wall, on the opposite side of the rim from the entrance hatch, was a statglass port through which a sizable rectangle of black and starry sky was visible.

Redpath, twisting his neck so he could face in the direction of the blazing magnificence of the distant Core, did his best to threaten Harry with the curse of Malakó.

Then he added for good measure: "You are a miserable son of a diseased whore!"

Harry shook his head, expressing mild disapproval. It always made him feel uncomfortable listening to people who tried to be eloquent and had no idea how to go about it. "I've had blessings that sounded deadlier than that."

He had dragged the castaways' backpacks, contents still intact, out of his ship along with their squirming bodies, and he let the bags go drifting about the shabby and uninviting interior. They looked like a couple of tired party balloons in the ultrafeeble gravity.

He thought his customers might eventually be able to work themselves free of the binding tape, but then again they might not. Harry got a couple of his suit's servo-powered fingers inside the ligature confining Dietrich's wrists and carefully snapped it so that the tape could be peeled off. He repeated the process for Redpath. Slowly and painfully the men began to move their arms, getting some life back into them, and loosening and unwinding tape at the same time. As long as Harry was in the suit, he wasn't worried about any physical resistance his prisoners might put up.

Both of them were keeping their mouths going, mostly spouting abuse. Redpath complained bitterly, claiming he had suffered scratches and bruises from Harry's dragging him around.

And Dietrich: "You're killing us, leaving us here! If you had any guts you'd kill us outright!"

"If you had any brains, you'd know how close you came." But now the pair of them looked so utterly forlorn and inept, sitting on the deck and trying to work life into their arms, with each movement bouncing a little in the low spin-gravity, that Harry found himself trying to be reassuring.

"You know, there could be worse places for you to wind up your miserable lives. The gauges show reserves of air and water aboard, and who knows, you might even discover some food. If you don't like the odds with the little boat, there's a chance that another ship will come along, sooner or later."

Redpath raised his head and wailed: "Yes, maybe in a hundred years!"

"Could be that long. But you might get lucky, and it's only fifty."

Dietrich said: "The berserkers will get us first!"

"Entirely possible. This little system is just about in the middle of a zone that everyone's being warned to stay away from. They probably know this station's been evacuated—but they might figure the dirty humans left behind some bacteria that need to be expunged."

The machines were generally thorough, as only machines could be, in obedience to their basic programming, which commanded them to destroy all life wherever they could find it. But there was so much life. Truly a berserker could never rest—except maybe, Harry supposed, when lying in ambush. As soon as its immediate environment had been rendered as sterile as an operating theater, it had to move on, seeking new territory to free of the corruption called life.

Suddenly Redpath was trying seriously to make a deal, promising Harry obscene amounts of money, in exchange for life and freedom.

"I can tell you how to get it. More than your ship is worth."

"See? You could have just bought the *Witch* from me, saved yourselves a lot of trouble."

"No, man. You don't get it. To get the money, we needed the

ship. A little ship like yours." Somehow, now that the world had fallen on his head, Redpath seemed less nervous than before.

Harry looked at him. Something had suddenly altered in the man's face; he had run through all the reflex reactions to the threat of death, and none of them had saved him. So now we were getting down close to bedrock.

Redpath was whispering: "Take me where he can't hear." With a little jerk of his head he showed that he was referring to his companion.

But Dietrich had already heard. "Hey, none of that shit."

Harry came close to just turning around and walking away. But instead he folded his arms and waited.

The two looked at each other. After a moment Redpath said: "All right, we give up."

"Aha, that's good." Harry nodded. "That relieves my worries. But what do you think you've got left to give up?"

"Information, man. I will tell you. Let me go, and I will put you onto something—the money, yes, just like I said. I'll do that. But also something better than money."

"Let us both go," Dietrich amended.

Redpath looked at him. "Yeah, that's what I said."

Harry stopped looking out through the port. "Really better than money? I'm curious to know what you think that would be."

"*Stuff*, man. You can put this stuff in your mouth or up your nose, or in your veins, wherever. Will give you a sensation such as you have never experienced before. The finest shit that anybody ever tasted."

Harry was looking at him.

Not interpreting the look correctly, the man just babbled on. "There's a deal coming up on Maracanda. A big drug deal, the biggest ever, and we'll cut you in. That's why we want your ship. It needs a ship like yours, one that's not too big."

"If you used too big a ship, I suppose it would just get in the way."

The man was shaking his head. "You don't understand, Silver. Don't understand about that place, Maracanda, what it's like. You don't have the first idea. And the woman in there?"

Harry had been gazing out the port, through which he could just see part of his own ship's unmoving hull. He turned his head back. "What about her?"

"It's all bullshit about her looking for her husband. She is in on it, too, the big deal, the special stuff. She came out with us from Maracanda. The three of us were all sent out to get a ship, whatever means we had to use."

It sounded very confused, a long way from believable. But real life often gave that impression. Harry's voice dropped a little lower. "To get my ship?"

"No. No! Any ship, man. It just has to be about the size of yours." The man gestured, with arms that were starting to regain a passable degree of function.

Harry watched him warily. "You're saying there's no Alan Gunnlod?"

"There is no bloody fucking Alan. And Gunnlod's not her real name. I tell you that's all bullshit. Redpath and me, we were just gonna take your ship. But if you leave us here, that woman will kill you to get it. She's one mean bitch."

"She was trying to stop you."

The man laughed bitterly. "You had us stopped—she must have figured that you would. She's smart, all right. You're smart, too, but she's one mean bitch!"

Harry took another step back. "You're one mean storyteller."

The other man chimed in. "All right, give her a chance, turn your back on her, see what happens. Pretty soon you'll be dead, she'll have your ship. Or have you doing what she wants."

And the first again: "Man, I swear by all the gods—lock me in that closet again, but take me somewhere where I can live!"

Harry surveyed the pair of them with distaste. "One thing you're both right about—my deprived status regarding drugs. Good old stuff, marvelous shit, to put in my veins. How could I miss out on that glorious experience?"

He smacked his lips inside his helmet, thinking how good a shot of scotch was going to taste, once things settled down. He promised himself he'd make it a double. "My trouble is, I've led a sheltered life. Well, goodbye, gentlemen."

One of them gave a despairing cry: "I wouldn't treat an animal this way!"

"Neither would I."

At the last moment, just as Harry had half expected, the two of them came tottering on stiffened legs, making a despairing, hopeless attempt to rush him, just as he was about to close the door on them.

Harry saw no point in getting really rough. Not at this stage. He caught the front of each lurching body with one of his servo-powered arms and shoved the stumbling pair away, just hard enough. The push sent them reeling and falling in the feeble gravity, far enough away to give Harry time to get out through the hatch and close it after him, abruptly cutting off their last despairing yells.

Lily had offered no advice and no suggestions while he was disposing of her erstwhile fellow passengers. He kept a sort of watch on her from the corner of his eye. He had fixed things so that even while he had been busy on the station, his helmet communicator kept projecting on a corner of his faceplate a small view of the *Witch*'s control room, with her inside. But she offered neither help nor hindrance. Briefly Harry wondered if she, too, might be praying to Malakó.

When he came back through the mated airlocks into the control room again and set about the brief routine of undocking, Lily was sitting just where he'd left her.

She greeted him brightly enough. "So we are rid of them?"

With separation from the station complete, Harry heaved a sigh of relief, and started the process of disassembling his suit, which began with loosening certain interior fasteners. "We are. If great Malakó is kind, maybe the world at large won't have to lay eyes on them again."

Lily shifted her position, as if she found her chair uncomfortable. "Speaking of laying eyes, why are you looking at me like that?"

"Was I staring? Sorry."

Lily shook her head. After a while she said: "It occurred to me that you must have decided to trust me, for you left me all alone on your ship, with access to the controls."

"Yeah. So I did."

"How did you know I wouldn't steal your *Witch*?"

Harry seemed to find something about that remark amusing. "I couldn't imagine you doing anything like that. Why would you?"

"Why? Your ship must be very valuable, Mr. Silver. Obviously there *are* people who want it. But you didn't seem to worry that I would just drive it away and leave you marooned with my— traveling companions, as you called them?"

"Call me Harry. I had faith in you, kid." Harry smiled, easing off his helmet, drawing a deep breath. He sighed with relief, breathing good, familiar, well-filtered and processed shipboard air.

"Call me Lily, then. What was it you couldn't imagine—my having pilot skills, or my wanting to take over your ship?"

He shook his head. Chuckled a little, as if at some joke that he did not intend to share. "What I couldn't imagine, Lily, was you being dim enough to try anything of the kind, having seen what happened to contestants number one and two. You haven't learned all my secrets yet."

Lily smiled. "Perhaps you have not yet learned all of mine."

"That is quite possible."

"Whatever may happen on the remainder of this journey, Harry, I do not believe that either of us will find it dull."

He looked at her and gave it some thought before he answered. "Amen to that."

The autopilot was nursing the *Witch* back out toward the periphery of the Thisworld system, seeking a lane of normal spacetime sufficiently empty of particles and gravity to furnish a good, safe springboard for a c-plus jump. If Harry had melded his mind into the thoughtware and applied his judgment, the process would doubtless have gone a little faster, but it seemed to him that he had earned a rest.

There had been silence in the cabin for a couple of minutes, not even a background hum of anything at all, when Lily spoke up suddenly, asking if they could have some music.

"Sure. Probably the *Witch* has got a hymn to Malakó somewhere in storage."

"All right. But no, on second thought, make it something

totally secular. I'll probably be hearing more hymns than I can stand after I catch up with Alan."

" 'Secular' covers a lot of territory."

"I'll leave the choice up to you. Or to your *Witch*."

Harry felt safe in leaving the choice of music up to his ship, which by this time knew pretty well what he liked and what he didn't. The result this time seemed to him satisfactory, as usual.

With a light tune playing in the background, the *Witch*'s pleasant voice cut in, providing some information on the music— not singing it. Once Harry had told her that recorded human voices did a much better job of that.

But then the voice just cut off in midsyllable, and in the same instant the music stopped in midnote.

A second later, Lily looked up, mildly startled.

Harry didn't look up. He was already gazing intently at the holostage that stood beside his pilot's chair. His moment of surprise had come in silence, a few seconds earlier.

Lily looked at Harry, then back at the display, the little stage on its pedestal positioned almost between them. She shifted her position in her chair. There was something on the stage that she had never noticed before.

When she spoke, there was the start of a quaver in her voice.

"That little bright red image. Is that another ship, or—"

Harry didn't respond, or move, until he had spent another fifteen seconds steadily watching the little image. When he answered, the best he could find to tell Lily was: "No, it's not a ship. It's just what you're afraid it is."

The young woman let out a preliminary kind of gasp, as if she might be going to scream. But quickly she got herself under control and huddled silent in her chair.

"It's not going away," Harry added in a calm voice. "Which I take to mean it's probably spotted us."

Since the moment when the berserker had appeared, Harry had been very busy doing several things. Among his other activities was a steady and methodical swearing, at the subvocal level, at the small blur on the holostage. That served to relieve his feelings, while the more practical part of his mind was riffling thoughtware in a blur, much faster than a cardsharp's fingers.

By all the tests of logic and technology, the cancerous little blur that had just shown up on his stage could hardly be anything but a berserker machine—but at least, thank all the gods of all the planets, there was only one of them.

"Can't we jump?" Lily was asking, her voice gone up in pitch. "Get out of here?"

"If we tried to jump right here and now, we'd kill ourselves." By interstellar standards this region on the outskirts of a system was a virtual dustbin, space choked with deadly dust and gas, maybe as much as a hundred trillionth of the density of the air inside a spaceship's cabin. A few more minutes, and he would have had the *Witch* in cleaner emptiness, then quickly into the comparative security of flightspace, where the likelihood of any enemy locating them would be enormously reduced. But there was no use crying or cursing about lost chances.

As matters stood, they were just on the point of getting clear of the Thisworld system, and the berserker was no more than eighty thousand kilometers away, so optelectronic pulses could leap from the *Witch*'s hull to the enemy's, then bounce back again, bringing information, in less than a second.

Harry already had his ship well into a routine of evasive action, while at the same time working to increase their distance from the killer.

Lily needed less than a minute to recover from her shock sufficiently to fasten herself into her chair, which, like Harry's, had automatically changed its shape to become a true acceleration couch. Its built-in pads and extra forcefields might or might not be enough to do her some good if the ship's artificial gravity should stutter during the stressful maneuvers that now seemed inevitable.

As soon as Harry had a moment free of intense mental concentration, he gave Lily what he hoped was a reassuring grin and made his voice relaxed and careful.

"That object hanging just above your right ear is a gunner's helmet, and it's connected to a couple of modest weapons we have that might be useful. But don't put on the helmet unless you've had some training. If the answer's no, for God's sake tell me now. We're at a point where one good lie on your part will probably kill us both."

"No gunnery training, no." The young woman put up rigid fingers and thrust the helmet farther away. "I did go to pilots' school for six weeks—and I was pretty good. That was where I met Alan. At one point we were both going to be professional spacers."

"But you can't do gunnery."

"I can't. I'm sorry."

"Don't be sorry. It's all right, we'll manage." Harry nodded, smiling. "As long as I know." Wishing he could feel as confident as he was trying to sound, Harry mentally flipped the thoughtware switches that brought the *Witch*'s nominal armament, such as it was, under the pilot's control.

He could tell from the berserker's darting movements on the stage that it had certainly detected the *Witch*'s presence and was coming after them. The damned thing seemed to be gaining ground with every heartbeat of its prey; yes, it was small, thought Harry, almost certainly not as big as the *Witch*, but equipped with a powerful drive. Even at this distance, he thought he could tell that it had a different shape than any spacecraft ever fashioned by Earth-descended humanity.

How soon would there come a reasonable opportunity to

jump for flightspace? Studying the configuration of the clouds around him, it seemed to Harry that the course he had begun to follow toward Maracanda was taking them in the wrong direction, but how could he have known? While the artificial gravity held everything rock steady inside the hull, the *Witch* was speeding, lurching around the fringe of some kind of nebula. They were heading almost straight away from the berserker, and space around them was thickening with each second of their flight, growing dense enough with dirt and gas to make direct superluminal jumping virtually suicidal.

Bad luck.

Or was it luck? Had the machine already scouted out this territory? Was it deliberately maneuvering to drive them into a zone where the overtaking and killing would be easier?

The berserker was closer now, and the *Witch*'s sensors could form a clearer image of it. According to what Harry's instruments were trying to tell him, the killer machine was actually smaller than his ship. There might be some advantage to the human side in that, but there was a downside, too—the smaller object could be driven faster in this gassy, dusty environment. And it needed to waste no space or energy on lugging along a peaceful cargo or keeping a human crew alive.

Harry considered jettisoning his valuable freight, but the benefit would be minimal; and right now carrying the extra load was less dangerous than risking even a millisecond of distraction.

The range was getting so short that it was even possible to make out some details of the enemy's shape—not that it mattered very much. On one end there stuck out a protrusion like the head of a rooster, holding some kind of crossbar in its beak. Just what the significance of that might be, Harry could not guess. A beam weapon blasted from the enemy, flicking after his ship at the speed of light.

The *Witch*'s shields, which Harry was particularly proud of, glowed fiercely for a moment, managing to protect the ship and its passengers from the berserker's weapons. The only effect perceptible inside the cabin was a strange sound that reverberated through shields and metal, like a handful of fine gravel tossed against a thick window.

Lily stiffened in her chair. "What was that?"

"Nothing to worry about, no harm done." Harry's words were slow, almost drawling—trying to make things as easy as possible on his passenger's nerves. "I'll slug him back."

It was worth a try. But the berserker's shields were also, as expected, very tough, and the modest projector on Harry's ship could do it no harm. Dust and gas in the berserker's vicinity flared into incandescence, but that was all.

There followed a brisk exchange of missiles, also ending in a scoreless draw, and subjecting the two humans to nothing worse than one more strange noise.

Lily had begun making her own peculiar noises; on a merely human scale, they sounded insignificant. Harry didn't look at her. He wasn't far from the stage of making strange little noises himself.

The *Witch* wasn't going to be able to outrun this killer in normal space, that was growing discouragingly obvious. What worried Harry most immediately was missiles at point-blank range, or an actual ramming.

"Here the son of a bitch comes," said Harry. Then he added rhetorically: "Hold on."

Within the next minute or so, at a range of only a few hundred kilometers, the berserker almost succeeded in snaring the *Witch* in a deadly forcefield entanglement. Harry's thoughtware awoke a resonant image in his brain, drawn from some historical drama, or purely his imagination: that of a gray net hurtling, the weapon of some ancient gladiator.

Meanwhile he had made a smooth and practical adjustment

in the deployment of his ship's own shielding fields, so that the attacker's could find no purchase on them, and the harsh but immaterial net slid away. The human mind, when born with sufficient talent and properly trained, then melded with the right machines to make up for the excruciating slowness of organic nerve signals, could under the right conditions outperform in the dance of combat any mere computer—most of the time.

Harry kept twisting the *Witch*'s tail, doing his best to get out of there.

For the time being, he had to give up even trying to strike back. He parried a missile, parried a projector beam, eluded another forcefield grab. Again a missile blast that did no harm. Under his skillful piloting, the *Witch* managed to slide away somehow, again and again, just in time.

Over the next twenty seconds, he even managed to gain a little ground in the pursuit.

The gain was illusory, for quickly he was losing ground again. The chase dragged out for a full minute, then another. Still he was constrained to hold his ship in normal space, working deeper and deeper into the brier patch of a gradually thickening dust cloud.

Harry could feel how his whole body had gone wet with sweat over the last few minutes. He was also feeling intensely naked without his armor. He hated the computers that drove his enemy; they were secure in the certainty of their programming, they never had to sweat or tremble. The berserker's brains, of course, did not hate him, or anyone. They just went ticking on about their job without feeling, without true thought. No animosity, just business. Planning the next move without fear or hate or triumph, dead things fixated on their wired-in purpose of creating yet more death.

Contrary to what Harry had more or less expected, his passenger seemed to be gaining better and better control of herself as the strain dragged on.

After several minutes she spoke again. "Harry?"

"What?"

"Is there anything I can do?"

"Talk to me. It might help. Just don't worry if you don't always get an answer."

"Talk about what?"

"About things on Maracanda."

"Never been there."

"That's right, you told me that. Then about something else. Anything but your favorite subject."

A brief silence ensued while Lily tried to find some cheerfully soothing remark that would have nothing to do with Alan. The best she could come up with was: "Harry, are we— Do we have a chance?"

"We do."

It took Lily a moment or two to decide what else would be good to talk about. Then she offered: "I suppose you're wishing you still had that c-plus cannon?"

He muttered to himself, coming to a decision. Not that it had been all that difficult to reach. Then he said: "That's what I meant when I said we still have a chance. Now is when we have to use it."

"What?"

"The cannon. The one you suppose I wish I had." He flipped on the autopilot and got up from his chair. A moment later, shaking somewhat with ongoing strain, he was stuffing his reluctant body back into his space armor. He hated the process, but few people could have managed it more quickly.

The fact that he had just, only minutes ago, taken off his armored suit didn't mellow his mood or his attitude toward the berserker that was forcing this distasteful task upon him.

He pointed out to Lily the locker from which he had taken his own suit. "There's another suit in there. One size fits almost everyone. It's self-adjusting. It might possibly save your life.

Hope you know how to put it on. If not, do the best you can with it, I'm busy."

She jumped from her chair and got busy, too.

Lily had the spare suit out of storage and was struggling nervously to get it on over her coveralls—fortunately, she seemed to be managing unaided. She was also talking to him again, as he had encouraged her to do. Alan had rejoined the conversation, and she was telling Harry something about how much fun she and her husband used to have when times were peaceful and they had been starting out together in pilots' school.

Meanwhile Harry, back in his chair (which had readjusted itself to fit the shape of the heavy suit), was lost in concentration on his task and heard only snatches of what she was saying.

In response to Harry's gentle mental touch upon the thoughtware, the *Witch* was once more making incremental gains in her flight from pursuing doom. The only thing wrong with making this kind of progress was that, in order to pull away, the ship kept driving deeper and deeper into gas and dust. If they kept on, they would quite soon find themselves in a region of space in which the pursuing berserker, being smaller, would enjoy a clear advantage.

In a few truncated sentences, he communicated the gist of this unhappy situation to Lily, who had conquered the suit and was back in her chair.

Probably she at least felt a little better protected now. Her response was: "What can we do?"

"We're down to about one chance. Don't bother me!"

Maybe, he thought to himself, we have three minutes. Quite possibly somewhat less.

"Only one thing we can do now," he repeated, muttering more to himself than to her. "No choice now, no choice at all."

He was going to have to somehow unlimber the cannon that he had taken such pains to conceal in his vessel's prow, not that long ago, in a different sector of the Galaxy.

*   *   *

If his current enemy had ever bothered to compute the likelihood of such a mule-kicker of a weapon appearing on such a small ship, the answer must have come out at very nearly zero. For the simple reason that using it in this fog of dust was going to put the gun platform in almost as much danger as the target. But if Harry failed to fire it now, and quickly, the odds against survival would be even worse.

"Stay in your chair," Harry advised. "I'm turning down the gravity." That was a necessary preliminary, to allow him to work up in the prow, a couple of meters above his combat chair, an area otherwise just about impossible to reach. He couldn't, of course, turn the gravity off altogether, or the next burst of acceleration called for by the autopilot, at a thousand gravities or so, would instantly accomplish the berserker's purpose.

In the dreamlike, underwater movements engendered by weak gravity he darted as swiftly as he could about the control room, hastily ransacking drawers and cabinets, collecting the special tools he was going to need. Then he launched himself in a slow and gentle, nearly weightless dive up to the cabin's arched overhead, clamping his suit to a featureless section, where he immediately got to work on the paneling.

With his helmet still keeping his brain in close touch with the *Witch*'s circuits, he called up a projected view, on the inner surface of his faceplate, of a certain area of the *Witch*'s outer hull. A spot about a meter wide in the featureless smooth surface was in the process of turning itself into a small hatch. Presently the hatch opened and a gun muzzle emerged. This protrusion was somewhat thicker than Harry's arm. It looked dark and crude, more threatening than effective, like some antique cartoonist's idea of a massive weapon.

The next step was to connect the weapon to the *Witch*'s gunlaying system, which had already locked onto their pursuer.

Step one accomplished. Two coming up.

*   *   *

Following a recent skirmish on a world called Hyperborea, the supply of cannon slugs on board the *Witch* was down to a single projectile. The magazine containing it had been concealed behind a solid-looking panel on the other side of the control room, while the breechblock of the cannon was empty when it was folded away. Therefore it was now necessary to open both magazine and breech, and load.

The sole remaining missile was about the size and shape of Harry's fist and forearm, and very heavy, being formed of pure solid lead. Very pure though not so simple, a cunningly balanced mixture of lead's four stable isotopes, sealed inside a thin film of oxidation. The slug was machined and shaped down to the thousandth of a gram, and it looked as blunt and simple as the muzzle of the gun itself. All the weapon's computer-cleverness and power lay buried in its breech.

To get at the ammunition, Harry had to undo another set of secret fasteners. Then he opened the magazine and dragged out the remaining slug, grateful for the augmented strength the suit gave to his arms and hands.

Lily, with only the vaguest idea of what he was doing, couldn't stand the suspense. "Harry? Can't we try to run? What in all the hells—"

"No, that's one thing we can't do any longer. Not if we mean to stay alive. Now shut up." Yes, he knew that a minute ago he had been telling her to talk. That was then, this was now.

The next twenty seconds seemed an eternity, but at the end of that time, still working inside the inner hull, he had opened the breech of the weapon and slid the slug into the chamber. Now that the cannon's circuitry was integrated with the ship's systems, Harry was doing a quick, nearly weightless dive back to his combat chair. During the few seconds of his passage, the output of the hydrogen power lamps that drove the ship and everything in it was mounting silently, surging up rapidly to maximum, forging an insanity of coiled-up forces inside the cannon, a knot beginning to warp all nearby time and space.

Now Harry had himself clamped into his chair again, and none too soon, for the berserker was hardly fifty kilometers away, closing at six klicks per second on a quick countdown to ramming.

"Here goes," Harry announced to the universe in general. For just a moment he wondered if it would be worthwhile praying to great Malakó. But he thought he preferred his old favorite, To Whom It May Concern.

The *Witch*'s gunlaying system was not the finest in the Galaxy, especially when it had been hooked up by a semi-amateur to this brute of an odd weapon, but at this range he thought that he could hardly miss.

The real danger was not that he would miss. The real trouble was that firing a c-plus amid the natural gravitic haze of the surrounding sea of dust would be a move fraught with uncertainty, to put the difficulty mildly. Whatever else happened, whoever survived, the result ought to be spectacular . . .

The firing itself was invisible and inaudible, and it happened the instant Harry pressed the manual control to arm it fully.

It was an experience Harry Silver had had once before in his ship's cabin, and it was no more enjoyable now than it had been then. A jolt of physical recoil, felt on a natural and human scale, would have been something of a relief, but that was not what happened. Instead the world turned strange around Harry Silver, the energies released passing twistily through all his bones. Lily's, too, for he saw her suited body stiffen in her chair.

For just half a second, he thought that he saw certain old familiar faces in the cabin . . .

One in particular, that almost made his heart stop for a moment . . .

A second strange scene passed through his mind.

Another one followed.

He saw yet one more, including the image of a certain face that always made his heart beat faster.

Then the effect had passed, the nerve cells in Harry's brain returned to something like their normal activity, and the version of the world claiming to be reality was back again.

Lily's voice came to him through his helmet, saying something that showed she, too, had been strongly affected. "I've just seen Maracanda . . . but maybe it wasn't that."

Outside the ship, and in the image on the holostage, the result of the cannon blast was instantaneous. What the death machine ran into was not so much a hit as an obliteration, its image instantaneously transmuted into a sleet of particles and rays, a shotgun blast of dust that bloomed in radiant glory as its particles collided with those of the vastly thinner, slowly drifting nebular cloud. A swift cascade of secondary collisions produced a truly beautiful, utterly silent blast, a glorious and cataclysmic rainbow.

Actually, no mere collision with thin gas and dust could have achieved quite that effect. The culprit had been a slug traveling at de Broglie speeds. Only relativistic time retardation allowed the mass of stressed metal to survive until it reached its target.

By the time (and time, too, had been warped) it got there, its mass had been magnified awesomely by its velocity, one aspect waves of not much more than mathematics. The molecules of lead were churning internally with phase velocities greater than that of light.

Deep down in the *Witch*'s lower hull, the hydrogen power lamps still surged, compelled to make up some of the energy they had so recently borrowed from long seconds in the future. It was all done in silence, and Harry could sense the roaring flow only through the *Witch*'s circuits. Some large component of the energy could never be made up, and the deficit thus created went on chasing itself into the future in the form of an eternal negative. Or so the experts seemed to be saying when Harry listened to them. Just how the damned thing worked was more than he had ever been able to understand, but it seemed that as long as the ship's systems could stand the strain, the *Witch* and her occupants were going to be all right.

Harry Silver was lying back safe in his pilot's chair, gasping, about as safe at home as he ever got. Inside his armor, its micro currents of air were busy drying out his sweat.

One problem solved. But now that it was settled that he and his passenger were going to survive for the time being, returning life brought with it its own set of difficulties. He had been forced to reveal to his passenger that his ship was still carrying a monstrous weapon, strictly forbidden to any civilian vessel whose crew might be desperate or near suicidal enough to want to use it. The mere possession of it could conceivably be enough to earn him a year or two in prison, from some judge who made a strict interpretation of the law. Lily would hold a power of blackmail over him as soon as they came under Space Force jurisdiction again.

But at least there was no longer any red dot swelling on the holostage. And for the moment, that disappearance was all that counted.

"It's gone?" Lily's voice was barely audible.

"It's gone. We killed it." Harry got out of his chair and with shaking fingers started to take off his armor. He was looking forward to a good stiff drink.

Some time later, when they were smoothly under way again, and Harry was on his second drink, Lily surprised him. He had been expecting some question or accusation about the cannon. Instead she observed: "You don't have a regular partner." That was really a question, though she made it sound more like an accusation.

"Not right now."

"Except your ship, I suppose. Sometimes you speak of her as if she were a woman."

"Oh, I can tell the difference." Harry looked his human shipmate up and down. He had long experience of the way battle, terror, and destruction sometimes worked as aphrodisiacs. From the look on her face, the position of her body, he judged that she was in a kind of balance, ready to be tipped this way or that.

His passenger was looking steadily at him. He couldn't tell what might be going on inside her head. Could anyone ever really tell about anyone else?

Finally he asked: "Great Malakó won't mind? Or Alan either?"

Her voice was faint and querulous. "I don't know anything about Great Malakó. I try to read about it, but . . . and sometimes I think I don't know anything about my husband, either." She paused. "You have just saved my life. Again."

Harry grunted. "Right now you can be my partner in conversation. How come you dropped out of pilots' school? You said you only went for a standard month and a half."

"Alan was very enthusiastic about going into space work, back when we started school. Then he lost interest. So we both dropped out. If you are wondering whether he will be jealous, when he finds out you and I have been traveling alone together—"

"I wasn't wondering. Not particularly."

"The answer is that I don't know. I fear there are days when I am not one of his enthusiasms."

"And maybe you have days when he doesn't excite you so much either."

Lily flushed. "I love my husband very deeply."

"Yeah. This new religion he's got, it doesn't necessarily mean he's going to drop you. Does it?"

"I don't know." Then she shook her head. "No, I can't believe Alan would do that. But all religions have splinter groups, don't they? I think there are some followers of Malakó who try to attain great holiness by being celibate."

"I guess all religions have splinter groups," Harry agreed.

"That's what really worries me, makes me afraid that when I get to Maracanda, maybe they won't even want me to talk to him. That there's usually one sharp, pointy little splinter that tends to become more and more fanatical."

"And you think that Alan might be attracted to that kind of thing."

She nodded. After giving Harry a thoughtful look, she said: "He's like you, in one way at least. He's not the kind of man who wants to do anything halfway."

Harry raised his glass. "Since you're madly in love with him, I'll take that as a compliment."

"It was meant to be. But I suppose you don't have a regular religion."

Harry grunted again.

Now she was annoyed. "Tell me, Mr. Silver, what *do* you have?"

He cast a glance around the cabin. "For one thing, I have this ship. It's all mine, free and clear, along with its attachments and its cargo. Which may not amount to much in the cosmic scheme of things, but a fair number of people would like to own it. Or at least want to ride in it." He turned in his chair. "Also I have something of a thirst. Join me in a drink?"

"From your inflection on the word, I presume you speak of alcohol? Malakó has no objection to that either. In moderation."

"I'm all for moderation. Though some people carry it too far."

Half a minute later, savoring his first postcombat sip of scotch and watching Lily quickly swallow hers, Harry remarked: "Whisky is my favorite drug." The mention of drugs brought no particular reaction. At some point he meant to raise the subject of smuggling, too, but he hadn't yet thought of a good, smooth way to bring it up.

The subject of traveling seemed to come up naturally. Harry expressed his curiosity as to whether his remaining passenger had ever actually been within ten thousand light-years of the Core. Sagittarius A, the ancient and still somewhat mysterious radio source, was there. So were other, greater mysteries, among them the one that humans called the Taj.

"No, I haven't been anywhere near there." It sounded as though Lily really wished she might have been. "Have you?"

"Not close. Not really close. From all I hear, just getting into Core Sector's not easy, let alone exploring it." Over the years there had been several famous, partially successful expeditions organized to go probing at the center of the Galaxy. Each of them had brought back more questions than answers. "Normal space and flightspace both tend to get a little twisty there. Travel is sometimes possible, but never exactly easy or routine."

Lily said: "From all that I've been able to find out, believers in great Malakó, or some of them at least, look forward to visiting the Core on a true pilgrimage. That's why Maracanda's a holy place for them."

"Maracanda's nowhere near the Core." Harry was gently sipping the refill in his glass.

"True, but it has something called the Portal."

"What's that?"

"Some kind of visual phenomenon, it seems. Sometimes it's described as if it were a giant telescope." She smiled lightly. "But anyway, I don't suppose your ship will ever go on any pilgrimage."

"Hard to say where the *Witch* will go." Harry sipped again. "If she brings me along with her, no doubt my presence near the Core would spoil any ennobling effect."

"But Harry, great Malakó aside, don't you want to go there, too? Just to go there, just to *see?*"

"Well, yeah." After a while Harry added: "But the Taj is one thing I might be afraid to look at. There are a lot of wild tales about the Core, even among people who don't make a religion out of it."

Both of them had heard the stories about the Taj, and the legend of the boy Michel Geulincx, who was supposed to have gone there in an incredible way, and to have undergone an even stranger transformation.

Before long the subject of Alan came up again, as it always did with this lady. Harry thought that if they had to talk about the missing husband, he might as well try to make it interesting.

He suggested: "Maybe Alan won't be eager to come home. What then?"

Lily was shaking her head, slowly and forcefully. "He will be, he must be, willing to come home, when I have talked with him. He is a good man in his heart, and so he must."

"But if he doesn't. Sure you won't have another drink?"

She accepted mechanically. But when the drink was ready, she just held it in her hand, frowning at the glass. She said: "In the unlikely event that he doesn't want to come home . . . but no. He will. He will."

The *Witch* was purring through flightspace, her statglass ports all tuned for opacity. Looking out would not have inflicted any serious harm upon the human eye or brain, but there was nothing to see, except what had often been described as eye-watering, nerve-grating irrelevance.

Harry and Lily were seated in the control room, in their very comfortable, almost infinitely adaptable combat chairs, enjoying a meal of tender pseudo beefsteak and new potatoes, raw materials provided by the ship's recycler.

At least Harry was enjoying it, with an accompanying glass of wine. The lady had nibbled a bit on a couple of Harry's suggestions, but seemed to quickly lose her appetite.

Somehow the fact that she didn't seem to be eating properly

was a source of irritation. It bothered him to think he was turning into some kind of a damned uncle or something.

Finally Harry asked: "Don't care for my chef? She does get a little idiosyncratic sometimes." The chef, of course, was only a facet of the *Witch*'s very capable and knowledgeable optelectronic brain, and the cooking and service were performed entirely without the touch of human hands.

She shook her head. "Not exactly what I'm used to. But then what I'm used to is not all that great." She pushed her tray away and turned her chair. "Where did you get these chairs? They're very comfortable."

"They ought to be. I paid a lot for 'em."

Lily pulled back the tray, toyed with her food again.

Harry wondered aloud: "I wonder what people eat on Maracanda."

"Just about everything that people use has to be imported, I understand. Food and air and water all recycled, as on a ship." She took note of Harry's intense gaze. "Before I left home, I looked the place up as best I could."

"The recycling sounds good. What else did you find out?"

"Not much. I left home in a hurry."

"Traveling alone, until you got to Hong's World?"

"Yes. And then I got there just in time for an evacuation." Then Lily burst out: "What do you suppose has happened to Redpath and Dietrich?" At the same moment she dropped her mostly uneaten meal, tray and all, into the disposal.

"That's one of the subjects on which I don't care to suppose anything."

"Harry, I don't blame you for what you—for the way you handled the problem."

"That's good." Harry sounded like he didn't care much one way or the other.

Still she wouldn't let it alone. "I'm not sure what else you could have done with them. But still it bothers me to think of how they . . ." She let it trail off.

"All right, let's talk about it. I don't mind. If you're asking seriously, I wouldn't give much for their chances." Harry sipped and nibbled, judiciously balancing flavors. "But no need for you to feel guilty over something I did. In fact, you can take credit—if you want to call it that—for their being still alive when we told them goodbye." Harry's tray, polished almost clean, went to its doom, and a moment later his wineglass and napkin joined it.

"You're serious, Harry."

"Very much so. About some things."

The *Witch* had encountered the berserker on the outer fringe of the Thisworld system, actually within line-of-telescopic-sight, and less than one light-hour's distance, of where Harry had marooned the two men. That led him to assume that other bad machines had been in the vicinity, and that, by now, it was quite possible Redpath and Dietrich had gone where all humans, good or bad, eventually wound up. Well, if that was the case, at least berserkers were almost always quick and efficient in their killing.

Lily didn't want to discuss the matter any further, and neither did Harry. Well, he wasn't going to lose any sleep over it. He couldn't tell whether she eventually would or not.

Distantly he wondered again if she was locking the door of her little private cabin when she went to sleep. Of course, the *Witch* would find out for him if he should want to know—just out of curiosity. The *Witch* would even unlock the door again if her master made such a request. But he did not.

Harry went to his own cabin from time to time, always alone. And he routinely locked his door, using a code word to ensure that it would stay that way. That had become a habit with him, even when no one else was aboard the ship.

*   *   *

It was morning again, ship's time, and they were back in the control room, talking.

"Do you love space, Harry? Traveling in it, looking at it, thinking of all the endless infinities just outside the hull?"

"No."

That took his passenger somewhat aback. "No? Why not?"

"Because there's nothing there."

"*Nothing?*"

"There are some beautiful sights, I'll give you that. An exploding star, a nebula, a firestorm of radiation. I bet the system we're going to visit is somewhat spectacular. But you can't get close to most of them, and if you could, the beauty would be gone. On top of that, they'd kill you."

"But—Harry, I've been getting the impression that you spend most of your life in space."

He thought about it. "That's not the way I look at it. What I'm really doing is spending a lot of time inside my ship. By now I've got everything in her set up just about the way I like it."

She thought about it. "Is that all you want from life? A comfortable ship?"

"I could do worse. It's more than a lot of people get."

Long experience had convinced Harry that whenever a pilot or a passenger was in a particular hurry to get to someplace, anyplace, the normal complications involved in astrogation tended to grow into fiendish puzzles, sometimes equipped with menacing claws and teeth. That was just considering nature, before you factored in berserkers. The tides of dark matter, dust and gas, though no more than a hard vacuum by breathers' standards, were continually ebbing and flowing in ordinary spacetime, and sometimes threw up corresponding obstacles in nearby flightspace.

Harry's remaining passenger had little more to say about her destination, or her plans for when she got there, but she seemed to be counting down the hours and minutes. Meanwhile events ran true to form, regarding technical delays. But with perseverance and a little luck Harry overcame the routine difficulties. With Lily spending most of her time in the next chair, alternately stiffening and slumping in apparent anxiety, he put up a holostage display to let her see something of what his helmet showed him as the *Witch* dropped out of flightspace and began decelerating in her close approach to the Maracandan system. They were, or ought to be, within an hour or so of landing.

There were a few small outlying planets, commonplace and virtually uninhabitable, in eccentric orbits. They were the least eccentric thing about the place. The system the *Witch* was approaching was so odd that Harry was damned if he could be certain at what point his ship had entered it. The most glaring peculiarity was that it lacked the normal arrangement of one primary star at the center. Instead it presented an alternate formation whose weirdness raised in Harry's imagination the image of a bored Creator who was pleased to think up little jokes.

The Maracandan primary was not one object, or even two, as would have formed a decent, normal, close binary sun. There were three, none of them routine. Here the visitor was confronted in the first place by a sizable black hole, blessed with the name of Ixpuztec, and in the second place by a neutron star, called Avalon, of the fast-spinning pulsar variety.

In the third place, there was Maracanda itself.

Even in the company of Avalon and Ixpuztec, Maracanda was the oddest of the trio. It was something the *Witch*'s data bank refused to call either star or planet, but referred to cautiously as a "habitable body." It was vastly more massive than any normal Earth-type planet, but portions of its surface were rendered comfortably habitable by stable zones of natural gravity inversion.

All three components of the primary were perpetually chasing each other in a most peculiar orbital dance, one that traced out a nearly perfect figure eight. Together they formed what researchers called an azlaroc-type system. Long ago Harry had heard of such rare things, as distant curiosities. He turned to his data bank to refresh his memory on the subject. There were exactly four such objects known to exist, including the eponymous and remote Azlaroc itself, among the millions of solar systems so far studied in the six or seven percent of the Galaxy that Earth-descended humans had more or less explored.

The celestial mechanics of a three-body primary looked wildly improbable, not to say artificial. But a history of observation strongly suggested that the stability of the four known examples could be relied on.

Further consultation with the *Witch*'s data bank assured Harry that the celestial mechanics had actually been worked out in theory centuries before any such system had been discovered, even before serious space travel had begun.

Given the diverse and exotic natures of the three bodies composing the Maracandan triple primary, Harry couldn't understand how they could really be all of approximately the same mass, as the laws of celestial mechanics would seem to demand. But that was what their behavior implied. To his surprise, his data bank waffled on giving that question a straight answer. Harry had to assume the figure-eight orbital track meant that the system's common center of mass kept shifting around somehow through the space between them.

The data bank also noted that the "habitable body" had a human population somewhat in excess of half a million, and steadily growing. More than half of them lived in Port City, the capital. Somehow it was no surprise to note that a Space Force office had been established in the capital, which meant the Force would very likely have some ships in this solar system, too. This information added nothing to Harry's peace of mind. But it would not prevent his landing; he had what he thought were reasonable grounds to suppose that the news of his being wanted on criminal charges had not yet reached this backwater.

The *Witch* was still hundreds of millions of kilometers from the center of the peculiar figure eight when transponders aboard began to acknowledge signals from robotic outposts of the local early warning system. Harry had been expecting this; something of the kind had been established around any world whose people knew dread of berserkers, which meant almost any that had people on it. From the spacing and timing of the signals, Harry judged this warning network to be no better than second-rate.

There also came a terse robotic message alerting the visitor to prepare for a somewhat unusual final approach and suggesting that the ship's captain might want to wait in a carefully chosen orbit until a human pilot experienced in Maracandan space could be provided.

Harry promptly sent his answer. "No. Hell, no. Look, you people have an open spaceport down there, don't you? Just give me the regular approach instructions, I don't need to be piloted in."

He was going to have to wait a while for a reply to that. The *Witch* was still at a distance where the exchange of light-speed messages occupied the better part of an hour.

Lily had been silent while Harry was talking to the early warning system. But now she commented: "That's really unusual, isn't it? Offering to send a pilot?"

"Very close to unheard of—except when there's something as tricky as a black hole or a pulsar nearby. Here we have both— not to mention that thing that's the real oddity. We'll probably get a string of special instructions. But I have no doubt the *Witch* can handle it."

Harry had already begun the job of stowing away the c-plus

cannon, and he was going to have to speed it up. He disliked being forced to hurry anything, but he knew that he probably had less than an hour in which to finish the job. It was vital to make sure that the weapon's presence aboard was disguised as thoroughly as possible.

Lily asked in an innocent voice: "Can I help?"

"Not skilled in armaments, are you? No. So your best method of helping is just to keep out of the way."

She moved a little closer. "What would happen if they discovered you still had their cannon on your ship? And while we're on that subject, I wonder why you do still have it? I know you started some explanation back on Hong's World, but my mind was elsewhere then."

Her voice had taken on a challenging, speculative sound that made Harry pause with tools in hand. "The answer to your first question, lady, is that neither of us would be smiling. I'd be arrested and put on trial in some kind of Galactic Council court, maybe just in front of a Space Force magistrate, and they'd be sure to call all available witnesses, which means you. The trial would take some time, because I'd have the best lawyer I could find. You couldn't very well concentrate on your search for your dear husband."

"That's what I was thinking." She swung her big chair, rotating to right and left, in a manner that might have been playful, except that her face was grim. "We can avoid those kinds of problems, I'm sure. I do want to get on with the search for Alan, as quickly as possible." She drew a deep breath. "Harry, I mentioned this before, but you didn't really answer. I can't afford to pay you any more, just getting here took almost all my money. But will you help me find him? Just stand by me until I've done that? I mean, assuming all the business about a trial can be avoided?" Her eyes as she asked the question displayed an utter innocence.

A chain of emotions passed through Harry Silver's mind,

some so quickly that he couldn't be sure just what they were. Anger briefly dominated, but uncertainty kept anything from really taking over. He stared at her, and he still couldn't be sure of anything about her. But more and more he wanted to find out, even if doing so cost him time and effort.

Finally he said: "Okay, I can put in some time helping you locate your husband. Then, if just getting to see him proves to be a problem, maybe—I say maybe—I can help with that, too. If that's what you really want."

She pulled herself up straight in the chair. "What else do you suppose I want?"

"I don't know. You tell me."

Lily shook her head, as if to clear away some misunderstanding. "Thanks. Thanks, Harry. If I could pay you more, I would. Listen, when I talked about avoiding a trial, I didn't mean to make it sound like—like I was blackmailing you."

"I was trying not to hear it that way. Thanks for putting your request so nicely. Now I can feel that I'm just satisfying my own curiosity."

After a pause, Harry went on: "As for your second question, the reason I still have the cannon on board is that I haven't found any reasonable way to get rid of it. Can't just chop it out of the hull without wrecking my ship. And even if I was willing to do that, I don't have the tools that would cut this hull. Removing it properly will take special equipment, and special skills which I don't have either.

"There aren't many people who could make a neat job of it. And the only ones I know outside of the Space Force shouldn't be trusted with the weapon."

His passenger seemed to be thinking his situation over, trying to come up with something helpful. At last she offered: "What about the Templars?"

"A thought. But I haven't had time to think about it." That

was something of a lie; but he was a long way from having a serious Templar plan as yet.

Lily went on: "So, you'll say nothing about having the cannon on board, and of course I won't either. Are you going to report that we encountered a berserker?"

"Sure. That's not only required, it's the only decent thing to do. No problem. I'll make a report as soon as we get to where someone can listen to me."

"You'll just tell them we saw one and managed to get away from it?"

"Better than that. I've got a recording that'll give the interested authorities a pretty good look at what happened."

"Oh?"

"Yeah. It's obvious that the damned machine took a calculated risk, making an all-out effort to catch up with us inside a dust cloud. It had bad luck and wrecked itself. That's what generally happens when ship or machine tries to go too fast in the wrong place. Made a real spectacular smash-up."

"Is that what the recording shows?"

"It does now. Destruction is basically destruction, and the *Witch* and I've just touched up the pictures and the data a little bit. Making sure the key points show up clearly. No big changes were necessary." Harry seriously hoped that any traces the c-plus firing might have left in the *Witch*'s onboard systems had been erased by now.

The Maracanda system offered its visitors a rich assortment of things to marvel at. This became more evident as they drew close enough to get a good look at its triple primary.

The black hole was not directly visible, its jealous gravity too powerful to allow the escape of any image-bearing light. But its location was perfectly easy to spot by its broad accretion disk spreading out tens of millions of kilometers on each side, an accumulation of material on the verge of being sucked into the ravenous, spinning vortex that hid beneath the blackness of its event horizon. The stuff was falling so fast and heated so intensely in the process that it glowed with radiation all across the electromagnetic spectrum, but was especially ferocious in the X-ray band.

Here, within the labyrinthine complications of the Maracanda system, any orbit a ship might take had to contain some element of risk. This was why the routine approach directions for Maracanda itself were so stringent, forceful, and detailed. No one had to tell the experienced pilot that gravitational anomalies could swallow spaceship-sized bodies in less than an eye blink. The smallest miscalculation could send a ship into a knot, or over a slippery, invisible brink, into a domain where engine power and artificial gravity would be overwhelmed before even a quantum computer could react.

In this neighborhood, the outcome of a slight mistake might be the smearing of ship and occupants together into a thin film of newly created neutrons on the pulsar's surface. Or tidal forces could spin them into thin threads of exotic matter, crushing even neutrons into quarks, before spattering them down into the black hole's event horizon, as heavily redshifted, eternally fading images.

The hole itself was never visible, even at this close range. What one saw was the event horizon, a fiercely spinning, slightly and swiftly wobbling chunk of blackness, dark as a berserker's heart. This ebony core, bulging on one side, was outlined by a tight-fitting, narrow ring of scalding brightness.

Harry's passenger said: "I want to know everything about this system, everything I can. Where do they get such names? I mean, Ixpuztec?"

"Usually from someone's ancient god of the underworld."

The bulge was visibly wobbling as they looked at it, a much slower cycle imposed on the incredibly rapid spin.

Lily was fascinated. Most people would have been. "What makes it look like that, kind of lopsided?"

"The way it spins. That makes it suck in passing starlight faster on one side than the other."

" 'Suck in passing starlight.' I don't understand."

Harry grunted.

"How fast does it spin?"

"Would you believe me if I told you?"

Lily turned away from the port, leaning on the bulkhead as if she needed it to prop her up. She was giving him a long, thoughtful look. "I think I would tend to believe almost anything you told me, Harry."

He cleared his throat, feeling suddenly uncomfortable. "Then over here, by contrast, we have a pulsar."

By contrast, the neutron star called Avalon did not look all that strange—not for a pulsar. Not, at least, when seen from a distance of a quarter of a light-hour. When you were simply gazing at that body through the *Witch*'s optical telescope, it was possible to miss the fact that the star contained the mass of a normal sun, packed into the circumference of an Earth-like planet. To the unaided eye it seemed to glow fiercely with rather ordinary light, in almost the spectrum of a dutiful, ordinary star.

Eventually, after a long long time in human terms, it would lose its fire and cool off. Even now the source of its visible radiation was different from an ordinary star's. Light was not erupting from the stellar surface, which looked polished and metallic, almost dark, when Harry dimmed down the scope's optics enough to let him see it. Most of the radiant glare of the neutron star came from the superhot thin gas that fell in endlessly toward that surface, drawn from nearby space by the star's horrendous gravity—a kind of solar wind blowing in reverse.

The *Witch*'s autopilot had discovered and locked on to one of the prescribed safe paths for spacecraft approaching the system. This avoided the plane of the monster beam of X rays that swept space in time with the pulsar's spin—one rotation every two seconds, a peculiarly slow rate for a neutron star.

Ordinarily Harry would have found any system containing both a pulsar and a black hole interesting, well worthy of some time spent in contemplation. But all of the Maracanda system's other oddities paled to insignificance when Harry got a good look at their destination, the "habitable body" his data bank still refused to call a planet.

Lily appeared to be just as astonished as Harry when she studied the image taking shape on the holostage—if "taking shape" was an accurate description of the process. If asked to be candid on the subject, Harry would have said the object was only attempting to take shape and not succeeding very well.

It deviated from the spherical even more than the black hole did.

As if this might be some new, especially outrageous trick intended to keep her away from Alan, Lily protested: "But it isn't round."

Harry was slowly shaking his head. "No, it sure ain't." In fact, Maracanda was notably more lopsided than the black hole.

They couldn't call it even approximately spherical. No, it was more like a long, thin hen's egg. From certain angles it appeared to be only one or two hundred kilometers thick. All right, maybe that was an illusion. Maybe. But . . .

And was Maracanda rotating or not? Trying more or less optical magnification did not help. Was the habitable body more like a thin egg, a doughnut, or a pancake? In Harry's eyes its sprawling presence seemed to assume these shapes and others, successively, in a progression that was obviously part of some optical illusion.

When called upon, the data bank offered calm explanations. But they were not entirely satisfactory.

A computer could offer explanations, but it couldn't very well judge whether you were capable of understanding them or not. After listening, Harry tried to come up with his own.

"What we're seeing is only a type of mirage, due to a certain—what they compare to a reverse solar wind. Infalling matter, and not all of it normal matter by any means, moving between us and that—*thing*, whatever it is, where there's supposed to be a place where ships can land. You'll notice that the apparent shape changes not only with our position, but with our relative motion."

If the celestial mechanics of the system ever brought the habitable surface of Maracanda into the way of the pulsar's periodically slashing X-ray beam, the peculiar body evidently enjoyed some effective natural protection, or it never could have been considered habitable. Harry's data bank was sternly emphatic about the astrogational hazard presented by the veils of infalling gas.

The data bank had more to say, its voice slightly louder than usual, as if to emphasize that this was important. It was prescribing exact approaches, issuing warnings that Harry heeded, though he didn't understand them right away. The same forces that protected Maracanda's surface, effectively creating a livable world in a place where such a thing had no business to be, also tended to disable many kinds of complex machinery. There were large portions of the otherwise habitable surface, known as breakdown zones, where such modern tools as groundcars, radios, and spaceships almost always failed to operate.

Harry puzzled over that statement for a moment, then put it aside. "All right, as long as we can be sure of a safe area to land, we'll figure out the rest later. Let's get back to basic questions, like what *shape* does this damned place have?"

Harry's data bank still seemed somewhat out of its depth in this discussion. It informed him soberly: "The real shape, that is, as mathematically defined, is somewhat more ordinary, almost spherical in fact, except flattened somewhat at the three poles."

Three poles. Sure. Harry's mathematical education was comparatively limited, and right now he had other things to be concerned about, and besides, he hated arguing with machines. Instead of arguing he said: "This I want to see. Dispense with the live video for the moment. Draw me a diagram."

"The holostage can present only a relatively crude approximation," the ship's pleasant voice warned.

"I understand. Go ahead."

Immediately there began to take shape upon the stage an image that looked like some clever madman's proposed design for an optical illusion. This looked even crazier than the triple primary. Harry thought the object might have been meant to represent a slowly rotating sphere, except that it was not only turning but seemed perpetually on the verge of turning itself inside out. Harry wanted to keep staring, and at the same time he was glad to tear his gaze away.

He waved it aside. "All right, I'll take another look at this later. There is an area where we can land safely?"

"There is."

"Can you handle this landing, autopilot?"

"Certainly."

"Then do so."

Lily looked suddenly relieved, as if the issue had been in doubt. A smile twitched at her lips, as she said: "You must repeat one hundred times: This is not a planet. This is not a planet. This is not . . ."

SEVEN

"It looks like at least a few other ships have recently made it down in one piece," Lily observed, nodding at the display that had just winked into existence on the holostage. It showed what was obviously a landing field, a flat expanse dotted here and there with symbols representing stationary spacecraft. The *Witch*'s assigned berth was conveniently marked.

Harry didn't comment. His ship's data bank, which Harry updated at every opportunity, was firm on the subject: there was only one spaceport on Maracanda. Examining what little he could see of the flattened surface in the general vicinity of the landing field, Harry could see a sizable settlement, clusters of strange-looking buildings. The oddity was that they seemed to be made entirely of the same material as the ground on which they stood.

When they were a few minutes closer, near enough for a telescope to give them a good look at the city, it seemed not to have been built up so much as carved out of the surrealistic land. The place looked more like a crude computer graphic of a landscape than any real place Harry had ever visited. To Harry, the look of this place suggested a crude attempt by some reality-designer to imitate the fine detail and subtle colors of good computer holographics, the type that aimed more at artistic effect than realism. Streaks of color, distributed according to no visible plan, ran across the varied surfaces in random patterns.

Lily put a hand on his arm. The gesture seemed perfectly natural. "Look at that."

What the two people in the approaching ship had first taken to be vegetation, trees of some kind, appeared as they drew closer to be bizarrely shaped outcroppings of the land itself.

Moments later, the *Witch* had set herself gently down near the middle of a large and almost disappointingly normal landing field. It was smaller than their departure site on Hong's World, but otherwise very similar.

Within a minute after touchdown, the ship requested captain's permission to turn off artificial gravity altogether. The local gravity was so precisely close to standard normal that keeping it on would be simply a waste of power.

"Permission granted," said Harry after a moment. Then he wondered aloud: "Why should it match so closely? This isn't even . . ."

"A planet," Lily finished. "But typical of azlaroc-type objects. I've been doing a little reading up on them over the past few months."

"You didn't tell me that before."

"I was afraid to sound like an idiot, repeating the things I'd read."

Two minutes after touchdown, Harry and Lily, each carrying

one meager pack of personal baggage, walked out of the *Witch*'s main hatch and down the little landing ramp to stand under what looked more like smooth, continuous cloud cover, or the interior of some huge artificial dome, than it did a sky. From high above they had been able to see the landing field, but looking up from the field was a different story. The gravity was evidently completely natural, yet he could feel in his bones and muscles that it matched the standard of Earth-surface normal with eerie precision.

There were some ten or a dozen other ships visible on the broad field, which still had room for hundreds more. In the distance, a few people and groundcars moved about. Beyond that, a couple of kilometers in the distance, rose the modest towers of a peculiar city that, judging by its colors, seemed to have been built entirely of slabs and blocks of the strange ground.

An ordinary people transporter, a comfortable-looking machine, roofless as if it were intended only for indoor use, and somehow incongruous in this setting, came rolling toward them from the direction of a distant building. It rolled on smooth treads, as it might have done on the majority of public spaceports across the settled Galaxy.

The machine stopped in front of the waiting couple, and its scanners inspected them briefly. Then in a smooth voice it invited them to climb aboard for a ride to the office of the local Port Authority, where all visitors were requested to check in on landing.

There were only open-air seats, tending to confirm something Harry's data bank had told him, that this world saw neither rain nor snow. Space was provided for ten or twelve people, but no other riders at the moment.

While being borne smoothly across the plain of the landing field, Harry looked around.

"What is it?" His companion was suddenly alert.

"The silence." He made a vague gesture. "As if we were in a—sealed chamber somewhere."

Lily nodded. The quiet seemed unnatural for any out-of-doors location, anywhere in atmosphere. There was very little wind.

"There are no birds," she added suddenly. She was leaning a little closer to Harry in her chair, as if unconsciously.

That was right, Harry thought, no birds. Nor any bugs either, as far as he could tell so far. No life forms casually present, at least on this part of Maracanda. Even the gradually approaching city and its people seemed too quiet, though now they could begin to hear some ordinary sounds of traffic.

Harry also took note of the fact that one of the landed ships was a Space Force vessel. Only a scoutship, but enough to give evidence that the Force was active here. Smoothly rounded, house-sized mounds in the middle distance were identifiable as some of the ground defenses.

Lily was silent for most of the ride, mostly leaning forward in her seat, as if trying to pull the rolling vehicle a little closer to her Alan. Harry could see nothing in her behavior to suggest that she had visited this world before.

A scattering of traffic moved around the edges of the field, as it would at the spaceport of any normal planet. The people moving about on foot, ignoring the two new arrivals, looked much like travelers on any world with a mild climate. A minute later, the transporter deposited Harry and Lily at the main entrance of a building of modest size that seemed, like all the other visible structures, to have been built out of slabs and blocks carved or molded from the land itself, alternating with windows of imported glass. ADMINISTRATIVE CENTER read the graceful sign over the main entrance.

Smaller signs indicated the way to various tenants of the headquarters, including the Port Authority office. Lily was carrying her pack as they started up to the entrance, attracting no attention from the people going in and out on business. She told Harry that she had brought with her a list of names, of specific addresses where she thought Alan might be found, and of religious officials who might be here and, if here, might be expected to know his exact location. Beyond that, Lily had only a vague idea of where to start looking for him.

She tripped quickly up the gracefully shaped ramp and into the building, with Harry pacing less hurriedly behind. Inside, they found their surroundings reassuringly normal. This building had a roof, was fitted with more or less standard office decor, and was moderately busy. Half a dozen civilians, clothed in a cosmopolitan variety of styles, were trying to hold face-to-face meetings with two or three low-rankers in Space Force uniforms. Evidently the Force occupied a good share of this facility's ground floor.

Signs giving directions and advice were posted everywhere, their little arrows and fingerposts pointing in every direction, and Harry noted several signs marked with the stylized spiral that was the most common symbol of Malakó. These, in a script that changed from language to language while you watched, advised newly arrived pilgrims where they could go to establish contact with their fellow worshipers.

Lily looked indecisive. Harry asked her: "So, where would you expect your man to be?"

But Lily was already moving toward the map.

All across one broad wall, so that everyone who came into the building saw it at once, stretched a long, rectangular holomap, twice as broad as it was high. A small printed legend proclaimed the entire livable surface of Maracanda. There was no suggestion that the domain portrayed was really not practically flat.

No lines of latitude or longitude had been drawn, but directions of east and west, north and south, were clearly shown, as was the scale. The area marked as habitable, an enormous oval, extended for thousands of kilometers, not over the surface of a sphere, but across a vast plain. The area outside the oval, at the extreme edges of the map, was filled with a chaos of symbolic

little lines marked here and there with the terse comment:
UNINHABITABLE.

The east-west dimension of the oval was considerably
greater than the north-south. Harry wondered on what basis the
directions had been assigned, when just determining the poles of
rotation seemed to be far from a simple matter.

Lily had gone immediately to the map, and was pointing out
some of its features, with the intent, abstracted air of someone just
discovering them for herself. She was fretting about how far away
the other settlements seemed to be. They were distant indeed,
more than a thousand kilometers east of the only marked spaceport, where they had just landed.

"The what?" Harry hadn't heard the first time.

"The Tomb of Timur. Also called the Portal, not to be confused with Port City, which is where we are now. Alan will be way
over there, a thousand klicks from here, at the Portal. Or as near to
it as he can get."

"How can you be so sure?"

"When he gets enthusiastic about something, he becomes a
real fanatic. Where else would he go?"

Harry didn't want to try to guess. Once more he scanned the
map, thinking there was something wrong about it. It finally sank
in on him that there were no other cities or towns marked anywhere. Not one. Port City on one edge of the vast oval expanse,
and at the other end, Minersville and the Portal, separated by less
than fifty klicks. And that was it. Oh, except for one small dot,
four-fifths of the way across, labeled CARAVANSERAI. He wondered
if, for some reason, a large part of the population had simply been
left off the map.

He observed: "All those other places are a long haul from
here, well over a thousand klicks. And it seems spacecraft can't or
don't land over there. How will you get there?"

"When I was reading up on Maracanda, the sourcebook said

something about caravans, and ground transport being generally difficult, but I couldn't really understand what it was talking about."

Harry was puzzling over another symbol on the map, a long and wiggly line labeled SUBDUCTION ZONE, when Lily gave a sharp tug at his sleeve.

He turned to discover two men in Space Force uniform, wearing sidearms, approaching him on foot, smiling pleasantly.

"Mr. Harry Silver?"

"Yes?"

"We'd like you to come with us, please."

He looked from one youthful face to another. "Is this an arrest?"

"No sir, nothing like that. A request only."

Evidently his ship had been identified, on approach or on landing, and some sort of official notice taken. Harry gave his welcomers a smile. "Why not? I always enjoy a chat with the Space Force."

He didn't look at Lily, and was ready to walk away from her without a word, as if they were two strangers only standing next to each other by chance. But she wasn't having any of that.

"What about me?" she spoke up sharply.

One officer kept a steady eye on Harry, but the other turned. "Ma'am?"

"My name is Lily Gunnlod. I was a passenger on Mr. Silver's ship."

The two exchanged glances. "We don't have any orders regarding you, ma'am. But if it's convenient, maybe you'd better come along."

Little was said among the four of them as they took a short walk down a corridor paneled in something that looked like false marble, to arrive almost immediately in the Space Force offices.

Harry left her sitting comfortably in the little anteroom when he was ushered in to see the local Space Force commandant.

Commandant Rovaki's eyebrows, bushy and silvery, were the most prominent features of his small face. His body was on the small side, too, nervous and energetic, seeming well suited to the dimensions of his small private office. Decoration was at a minimum in here, lighting was bright and direct, order and efficiency were paramount. There were no pictures on the plain walls, or even windows, but only charts that moved and crawled with information.

The commandant did not bother to rise when Harry was brought in. The greeting from behind the small, efficient desk was terse and to the point, accompanied by a knitted frown of eyebrows. "We've got a dossier on you, Silver."

"Good afternoon to you, too." Harry helped himself to one of the two unoccupied chairs and soon discovered it was not designed for comfort. "Yes, thanks, we had a pleasant trip. Nothing good in your file on me, I hope." He tossed a small recording cube on the commandant's desk. "A little something to bring you up to date."

"I wouldn't advise you to be antagonistic, mister!" Rovaki gave the little cube a brief, suspicious glare, as if he dared it to explode. "What's this supposed to be?"

"Some pictures of a berserker. Ever see one?"

"Pictures taken where and when?"

"On the edge of the Thisworld system, when I just passed through."

The officer stared at Harry for a full ten seconds without speaking. At last he said: "Not in my territory. I know your type, Silver. You've been lucky in a berserker fight or two, and also in getting away with some illegalities. So you think that you have special rights and privileges. That's not going to work in the Maracanda system. I hear you have a passenger."

"Had one. She's now reached her destination."

"And just what are the two of you up to here?"

"So far we're just wasting time—me in here, she in your outer office."

"All right, mister, have your fun. Maybe I'll have some fun of my own before we say goodbye. Now I want to know what kind of business the two of you are in. Here to get rich digging up the ground? Or maybe you have spiritual goals."

"You'll have to ask the lady about her business. I just told you mine."

"Mm-hmm. So, you came here with only one passenger. What's your cargo?"

Harry told him. "Six large boxes, said to contain food-processing machinery. I haven't looked into 'em. The shipment was consigned to Hong's World, but I guess nobody there had need of it any longer. Couldn't find anyone who wanted to pay for it."

"I'll want to inspect your cargo. And the rest of your ship."

Harry nodded. "Sure. I'll give you the personal tour, any time you say."

For a time Rovaki sat nodding to himself in meditative silence. "So you have no contracted deliveries to make on Maracanda?"

"Just one passenger, as already described."

The commandant leaned back in his chair. "Then I'll make that inspection of your ship when I get around to it. Meanwhile we're just going to seal her up, pending inspection for possible contraband."

It was Harry's turn to sit and think, while Rovaki looked at him from across his desk, letting Harry ponder the implications of not being able to move his vessel or unload it here.

Harry sat back in his chair and closed his eyes.

"I'd pay attention, Silver, if I were you."

There were metaphysical depths in that response that Harry decided to avoid. "I am paying attention," he answered mildly. "More or less. I don't know *what* I'd do if I were you."

Rovaki blinked. "Tell me more about your passenger."

"I'll tell you all I know, it won't take long. In effect, she chartered my ship to come here. Says she's looking for her husband."

The officer seemed to take sharp notice of something in Harry's tone. "Any reason to doubt that?"

Harry shrugged. "No special reason either to doubt it or believe it. She paid me and I earned my money."

"And the trip was uneventful?"

"Oh, quite. Unless you count the berserker. If that subject really doesn't interest you, I might as well take my recording back."

"Not so fast. I'll look at it in good time. When I'm ready. I have some people and some programs that are very good at detecting fakes. Tell me about this alleged missing husband. What's he do?"

"What I hear from his alleged wife is that currently he's much involved with the Malakó religion. But you'd better ask the man himself. I've never even met him, I just drive the alleged ship."

The official did not seem to find Alan's purported motives strange. He became almost conversational. "About half the people arriving at our spaceport claim to be coming here for religious reasons. The proportion used to be higher, but now there's quite a crowd coming to prospect for minerals, or to put in a claim on a section of land, just on speculation. What business arrangement did you have with this Alan Gunnlod?"

"None at all. I just told you, I've never met him, or communicated."

The officer switched topics abruptly. Somewhere he must

have taken a course on how to be a skilled interrogator—keep the guilty subject off balance, tangle him up in his stupid lies. Well, the conversation so far was unbalanced and tangled enough.

Gesturing at a blank space on his office wall, Rovaki called up an intricate 3-D astrogation chart. "So, you claim to have encountered this berserker in the Thisworld system?"

"That's what happened."

"If your record proves to be authentic, it will be passed on to the appropriate authorities. What were you doing there?"

"I just told you. If you doubt I was really there—"

"Now, would I have any reason to do that?" Rovaki made an adjustment, and the chart on his wall switched scales and point of view. A hundred or so solar systems vanished, others were brought into the foreground.

"It does seem just a little out of the way, doesn't it?" the officer commented. Rows of numbers, and curved lines, flickered and came to an understanding among themselves. "In the conduct of normal business, setting a course to Maracanda from Hong's World, Thisworld wouldn't be likely to show up on your route."

"When I put my ship on autopilot, she sometimes seems to have a mind of her own."

Commandant Rovaki resettled himself in his chair. He took his comfortable time about it, as if to make the point that he had just got started asking questions.

"You say you came here from Hong's World. Where were you before that?"

Harry told him.

"And before that? Your previous port of departure?"

Over the next few minutes they worked their way back through several months of standard time, until they had arrived at a place called Hyperborea.

When Harry pronounced that name, the commandant leaned back in his chair and gave him a strange look.

"Yeah, I know," Harry assured him, "it's one of your big bases. And that was just when all the fuss was going on there. You can check with the commanding officer, Commander Claire Normandy." To himself he thought, You'll probably be hearing from her about me anyway, soon enough.

The officer refused to be impressed. "You can rest assured that I'll do that."

Rovaki spent a few minutes going back over the same ground. Then suddenly he seemed to tire of the interrogation game. "All right, Silver, you can go. For now. I would advise you not to leave town."

Lily, still sitting where Harry had left her, tossed aside a smartpaper magazine and looked up at him expectantly. The low-ranker who escorted Harry back to the waiting room politely asked her to step in for a separate interview.

When she shot a questioning look at Harry, he tried for a reassuring smile. This would seem to be an ideal chance for him to say goodbye and disappear. But without his ship he had no place to go.

Instead he said: "Go ahead, talk to the man, Ms. Gunnlod. I'll be waiting. I'm not going anywhere."

"Thanks." It sounded like she meant it.

Settling into a chair, Harry
picked up the smartpaper magazine Lily had been looking at,
glanced at the title page to see what range of content it could provide, and tossed it aside. Evidently no new information had been
loaded into it for more than a standard year.

There was a small holostage in one corner of the waiting
room, tuned and positioned to avoid distracting the low-ranker
receptionist at her work station. A presentation of local news was
currently on stage, and Harry began to watch and listen with some
attention. It would probably be a good idea to absorb whatever
details he could about the ways of human life on Maracanda.

So far, the newscaster, who sounded weary, had been talking
almost exclusively about what she called the usual disputes over
access to the Portal. The images of various people Harry had

never heard of came and went on the little stage, staking out their positions. The first speaker claimed to represent the scientific community, the second one the true Malakó religion—never mind about those schismatic heretics who were causing all the trouble—and a third the local civil authority. No two speakers seemed to agree about anything; Harry had no idea if any of them were right.

The times allotted for Portal access by the general public seemed to be severely limited. So were the disputants' times on stage. There wasn't going to be any long discussion, nothing that might allow an outsider to deduce just what they were talking about. On with the news. The amount of high-grade mineral exports had reached a new high in the last standard month. Investigators had still uncovered no clues in the disappearance, a standard month ago, of a certain Dr. Emily Kochi, an astrogeologist. Dr. Kochi had no family on Maracanda, but many friends who by now had just about given up hope. She had been working alone in a remote area, and it was feared that she had been caught in a subduction zone.

On the brighter side, it seemed a new school was about to open in Port City.

Harry's attention wandered, and he checked the local time. Lily seemed to be spending a good amount of time talking to the Space Force—or maybe she would just be listening as Commandant Rovaki practiced his interrogation skills. Harry wasn't much worried about what Lily might be telling him. If she was the innocent person she claimed to be, she wasn't going to say anything that would delay her search for Alan, and if she really was secretly the queen of smugglers, she certainly wasn't about to sign up for any unnecessary appearance in a courtroom.

No, the two amateur hijackers must have been lying about her, just trying to save their miserable lives. Harry couldn't really find her credible as a master criminal.

At that point, experience kicked in, reminding him of a

number of things in the past that he had not been able to believe, not until they ignored his predictions and happened anyway.

What he did have no trouble at all believing, and found a serious annoyance, was Rovaki's announcement that his ship was being sealed, that the *Witch* was condemned to sit idle on the ramp of this out-of-the-way port for some unknown time, just waiting for his lordship of the local Space Force to get around to inspecting it.

Harry was pondering, gloomily and unproductively, the various ramifications of this problem when a new face appeared in the entrance to the waiting room. It was a dark, masculine countenance, showing a lot of ancient Asian ancestry, and set well above the floor, atop a kind of uniform that was probably not often seen inside this Space Force office. Each of this man's shoulders bore the single small silver star of a Templar brigadier general.

The general had come to a halt, hands gripping the sides of the narrow doorway. His dark epicanthic eyes were staring at Harry—not exactly with recognition, but some kind of anticipation. The scrutiny was intense, but did not seem unfriendly.

It took another moment for the attendant clerk to catch sight of the visitor. She looked up, startled, from her work. "General Pike? The commandant is currently engaged. If you'd like to see—"

A large hand waved dismissively. A harsh voice rasped: "That's all right, didn't much want to see him anyway. Not today. You'd be Harry Silver?"

Harry got slowly to his feet. "That's right, general."

"Word has got around that you just made a berserker kill."

"Word gets around quickly then. I'm glad someone's taking notice. Let's just say I watched a berserker die."

The general moved a step into the room, to stand with arms folded. There was excitement in his voice. "But I understand that you engaged the bloody thing in combat?"

Harry nodded. "Except I'm not sure if 'engaged' is the right word. We exchanged fire, but I was doing my damnedest to get away."

"By thunder!" The newcomer's eyes were glowing. He stepped closer, put out a hand, caught Harry's in a crushing grip. "Need I say that I'm keen to see any record of this exploit that you might have managed to retain—and to offer my heartfelt congratulations to the winner!

"My name's Robledo Pike." Breaking off the handshake, he stepped back to make a sweeping bow, flourishing a broad-brimmed hat, one of the optional adjuncts of the Templar dress uniform.

"Harry Silver."

"So I've been told." Then the general jerked his chin toward the inner office. "Still waiting to see the man, are you?"

"Actually, I've seen him. I'm just waiting for a friend who's in there now."

"Ah. Do you suppose you could wait in my office as well as here? My chairs are softer."

"Why not? I can show you that recording if you like." Harry was prepared with another copy to hand out.

"Excellent!"

"I'll be glad to go over it with you, in case you have any questions."

"Could you possibly spare the time right now? My office is just upstairs. Free-zone space is at a premium here, you see, and everyone shares a building. Beth, my dear?" This last was addressed to the clerk. "Suppose you could point Mr. Silver's friend in the right direction to catch up with us, when His Nibs is finished with her?"

"Certainly, general."

But no sooner had the clerk said that than Lily emerged from the inner office, not exactly storming, but moving along energetically.

She was talking as she walked. Over her shoulder she told the commandant, who was still out of sight somewhere behind her: "I'm going wherever I want to go, and doing anything I want to do! As long as I'm not under arrest, I'm going to Portal City to meet my husband. If you want me for anything, you can find me there."

Then an afterthought, lifting her chin at Harry: "And if Mr. Silver wants to come with me, and I hope he does, I'm going to see a lot of him!"

Commandant Rovaki's voice could be heard, calling after Lily: "And when you see Harry Silver, tell him I'm putting a seal on his ship, until this little matter is straightened out. He'd better not go anywhere either."

Lily said to Harry: "So, it seems that, if I am really a decent young lady, I will be well advised not to associate with you."

Harry performed brief introductions, and the general made another sweeping bow. A couple of minutes later, they were all three in the general's office. Pike's office was somewhat bigger and considerably more disorderly than Rovaki's. The walls were hung with portrait after portrait, mostly of veteran men and women in Templar uniforms. There was a variety of mementos, including an old recruiting poster:

THE FIGHT FOR LIFE HAS NOT BEEN WON

THE TEMPLARS NEED YOU

Just underneath the legend a lifelike graphic, appearing three-dimensional when viewed from the proper angle, portrayed an attractive child cringing away from a grasping metallic menace. The berserker in the image was far more barbed and angled and poisonous-looking than the one in Harry's brief recording.

But it was, of course, the one in the recording that the general was watching, for about the tenth time.

Robledo Pike, in contrast to his Space Force counterpart, proved eager to see the berserker blasted over and over, in shower after shower of multicolored sparks. Pike was nodding judiciously, as the spectacular climax appeared again. "Must have hit a clot of dust head on—a veritable lump of the good hard stuff— only other time I can recall seeing one disintegrate like that was a direct hit from a c-plus cannon."

Harry nodded in agreement. "It sure had a decisive effect."

"Let's see that just once more—hah! Beautiful!"

Leaning forward in his chair and fixing Lily with a curious eye, Pike spoke in what he obviously hoped was an encouraging tone. He would be glad to hear any additional details she might be able to provide about the recent skirmish.

She protested that she had been only a bystander, unable to interpret the little symbols on the holostage. "Until the red dot vanished, and I knew that we were going to make it. Thanks to Harry." And she gave him a warm look.

There was a little silence, which Harry broke by saying: "Well, folks, I've got to start trying to do something about my ship. Looks like my next step is to go out and find myself a good lawyer."

The Templar frowned and leaned back in his chair. "Might not be necessary, Silver. Let's talk a little first. It could be that I have a better idea."

"If there are ideas to be offered, I'm listening."

"By thunder!" Pike leaned forward again, pounding a fist softly on the arm of his chair. "I want to do something for you, sir—and you, too, madam. Two brave people who have courageously faced and fought a berserker machine. Successfully!"

"Sheer luck," Harry murmured modestly.

"Ah, but it's results that count—and here you've shown me the recorded evidence. Now, as to your current problem. I could give you the names of one or two good lawyers, but perhaps I can do even better." Pike fixed Harry with a frowning, scheming eye.

"How's that, general?"

"I'm on good terms with the federation prosecutor here on Maracanda. Mind you, I promise nothing, but it might be possible to expedite the unsealing of your ship."

"Sounds good," Harry admitted cautiously. "Maybe, some day, in return I could do some little thing for you."

"Oh, not for me, my lad. Whatever I might ask of you—and of you, young woman—will not be just for me. Say, rather, for all humankind."

The general paused, and went on. "You know as well as I do that there exists in the Galaxy a certain class of men and women—no, I shouldn't dishonor the names of women and men by putting them in that category. Of *creatures*, say, so-called humans, who find their object of worship just where they should not—creatures you don't like any better than I do." Pike paused dramatically. "I'm speaking, of course, of goodlife."

Harry grunted. Lily looked thoughtful. Goodlife was the berserkers' own name for humans who wanted to help them destroy humanity. Such renegades were rare but by no means non-existent, and the general was right—Harry had known some of them to make a dark religion out of their alienation.

Pike was going on. "It has come to my attention that in the eastern cities—Minersville, and the settlement usually called Tomb Town—goodlife activity is carried out almost openly. Speeches in the so-called sacred square, before the Portal. I'm damned short on people just now, and I appeal for help to those I know are not unwilling to take a shot at a berserker. Are you with me?"

Lily was shaking her head doubtfully, but certainly had not turned down the general as yet.

Harry said: "I'm out of practice as a secret agent. But if you just want people to keep their eyes and ears open—"

"That's it exactly!"

Lily murmured something in agreement; and a moment later, Pike was offering to provide his agent, or agents, money for necessities.

Harry didn't want to be in the man's debt any more than he could help. "I'll bill you later, if I think I have it coming."

Lily cleared her throat. "I appreciate your gentlemanly atti-tude, General Pike. I'll be pleased to discover goodlife for you if I can. But you must realize that my reason for coming to Maracanda is to find my husband. Everyone agrees that the east side is the place to look, and that will remain my priority."

"Yes, you've come a long way to locate him, haven't you? A kind of devotion that is all too rare in our times, perhaps in any times . . . Well, I don't doubt you're right, madam. If he's here as a Malakó enthusiast, he is undoubtedly over in Tomb Town, or somewhere near it. Gone for a look into God's Eyeball, as some have been known to call that strange thing there."

Harry and Lily were ready to get up and go. But General Pike, having established contact with sympathetic listeners, wanted to talk some more on his own favorite subjects.

"I tell you, Silver, Ms. Gunnlod, goodlife are only part of the problem. The worst part, but not the whole of it, by any means."

The Templar's fundamental argument was that people, the various components of Earth-descended humanity, should not be feuding among themselves, but should unite in fighting the real enemy, berserkers—and his face grew red when he spoke of the fiendish, loathsome, demonic perverts who had sold their souls to become goodlife, in effect worshiping the essence of evil.

Lily broke in, obviously hoping to extract some practical

information. "Have you been to the east side, general?" Everyone knew that Templars tended to be religious.

"Not for some time. Duties keep me busy over here. And begging your pardon, ma'am—not knowing exactly how deep your own commitment to the thing may be—but this Malakó business is not for me. The great Eyeball, or whatever . . . no. My own religion is very simple—I worship Life!"

"And speaking of life—" He warned his new agents to watch out for their own.

"How're we supposed to report back to you?"

"There's only one quick way, unfortunately not the most convenient, or the most foolproof. I'll show you. Step this way, if you will."

In a moment he had conducted his two visitors into a small adjoining room. There they found a crippled man in Templar uniform seated at a plain, small table. Thin cables emerged from holes in the table's top, then connected to a small, odd instrument of brassy metal, mounted in its center. From time to time, something in the little machine would vibrate fiercely, while the man watched steadily. More elaborate equipment, connected to the brass, produced a kind of printout. The lines on the continuously emerging graph zigged and zagged in time with the chattering of the simple machine.

"Our central telegraph terminal." Pike's voice held a note of pride. "Anything new, Kurchatov?"

"No sir." The scarred Templar looked up and smiled vaguely at his visitors, but in the next moment was concentrating again on the machinery.

Pike was explaining. "Our sole means of communication with the other cities on this world. All that comes in, you see, are simple dots and dashes, through a fiberoptic line. It's the only way we know of to get a message quickly through the breakdown zone."

Harry felt somewhere between dazed and lost. "This is the best anyone on Maracanda can do in the way of communication?"

"Between here and the far east, Minersville and Tomb Town, I'm afraid it is. Radio's been shown to be hopeless, away from the free zones. Biggest free zone is right here, of course, encompassing the spaceport and Port City.

"People keep trying to find a better way, of course. We need more resources for research. But our Superior General probably sees no reason to have much of a Templar presence on Maracanda—except to keep the Space Force from having a monopoly. There's nothing much here that needs to be defended against berserkers, and no berserkers to attack."

Lily asked about the fastest way to reach the vicinity of the Tomb.

Pike told his visitors: "There's basically only one mode of travel on this world. That's overland, by caravan, or pedicar, or on foot, if it comes to that."

"Someone was trying to explain that to me, but—"

Harry cut in: "Nothing goes back and forth by air, or spacecraft, between here and there, west and east? Nothing at all?"

Pike was shaking his head. "There just isn't any air transport on this world. Here, let me show you on the map."

The Templar's map looked like a good copy, though considerably smaller, of the big one on the ground floor of the administration center. Using a laser pointer, the general called their attention to the spot where, he said, Lily wanted to look for Alan.

Harry commented that the map showed no other cities or towns anywhere.

"That's because virtually no others exist."

"Here is the famous Portal, also known as the Tomb of Timur, the human founder of the worship of Malakó. A great many people are not convinced that anyone is actually buried there."

A moment later, Pike had summoned up the caravan route, a long thin line springing into visibility, winding across the map from one edge to the other. He also pointed out the settlement of Minersville.

"About half the population on the other side of Maracanda is centered in the vicinity of the Tomb—sometimes called the Portal, and sometimes, by the especially irreverent, the Eyeball, or Eyeball of God. The other half is centered in Minersville, just a few kilometers away, on the land office, which is very near the Tomb. Also the richest land, in terms of mineral wealth, is in the same vicinity. The only feasible way to reach any of these places is by going overland. In practice, for most folk, including you, that means joining a caravan."

General Pike was just beginning an explanation of something he called the caravans, which sounded to Harry like some truly demented system of ground transportation. Harry, still not getting it, cut in. "Any reason, legal or physical, why I couldn't just take my ship over there and land it? Assuming, that is, that the Space Force doesn't already have her sealed? And by the way, is there anything you can do about that?"

"If the commandant said he'd seal your ship, it's probably done by now. I said I'd try to be of some help there, and I will. But I may not be able to do much. In practice, the Space Force can seal a ship for thirty standard days, or until the owner goes to court and gets an injunction of relief."

The general sighed. "To return to your main point: there's no legal prohibition against trying to land a spacecraft or aircraft on the other side of the continent. Almost everyone asks, and we might post a sign or two. But again there are the breakdown zones, you see, so in practice the thing's impossible."

"I still don't understand this business of breakdown zones."

"Join the club. I can tell you what everyone knows: They are regions, domains, on this world in which modern technology simply does not work—for reasons that are still being investigated. They are also something you must understand before you try to go anywhere or do anything on Maracanda. Across much of the surface, the 'sky' is simply too low, the breakdown zones too nearly continuous, to allow anything like practical air travel."

"All right, then I suppose the caravans are some kind of system of groundcars?"

"More like overland trains, necessarily very low tech. You'll see. They're efficient, most of them reasonably comfortable, if your standards of comfort aren't too high. I've made the trip. But your journey will take several days. There is simply no faster way."

As the couple walked out of the administration building, under the deceptive natural canopy, afflicted with a perpetual mild overcast, that served on Maracanda for a sky, Harry said: "I'm beginning to think you may have a tough time finding your man, kid. It looks like just getting near him will be a chore."

"It hasn't been exactly easy up till now. Are you still coming with me, Harry?"

"Said I would, didn't I?"

"Commandant Rovaki will be upset if you leave town."

"That's another reason."

She shook her head. "Harry, it would seem that you'd be awfully easy to manipulate, once someone understood that you could be counted on to do the opposite of whatever you were told."

"Don't count on it, lady." But he had to smile.

After a few more steps, Lily said: "Harry, you haven't asked me what Rovaki questioned me about."

"That's easy, he wanted to talk about me." Harry looked around him. "Nobody's come to arrest me, so I guess I'm not accused of any crimes."

"You're right, of course. He asked if I'd observed any suspicious behavior on your part, and I told him that I hadn't." She smiled faintly. "He seemed to be leaving it up to me to define 'suspicious behavior.' I was the only passenger aboard your ship when it left Hong's World, and I had no idea what cargo you might be carrying. When he asked why you stopped in the Thisworld system, I told him I had no idea about that either—all that technical stuff was just beyond me."

"And he believed you?"

"As far as I could tell. And I kept pestering him for suggestions as to how I might locate Alan. A total waste of time, of course, except I think it kept him a little off balance."

Harry smiled. "So, now you're ready to get down to serious business. Really start the search for Alan."

The two of them were walking toward what appeared to be the center of Port City, whose streets began right at the spaceport's edge.

They had just got in among the peculiar buildings, and Harry was offering to buy lunch—though the clocks he had seen since landing showed the local time as early morning. Before Lily could react to the suggestion, a loud voice close behind them bellowed a strange, wordless cry.

In the next moment, a huge man in flamboyant civilian dress seemed to materialize out of nowhere to confront them. In a moment he had engulfed Harry in a boisterous greeting, pounding the smaller man on the back.

Harry stumbled, staggered, used what means he could, short of actual violence, to fend off the assault. He was muttering dark words under his breath.

The newcomer babbled, sounding breathless with delight. His clothes made the uniform of General Pike look drab by comparison. His voice went up and down the scale, as if he were trying to be all the characters in a play. "Dear Harry—what a delight to stumble across you here. Haven't seen you since—when was it?"

Harry couldn't have named the date if he had tried, and he wasn't going to try. He was willing to let their last meeting be forgotten. In fact, now that he thought about it, he had been making some effort to forget.

The other persisted. "Come on, I'm going to buy you a drink—and your lovely companion, too, of course. Can't you offer an introduction?"

Lily stared up at a mountainous body and a round face, cheeks partly bearded, somewhat pomaded, glowing with what might have been good humor, on either side of a well-tended and ornate mustache. And a lecherous, leering welcome to Harry's companion.

"Ms. Lily Gunnlod, this is Kul Bulaboldo—unless, of course, you're calling yourself by some other—"

"Not a bit of it, old chap, not a bit! I live here proudly under me own name."

Lily was looking from one of them to the other. Somehow she did not seem totally surprised. "An old friend of yours, Mr. Silver?"

"We've known each other a long time." It was a reluctant admission.

Bulaboldo's excitement had simmered down to the point where he could be coherent. "What brings you to this fair world, Harry, me lad?"

"It's a long story." Dryly, Harry asked: "I suppose you're here on a religious pilgrimage?"

"Oh, that's exactly it, dear heart! Very perceptive of you! Worshiping money as I do, I come to Maracanda to build a shrine to my god—or should I say to dig one out? Have you not heard of the treasures in rare earths available across the desert?" Kul gestured extravagantly.

"People keep talking about mining, prospecting, but—"

Bulaboldo, as usual, was not listening. "If I speak with attention to strict verisimilitude, I must admit that I have come to Maracanda to try to make a killing in rare earths. I may come a little late to the game for real success, but one has to make the effort, what?"

And with a nudge in the ribs: "What's happened to that little lady . . . You know the one I mean?"

"I might. Probably a lot of things have happened to her. And still are."

Presently Lily excused herself to go in search of a ladies' room. The Falstaffian one waited till she was out of sight and hearing before opening new subjects of conversation. Soon he was announcing, with a wink and a nudge, that he was more than a little interested in a story he had heard regarding a certain c-plus cannon.

"You and every bloody crook in the Galaxy, it seems," sighed Harry.

"Indeed, dear lad. The story I have gathered, from an impeccable source, alleges that one Harry Silver had somehow recently got away from the Space Force base at Hyperborea with such a weapon. Needless to say, we—in general, the community of those who understand such things—are all filled with admiration for the man who could accomplish such a feat."

Harry grunted.

"I suppose you've sold it already?" Bulaboldo suggested a couple of names as likely purchasers. Lily, returning, with mission accomplished, was close enough to overhear the names, but seemed to find them meaningless, to judge by her blank look. They were not meaningless to Harry, who recognized good examples of the dregs of Galactic society.

"Oh, go ahead," he assured Kul. "Discuss the subject. The lady knows."

"Ah, I see. Excellent. Get a good price?"

The man seemed to be able to hear about some things before they had actually happened. Harry said only: "If I had, would I be likely to talk about it?"

"Only to your best and oldest friend, dear lad." Bulaboldo moved as if to throw an enormous arm round Harry's shoulders, but caught himself in time to abort the gesture halfway through.

"If I did talk about it, you wouldn't like what you heard."

"My ears are calloused. Of course, I must assume that you *have* got rid of the thing somehow. It would be crazy to expect to go around peacefully trading, and submitting to Space Force seals and searches, with your ship's bow afflicted with a thing like that, sticking out like a sore nose." Bulaboldo mused, "Or something else . . . The protrusion must be how long?—several meters, anyway."

Harry offered no comment. Actually, the cannon he had concealed was a new model, hardly known to anyone as yet, and much less bulky than the old. Most people trying to imagine a cannon hidden on his ship would mistakenly discount the idea at once.

It was not that he had been conspiring or plotting to keep the damned thing. Selling it to pirates and terrorists was not an acceptable resolution of the problem either. It had crossed Harry's mind to dump the weapon somewhere, just to get rid of it, but that was a lot easier to say than to accomplish.

"And what business are you in, Mr. Bulaboldo?" Lily seemed to be asking it in all innocence.

"He's a crook," Harry explained succinctly. "The details vary from time to time."

Bulaboldo immediately protested, doing a bad actor's

impression of injured innocence, that he was not wanted for any crime at the moment. "At least not in this jurisdiction, old top."

Harry muttered that he had heard of his acquaintance that he was not above doing a little slave trading now and then.

Lily gave every impression of being outraged. "Surely that cannot be legal anywhere!"

Bulaboldo considered the point, frowning, gazing into the distance. The question seemed to put him on his mettle, a challenge not to his morals but to the depth of his knowledge of legal codes across the settled Galaxy.

"No, I don't believe it is." He shook his head. "Which, of course, poses difficulties, as one might expect. As a general rule, owning slaves really makes no economic sense. Ah, but in certain quarters, they are unsurpassed as a status symbol."

That answer silenced Lily for a time.

A good acquaintance, thought Harry, with every crime in the book . . . except one, probably. One crime that Bulaboldo would never commit was that of being goodlife. The bulky one enjoyed life too much to ever join that grim fraternity. But he would not be above dealing with the goodlife, or even with their metal masters, the berserkers themselves, if he thought he could make a reasonable profit.

Bulaboldo was making polite inquiries of his own. "And you, my lady, how are you enjoying your visit to our peculiar world?"

"So far it's not been dull." Lily appeared to reflect. "I must say that hardly an hour of my trip has been dull, especially since meeting Mr. Silver."

"Only to be expected! One must anticipate a certain piquancy in one's daily affairs when one travels with our dear Harry."

When Bulaboldo heard about Lily's missing husband, and

understood that she was not here simply as Harry's companion, he listened to her story attentively, and with an appearance of great sympathy.

Then he said, with an air of offering a revelation: "If this Alan Gunnlod belongs to the sect you speak of, I can tell you exactly where he'll be."

Lily only nodded. "Somewhere near the famous Tomb of Timur, right? I've known that for months. The trouble is in getting there. But I'm going to do it, if it takes me years. I'm going to get him back."

Bulaboldo had a pronouncement to make. "If they're putting a seal on your ship, old chap, the next step will very likely be to put one on a cell door, with you inside it."

"I don't need you to tell me that." Whether Robledo Pike was really taking care of that problem or not, it wouldn't do for Harry to act as if he thought he had help in high places. "Then where's a good place to keep out of sight?"

The bulky one looked concerned, and seemed to be thinking rapidly. Meanwhile, he stood facing both visitors, his massive shape forming a substantial roadblock around which the people of Maracanda detoured as they went about whatever business or nonsense they had in mind this morning. Few of them paid any attention to Harry and Lily, another pair of newcomers, maybe religious pilgrims or maybe prospectors, still wearing their ship-board coveralls.

"Old man, this is not exactly the most welcoming town for an outsider who wants to hide out. Even I have been in that spot a time or two—though fortunately at the moment I can walk the unpaved streets of Maracanda openly, looking each citizen boldly in the eye."

Harry said: "If you've got an idea, let's hear it. Keep me out of jail, and I'll owe you one."

Bulaboldo's eyebrows went up. "Is that a serious pledge? Mind, old chap, I'll hold you to it."

"Never doubted that you would."

"Well, I'll do my best. My only idea is simple and to the point. We've got to get you aboard a caravan. That'll buy us some time to work out a more permanent solution."

Lily brightened, as if the suggestion were a new one to her. "A caravan to the place they call Tomb Town, I hope."

The big man turned his benevolent gaze her way. "All the caravans that start from here go there, my darling. And vice versa, because there's really no other destination. Trains of vehicles wend their way from port to Portal, so to speak, and back again, across the wilderness.

"But we must get you, both of you, quickly to the departure point and aboard the morning eastbound. Wait right here, chaps. I'll slide my ample bottom into a groundcar and be back before you know it."

He moved away with surprising quickness, light-footed despite his size. Harry and Lily moved also, sliding more casually, a short distance to a doorway, where they waited, trying to blend into the adobe walls.

As soon as Bulaboldo was out of sight, Lily commented: "I must say I think you were serious about his being a criminal. How long have you known him?"

"Too long."

"Do you think we can trust him?"

"Absolutely not. But he can be very effective when he wants to do something—and I believe that for some reason he genuinely wants to help me. Maybe he can speed up our passage east. So for the moment I'm going to act as if I don't have any choice—and I'm not sure how much I really have. You see his eyes light up when I said I'd owe him one? He's already got a payoff in mind, and he's probably on our side until he gets it."

"I hope you're right. Harry? I can't thank you enough for what you've done. Just getting me here alive—and then volunteering to help me the way you have."

"Forget it, kid."

Pondering the somewhat vague commission he and Lily had accepted from General Pike, Harry decided he wasn't going to work very hard at looking for nonexistent goodlife on the east side of Maracanda. He doubted that his former passenger would spend much time spying for the Templars either. Harry would have been willing to bet that there were no actual functioning berserkers within light-years of this crazy place.

Pike had given Harry and Lily each a key that ought to provide them access to the Templars' private telegraph terminals in the east. Harry sympathized with the general's objectives, but had doubts about his shrewdness. Pike seemed to be the kind who saw goodlife and berserkers everywhere.

He said to Lily: "Here's another point we can be thinking about: general is a high rank to be commanding such a small detachment as the Templar force on Maracanda seems to be."

"Indicating what?"

"Suggesting that Pike has been more or less put out to pasture here. It's the kind of thing that's likely to happen when an officer fairly seriously screws up on a tougher assignment."

Lily thought about it. Finally she said: "But the general might be right. There could be some goodlife here."

"Sure, they could be anywhere. So could vegetarians, or nudists. But I can't see any reason why goodlife, or berserkers, would favor Maracanda as a target. If your goal is to destroy life, why plot against a world that has so little? Outside of a few humans, a very few pets, and a modest mass of intestinal bacteria, the total count of living things on Maracanda must be very close to zero. And there are the famous breakdown zones—I don't see how berserkers are going to operate in them."

Lily was ready for a little argument. "The humans here all seem to be concentrated on the few small parts of the surface that are not breakdown zones. And you told me berserkers love killing Earth-descended humans best of all."

"Well, they would if they loved anything—which they don't. And there are many, many worlds with bigger populations than this one."

Back in Pike's office, he had thought of hitting the general with those arguments, but had decided against it.

But of course Lily was right. The fact that Maracanda seemed an unprofitable place for berserkers to spend their time and energy didn't mean that goodlife couldn't be here. Some charismatic worshiper of death might have come along and drawn a following unto himself. Probably they'd be pretending to be something else among the other cults that were obviously flourishing. There were always sick and disaffected people, ready to commit some form of suicide, and some of those decided to worship the damned machines without even having seen one.

Harry was not particularly eager to have either Space Force or Templar Pike to see him in the company of, and apparently on friendly terms with, a shady character like Bulaboldo. So Harry had his back turned to the ramped entrance of the administration building, and was leaning his right side against the tavern's peculiar adobe wall, washed in the diffused sky glow that passed for sunshine, here in this solar system without a sun.

He wanted to look inconspicuous, without giving the impression that he was working at it. Lily was standing at Harry's left side, facing in the same direction he was. "Do you feel all right, Harry?"

"Sure. Great."

Except for her interview with Rovaki, Lily had been almost continuously in his sight, ever since they'd landed. Harry was keeping an eye on her, alert for any indication that she had spent time on this world before and was already secretly familiar with Maracanda. So far, Harry's alertness had been totally wasted. But still the castaways' last accusation refused to absolutely die.

Bulaboldo had been gone no more than two minutes when he reappeared, driving a sleek groundcar, which he pulled up directly in front of the doorway, minimizing Harry's exposure to observation as he climbed in. Maybe it was done just out of habit: the fewer people who knew when you did anything, the better off you were in general.

Lily was right after him, slamming the door behind her. At once Bulaboldo pulled out into the broad street's modest traffic.

The vehicle looked, sounded, and felt new and expensive. Judging by the prices he'd seen so far, everything was expensive on this world. "Your car?" Harry asked.

"Of course, old fellow. Did you think I'd steal one?"

Harry didn't bother to answer that.

Bulaboldo was driving on manual control, one-handed, while he used the other to facilitate a private conversation on his communicator. "Excuse me just a moment, old ones. Must give certain of my associates a few hints of what I'm thinking."

His communicator, like most others, was equipped with a

privacy device that kept any trace of the conversation from reaching his passengers' ears. The gadget even blurred Harry's line of sight to the speaker's lips, while Bulaboldo spoke briefly toward a spot on the dashboard.

His private talk on the communicator took less than a minute, and then he gave his companions his full attention once again.

"Tell me about these caravans," Harry suggested.

"Oh, you'll love 'em. But wait a couple of minutes and we'll be in sight of one, old top. Easier to show than tell."

During the next few minutes he gave Harry and Lily something of a guided tour of the city, as he drove smoothly through streets lined with houses and other buildings made almost entirely of the strange adobe, its colors varying in strips and panels. A number of these structures appeared to have been deliberately left roofless.

"So it's true that it never rains? Or do they use forcefields somehow, to—"

"It never rains."

There was a school. Yelling children in assorted sizes, evidently on some kind of break from lessons, filled a yard lightly fenced off from the street. That was something you didn't see every day, in most cities.

Bulaboldo said: "They tell me Maracanda has one of the Galaxy's highest birth rates. Can't think why, unless it's just a sense of all this empty space waiting to be filled, a lot of good air being generated that goes unbreathed."

The width of Port City from west to east proved to be no more than four or five kilometers. They had soon traversed that distance, and were pulling into a parking area, already about half occupied. Most of the other vehicles in sight looked basically similar to Bulaboldo's, though few were as elegant.

Climbing out of the car, Harry saw that they were only a

short walk from a long, low, roofless structure that put him in mind of a loading dock. Large signs at both ends cautioned:

ONLY VEHICLES

BREAKDOWN READY

PERMITTED BEYOND THIS POINT

"What's that all about?" Harry wondered, nodding at the warning.

Bulaboldo led his two companions forward. He seemed in a jovial mood, eager to play the guide. "The edge of town was established at this very spot for a reason, old sod. It's perfectly safe for people to travel beyond the sign—for thousands of kilometers beyond it, if they like. But"—he pointed dramatically into the peculiar desert—"as soon as one proceeds a few more meters in that direction, one immediately risks running into spots and strips of breakdown zone. See where that wire runs, mounted on poles?"

"It looks like some primitive telegraph," Lily said, squinting, as if the idea of this world possessing such a system were totally new to her. Harry nodded, silently approving. The thing looked like a mock-up of some ancient Earthly line of simple wire communication. A single strand, supported on a series of uprights spaced some twenty or thirty meters apart, went zigzagging off to vanish at last behind a hill, a kilometer or more away. He didn't suppose this was the Templars' private wire. More likely this was the public facility Pike had mentioned.

Bulaboldo went on: "The road itself is only faintly marked, and rather hard to see, but it generally follows the telegraph line. They both avoid the breakdown zones as much as possible. But every now and then the zone borders shift by a few meters. Usually the change is only temporary, but when it happens, telegraph service is likely to be interrupted. And if the road is overrun, caravans have to shift to primitive mode."

"How's that again?"

"Takes a bit of explaining. The engine that drives the caravan is the same type, hydrogen fusion, that's used in normal groundcars on most worlds, but the caravan also has an alternate system, much more primitive. Has to be seen to be believed. Private vehicles cleared for use in breakdown zones are lightweight shells, equipped with pedals, so the driver and passengers can . . . no, I'm not putting you on, old sod. Not a bit of it."

"So the telegraph only works intermittently?"

" 'Weirdly' or 'occasionally' might be closer to the mark. And the private lines, of which I'm told that one or two exist, are no better. There are instances on record of messages being delayed for months, even years."

Lily broke in: "When you get a chance, tell us more about the caravans."

"Of course." Bulaboldo leered at them both, as if about to launch into an obscene joke. "Let us concentrate upon essentials. The train of rolling wagons has comfortable seats. Needs 'em, because it takes two days to get to Tomb Town. There'll be lots of time for conversation." He turned a more benign gaze on Harry. "I'm sure that you and I, old sod, will have a lot to talk about."

"You're making the trip with us, then." Lily sounded startled.

"Oh, very much so. Didn't I tell you, my chick? I have extensive business interests over in the east—not in Tomb Town so much as in Minersville, which stands nearby—so yes, we will be mates, for a time, aboard the ship of the desert, fellow lodgers tonight at the caravanserai."

"What's that?"

"A hostelry of sorts. Not too uncomfortable, bit of an exotic experience. You'll see."

*   *   *

By now they were all three standing atop the loading dock. Harry was looking out into the open country—though "country" somehow seemed too natural a word for all these geometric curves and segments of straight line—beyond the city's edge. Bulaboldo had evidently told the truth, for civilization seemed to come to an abrupt end, right about here. To the west of the dock there were only a couple of small structures, whose purpose Harry could not determine.

Beyond those two small sheds, he could see nothing but a vast expanse of the odd land, stretching out to an improbable horizon. The horizon was not the result of any planetlike curvature, but only the apparent shrinkage of distant space between the strange land and the lowering sky.

It was very difficult to say exactly how vast the visible portion of the Maracandan surface might be, for it lacked a single human shape or other familiar object to give perspective. The scenery both far and near was so strange, so lacking in familiar visual clues, that Harry feared he might go dizzy staring at it.

Beside him, Lily was evidently experiencing some similar effect, for she clutched at his arm. Well, anyone could be upset, Harry thought, looking at this. Oddities of perspective, and the half artificial look of the peculiar overhead that was not quite a sky, made it difficult to judge distances.

She had shifted her gaze, and was pointing off to their right. "What's that?"

Just north of the loading dock stood another massive structure, even lower and wider in its profile, its volume stretching away for a city block or more. This one was mostly imported metal inside a partial facing of adobe slabs.

"That's where we get the stuff to breathe, m'dear." Bulaboldo explained that this was one of the vast atmospheric generators, installed a decade or more ago, that worked at keeping the air breathable, all across the habitable surface. Strangely enough, the first explorers had found the Maracandan atmosphere quite acceptable on their arrival; ever since then, time and energy had been devoted to keeping it that way. Another generator was implanted near the spaceport, most of its huge bulk also underground. Similar units were buried at a number of strategic locations, both here and in the east.

This was the installation General Pike had mentioned as a likely berserker-goodlife target. Harry assumed that oxygen and nitrogen were somehow extracted from the local land mass.

But now a sight of more immediate interest had presented itself. "There's your caravan."

Harry opened his mouth to make some comment, then decided he had better wait until he got a better look. Just coming into view from behind a nearby building was a small train of double-decker wagons, each with a lower level closed in by walls of sturdy mesh, and laden with what appeared to be miscellaneous freight, stacked crates, bags, and boxes. Adjoining the freight compartments, Harry could recognize a pair of small solid wall enclosures as relatively primitive chemical toilets, of a kind he had seen only in primitive conditions, and many years ago. The upper level of each car, entirely open to the air, held an array of passenger seats. This train was now being pulled up to the dock behind a transporter much like the one at the spaceport. A youth in coveralls, looking even younger than Lily, sat at the manual controls of the lead vehicle, which looked like a low-slung, house-sized, overgrown groundcar, carrying open seats for at least a dozen passengers, and running on smooth endless treads instead of wheels.

Harry and his two companions had soon boarded the train, amid a modest rush of other passengers. It was a simple matter of paying cash, or transferring credits, to a conductor who wore an odd, primitive kind of receptacle for coins hung round his neck and a distinctive logo on his coveralls. Other members of the small crew of transport workers were similarly dressed.

Harry had money ready to pay his fare and Lily's, but Bulaboldo insisted on picking up the tab for the two visitors. Then he helpfully explained the passenger accommodations. There were no reserved seats, but then there were no bad ones either.

Examining his chair, and the space in front of it, Harry observed: "No pedals on these."

"What? Oh, no. One would hate to try to propel anything the size of this train by pedaling. One might need a hundred active slaves, chained to their seats. No, when the caravan moves into the breakdown zone, it employs an entirely different system of propulsion. You'll see."

At the last moment a casually uniformed crew member came around asking all passengers if they had any advanced prostheses implanted in their bodies.

It seemed everyone on the train, Harry and Lily included, could answer no. "The breakdown zones again?" Lily asked.

Bulaboldo nodded. "That's right. Wouldn't do for your heart or brain to suddenly quit when its backup device shut down. For the first several hundred kilometers, there's just a possibility we'll hit a breakdown. After that, the problem is more or less continuous."

About three-fourths of the passenger seats were filled when the line of people waiting to get aboard had dwindled down to nothing. Looking over his fellow passengers, Harry decided that they seemed to be divided about equally between two groups. On one hand were traders and prospectors, some of them wearing odd-looking tool belts and dressed like ordinary folk for business or travel. On the other hand were the pilgrims of what Harry, judging by their diverse dress, took to be several different cults.

The mining engineers and workers tended to gather in one or two cars, while the pilgrims gravitated together in two other wagons, the population of each one dominated by one of the principal sects.

Bulaboldo grandly conceded that he was willing to join the religious folk if Lily wanted to be there. But she was quite willing to sit with the technocrats and dealers.

All seemed in readiness for departure, but there followed another delay, for no obvious reason. Bulaboldo used the time to hold one more brief conversation on his private handheld communicator, with someone a kilometer or two away in Port City. He said it was a contact who had accurate information about what was going on inside the administration building.

After making these calls, Bulaboldo assured Harry, in an almost inaudible whisper, that the Space Force people here on Maracanda were still not even aware that Harry was wanted for stealing the cannon.

"I guess that's something."

Trying to estimate his chances on a world he didn't know but Bulaboldo did, Harry soon thought of an objection. "Suppose Rovaki changes his mind and decides to arrest me. If there's no better communication system than yon telegraph, the cops shouldn't be able to radio ahead, to find out if I'm on the caravan."

"Right you are. By the time we're a kilometer from the city, the breakdown zones are so thick, no radio signal's going to find a way between them."

Lily put in: "Everyone keeps telling us about these zones. But I've never heard any clear explanation."

"Don't know if anyone could give you one, my sweet. This road winds around, avoiding major breakdown zones as much as possible, for the first thousand kilometers or so. But radio signal travels pretty much in a straight line, so radio's no good here, any more than it is in flightspace. Signals just can't get through."

That probably ought to have been reassuring, thought Harry, but it wasn't. He had something of the feeling of being caught up in an unpleasant dream. It seemed that only a few hours ago, entering the outer reaches of the Maracanda system, he had been fairly confidently in charge of his own life. The descent to practical near helplessness had been swift indeed.

"How the hell did this world get this way?" he burst out. "It's like somebody built it—or started to build it, then gave up when the job was only half finished."

Bulaboldo smiled. "Let it be my turn, old son, to employ a quotation from the ancients: 'You ain't seen nothing yet!' "

T E N

Lily, trying to extract more information from their guide, asked Bulaboldo how long he had lived on Maracanda.

He gave an evasive answer. "For the last few standard years, my dear, this strange place has been like a home to me, though I have not been continuously in residence. Maracanda, as you doubtless have discovered, already has a beauty, a fascination all its own. I'd say that if you like our Harry, you'll like it here. Above all, it is not *dull.*"

All the crew now seemed to be on board, and the transporter's drive was humming. The train of interconnected wagons gave a lurch, and was suddenly in motion, at the speed of a fast walk. Swiftly the loading dock and the outlying buildings of the city fell behind. The caravan was on its way across the almost trackless wasteland, gradually building up speed.

Even as their caravan pulled away from the dock, another transporter and more cars were being moved into position to form another train.

Lily asked: "How often do these trains run?"

Bulaboldo seemed to enjoy playing guide. "It's somewhat irregular. But there are usually two or three a day in each direction."

The steady acceleration continued, until the cars had reached a speed that Harry estimated at about a hundred kilometers per hour. Large wheels spinning smoothly, gripping the surface of Maracandan land, the caravan settled into a steady, quiet run, swaying a little on the curves. Given the winding road and the endless formation of steep, low hills, it was seldom possible to see more than a hundred meters ahead.

Lily watched, with growing fascination. "It ought to be fun to ride a bicycle or unicycle along this road."

Kul shook his head. "A lot of people have tried, but none of them get far. Gyroscopic balancing is very difficult in breakdown zones. The pedicars run on four wheels."

Looking ahead across the rugged and unearthly landscape, Harry observed little more than a suggestion of a winding road. For the most part the faint track followed the single strand of telegraph line, several times passing beneath it. Now that he was closer to the telegraph poles, Harry could see by the visible grain that they were made of natural wood, which must have been imported at considerable expense. Some of them had been infected near the base by streaks of land form, creeping up like some kind of alien kudzu. In place of leaves and tendrils, there appeared small extensions of the land itself. The growth appeared to be soaking into the substance of the wood and taking it over, as in some special Maracandan system of osmosis.

Still seeming to be guided by the line of telegraph poles

wandering off into the distance, the driver steered along a route marked by something less than a road, a little more than a trail. The ground was only faintly imprinted with wheel tracks, surprising given the number of people and machines that must be passing daily along this route. Only now did Harry notice that little wooden roadside signs, in the form of simple arrows, had been implanted at irregular intervals. These made a more reliable guide than the line of telegraph poles, which occasionally diverged from the roadway. The signs, like the telegraph poles, were infected by the creeping land, and some of the smaller signs had been almost entirely engulfed.

One of the other passengers was pointing out where natural objects, sprouting from a nearby hillside, had taken on the appearance of crude little imitation signposts. The resemblance to human artifacts wasn't great enough to seriously confuse a traveler, Harry supposed. But he wondered if in time it would become greater.

"Very odd," he commented.

"This is not a planet," Lily was murmuring, keeping up her mantra. "This is not a planet." But Harry got the impression that she enjoyed all the strangeness.

Here and there little branching trails, even fainter, curved away from the main route, to promptly lose themselves in the contours of the rugged landscape.

"If there's continual traffic, as you say, why isn't the road worn down more?" Harry wondered aloud. "The ground doesn't look that hard. And it can't be the wind that wipes out tracks. People keep telling us there is no wind."

"That's right, old sock. The air here is always moving about a bit, but very gently."

"I keep wondering if there's not some kind of rain, or at least fog. I thought maybe in certain areas—"

"We don't have fog either. No precipitation anywhere on Maracanda. You won't see any signs of ordinary erosion."

"Frost, maybe?"

"Nope. Air temperature never goes up or down by more than about five degrees."

"And all these are natural conditions? Or is nature beginning to give way to—something else?"

"For an azlaroc-type habitable body, at least for this particular one, they are natural. Hasn't someone proven mathematically that any real universe has to contain spots where the normal laws don't hold?"

"Not that I ever heard of." But it did sound to Harry like the kind of thing some twisted genius would want to prove, then brag about.

Bulaboldo assured his visitors, and a train crew member verified, that over time the land did change. Caravan tracks did disappear, about as fast as they were created, in accordance with the slow stretching or shrinking of the surface, which seemed to enjoy the property of being able to heal itself to some extent, tidy itself up. Natural surface activity seemed to follow the enigmatic processes that went on continually in the mysterious depths beneath the thin habitable region.

Harry could see the reason for the windscreens in front of the open seats. The speed of their train remained fairly steady at about a hundred kilometers per hour, on the straighter stretches perhaps a little more. Any normal vehicle would have had at least a simple optelectronic brain stocked with the answers to such questions, and a voice to announce them, but here there was nothing of the kind.

A member of the train crew, questioned in passing, gave the official version of their schedule: to reach Tomb Town and Minersville was going to take a good day and a half of standard measure, and the last hundred kilometers or so of the journey would be entirely within a breakdown zone.

Lily asked: "Do we keep rolling all through the night? But no, you mentioned something about a hostelry. By the way, there *is* a night here, isn't there? Back in Port City I did see what looked like streetlights."

"Oh, there is definitely a night. Light and darkness, alternating with a periodicity very close to that of the Earth-based standard day. Very interesting subject. Generally the caravans try to minimize night travel. We'll be putting in at the caravanserai around twilight."

"The caravanserai, yes, I saw that on the map. A strange name. Will we need reservations?"

"An old name, my dear, for an establishment whose like you will not see on any other world. It even provides a touch of luxury, in its own way. I should think you will not need reservations, unless business has picked up beyond all expectations." Bulaboldo closed his eyes, and adjusted his reclining seat. "Awaken me, if you will, when it is time to order lunch."

Harry thought of napping also, but there was still a lot to see. He was more worried over his ship than over the question of where he was going to spend the coming night.

His scalp was itching, which he took as a sign that his head wanted to get back into the pilot's helmet aboard the *Witch*. On most habitable worlds his ship could have paced off this cross-country journey in only a few minutes, even limping along at a snail's pace, mushing her way through a deep Earth-like atmosphere, using a muffler if necessary to suppress the shock wave that would otherwise have dragged behind.

Lily was pointing at something different in the passing scenery. "Harry, look at that."

At a distance of several hundred meters from the thin, winding road, the passengers could see the upper part of a pile of wreckage, protruding above a low hill. Jagged metal and composite materials were intermingled, component shapes distorted as if by violent impact. The size of the wreck was hard to judge with no good reference object near it, but Harry interpreted what he could see as the remains of a small spaceship. Harry would have thought most space hardware virtually proof against any kind of natural deterioration, but parts of the mound were markedly discolored, the hues of the Maracandan land forms seeping up into them like dye.

"I wonder who piloted that?" Harry mused. "How long's it been there?"

"Whoever the poor bugger was, he showed a certain lack of competence." Bulaboldo had awakened when their voices rose, and his headshake was superior and pitying. "No doubt he was certain he had a safe course calculated. But either the calculations weren't quite right, or his mind wasn't quite sharp enough on the controls. Came down in a breakdown zone."

"Yeah, that's what it looks like. But you were implying earlier that there were other good landing spots, waiting to be discovered."

"Officially, none at all are known, but I shouldn't be at all surprised if some exist, hidden among the invisible folds of a breakdown zone." The big man had folded his hands comfortably over his ample paunch. "Of course, under those conditions it would take some ingenious searching to find one—and a really good pilot to make use of it. A good pilot, with a good, small ship."

"Sounds like a challenge." Then Harry frowned at the wreck again. "Must have hit with a hell of an impact, to break up a ship like that."

"Not necessarily all that great. As you know, the bust-up would ordinarily be cushioned by the ship's own artificially generated fields. But the field generators on any ship are sophisticated machines, and naturally they would have stopped at the same time as the drive. In fact, they might have malfunctioned in a way to make the impact worse."

Harry was silent, looking and thinking. No amount of piloting skill would help on any ship when all the hardware failed.

A female member of the train crew had stopped in the aisle nearby and was commenting on the sight. "Every now and then someone comes along and thinks they've found a spot that'll work for a new spaceport." This woman evidently had a different view of the odds than Bulaboldo did. "Or a temporary landing field at least."

Lily asked: "No one's ever succeeded?"

"Not that I know of. I think it would be real big news if they did."

Harry had to try to figure it out. "How about using a light aircraft of some kind? Much smaller, a lot more maneuverable." Back in Port City he had asked similar questions; he wanted to see if he got a different answer here.

The crewman's expression suggested that he thought that idea might have some merit. But it was Bulaboldo's turn to be discouraging. "No good. To get in here at all, you need a true spacecraft, and not a simple flyer. Because, you see, it's not a simple matter of wings and plain air. There are layers of different kinds of space, which accounts for the peculiar sky. Much more complex than any planetary atmosphere."

The caravan road was traversing an area where more strange markings decorated the land. Bulaboldo explained that ever since the days of the first settlers on Maracanda, some people had persisted in efforts to colonize the remote areas, usually on land that had been ignored, or dug over and abandoned, by people filing mining claims. So far every effort to grow crops or raise animals had ended in total failure.

The only way to water the crops was to somehow extract enough moisture from the air—some was available, but difficult to isolate, especially with very small natural temperature changes in the Maracandan atmosphere. In a work zone, with modern machinery, it might be possible on a small scale.

Some predicted that as this strange world evolved, it would become steadily more and more Earth-like, even to the extent of developing clouds and rain. A few settlers actually claimed to have witnessed small clouds and spots of fog. Most people, the authorities included, scoffed at such reports.

Harry wondered. "And where exactly do they think all this water is going to come from?"

Bulaboldo grimaced, signaling that he had no helpful answer.

Lily was ready to change the subject. "I wonder how many people ride this back and forth." Then she added: "I have an impulse to start asking people, like members of the train crew, if they remember a man named Alan Gunnlod, who was probably a passenger a few months ago. But why would they remember one man? And no one asks your name when you get on."

It seemed that now, when she was less than a day from where she expected to find Alan, her impatience was growing, her nerves wearing down, as if the long strain must be getting to her.

Harry's suspicions of his traveling companion still wouldn't go away entirely, but he had not a scrap of evidence to back them up. Since landing he had seen no overt signs of an illegal drug trade on this world—which, of course, did not mean that it did not exist. Bulaboldo's prosperous presence here was indirect evidence that it might.

She was still carrying her traveling bag with her, containing the modest luggage she said she had brought from home. Harry, in contrast, lacked a change of clothing or even a toothbrush. All his personal possessions, except what he was wearing—and the money in his pockets—were on his ship.

Bulaboldo was reassuring. "You'll be able to buy some

necessities when we get to the caravanserai. They have a shop. By the way, if you should find yourself a bit short of liquid assets at the moment—"

"I told you, I'm okay, Kul. But thanks for the offer."

"Think nothing of it, old top."

But Harry couldn't keep from thinking of it. Even with plenty of other things to be uneasy about, it worried him that Bulaboldo was so enthusiastically willing to be helpful. It was not exactly like they had been the greatest of friends in the old days.

Soon it was time to order lunch. Prepackaged meal trays and drinks were served, while the caravan kept rolling.

"Nibble what you find absolutely necessary to stave off starvation, people, but no more. Because you may actually look forward with some confidence to the dinner table at the caravanserai. On my last trip I sent my compliments to the chef."

Between spells of dozing in his gently swaying seat, and glowering at the passing desert, whose unique scenery had begun to pall—every minute there was more of it between him and his suffering, lock-sealed *Witch*—Harry enjoyed intervals of swearing at the fate that had not only made him a fugitive, but also co-opted him into being a spy or the next thing to it.

Not that he would have had any objection to spying on real goodlife, or slaughtering them, for that matter. It was just highly unlikely there would be any goodlife here to spy on. For the moment, thinking up new variations of foul language to apply to the situation seemed to be about all that he could do.

Still, Harry could hardly have refused to cooperate with the general. If the Space Force on this world was out to get him, he needed a sturdy ally of some kind.

*   *   *

Lost in thought, Harry didn't notice the change in the light until Lily jogged his elbow. She said: "Harry. I think—I still don't understand what it can mean, on a world like this—but I think it's starting to get dark."

Harry looked. He had to admit that the false sky to the east had taken on a new and gloomier aspect.

Lily was deeply impressed—as well she might be, Harry thought. She said: "If we're actually going through some kind of cycle of day and night, then doesn't it seem there must be something like a normal sun, somewhere in this—"

"One thing this crazy system does *not* have is a normal sun. You saw that when we were on approach."

"I know. I'd like to think that I just missed it somehow."

A minute later, they passed a westbound caravan, a train of cars much like their own. Simple electric lamps were lighted on the lead car, the powered transporter. Both drivers edged to the right, to negotiate the passage on the narrow road.

The dimming of natural light in the east continued, dusk spreading across the sky until there remained only a last glow lingering in the west; and soon the visitors saw with their own eyes, that there was indeed an alternation of daylight and darkness on this strange world.

Bulaboldo, coming back from a stretching stroll along the aisle, commented that the first explorers—something like a standard century ago—had observed the beginning of the same effect, but at that time the diurnal change in illumination had been so slight that people argued about its reality. Over the years since the first human settlement, the effect had definitely become more pronounced.

Years ago, according to the old settlers ("They always tell you: 'You can check the records if you like.'") the changes had been sporadic and irregular, but gradually the pattern had settled into a close approximation of the twelve hours of daylight and twelve of night obtaining in the equatorial regions of old Earth and a number of other Earth-like planets.

"But how did that pattern get *here*?"

The big man was solemn for a moment. "The only answer seems to be that we have somehow brought it with us."

Bulaboldo said that he was continuing to give Harry's legal difficulties a great deal of thought. Before leaving Port City, he had got his own legal counsel started on figuring the best way to proceed if Harry's difficulties ever actually got into court on Maracanda.

"Be of good cheer, old chap. I still have high hopes of being able to work out a way for you to regain possession of your ship. The Force can't actually take it away from you without some legal process. I wonder, though . . . I suppose they might've searched her."

Harry shook his head. "I can readily believe they've slapped their seals over the hatches, but I doubt very much they've even got inside. The ship's fitted with good entry codes and downlocks, and they'd need to get pretty violent to force an entry. As I understand the law, they'll need some real evidence before they can do that."

"Commandant Rovaki is not above doing a sneaky and illegal search. When you say 'good downlocks,' old lad, I assume you mean—really pretty good ones."

"The Force people back on Hyperborea had a similar idea, and they didn't have much luck."

"That is reassuring." Bulaboldo settled back in his chair. "Then it would seem that as soon as you can return to your ship, and peel those seals, your dear *Witch* is readily available to take you . . . anywhere that you might want to go."

"Should be. Only problem is, I'm liable to get arrested before I can get near her."

"There is that." But in this matter, Bulaboldo seemed incurably optimistic. "Well, these things take time. Let me keep working on the difficulty, old bean. Meanwhile, of course, this caravan's the place for you."

Discreet electric lights had come on aboard the eastbound caravan—light enough to read by, as some passengers were doing. Harry assumed they would keep shining as long as the engine continued to function. Passengers got up from time to time just to stretch, or to visit the primitive chemical toilets on the lower deck, which presumably would keep on functioning when all the finest and newest optelectronics had sputtered to a halt. Reserve tanks of water for drinking and washing were also carried on the lower level of each wagon. The floor of the wagon lurched from time to time, more than the deck of any smoothly running spaceship.

With Lily half dozing in her chair, and no one else in earshot, Bulaboldo began a conversation, for once keeping his voice low. "Harry, old scout, now that we have some time to talk, let me tell you something about my business. You're sure to find it amusing."

Harry wasn't sure of that at all. He only grunted.

Bulaboldo turned to the lady. "Then hearing about it might amuse Madam Lily." He gave her a slight seated bow. "I'm sure you understand that not all of us have come to Maracanda in search of the high spiritual values."

Her eyes were fully open now, and she regarded him coolly. "I thought you understood that I had not."

Bulaboldo went on to explain that the rare earths obtainable in the remote corners of this world were rapidly becoming famous in certain quarters across settled portions of the Galaxy.

Harry mentioned hearing a newscast reporting last month's record output from the mines. He concluded: "I never got around to finding out exactly what kind of stuff it is that half the people here are digging up and selling."

Bulaboldo nodded. "Why, as to that, I can show you."

Digging in his pockets, Kul explained that the sought-after materials came in two basic varieties, both of which were quarried, with some difficulty, from two separate layers of Maracandan rock, that came close to the surface in a number of places, some known and others doubtless still to be discovered.

"That's the reason for the swarm of would-be prospectors. I expect that as word spreads across the Galaxy, we'll have another wave of 'em, and probably another after that. Until people are convinced that all the easy pickings have been picked."

A small amount of one variety of stuff, no more than a few grams, was not hard to find. Bulaboldo made no attempt to conceal it from other passengers. Some turned their heads to watch, while others, including a near majority who were dozing, ignored the whole procedure.

"This, my old friends, is what is commonly called 'fairyground.' It is quarried, quite legally though with some physical difficulty, in a number of small mining operations. Most, of course, are in the breakdown zones, which makes the extraction physically difficult."

Lily asked, in innocent tones: "It's not a drug, is it?"

Bulaboldo blinked. Anyone who didn't know him would have been certain he was shocked. "Drug? Whatever gave you that idea? No, perfectly harmless, my lady. An army of Earth-descended scientists have testified that you can wallow around in heaps of the stuff in perfect safety."

Harry poked at it with a calloused finger. "What would happen if I ate a pinch or two?"

"I'd say the odds are very high that you'd survive. Might not even get sick. But I shouldn't think it was really recommended for internal use."

Their guide offered more information. Fairyground had so

far proven impossible to synthesize, representing as it did a distinctly unique state of matter.

Configured and sold as a toy, it repeatedly reformed itself into various geometric shapes and changed colors. Once a small amount of it had been together for a while, it resisted being subdivided further.

One of the train crew made what sounded like a routine announcement: passengers must prepare to shut down all equipment depending on advanced technology. The domain of solid breakdown zone was only a few minutes ahead.

Lily was pointing. "What's that?"

Harry turned his head and looked; he could hear rumbling movement in the dusk. In the middle distance, the shadowy outline of a hill was blurred with motion. At first he thought he saw a herd of running animals.

All the passengers on the caravan saw a herd of wild spheres, first blocking a strip of the road ahead, then parting to give the machine clear passage. One of the big rollers banged a telegraph pole, hard enough to make it wobble.

"Great Malakó! I thought that we'd startled a herd of—what? I don't know. Deer?"

"Well, you might say we have."

Harry would never have imagined animals like these. Not that he was entirely convinced that they were animals.

Lily burst out: "I thought there was no native life!"

"If you mean carbon chemistry and DNA, genetic codes and all that, there isn't any of that. But . . ."

Suddenly passengers were pointing in excitement, and calling back and forth. The creatures, or objects, were back, as if drawn by something about the caravan itself.

Kul said: "They become completely inert if you take them away from the Maracandan surface."

Lily asked: "Do they display . . . purposeful behavior?"

"If you count just rolling back and forth as purposeful."

Several passengers whipped out recorders, trying to capture the distracting sight of a herd of rolling spheres, keeping pace with the caravan at some little distance. Others, perhaps old settlers themselves, had evidently seen this before and went on dozing or reading their books.

Harry was fascinated. "What now? They certainly look like they're alive. I mean, the way they're moving."

"You'll find some experts who agree with you on that, old son. Probably there are just as many who disagree. The spheres have no discoverable genetic content of any kind, no cells, no organs. No discernible sensory apparatus, though obviously they respond to their environment. So, life, maybe. Though it's not much like any kind of life I've seen on any planet."

Lily said: "Since this is not quite a planet, maybe what grows here is not quite life."

There was still enough light to see dim shapes, and the line of telegraph poles, when the caravan rolled past a grove of what Bulaboldo said were called nevergreens, tree-shaped fractals near pyramids of land, colored almost the same as the land from which they sprouted, that gave a good imitation of another kind of living thing. Harry was reminded of trees with autumn foliage.

Harry steered the talk back to an earlier subject. "You said that there were two varieties."

"What?"

"Two types of rare earth."

"I did?"

"Well, someone aboard this wagon told me that."

Bulaboldo found a way to quickly change the subject.

ELEVEN

Right on cue, the discreet hum that had been coming from the very modern engine of the caravan transporter turned suddenly harsh. A second later the engine died completely. The rolling wheels, simple machines indeed, supporting all the cars, still whispered smoothly. The train of wagons coasted quietly for a few more meters, long enough to carry them all into the invisible breakdown zone, then rolled to a dead stop. The driver, accustomed to this phenomenon, had calculated his speed nicely just before the engine died.

A few passengers noted that a similar fate had overtaken a few small items of modern equipment they had been carrying with them.

A young crewman was announcing: "We'll be under way again in just a few minutes, people."

How are we going to do that? Harry wondered. With everything else he'd had to think about, he hadn't got around to really pondering that question yet. But now it seemed he was about to find out. Disembarking from the wagon with Bulaboldo and Lily, he watched the majority of the passengers go scrambling on ahead. He stood there, boots crunching on this truly alien soil, and waited to see what would happen next. This couldn't be the caravanserai, the scheduled overnight stop; by Harry's calculations, that was still about a hundred kilometers to the east.

Right here there was nothing like a hotel in sight, only a peculiar structure the size of a small garage, but looking more like a corral or cage, made of loosely interwoven strips of tough and slippery imported material. The corral enclosed some ten or a dozen spheres like those that he had earlier seen rolling free across the landscape.

Harry decided he wasn't going to ask what happened next. He'd doubtless find out soon enough.

The people of the train's crew had opened up the cage and were somehow urging or prodding the captive spheres to leave it, talking to them meanwhile as if encouraging animals. The creatures, things, whatever they were, looked like so many neatly carved and polished boulders, seemingly formed of the same material as the land. But they were true spheres, mathematically perfect as far as Harry's eye could tell.

Bulaboldo, standing with his arms folded, was watching something he had seen a dozen times before, just waiting for this preparation, whatever it was, to be over, so he could get on with his business trip.

Harry gave up and asked. "What's going on?"

"They're just hitching up the team, old lad. Supplying our motive power for the next leg of the journey."

"Hitching up the team?"

Lily said: "I was wondering if we had to walk the rest of the way, pushing the wagons." And then, half seriously, she began murmuring her mantra: "This is not a planet. This is not a planet . . ."

How heavy the big spheres might be was hard to tell. The train crew, pushing moderately hard, seemed to have little trouble rolling and prodding them, one at a time, out of their roadside cage and into a lighter kind of inverted cage that had been dragged out from somewhere and attached to the front of the caravan, from which the transporter engine had been disconnected.

Now and then during this process, the spheres showed a tendency for spontaneous movement.

Harry was fascinated. "Damn. Then your rollers are alive?"

Kul shook his head. "I don't think so. No one's ever seen them eat, or die, or reproduce. The theory is that they draw their energy from the ground, somehow. The transport company does hear a complaint, now and then, from some society for the prevention of cruelty to animals."

"I take it that they're native here. Just look at them, they have to be."

"They're native. Catching wild rollers, which is the local term, is something of an adventure. Essentially, one has to chase them down on foot."

"I bet."

A crew member moved among the passengers, making sure everyone understood that the rest of the day's journey would be accomplished much more slowly. It would take five hours to travel the hundred kilometers between the changeover spot and the caravanserai, their lodging for the coming night. Meanwhile, the rest of the crew went expertly about the task of getting the transporter out of the way. Since the transporter's engine had entirely ceased to function, several willing and active passengers were enlisted to help—Harry did, Kul managed to avoid the effort—with the tug-

ging and pushing required to move the powered unit to one side of
the main road, and swing it completely around so its decorated
nose pointed back in the direction of Port City. Dragging the useless engine deep into the breakdown zone and out again would
serve no purpose.

Harry would have liked to open up some cowling and take a
close look at the idled engine, to try to pin down exactly where the
failure had been induced. But he was no expert in such machines,
no one else seemed to have a similar idea, and he was reluctant to
draw attention to himself.

The body of the transporter was constructed of very light
materials, so turning it front to back was easy enough after the
boxes and bags of freight had been unloaded from the lower level,
and reloaded on the lightweight sphere-drawn engine that took the
transporter's place. The wagons also were very light minus the
freight most of them were carrying; had there been any wind, it
would doubtless have been enough to set the empty wagons rolling.

When the movable cage and its population of spheres
(Harry hoped they were rested and ready for a day's work,
whether or not they were alive) had been attached at the front of
the train, and everyone was aboard, a small, glassy bowl filled
with some flammable material was set alight, then placed in a
sling set dangling at the end of a long pole. The driver had taken
his usual place, but was using an entirely different set of controls.

Again Bulaboldo was explaining. "The spheres, you see,
respond to a particular spectrum of radiation. The flame provides it."

Whatever the exact mechanism, the fire was undoubtedly
attractive. The caged spheres began a concerted movement. Pushing against the front wall of the cage, which was evidently made
of some almost frictionless material, they exerted a force that
moved the loaded wagons. Their collective movements in the cage

produced a distinctive, polyphonic noise, something between faint whistling and light scraping.

"I don't believe it," Harry murmured. He was back in his comfortable chair, once more watching the landscape as it rolled past. As they had been warned, their speed was much reduced. But it held steady.

"This is not a planet," Lily sweetly reminded him.

The driver was steering, keeping the train of wagons on the road, by swinging the lure of the attractive light to left or right as necessary. There didn't seem to be anything in the way of a speed control in use, but Harry supposed that if you quenched the fire in the lure, or moved it to where the spheres could not detect its glow, they'd stop.

He was still staring at the spheres. "Do they die? Are they born?"

Kul said: "As to how they come into existence, there are different theories. No one has ever observed the process. An individual roller eventually stops rolling, or so I'm told, and after that gradually blends back into the landscape. Some people consider that just about equivalent to what happens to us."

"What if you cut one open? Break it up?"

"I'm told you don't find any internal organs, only a practically homogeneous interior. Cut it in pieces, and all you have is a pile of Maracandan soil."

Lily said: "I've read something about them. The general consensus seems to be that they're moving landforms. They draw energy from some kind of field that permeates Maracandan space—here in the habitable zone, at least."

Harry asked: "The same field that creates the breakdown zones?"

Kul shrugged. "Probably related somehow. But you're asking the wrong fellow. I'm sure the boffins can show you pages of mathematics."

There seemed no way of communicating with the rolling landforms. Scores, if not hundreds, of people had tried that, some using truly imaginative methods. No one had had any success. The spheres were what they were, and did what they did, and that was that.

At last Harry said: "I know one way to tell whether they're alive or not."

"What's that, dear fellow?"

"Put them in front of a berserker, and it'll quickly take the decision out of your hands."

Moving more slowly made it easier to study the passing scenery. Now Harry noticed that the warning signs were made of imported wood, like the little fingerposts that marked the road. And Bulaboldo pointed out how these, too, were starting to be blurred and degraded by their strange environment, by an infiltration of the land itself. The patterns of the land were reproducing themselves in alien material. Wood, for some unknown reason, seemed most resistant to the gradual transformation.

And here, again, something like a reverse process was at work. The land in turn seemed to borrow patterns from certain kinds of imported wood.

Bulaboldo seemed to enjoy lecturing. "The first people to move here more or less permanently were researchers, who were simply delighted when they found stable conditions that allowed them to land—a truly habitable zone, even air that allowed them to take their helmets off, for a few breaths. The original, primitive atmosphere wasn't as good as the gravity, but it was close to the mark. It just cried out to be augmented."

Harry was shaking his head. "I still don't get it. Whatever these forces are, that disable advanced technology—how do they decide what counts as an advanced machine? A lot of complicated machines are only combinations of simple ones."

Bulaboldo shrugged. "Talk to a boffin about it—I've tried—and he or she will snow you solemnly with advanced math, dealing with extreme complexity. But you won't hear any real answer. No doubt the great brains of the human race will figure Maracanda out for us someday. Probably not until they resurrect some way of doing science that doesn't depend entirely on computers and elaborate gadgets. Currently, they have a hard time measuring anything at all inside a breakdown zone.

"There were some early settlers who were just fascinated by the idea of living in a place where machines refused to operate, who imported genengineered horses and camels to carry riders and pull loads. Didn't work, though."

"Why not?"

"Didn't see it tried myself, but they say it was very difficult to feed the creatures properly, importing and recycling food. Anyway, the animals tended to sicken and die—which people here do not, by the way. It's quite a healthy environment for humanity—as long as we make sure the water and air and food are up to standard."

The train was equipped with a few small oil-burning lamps, for those times when it was necessary to get through a breakdown zone in darkness. Just in case, as Bulaboldo explained, night should fall while the caravan was still on the road.

"There's another point I can't even begin to understand, that is why Maracanda should have night and day. This so-called habitable body doesn't spin like a planet. And even if it did, it's not exposed to anything like normal sunlight—"

"All I know is, the authorities say the illumination comes from some—some interaction between the layers of the sky. As to why it's gradually taking on the timing of some Earth-like planet's diurnal cycle—probably that of Earth itself . . ." The big man shrugged.

"But there's no doubt that's what it's doing?"

"So the records indicate."

Harry shook his head, marveling.

"The Malakó people, and several other cults, have explanations for it all. But there's nothing on a scientific level."

"I wonder," said Lily softly, "that people dare to live here at all. And even to raise children. I'd be wary of bringing mine to a place like this."

Harry was curious. "You have any?"

She shook her head. "Alan and I have made plans—No, *I've* made plans from time to time, and tried to get him to agree. But he's always got something else . . . Things keep coming up." Her hand gestured back and forth, like someone trying to clear a fog.

"Our lives just haven't allowed for any stability. You must know how that is."

Harry grunted. Back in Port City, waiting in Rovaki's outer office, he had heard the newscaster saying something about a new school being opened.

Dusk was deepening into night as a low, sprawling, palisaded building that could only be the caravanserai came into view ahead.

Harry asked one of the train crew: "Do we get a break from the breakdown zone here?"

"Not much of one, I'm afraid. There are a few square meters of free zone near the center of the building, but they're taken up almost entirely by a compact food-and-drink recycler and a public telegraph station."

Harry, for whatever reason, had been expecting the overnight accommodation to be a small, crude structure. But its single story, the outer wall a palisade of imported logs, sprawled over half a hectare or so of ground.

The walls were twice as high as a man, and appeared to have been fashioned from the same imported material—logs—as the telegraph poles. This gave the place the look of some ancient stockade, an effect spoiled by the numerous broad, low windows that had been cut in the walls, openings defended only by orna-mental metal grillwork. Several doorways were broad and unde-fended, too.

But then, who was going to attack?

The caravan stopped some twenty meters from the building, at just a little distance off the road.

The place seemed large enough to house all the passengers and crew of a large caravan in reasonable comfort, but word was that tonight all the sleeping rooms were going to be taken.

Harry noted that the telegraph cable went right in through a small hole in one rugged wall, to come out again on the far side of the building, and run into the distance beside the road.

Harry and his two traveling companions paused, a little way outside the compound, to watch the last bright glow of sunset— well, something vaguely like a sunset, Harry thought, a streaki-ness of light, and changing colors.

"This is the first time," Lily said softly, "I've ever seen a sun-set without a sun."

Leaving his companions behind for a time, Harry went scouting on his own, stretching his legs. Ordinarily he might have gone wandering off alone into the Maracandan back country, which was perfectly safe, by all accounts, as long as you didn't stay lost for so long that you died of thirst, and you didn't fall into one of the rare subduction zones, where the surface of the world was slowly drawn underground, to be eventually produced again somewhere else. But right now he stayed in sight of the building, wanting to keep an eye on Kul as much as possible—and on Lily Gunnlod as well.

*   *   *

A large common room, lighted pleasantly by thick candles and brightened by the many mirrors on its walls, formed part of the interior of the caravanserai. One side of this space did duty as a kind of general store, with two clerks behind a counter conducting business—cash only, please—computing prices and change with an abacus. Here Harry soon provided himself with a change of clothes, as well as a shaver and a toothbrush.

Carrying his purchases in a small bag, he let his curiosity lead him next to inspect the telegraph facility. This was a small room partitioned off from the large common interior space, advertising its presence by the wash of modern light coming over and under and around the barrier. Someone had marked the boundaries of the hostel's central live zone with paint. The fiberoptic lines of the public telegraph came into the small island of free zone from both east and west, to be connected to a bright brass-colored manual key. Harry didn't suppose that the Templars had any terminal here—no loss, because he had no message for General Pike anyway.

In the middle of the telegraph room, a simple machine very much like the one Harry had seen at Templar headquarters converted the impulse of distant keystrokes to pulses of light and then displayed them on a kind of printout.

Bulaboldo strolled into the telegraph room, nodded casually to Harry, and asked if there were any messages for him. The civilian operator sitting at the table checked a list, then shook his head.

At one side of the small free-zone space, a couple of technicians sat and squatted on the floor, surrounded by a small scattering of modern tools. They were steadily tinkering with some elaborate, low-mounted gadget that was connected by lines to the telegraph, though evidently not part of it.

Bulaboldo, not finding any messages, was gone again. Harry lingered, striking up a conversation with the technicians.

"Strange world, eh? Some strange machinery."

One of the men on the floor chuckled. He seemed ready to take a break in his struggle with a small tool that was refusing to perform. He sat back and popped a chewing pod into his mouth. "I guess you might call it that. But what can you expect from a place that has huge chunks of antimatter in its core?"

Harry squinted at him. "It has huge . . . what?"

The second worker, still trying to puzzle out his job, was shaking his head and smiling. The first technician grinned. "Fact. Only a couple of hundred meters below us as we sit here, the rocks go crazy, turning into layers of shit like you wouldn't believe. Among the other goodies there are antimatter capsules, mostly bundled antineutrons, several tons in a package, neatly wrapped up in what seems to be a permanent magnetic binding."

Harry was staring at the man. Anywhere else in the Galaxy, he would have been certain that his leg was being pulled. Here on Maracanda, all he could say was "I don't see how it's possible."

The tech seemed pleased to have shared a marvel. "We come back to the usual Maracandan explanation: 'Balance of forces.' That's what the scientists tell us. Seems to cover just about everything."

Harry said: "I'd like to talk to one of the scientists. One who's really working to understand the peculiarities of this place."

The second tech looked up from his work at last. "Well, you just missed your chance. Fellow who passed through just yesterday, came in here and wanted to see all our latest readings. Tom, what was his name? Cloberg, something like that."

Tom wasn't quite sure either. "But I know there's quite a large staff, at the research station over in Minersville." The tech's jaws worked, grinding the last remnant of the chewing pod to juice.

Meanwhile, Harry had been running his gaze over the telegraph instrument. The key chattered now and then, as if talking to itself, and wrote out light streaks on a slowly revolving drum, where sensitive paper recorded the coded messages.

The operator displayed a message. He seemed pleased, as at a rare discovery. "Here's one that looks intact. Maybe it makes sense."

Number One tech, still sitting on the floor, shook his head. "Maybe not. If you do decode a lot of them, you realize that some were transmitted years ago."

If Harry had been anywhere else, he wouldn't have been tempted to believe that.

It was time to prepare for dinner. After a visit to the row of chemical toilets, much like the units aboard the caravan, Harry washed his hands and face at one of the adjoining sinks.

Since nearly all of the caravanserai was in a breakdown zone, maintenance machines were disqualified from cleaning the toilets and performing the hundred other tasks of daily housekeeping. Live workers had been found for the jobs, and doubtless were well paid.

Dinner in the common room at the caravanserai came close to living up to Bulaboldo's recommendation. The resident human chef was something of a virtuoso in his use of the recycler, a unit almost as up to date as Harry's in the *Witch*. There was also some interesting talk, with the stationmaster and members of the train crew joining passengers at table.

It occurred to Harry, looking at the glow of electric light washing out of the free-zone room, that *this* might be the strange part of the universe, the portion where high tech and high science can be made to work. For all that humanity had discovered so far, the bulk of the Galaxy, and all the endless galaxies beyond, could be pure breakdown zone.

Within the small enclave of human presence, buried deep in Maracandan night, gas lamps, or oil lamps, gave a warm but faintly flickering, cheerful illumination. Outside the circle of the flames' illumination, a blackness of frightening intensity had come over the silent land.

After dinner and a brief walk around the compound, Harry retreated to his small assigned room, where he lit the single candle waiting on its stand, took off only his boots, and lay down in his spacefarer's coveralls on one of the room's two cots.

Bulaboldo's room was down the hall somewhere. Lily had the small room next to Harry's, and she retired at about the same time Harry did. He was still trying to keep half an eye on her, though more and more it seemed like totally wasted effort. The suspicion planted by the smugglers in the space station was very nearly dead, but still retained a breath of life in Harry's mind. He wanted to see if this woman and Bulaboldo were secretly in some kind of partnership, or if she might be going to meet some other coconspirator, and have a long and secret talk.

Stretching out on the cot, Harry was glad that the sleeping rooms were roofed. He assumed this had been done only for privacy, but there might have been other reasons. Blowing out his candle, he thought that he would much rather lie exposed to a natural planetary sky than to the continual dull overhead of Maracanda, beyond which something, something no human had yet managed to understand, ceaselessly played at counterfeiting day and night. Without a roof he might have been afraid to close his eyes. As if some unwelcome presence might come dropping out of that gray nothingness . . .

The berserkers had been chasing Harry for a long time, hounding him continuously, never giving him a break, for an epoch that seemed to stretch out into eternity. He was tired, so tired, of never being able to put them out of his mind. Right now they were at least out of sight, but that didn't help much, because he knew for a certainty that they were lurking nearby. He could feel their presence in his bones. They had chased him for an age, endlessly and relentlessly, and now they were about to pounce.

That, Harry realized, was the way things usually went in dreams. First came the fear, and afterward came the image, the presence, to give the fear a face and form. In some small corner of Harry's mind he already realized that he was dreaming, but the knowledge did not help much.

Suddenly he knew that the first of the death machines was about to attack, and simultaneously with the knowledge the metallic shape came bursting out of ambush, popping right up from the middle of a strange landscape that might have been somewhere on a world called Hyperborea.

In the next moment, with an abrupt shifting of the scene, Harry realized that he was not on Hyperborea at all, but standing on the much colder world that had once been his home. He hadn't been back to the place for many years, yet his booted feet crunched in the snow, and the land lay brilliant in the light of the three moons.

There sounded a loud, snapping clang, and Harry knew the sound came from the impact of the berserker's jagged grippers against the heavy armor he had willed himself to wear. But even though in his dreamworld he had the armor on, it wasn't going to do him a bit of good. In another second or two the fusion-powered arms of the berserker were going to tear him right apart . . .

The terror brought him upright in bed, gasping. The loud, sharp noise that had wrenched Harry Silver out of his dream had landed him in a waking reality that seemed even less probable than the dream, and more confusing.

He was not out on the rocky waste of Hyperborea, nor had he returned in some mysterious way to his home world. He was waking up on one of the narrow cots in a small room in the caravanserai on Maracanda, and people—live, solid people—were forcing their way in through the window.

Around him, the darkness that passed for night on this strange habitable body had been comfortably quiet—until now. The harsh clanging, snapping noise was repeated, loud enough to awaken anybody, and this time Harry realized that it was made by one of the window bars being broken out of its socket.

The window, like all the others in the low, sprawling building, lacked any kind of glass or screen, and the metal bars were more ornamental than serious. They might discourage a casual trespasser, but were too flimsy to withstand a determined assault. A prying attack with a strong, simple lever had broken loose first one of them and then another. Someone just outside the window was holding a long, thick bar of wood.

At some distance outside the building, near the area where the caravan had parked, an oil lamp on a tall pole was burning, sending a faint wash of light into the room. Another dim glow came from Maracanda's cloudless, spaceless sky, which, like the sky of Earth, had never gone completely dark. Streaks of interior lamplight, fainter still, came sliding in under the closed door leading to the hallway.

By the time Harry's eyes were fully open, it seemed to him that a small army of enemies was streaming in through the violated window. The first pair of dark-clad figures, showing something woodenly peculiar about their faces, were standing beside Harry's bunk even before he was fully awake. In another moment they had laid hands on him. Each of them had one of Harry's arms, and they were attempting to drag him away. The narrow bed sat close against the small room's wall, and the man trying to grip Harry's right arm had to climb onto the cot to do so.

Harry's first reaction of fear and outrage was mixed with something like relief, on realizing that in reality he did not face berserkers. The hands grabbing at him were strong, but had no more than human strength. Only the invaders' strange faces gave him doubt, and it took him another moment to realize that they were artificial, subtle masks, no two alike, that offered, almost convincingly, the impression of natural humanity.

Training and instinct had already taken over, and the fight

was well under way even before Harry was fully awake. Both of his arms were caught; neither of his immediate assailants was a weakling, and for the moment he had to do what he could by using his bootless feet alone. There were yells and gasps, and the third and fourth figures to approach him were sent staggering back.

The intruders had him outnumbered, about five to one, as near as he could tell, in the midst of what had swiftly become a crazy melee. But their trouble was that they were anything but a practiced, well-coordinated team. Too many of them had come crowding into the unfamiliar little room, so that in the semidarkness they kept blundering into each other's way. They were all dressed alike, in dark, tight-fitting garments, and Harry had the impression that all carried short, primitive weapons sheathed at their belts. But so far, in these first moments of voiceless struggle they had drawn none of their knives or clubs. The two men who had seized Harry kept trying to wrestle him, rather than stabbing him or hitting him over the head.

As soon as he could spare the breath, he got out one good karate yell.

As if the noise had broken some spell, suddenly all of the attackers were loudly vocalizing, too, jabbering warnings and barking confused orders at each other.

"Hold his head . . . this way." That sounded like a woman's voice, trying to give directions, coming from behind a mask that showed a molded imitation beard. She was cradling what looked like a piece of cloth in one outstretched hand, holding a soft pad loosely, as if in readiness to slap it over Harry's face the instant she got the chance.

She wasn't going to get it. Harry twisted his head and neck from side to side. He kicked out again and again, as methodical in his viciousness as he could be. No way he was going to get full power behind the kicks in this position, but there were so many bodies around him he could hardly miss, even if it was hard to see. One figure reeled back, groaning, another dropped to one knee.

Yet another struck at Harry, but ineffectually, with an empty, untrained hand. They seemed to be going to great lengths to keep from doing him any serious damage. All their efforts were concentrated on dragging him away.

The man holding Harry's right arm made an attempt to shift his hold, and in the moment when his grip was slackened, Harry got that arm free. His backfist strike, snapped from the elbow, caught his fumble-fingered assailant on his masked right cheek with an impact that must have loosened a tooth or two, and sent the fellow tumbling off the cot. With his right arm free, Harry saw about getting the left one loose.

Only a few seconds had passed since the second window bar gave way. The door to the adjoining room slid open. Lily's head appeared in the aperture, followed by her shoulders still clad in the top of her coveralls, and like any normal person she was coming to see what in the name of Malakó could be going on. In the slow way that things seemed to move when a fight was on, Harry saw one of the intruders turning away from him to confront this newcomer. Lily's mouth was opening, and in another instant she would be yelling, too.

By this time a couple of the villains had regrouped enough to make another effort to hold a saturated cloth over Harry's nose and mouth. That plan had not succeeded even when Harry's arms were being held, and it had no chance of working now. The cloth was soon on the floor again, along with one of the people who had been holding it. Others were starting to regain their feet.

Now Lily, her mouth gone wide and screaming, was being pulled into the room. Harry was off the bed at last and standing on his feet. Ducking under ineffective blows, fighting off what seemed a score of clutching arms, he could hear someone rattling the other door, the one to the corridor, which he had locked before retiring. From out there in the hallway, Kul Bulaboldo's voice, much louder than Harry had ever heard it before, was calling out to know just what in all the hells was going on?

Lily meanwhile had started fighting with the temper of a small fiend, kicking, biting, scratching. But either she hadn't much skill at this kind of thing, or the room was just too crowded to let her show it. Judging by the way she yelled, she had not yet been seriously hurt.

One intruder was saying, or at least Harry seemed to hear: "If you don't struggle, Doctor Kloskurb, your wife won't get hurt."

At the same time, another of them was managing to get Lily's two arms pinned behind her back.

"Come with us, Doctor Kloskurb, or she gets . . ."

Harry, having got both arms free at last, was not impressed. Dr. Kloskurb, whoever he might be, was probably home safe in bed, and his wife likewise. The man who had been holding the knife at Lily's throat caught a smashing elbow under his chin, and went down groaning. The knife went flying somewhere, and Lily grabbed at her throat as if she had been nicked.

The rattling of the door had grown more violent, and now came to a stop, in a pause followed instantaneously by a crash. The whole panel, formed of some imported plastic, came bursting in, admitting the relatively bright light of the corridor. Where the door had been, a bulky outline, Bulaboldo's, clad in a long, strange-looking, netlike shirt or gown, stood outlined against the brighter illumination.

From that moment it was all downhill for the attackers.

Bulaboldo had come in carrying some kind of a short club—with a second look Harry could see that he was holding a pistol reversed so he could strike with the butt—the odds had definitely shifted.

In only another moment the surviving attackers had broken

and were scrambling away in panicked flight, some struggling to get back out through the broken window, some taking good advantage of the open doorway.

At absolutely the wrong time, in the key moment, with full victory in the defenders' grasp, Kul, as if reeling back from some assailant's blow, or dodging the thrust of a knife, somehow blundered into Harry.

Harry fell, tripping over something—he couldn't tell what, maybe a fallen body, or maybe a broken chair or upended candle stand. Bulaboldo kept struggling to get up and sliding back. The great bulk of Harry's helpful rescuer kept squashing him down, pinning him in place long enough to keep him from grabbing any of the intruders who were still active, as they went out by door and window with amazing speed.

Spitting oaths, grabbing handfuls of Kul's netlike garment and manhandling his great bulk out of the way, Harry at last regained his feet. Kicking broken furniture from his path, he lurched and stumbled across the small room to the window, but, having got that far, all he could do was hang there, panting, on the sill.

One of the five attackers was still writhing on the floor, but the four others had got clean away. Harry was just in time to see the last escaping enemy vanish into the shadows surrounding a darkened pedicar, a moderate-sized vehicle already moving, picking up speed. The enemy had been beaten and routed, and Harry wasn't going to run out into the night in hopeless pursuit of a bunch of lunatics.

Besides, three places on his body, maybe four, were starting to send out signals that he had been strained and bruised. None of the sore spots seemed likely to need professional help.

He went to Lily, checking to see that she had not been seriously hurt. She was gasping and blubbering, but Harry could see that the knife nick on her neck was superficial.

Kul was the loudly groaning one, as he stamped about with his pistol still in hand.

How many sleeping rooms did this facility afford? Maybe one hundred? Harry had the impression that all, or most of them at least, were occupied tonight. He had observed on his way in that none of the visible entrances to the building seemed to be locked, and the main entrance stood open and unguarded. But rather than enter the building that way, the intruders, whatever their purpose, had chosen to break their way in through Harry's barred window.

Not all of them had got away; he had one captive still on hand for questioning. Harry turned and looked at the body on the floor. One leg and one arm were moving slightly, so the man was still alive.

THIRTEEN

In the light spilling in through the empty doorway from the corridor, Harry could make out several items abandoned by the desperadoes in their flight. There on the floor lay a short cudgel, over there beside the wall a knife, and there, beside an upended cot and candle stand, the scrap of cloth they had been trying to plaster over Harry's face. He presumed the fabric was laced with some kind of poison or anesthetic.

Bulaboldo was back on his feet now, stretching his back and testing his joints, his groans subsiding; he seemed to have got the worst of them out of his system.

The big man came closer. "Harry. You're all right?" His concern sounded genuine.

Still panting, Harry took a quick inventory, checking out his sore spots one by one. They all turned out to be no worse than bruises. "Nothing broken, not even any blood. Good thing you came in when you did. How about yourself?"

A massive shrug. "Nothing worth mentioning. A mere scratch."

Harry couldn't see even that much damage, but he said: "I owe you another one."

"I will be proud to collect that debt, dear lad." Then Bulaboldo, mumbling to himself what sounded like exotic curses in some alternate language, moved about the room with his head bent, studying the various items dropped by the invaders.

Harry had turned back to Lily, who was still huddled on the floor in one corner of the room, making her favorite strange noises. Bending, he touched her gently, and asked: "You all right?"

She choked out some answer that Harry could not hear clearly. By this time other people, guests and workers of the caravanserai, roused by the uproar, were crowding in at the empty doorway, walking on the fallen door, beginning a clamor of comments and questions.

Bulaboldo had discovered that one of the cots was still intact enough to let him sit on it.

The stationmaster was among the first to enter, with a kind of billy club in hand. When he saw that the trouble, whatever it had been, was over now, he stuck his billy club back in his belt, with a firmness that seemed to permanently forswear the use of violence. A moment later he had picked up the cloth dropped by the invaders. After taking one whiff at arm's length, he threw it back on the floor. "Enough to make your head spin."

"That seemed to be the general idea," Harry agreed.

"What happened?"

Harry pointed at the evidence. "People broke in—look at your window bars—and tried to kidnap me."

"Kidnap?"

"Don't ask me why."

There followed a barrage of questions from several new arrivals.

Harry could testify that at least a couple of the intruders who got away must also have been seriously hurt, and must have needed help in making their getaway.

Lily said she had been on the floor when the fight ended, unable to see which way any of the escaping people went.

The stationmaster looked as if he had hoped to find some innocent explanation of it all; but by now it was plain that wasn't going to happen. With a sigh he asked: "Can we be sure how many there were?"

"There were five," said Harry.

"Can we be sure?"

Harry looked at him. "What did I just say? Did my best to keep track while I was hitting them. Four got away."

Kul interrupted, with a mighty clearing of his throat. "When I looked out the window, it seemed to me there were two cars, already starting to move away."

"Which way did they go?" the stationmaster wondered. "East or west?"

Bulaboldo shook his head. "I don't know. They were moving out of the parking spaces, toward the road. Light's bad out there, and I couldn't see which way they turned."

None of the three participants in the fight who were still conscious could contribute anything immediately helpful. When people kept looking at Harry, he added: "It was just sort of flee-ing bodies, vanishing in the gloom. But one didn't get away." Quickly Harry turned his attention to the body feebly moving on the floor.

By now, there were more people in the room than there had

been during the fight. Guests of the caravanserai jostled for space with members of the staff. All were questioning each other, to no avail, while a couple hovered in ineffective sympathy over the kidnapper still on the floor.

"What happened to this one?" someone wondered. The man showed no obvious wounds.

"He ran into a door," Harry grunted. Then he looked over at Lily. "Sure you're all right?" Only now did he see that blood was trickling, very lightly, from her pretty neck, where the menacing knife had made a nick.

"I guess I'll live," she got out quietly.

A couple of people had started fussing over her, administering first aid.

Someone had set up the candle and relighted it, and at last someone else was bringing a brighter lamp into the room. In its efficient glow Bulaboldo got busy, pointing out to newcomers the weapons that the intruders had dropped on the floor.

Harry was also able to get a better look at the big man's protective garment, which had been fabricated of some fine, lightweight plastic chain mail. Harry had seen that stuff before—it was tough enough to repel almost any point or blade.

The stationmaster and others were working over the kidnapper who had not been able to get away. One of them was gently peeling off the fellow's mask. The face revealed was one that Harry had never seen before.

Looking at it from across the room, Harry thought he could detect certain signs of serious head injury: the fellow's pupils were of unequal size, and he seemed to have blood oozing from one ear. Harry would have liked to drag him into a brighter light somewhere, and try some homegrown methods of resuscitation. But no, it looked like any questioning would have to wait. The man was still breathing, but that was about it.

A bunch of people were still in the room, and more hovered

at the door, vacillating between wanting to look at what was happening and trying to remain uninvolved.

Lily, who obviously needed no ambulance, was standing up and had a small bandage on her throat to stop the bleeding. She told her version of events, and then repeated it as more people started asking questions. The story she told meshed pretty closely with the scenario as Harry recalled it.

She was backed up by the respected Maracandan businessman and dealer in mining properties, Kul Bulaboldo, who was eager to identify himself—he had begun handing out smart business cards—and to vouch for the integrity of his two friends.

The stationmaster rose and turned away from the man on the floor, muttering that he was in bad shape. "We don't even have a decent medirobot here; transit authority says it would take up too much free-zone room. All we can do is get this fellow to the hospital, quick as we can, I say we don't wait for an ambulance. And I'll try to get off a couple of telegrams." He started trying to shoo people out of the room. He turned to look at Harry. "Maybe they'll want to send out some kind of investigator from Minersville."

Harry stared right back. "Obviously they were mistaking me for someone else, this Doctor Somebody. What gets me is, when you decide to kidnap someone, why do it here?"

Bulaboldo made a thoughtful murmur that might or might not have meant he considered the question a useful one. "You mean, why at a caravanserai?"

"Well, that. But in particular I was thinking, why do it in a breakdown zone?"

Kul frowned ferociously. He seemed genuinely surprised and outraged at the kidnapping attempt. "Oh, I suppose it makes sense. Getting at the victim would be easier. It would probably have been much harder to force their way into a modern building, equipped with some high-tech security system. In a free zone, the predators would have been able to escape much faster in a powered vehicle, but any pursuit that followed would be faster, too. And news of the crime could be sent ahead to cut them off."

Privately, Harry was trying to tie the incident to his lingering suspicion that Lily was after all involved in something shady. But he couldn't come up with a connection.

The stationmaster seemed afflicted with lingering shock. When the case of head injury had been dispatched to Minersville in a pedicar, propelled by two hard-muscled young employees of the caravanserai, he came back to Harry's room to talk some more.

"Nothing like this ever happened here before," he repeated several times, sounding half apologetic and half angry.

Bulaboldo, listening with every appearance of great sympathy for the beset official, had begun to exert his considerable skills at soothing authority and establishing an indirect dominance of his own.

He forestalled any attempt, quashed any suggestion, to hold Harry here at the caravanserai until some official investigator arrived.

"We'll all be in Minersville tomorrow anyway," he assured the official. "But perhaps you should telegraph in that direction, have them be on the lookout for the fugitives."

"Ah, when you really need the damn thing, it never works. But I'll see if we can get a signal through."

The stationmaster's helper, a nervous youth carrying a pad and stylus, began to try to write down the names and addresses of the principal witnesses.

Harry gave such personal data as seemed pertinent. Then he said: "What puzzles me is that one of them called me by name."

"Oh?"

"Yeah. But not by my right name. 'Doctor Kloskurb,' or something close to that. What kind of sense does that make?" Then he fell silent, jogged by a certain memory that he didn't want to talk about just then.

No one else had a good answer to his question. As word of the attempted kidnapping spread through the caravanserai, every face that he saw seemed to be looking at him strangely. He glowered back at them, and no one except the stationmaster bothered him with questions.

In the common room, the smell of yesterday's cooking lingered in the air, and a row of broad tables awaited tomorrow morning's breakfast, now not many hours away.

A quarter of an hour later, the official announced with some satisfaction that the morning's eastbound caravan would be departing at its scheduled time, and crew and passengers alike should attempt to get back to sleep. Harry decided he would try.

Lily had announced she was more than ready to make that effort, and closed her door. But only seconds later, the door between her room and Harry's slid open again, and she put her head through, taking another look at the cheap shattered furniture, the other door still on the floor, the broken barrier of the window.

"Looks a bit of a mess," she commented. "Harry, I've got an empty cot in my room, if you'd like to use it." She paused, fingering her throat, where the small bandage was almost invisible. "Unless you're going to your friend's room?"

"My friend? Oh, you mean Kul?" Harry had to chuckle. "But he was some help, wasn't he? Thanks. I'm sure I'll like your room better." He began to throw his belongings into the little bag from the general store. Packing took about five seconds, including picking up his boots. "Sorry about your neck; I didn't mean to joggle the fellow's arm. I guess my aim was just a little off; but my intentions were better than his were."

"You probably saved my life—again." She was holding the door to her room open for him. "I don't know if either of us will get any sleep." Then she considered how that might sound. "I mean . . ."

"I understand. If I snore too loud, just kick me."

He had just stretched out and closed his eyes, when Lily's voice asked from the other bunk: "What were they after, Harry? It wasn't really anything to do with you, was it?"

"Not that I know of. Except that kind of stuff seems to follow me around." He paused, wondering whether to open his eyes or not, and deciding against it. "Still want me to help you find your husband?"

"Yes. I do."

The rest of the night passed uneventfully.

When Harry woke up, suddenly and peacefully, the first gleams of what passed for daylight on Maracanda were brightening the window of Lily's room. She lay sleeping, face half buried in her pillow. Like Harry she was fully clothed except for boots, but she had pulled a blanket round her, probably more for symbolic security than for warmth.

For a few moments Harry lay studying her face, thinking he knew not much more about her than he had two days ago. Then she began to stir, and it was time to get up. In a few minutes, they were joining their fellow passengers in a kind of cafeteria line for a good recycler breakfast.

The signal for boarding the eastbound caravan was given almost on time. Soon the travelers were back in their respective wagons, most choosing to occupy the same chairs as yesterday. The lure lamp was lighted and dangled on its pole in front of the movable cage of massive spheres. The spheres trembled for a moment, then began to roll toward the source of special light. Harry wondered if they had got a good rest during the hours of darkness.

Again the pace was moderate. It seemed to Harry that a good long-distance runner would probably have been able to keep up.

* * *

Full daylight, or its analogue, came from the brightening east to meet the travelers on the road. By then, they had reached a place where they had a good view of the several distinct layers of atmosphere—for want of a better word—each displaying gaps of apparent emptiness, that made up the imitation sky of Maracanda. No one with the caravan seemed to know exactly how far up between these layers the breathable atmosphere extended.

The closest layer hovered, somehow self-supporting, no more than a few meters above the crest of a rise of land.

Harry mused, "Looks like it should be possible to climb up there and touch the sky."

Bulaboldo shook his head. "Actually it could be possible, but I wouldn't advise making the attempt. No one's done that, to my knowledge, and survived."

That got Lily's attention. "What happens?"

"As I understand it"—Kul made a finger-snapping gesture—"like lightning, only more so."

The morning was spent in following a winding road, or trail, between chains of towering hills, and across and around other landforms more than ordinarily spectacular.

As the journey wore on, Bulaboldo was ready to converse again, but not about the kidnapping attempt. He had several times already expressed his concern about what the Space Force might be doing, legally or otherwise, to Harry's ship. Harry himself wasn't particularly worried, and was able to reassure his associate. He thought his ship and his cargo should be safe till he went back to get them. But whether that would be in days or years he didn't know.

Elaborating on their earlier discussion, Harry told Bulaboldo that taking control of the *Witch* would not be an easy task for the Space Force, even if they brought in clever engineers. Not with the automatic defenses and alarms Harry had in place. The thoughtware also bristled with truly fiendish downlock codes, practically guaranteed to stop anyone but Harry from getting his ship to lift off, or even turning on her engines.

"I told you. The Space Force has had a shot at it before, without any noticeable success."

But it seemed inevitable that the Space Force would now be keeping watch on Harry's ship, ready to arrest him the moment he went near it.

Bulaboldo asked how much cargo space Harry had available.

"Depends what kind of additional cargo I'd be attempting to fit in. I've got some machinery in there now. Maybe you'd like to make me an offer on that?"

"Machinery. Ah. Can you testify as to its nature?"

"Supposed to be food processing, of some exotic kind, I think. No, I haven't seen any of the crates open."

"Well, let me consider it, old chap. When I've had a chance to eye the merchandise, I might make an offer. Creative trading can present a fascinating challenge."

Gradually the talk turned to other kinds of hardware. Harry was still seeking information. "What about weapons? Their use in the breakdown zones, I mean."

"No different from any other machines. Complexity fails, almost every time. I believe it's been demonstrated that a bow and arrow remain dependable—a longbow, that is. The crossbow is a little too complex. With anything more complicated than that, it's hopeless. They say that in the early days on Maracanda exhaustive tests were made, on everything from slingshots up to alphatrigger carbines.

"But no need for concern. One has yet to encounter any dangerous native forms of life—with the exception, it would seem, of kidnappers. There are no voracious beasties here."

"And no berserkers."

Bulaboldo looked startled, as if that particular idea had not even crossed his mind. "No. Not yet. And they're certainly complicated machines. I don't see how they could expect to have much success at all, on a world full of breakdown zones."

"And not much here in the way of humanity. No bait to tempt the predators."

The conversation moved along again. Harry was reminded of an ancient poem that had something about caravans in it.

"Poetry, old spark? I've noted in the past you have a certain tendency to quote the stuff."

"Learned that from my ship."

Bulaboldo only looked at him. It was perfectly obvious that the ship wasn't going to display any tendencies it hadn't learned from Harry.

It was late in the local afternoon when the train of cars, pulled tirelessly, if not very swiftly, by the cage of rolling spheres, drew near its goal.

On this last leg of their journey, signs frequently appeared at roadside, warning in several languages, of BREAKDOWN ZONES ahead. The signs here struck Harry as rather pointless, as the travelers had been largely in such zones since sometime yesterday.

At last there came an hour when the caravan emerged from a deep notch between tall, irregular landforms, each a different color, to confront a sprawl of the peculiar Maracandan buildings, and it was obvious that they had found their destination.

As the train of cars pulled up to a loading dock very much like the one it had departed from back in Port City, the lure lamp was shaded, and the massed spheres under their cage of basketwork rolled gently to a halt.

This was a bustling free zone, and the sounds and sights of high technology reached the travelers before they were close enough to get a good look at the town itself.

Tomb Town occupied a free zone almost a kilometer square. Unfortunately, the Maracandan sky above consisted of a solid dome of breakdown, preventing the establishment of any kind of spaceport, or even the erection of buildings more than three or four stories high.

Harry supposed that the difficulty of getting to these remote towns only made them more attractive to certain people. Occupying a slice of precious space at the rim of the Tomb Town free zone was a vast but inconspicuous recycling plant, a large-scale version of the system that produced gourmet wonders on Harry's ship. Harry supposed the plant was kept in steady operation. Hydrogen to keep its power lamps alive could be pried loose from the Maracandan substrate.

Even at first glance, Tomb Town radiated a crude energy that had been missing from Port City. The loading dock was bustling with traffic coming and going from Minersville, only a few kilometers away.

It seemed clear that this settlement was considerably smaller than Port City, but it showed signs of rapid growth, including heavy pedestrian traffic on the streets visible from the main gate. A map posted at the gate suggested that the town was laid out in an odd plan, doubtless to take advantage of as much of the free zone as possible.

The caravan only stopped here briefly, for partial unloading, and would soon be rolling on along the road to Minersville.

Actually, before the caravan had fully stopped, a small rush of men and women, traders and prospectors, were jumping off the moving wagons. The object of the rush was to get as quick a look as possible at the latest version of a map showing what lands were still considered available. Dealers in land had sprung into existence, and with the blessing of the public office were subdividing lots.

Bulaboldo on the other hand was in no hurry and seemed

scornful of anyone who had to rush around like that just to meet someone else's schedule.

A large and badly faded banner of plain dumb cloth said WELCOME above the symbolically gated entrance to the town. From what Harry could see of the settlement, it looked a bigger place than he had, for some reason, been expecting.

Harry held back a little from the rush to disembark, preferring to avoid the crush of bodies at the exit door. A few passengers, unwilling to wait in line, were just leaping out over the car's low sides. But Lily was in the forefront of those using the designed way out, with some of the business-suited passengers giving her the most competition. The business people seemed to be even more eager to get off than the religious pilgrims, as if another half minute or so might make all the difference in the kind of claim they would be allowed to file.

While waiting, Harry surveyed the scene, looking for any sign of a Space Force presence, wondering if Rovaki might have telegraphed ahead with orders to harass him some more. So far he couldn't see any.

Whether or not the Force was here, Pike had assured him that the Templars were, jealously maintaining some presence, too. Harry had also been told where to find their private communication line, which he was supposed to use to get any necessary messages back to Pike.

Lily had been quickly off the caravan, but then she just stood there for a moment, carrying her small baggage. As if, thought Harry, she had been imagining Alan standing here to meet her when she arrived, and now was shocked when that didn't happen.

Harry, even more lightly burdened, came to stand beside her.

It wasn't hard to tell, from the glaring signs, that most of the buildings facing the newcomers, and the biggest of them, were casinos that seemed to be doing a good business near the mining town. The casinos had palisaded walls, with only a few high, small windows. They looked well-to-do, and fortified, in a way that the caravanserai had not been. Evidently not everyone in Tomb Town was focused on spiritual values.

On the caravan he had heard stories about how the crews of some civilian vessels jumped ship when they arrived on Maracanda and heard the rumors of mineral wealth. Some of them had gone tearing off into the interior with little or nothing in the way of preparation, and no one who told the stories was sure what had become of them. The local authorities could put up warning signs, but they were not equipped or inclined to use sterner measures.

FOURTEEN

It seemed that last night's tele-
graphic messages sent out by the stationmaster had not been too
badly garbled. Some local official, wearing a vague smile and a
uniform that Harry could not recognize at all, was waiting to
escort Harry and his companions to the Tomb Town central hospital, where the battered and unsuccessful kidnapper had been
hauled by pedicar last night.

The official nodded pleasantly to Kul. "Mr. Bulaboldo, good
to see you again. We hear you had a little difficulty on the trip."

"You might say that, old top."

"Well, sir, we'd like you to take a look at the man who was
injured at the caravanserai last night. You and your companions
who were there, of course." And the official fixed his eyes uncertainly on Harry.

Harry would have expected Bulaboldo to protest at this distraction, but on the contrary he seemed eager to come along. Lily came also, with an attitude of wanting to get the business over with as quickly as possible.

The hospital, in easy walking distance from the caravan terminal, was a low, typically Maracandan building, built of slabs of local rock. Inside, electric lights glowed with gentle efficiency; it was a relief to be back in a free zone. The seriously injured victim of last night's brawl, now unmasked and looking about as harmless as patients in beds generally do, lay folded in pastel sheets with the thin, shiny tentacles of a modern medirobot still attached to his head in several places. When one of the tentacles occasionally moved, he looked as if he might be trying out for the part of Medusa. A youngish woman wearing physician's insignia stood by the patient as if on guard.

The man in the bed gazed back at Harry stoically, his face showing not a trace of recognition.

Studying the would-be kidnapper in turn, in the full light of day, Harry could only shake his head.

"You sure you've never seen him before, Mr. Silver?"

" 'Never' is a big word. Maybe as a face in a crowd, somewhere, sometime. But I don't think ever on this world. Not until last night. Who is he?"

The official gave a name, one that meant no more to Harry than the unfamiliar face. He added: "Been working as a miner here for about a year. No criminal record."

Taking his turn at the foot of the bed, Bulaboldo glanced briefly at the patient, then turned away shaking his head.

Lily in turn took a quick look, as if the sight were painful, and said that she had never seen him either. Apparent sympathy in her face and voice, she asked the attendant doctor if the man was going to recover.

The doctor standing at bedside said that treatment had been

effective, and a full recovery was eventually to be expected. But the victim remained totally clammed up, refusing to say anything about the events of the night before.

"Can he talk now?" Lily asked.

The woman physician said: "He can, but he hasn't said much."

Speaking slowly and distinctly, and pointing at Harry, the official asked the man in the bed: "Do you recognize this man?"

"I can't remember anything." The responding voice was an awkward croak, his unfamiliar face was wooden.

"I know one thing he remembered," the local official said. "He's asked for a lawyer."

As soon as the three of them were out of the room, Bulaboldo, operating in his won't-take-no-for-an-answer mode, announced firmly that Harry and Lily were of course going to stay with him as long as they were in town. "Believe me, dear friends, temporary housing is not that easy to come by in this city. The hotels generally have long waiting lists."

Harry and Lil looked at each other. Harry said: "I accept, but I want to do one other thing first. Those people were after Dr. Somebody, and I still think the name was Kloskurb."

The hospital's information desk seemed a logical starting place. The local roster of physicians listed no Kloskurb or anything like it, but a check in the city's professional directory came through. Emil Kloskurb, with an advanced degree in physics, worked in the astrogeology research lab. The address shown was almost in the center of town, close to the Square of the Portal.

A pedicab conveyed the travelers swiftly to Bulaboldo's residence in Tomb Town. This turned out to be a large and elegant townhouse, in what was clearly an upscale section of the city.

Harry found that he had about given up on trying to keep an eye on Lily. Whatever time and effort this saved him, he could now spend on worrying about some way to get his spaceship back.

Bulaboldo had repeatedly pledged Harry his help to do just that. (Of course, Templar Robledo Pike had also promised something along that line, but Harry didn't want Bulaboldo to know anything about Templar Pike.)

Bulaboldo had practically promised that he could arrange to pry the *Witch* away from the authorities back in Port City. But so far he had refused to discuss any details of the plan. When they were in the house and could presumably talk freely, Harry brought the subject up again.

Kul shook his head. "I just wish you'd leave that to me, old chap."

"It's my ship. I want to know."

Bulaboldo started to say something, took a look at Harry, and said something else instead. "I can assure you of this much. Very delicate negotiations are in progress."

"Conducted how? By telegraph?"

Kul looked right and left, as if making sure they could not be overheard. "Not the sort of business one would ever want to trust to even a private wire. The telegraph has been known to give up information to the wrong parties, besides keeping it from the proper ones. No, the details have been delegated to a certain associate of mine, back in Port City."

"Who?"

"His name would not mean anything to you."

"Who says?"

"Trust me, lad, I know what I'm about."

Harry answered quietly and slowly, as if he were weighing every word. "I hope you do, Kul. I really hope you do."

The other looked a shade uncomfortable. He licked his lips. "Old times' sake, and all that."

"You're going to want some kind of a payback, sometime."

"Glad to be of service, Harry. Of course, one never knows when one will indeed need help in turn."

Harry gave him another look, but that was all he could find out for the moment. All right, so Bulaboldo would try to arrange to get the *Witch* unsealed and released, just out of the goodness of his heart.

Harry was sitting in the common room of Bulaboldo's elaborate house, sipping coffee brought by an elegant robotic servant and reading a pamphlet he had just picked up. "A lot of people come to this world on pilgrimage because the Tomb of Timur is here. What I want to know is, does this Timur have anything to do with the founding of the Malakó system? Or is he separate?"

"As far as I can figure this out, most Malakós believe the two have no connection." Lily, on a nearby sofa, was studying a larger Malakó guidebook, one she pulled from a nearby library shelf. She had announced her intention of setting out very soon for the Square of the Portal, which seemed to be in easy walking distance.

Harry hadn't got the whole story of Timur yet, and it seemed he wasn't going to get it from the turgid prose of the little pamphlet. Only that the man had been an important prophet or leader, or both, who was supposed to have been buried in some exotic way.

Lily was suddenly worried about the religious details, as if it might be important for her to have them right. "On the spot where the spirit of the Galaxy first spoke to him?"

"Something like that. Does it matter?"

"It might. I want to be able to talk about these things with Alan." She sighed. "I guess I'm ready. Harry, are you coming with me?"

"Said I would, didn't I? Provided we can stop in at the

research center on the way. I still want to talk to this Dr. Kloskurb if I can." He looked at her and added softly: "It should only take a minute."

The doctor wasn't hard to find. The first thing Harry noted, while introducing himself and Lily, in a computer-intensive laboratory at the research center, was the man's general resemblance to himself. No one seeing them together would have mistaken them for twins, but in size, coloring, and apparent age the match was close.

Lily agreed. "The two of you could easily be brothers. Only you're just a little younger, I think, Harry."

The scientist listened to the story, and agreed on the fact of the likeness. "But what you tell me about an attempted kidnapping seems absurd. I can't think of any reason why anyone would want to abduct me." He paused. "Are you sure it was my name he spoke, and not just something that sounded like—"

Harry said: "People have called me a lot of things, but usually not by any high academic titles. No, one of these people called me by your name. And here we have the resemblance, as supporting evidence. You stayed in the caravanserai just a night before I did, and somehow they got their timing wrong."

Kloskurb was still incredulous. "Why would anyone want to kidnap me?"

"Possibly you've got something they want. Or someone close to you has got it."

"Ridiculous. I'm not a wealthy man."

"Maybe what they want is not necessarily money."

"Then I can't imagine what. Revenge? But I have no enemies."

Harry, crunching a chewing pod between his teeth, looked at him thoughtfully for a little while. Then he said: "People in your field seem to lead hazardous lives on this habitable body. The scientist who disappeared a standard month or so ago—what was her name?"

"Yes, of course. Dr. Kochi." Kloskurb nodded soberly. "We were colleagues, worked on the same project for a time."

"Maybe Dr. Kochi did not fall down a subduction zone. Maybe it was people who pulled her away."

"Well." The doctor looked around him, at his computers and other busy machines. Obviously he wanted to get this intrusion over with as quickly as he could. "What would you suggest I do, Mr. Silver?"

"First, talk to your local law people—though they'll probably say there's nothing they can do. Then keep your eyes open. I don't know how you feel about hiring bodyguards, or what they cost here, or if they're any good, but it might not be a bad idea."

"As, for instance, possibly yourself?"

"Me? No!" Harry hadn't been trying to give that impression. "I've got a different career, one that keeps me very busy."

The scientist muttered something. He still looked yearningly at his machines. Harry asked him: "Onto something good?"

"There are discoveries of really major importance waiting to be made." Once started on his favorite subject, Kloskurb tended to keep going. It seemed that the deeper layers of the mass called Maracanda, starting at a depth of a hundred meters or so, contained many nodules of exotic matter. There was a note of wonder in the scientist's voice: "Even nodules of antimatter are a theoretical possibility."

Lily was showing signs of restlessness. Harry nodded. "That's what the techs at the caravanserai were telling me, only they made it definite. How in all the hells can you have chunks of antimatter buried in the middle of a normal world?"

"That, of course, is what we hope to discover. I assume some kind of natural force shielding, probably magnetic, would have to be in place." Kloskurb smiled. "Of course, it's probably a mistake to ever think of Maracanda as a normal world."

When the two of them came out of the research lab, Lily said impulsively: "The square is only one short block from here, if the maps are right. I've got to take one quick look." Her breathing was heightened, and there was more color in her face.

"Sure." Harry stayed right with his client, playing his promised role of escort. Alan or no Alan, having come this far, he had an urge to see the thing.

Only about fifty paces, on a walkway crowded with others seeking the same destination, and they were in the Square of the Portal. Vehicular traffic was forbidden here, and the whole space was thronged with people. The square was fifty or sixty meters on a side, and three of the sides were more or less ordinary Maracandan buildings, of two or three stories each, housing a mixture of stores, offices, and apartments. The fourth side of the square was the nearly vertical face of a Maracandan landform about the same size as the buildings, striped with a converging pattern of natural grooves and ridges that looked very artificial. The pattern converged in the middle of the ridged surface, four or five meters above the ground. At the center of it was something that at first glance seemed to be the entrance to a cave, filled by the glistening transparent surface of a bulging bubble.

Days ago, when he'd still had his ship, Harry had called up from his ship's data bank a holostage image of the miraculous Tomb of Timur, and this was basically how it had looked: a clear, transparent bubble. But, as often happened, the thing itself was much more impressive than any image. Looking at the reality somehow suggested that the mouth of a tunnel might lie behind the glassy smoothness of the bulging surface.

Lily had given the marvel one quick look on entering the

square, and that was about all. Now she was scanning the faces of the surrounding crowd, her own face eager.

Harry was watching her. He said: "You know, he may not be here just at this very moment."

The young woman didn't answer. So intent was she on her search that Harry wasn't sure that she had heard him.

"Well, give it a little time." He couldn't be sure that she had heard that either.

Lily seemed to be drooping, and at last she spoke. "He'll either be here or at the Malakó temple. That's only a block away. But I want to get some rest before I go there. And I must look like hell."

"You do look kind of worn out."

"I feel kind of worn out. Last night was not exactly restful. And when I confront those people at the temple I may have to do some arguing."

"I hope he's worth it, lady," Harry surprised himself by saying.

She gave him a twisted little smile. "He is to me."

Back at Bulaboldo's house, his two guests were assigned adjoining rooms, following their preference at the caravanserai. No rickety cots in these bedchambers, but high-tech sleeping platforms, along with the latest in other types of modern furniture. The windows in these high walls were sturdily protected. The modern, high-tech partition between Lily's room and Harry's discreetly displayed a faintly visible outline where, with the cooperation of people on both sides, a communicating door could be readily dialed into existence. Just beyond it, Lily had quickly plunged into a regimen of rest and revitalization, a few hours' respite that she thought she needed before undertaking the final push in the Great Husband Search.

Harry, having decided that a nap might not be a bad idea, lay sprawled on the bed in his own room. Looking drowsily at that potential doorway on the wall, he couldn't help being somehow reminded of the sealing Rovaki had said he was slapping on the *Witch*'s main hatch. Harry had never laid eyes on that outrage, which was probably just as well. He could picture it, though: probably some kind of damned plastic that would be nastily hard to remove completely. It was as if some friend of his was locked up with tape slapped over her mouth.

Before Harry knew it, he was dreaming about berserkers again.

This time he knew that the bad machines were coming to kidnap him, not just to kill him, and he was terrified. For once, it was not their impersonal robotic efficiency, their mechanical certainty, that frightened him. This time it was their anger and their hatred, because he knew that something had happened to arouse their metal spirits, and at long last they were enraged.

He, Harry, had hidden something from them, something they dearly wanted. And the bad machines were also seeking an accounting from him, for all the harm he'd done them through the years.

The members of this particular berserker horde were all the scarier, because they cunningly remained just out of visibility, concealing their shapes and sizes from him. But Harry knew with all the certainty of dreams that they were there, moving about just under the surface of the Maracandan land, like children playing ghosts under a sagging sheet—and it was, as it always would be, his, Harry's, duty to warn the world about them.

And, of course, he found it impossible to move—

Harry awoke with a sudden wrench of mind and body. He wasn't screaming, but he had the feeling that he'd just cried out. There were no berserkers to be seen, and not even any kidnappers. Only the unfamiliar lodging of Bulaboldo's house in Tomb Town. Kul's business, and Harry didn't want to know just what it was exactly, must be good. His house, or mansion rather, was equipped with a solid roof, in contrast with most Maracandan buildings. Maybe, Harry thought, he was not the only one who feared the unknown dropping from the sky.

He got up from the elaborate sleeping platform, stretched, and went to his room's window to look out. He gazed on houses, mostly high walled and lacking roofs, built on a slightly lower level than Kul's fortress, along nearby streets and zigzag alleys.

Surveying the strange world outside Bulaboldo's one-way viewing wall, he could tell that, sure enough, the local day was progressing on schedule, with a vague brightness spread through the multiple layers of energy and odd matter making up the Maracandan sky. Maybe in a few more standard years the place would manage to generate an apparent sun.

Checking on the lady in the next room he found her up and about. A few minutes later, cleanly dressed and fresh from his own shower, Harry descended from his room to join Lily and Kul downstairs. They were just sitting down to lunch. Lily looked rested and refreshed and had garbed herself in new, attractive clothes.

She looked up as he appeared on the stairs. "You know what, Harry?"

"Tell me what."

"None of those children being born and raised on this world are ever going to see a star. Not until they go out into space."

Harry grunted. He always enjoyed looking at the stars—provided he could see them safely dimmed and filtered through a few miles of Earth-like atmosphere, or, better yet, through the elaborate optics of some stout ship's ports. From that secure position it was rather like being snug and warm inside your cheerful house, while rain or snow came pelting down outside.

On the sideboard in the dining room awaited hot dishes holding tempting food. Harry went for some kind of eggs and thin, crisp, meaty slices, all artistically synthesized.

When the three of them were seated, Kul added: "I suppose you're heading for the square again this afternoon, old thing?"

Harry glanced at Lily. "I suppose we are." He thought, Bulaboldo's keeping me under close observation, and he's going to do that until I'm needed. Whatever it is he wants, he's not ready to tell me yet. When he tells me my ship is ready, that's when he'll let me know.

Serving machines rolled and reached discreetly around the three people as they ate, tending and tidying and pouring. Harry hadn't yet seen another human being, besides Kul and Lily, since entering the house; though once a woman's distant, silvery laugh had suggested there were some around.

Since the attempted kidnapping had already been reported to the local authorities, Harry supposed that the Templars must have heard of it, too. Of course, it would give him something, a bit of real content, to put in a report to General Pike. He would first have to find the Templar communication terminal here in Tomb Town and then see if the secret key he was carrying really allowed him to use it.

Harry thought the general would probably be pleased if he could find some way to blame the attempted kidnapping on goodlife, though that theory would seem quite a stretch. Members of that morbid cult were occasionally active as suicide bombers, but not, as far as Harry was aware, as kidnappers.

But the Templars could wait; first Harry was going to escort Lily back to the square.

Having disposed of a quick lunch, the lady eagerly shouldered her small pack and graciously thanked Kul for his hospitality. If she found Alan, or maybe even if she didn't, there would be no need for her to come back to Bulaboldo's house.

"And thank you for the flowers, also." She had gathered, at Kul's invitation, a few sprigs from the carefully cultivated pots in the mansion's roof garden and was wearing them as decoration on her fashionable but inexpensive broad-brimmed hat, just ordered from a nearby shop.

"My pleasure, m'dear. Harry, you won't dally too long, will you?"

"I expect I'll be home for dinner, Daddy." Suddenly Harry was sure that the fat one was going to have him followed and watched by some robotic gadget or clever human. All right. All right. Just so he somehow gets my ship back for me.

Turning to the woman at his side, he complimented: "Flowers look nice."

"Thank you. Alan likes this kind. We once planted some at home."

Lily was ready to march off briskly, but then she stopped, impatient as a child, waiting for Harry.

As the two of them walked toward the square, retracing the path they had taken earlier in the day, Harry asked: "Did you try the city directory?"

"Of course. No luck. But it seems that a lot of people who live here just aren't listed."

They had gone a few more strides along the busy walkway when she turned to Harry suddenly and said: "Thank you."

"What have I done now?"

"You got me here in one piece. It's just gradually sinking in on me what might have happened—probably would have happened—if you hadn't snuffed those hijackers."

"That's all right. When I contract to deliver a passenger

somewhere, I like to see that she gets there." He paused, then went on. "You know, when I was tucking them in, there in the abandoned station, they admitted that they were smugglers, they wanted my ship for some kind of special operation. Said they had a real good deal going, here on Maracanda. Of course, some other people were in it with them."

He was watching Lily carefully while he pronounced that last sentence. He could have saved himself the trouble, because none of it mattered in the least to her. Harry wasn't sure she even heard it. Only Alan mattered, as always. Alan, Alan, Alan.

Since arriving on Maracanda, even while having his hands full with other problems, he'd been keeping his eyes open for some sign of illicit drugs for sale or in use. So far he'd spotted nothing. But it would be hard to find an inhabited world anywhere in the Galaxy where no trade of that sort was ever carried on. On the other hand, Maracanda didn't seem a very likely place for growing organic drugs or anything else.

Meanwhile, Lily was back again on subject number one. "For as long as I've known him, he's been pinning his hopes of— of salvation, I think it amounts to that—on one thing after another. I told you how we both went to pilots' school."

"You said something about 'sports rituals,' too."

"Oh. Oh yes, when I showed you the holo. Maybe he's been unconsciously looking for some kind of religion all along."

Harry grunted. He tried to make it an upbeat sort of sound.

"But this is the first time he's actually taken to a religion, in the conventional sense. I suppose he can't help it. Maybe there's some scientific, psychological name for his condition. But I don't care about that. I just want him back. If I have to take Great Malakó with him, I can handle that."

*   *   *

On entering the square this time, Harry accepted a handout from a robed religious acolyte and found himself looking at a pamphlet printed on smartpaper, the words on the cover flowing into other words even as Harry looked at them. After a few seconds, text alternated with a holographic image of the Galaxy. The printed image on the white page moved in a swirling effect, which reminded Harry of nothing so much as the cycling of a certain kind of waste disposal device.

Before he could crumple the thing and throw it away, there was another change. On the paper appeared the face and voice of an anonymous lecturer, the appearance of the printed words lip-synched with the speaking image.

The burden of this silent monologue was that down through the years human investigators, human searchers, had somehow (unintentionally, by observing it and thinking about it) constructed the Tomb of Timur as a composite model of all the things that they were looking for. True believers, guided by their faith, would understand that the Portal was really the reason for the existence of Maracanda, and in fact it was pretty much the center of the universe, or at least the Galaxy, which to the true followers of Malakó was pretty much the same thing.

The printed voice went on: *There exists an ancient parlor game—maybe you've heard about it, maybe you've played it. The central player—or call him the victim of the joke—tries to determine the nature of an imaginary object by asking questions of the other players. But it is only the questioner who determines what the object is—not consciously, not deliberately, but by means of the questions that his imagination urges him to ask. The other players only answer yes or no according to some pattern that they have prearranged among themselves, without the knowledge of the questioner.*

Interesting. But Harry stuffed the paper in his pocket; he wasn't going to take the time to read it now.

The square was even more crowded now than when they had seen it a few hours earlier. Some of those present probably lived or worked here, and appeared to be intent on business. Others were worshiping in a variety of ways, some quiet and some flamboyant. And it was plain that many more had come only to gape.

The people were worthy of study, but Harry's gaze kept coming back to the Portal itself. When he raised his eyes above it, he wondered whether there might once have been some gravitational anomaly associated with this spot. Because the sharp peaks of neighboring hills, just outside the city, all leaned in this direction, as if offering homage. Somehow, as if through a great magnifying lens, or a porthole looking into a wormhole, it provided a close but distorted look at the Core, the Galaxy's great glowing heart, which through the normal paths of space, or even flight-space, would be thousands of light-years distant, a journey occupying standard months, if conditions obtaining along the route would allow it to be made at all.

Scientists who had seen this view thought it interesting, but not of very great value as a true window on the Core, because of the obvious distortion.

A bubble that always looked as if it might be about to pop, but never did, emerged from a gateway, an opening maybe three meters high, and equally wide. The exact shape of it kept shifting, so it was always nearly a circle, but never quite.

Harry divided his attention between the Portal and Lily, but she ignored the thing almost entirely. Generally, her eyes kept sweeping the crowded square, sweeping swiftly over a hundred faces, and then a hundred more, trying to keep up with the ceaseless flow.

Lily had found a better place to stand, slightly elevated, from which she could see more people. She was on the lip of the entrance porch of one of the office buildings. Harry stepped up beside her.

Looking at the wonder from a different angle, he got a different impression. The glassy bulge seemed perpetually about to burst out of the contorted land in a strangely inclined hillside. Directly in front of it, an area of about twenty meters across was fenced off by some low but solid barrier—maybe the artificial fence was starting to show signs of strain, as if it might be in the process of melting, not from high temperature but from sheer strangeness, the exotic forces that had created and maintained the Portal. Little icicles were protruding, all of them pointing directly toward—or away from—the Portal.

Hucksters of souvenirs, and religious chanters, cried out in their different voices. In this designated area, offerings of papers and coins, flowers and food, had been placed in honor of the god.

Guards in the strange uniforms of the local authority were standing by, evidently to keep people from actually trying to reach the Portal. He supposed that some arrangement must have been worked out to let scientists and other responsible folk have a turn at close examination. Harry assumed that protection was also necessary to deter the lunatics and violent demonstrators who would be drawn to any unique object as famous and mysterious as this.

There were also, of course, souvenir sellers of one kind and another, who had set up their shops or folding stands nearby.

Lily, who had lately been studying the subject intently, told Harry that time and again some people had tried to go through the Portal, or Tomb (the members of one small subsect insisted on calling it the Cromlech) or at least insert a hand or a foot. A few determined fanatics, hell-bent on finding union with the One. Some had even devised machines they thought would carry them in safety to their god.

Lily observed: "Several times plans have been drawn up to enclose the Portal entirely in a building. But there is always too much religious protest."

Harry was still intrigued. "What happens to the people who try to jump into it?"

"The very few who have actually managed to get in are gone, no one knows where. Every time someone succeeds, the authorities do something to make the feat even more difficult. Yes, I know what you're thinking. Alan may have done something like that. But I refuse to accept the possibility."

Harry actually hadn't been thinking that at all. Somehow what he had learned about Alan up to now didn't seem to qualify him for such gloriously irrevocable deeds.

And here came a pair of cultists of yet another kind, just what kind Harry had no clue. They were a man and woman wearing robes of black and working as a team.

Something about Lily and Harry must have caught their eye, for they stopped to harangue the couple, the man demanding: "What is really at the core of the Core of the Galaxy? An enormous black hole."

Lily just shook her head and turned away, her eyes searching, searching. She had no time for nonsense. But Harry felt a little bit like arguing. He said: "Opinions vary on that. Theories come and go."

The black-robed woman said: "Not anyone's tomb, not yet. But it will one day be the final resting place of all humanity, all our hopes and dreams."

Harry was still game. "Maybe. Some of us might have a different idea about that."

Crowd noise almost drowned out what the woman was trying to tell him: ". . . servants of the Black Hole . . . the Infinite Emptiness."

There Harry felt on firmer ground. He said: "You've got it wrong. Black holes are the very opposite of empty."

And the man chimed in: "What would you not give, what would any human not give, to be able to save some of the time and energy wasted on what is called life?"

"Yeah. I might go back five minutes, and not be standing here when you came by."

Harry had just turned away from the black-robed pair when his attention was suddenly caught by the figure of a youngish man in a white shirt, the kind a lot of the cultists favored. The fellow had just emerged from the milling crowd, ten meters or so away, and seemed to be staring at Harry with great intensity.

No, on a second look, he wasn't looking at Harry, but directly over Harry's right shoulder.

"Hello, Lil," the newcomer called softly. Alan had lost his little black mustache at some point, and he sounded tired.

FIFTEEN

"You—you—" Words dissolved in a small scream, as the young woman dashed past Harry to grab her husband and hug him fiercely.

Alan hugged her back, but he also wanted to talk. "Lily, I wrote you a letter, a few days ago, explaining some things that have happened, but here you are. You must have left home before it arrived."

Now Lily, in the excess of her relief, was turning angry. "What in hell was the idea, running off the way you did? I thought you'd been kidnapped!"

"Well, no, not really. Not exactly."

"I could murder you," Alan's wife told him, then she abruptly fell silent, shot out a hand and grabbed the full sleeve of the distinctive religious garment Alan was wearing, a kind of long shirt. Harry had noticed that other people in the crowded square were dressed in the same way.

Lily shook him by his sleeve, then pushed him off at arm's length. "What've you done? Taken some kind of vows?"

"Vows? Oh, this?" He brushed his fingers over the pale fabric. "No, it's just that this is more or less required, as long as I'm still living in the Malakó dorm—it's a kind of bachelor quarters, for men in training."

Her anger gone as quickly as it had come, Lily was sobbing. Harry could understand that; he even thought he might be entitled to a good cry, too—though probably not in public. He was thinking of all the time and energy he'd wasted, conned by a smuggler into almost believing the worst of this unhappy girl. It was no longer possible to doubt that she was straight and innocent— unless she was not only the queen of smugglers, but had hired someone to play the part of Alan, and was also the greatest actress in the Galaxy. Anyway, the greatest actress was not going to break her neck and strain her tear ducts just to convince an obscure space pilot of her virtue.

Alan's response to his wife's outpouring of tears and emotion was mainly to look numb, and maintain a slightly confused attitude.

Tentatively approaching Lily again, the husband held her and patted her on her back. Alan, looking over her shoulder at Harry, at last showed some curiosity. "Who's this?"

Lily turned and looked. Then she let go of Alan and backed away from him a step. "Alan, this is Mr. Silver. Harry Silver. He's the pilot who drove me here, he's been helping me look for you."

Alan extended his hand and muttered a greeting. Harry stepped forward to briefly take the hand, which was almost limp, and grunted something back.

Lily had seized her long-lost man again, and was holding him at arm's length, gripping him fiercely by the shoulders. "Let me look at you. That silly shirt . . . And you look thinner. Have you been fasting, or—"

"Fasting?" It was as if Alan had no idea what the word might mean. "Oh. No, not really, they don't require anything like that. But"—he paused for a deep breath—"Lil, there are some things I have to bring you up to date on."

But before he began any explanation, a new thought seemed to come to him, striking a spark of excitement. Alan turned back to Harry.

"Look, Mr.—Silver, is it?—did you, by any chance, come to Maracanda looking for an investment opportunity?"

Harry blinked. He leaned back against a wall of strange Maracandan stone and folded his arms. "Well, no. That's not why I came. But I might consider something. What've you got in mind?"

"What do I have in mind? Just a break like nothing you've ever seen before. One of the greatest opportunities that any human being has ever been offered. The chance of a lifetime! Literally!" As Alan spoke, new animation grew swiftly in his voice. He put his arm around Lily again, as if she might be the prize to be awarded. He seemed totally unconscious of her growing confusion as she listened to him.

"Tell me more," said Harry, watching and listening with fascination.

Alan's face was glowing with enthusiasm. "There are opportunities here on Maracanda that ninety-nine percent of the people in the Galaxy have yet to learn about . . ."

It was a real sales pitch, Harry thought, and a fairly good one. Something to do with land and property and minerals, though Alan was slow to specify exactly what it was he had to sell. Meanwhile, the real show was Lily. Her expression was slowly changing, joy so intense as to be painful passing slowly through confusion, sliding downhill into a kind of outrage.

Finally she managed to interrupt the pitch. It took her a couple of tries to get the salesman's full attention back. Her voice had turned dangerously mild.

"Alan, you're babbling. Minerals and properties? What in hell are you talking about?"

Turning the spiel on Lily, Alan seized one of her small hands in both of his. "Honey, now I can understand what the real meaning of it all is."

"Of it all?"

"Of life, and everything—you must see it, too!"

"See what?" It seemed possible that she was going to faint.

Alan was a long way from fainting. He might be thin, but he was bursting with energy. "I mean what fate had in store for me. The real purpose of my coming to this strange world. I was led to Maracanda. Consciously I didn't understand it myself until these last few days, but now everything is coming clear."

"Clear?"

"Yes!"

"But—Alan, That note you left me, what about that? Saying that the only thing in the whole universe that had any genuine importance, any meaning for humanity, was—that." She shot an accusing gesture across the busy square, toward the looming Portal. "Malakó."

Alan cast one brief, bored glance in that direction, humoring his wife. Then he turned back to her. "That's what I *thought*, then, Lil. Of *course*, that's what I *thought*." He might have been trying to explain to her some foolish exploit of his childhood, decades in the past. Now he could be tolerant of such youthful folly, because, after all, it had ultimately led him in the right direction.

Enthusiasm came welling up again. "But now, since I've seen Maracanda, been exposed to the possibilities, it's hit me. What Malakó represents is no more than a kid's dream. An important symbol, maybe, but no more than that. The real value of this world does not lie over there across the square, or off in the center of the Galaxy, in places where people can never go. No!" He made a gesture, thrusting something violently away.

"Noo! What people need, what we really need, it's here! Right here!" Alan stamped his foot hard on the pavement. "The truth we need is real and accessible, part of the world we live on. Minerals, Lily, hard, solid minerals. This world is a treasure trove of awesome wealth. Literally! And we, you and I, can have our share."

"Oh." Alan's wife was backing away from him again, one step and then another, her face a study in horrified understanding. "You've done it again. Haven't you?"

Now her voice was mounting to a scream. "Do you know, do you know, you fool, you almost had *me* thinking Malakó, believing it? Getting myself ready to kneel down and pray?"

"Actually, they don't kneel down. They—"

"Shut up, you imbecile! I should have known. I should have known you were going to do something like this. After all the years we've been together, all the plans you've made and dropped, I should have known."

Alan blinked at her, waiting until she should be ready to listen to him again.

"I should have known," Lily repeated in a murmur, as if mostly to herself. "But let me make sure. Once more I ask. What about that note you left me?"

"The note I left you," repeated Alan. He had to make an effort to remember. "Didn't I just explain about the note?"

"Did you?"

"Oh yes, I can see how what I said in the note would have misled you. But never mind that now, Lil. Or, if you want to look at it that way, just think that my coming here might really have been divinely inspired—because this world, Lil, is like no other. What we have on Maracanda can transform our lives, and the universe, right here and now!" He paused. "How much money have you got available?"

She moved away from him, stumbling back toward Harry, leaning on the wall where Harry leaned, closing her eyes briefly. Then she looked at her husband again.

"Practically nothing. I spent it all, chasing you halfway across the Galaxy. I'm almost broke!" The last words came out as a cry of fear and anger.

"Well, if there's anything at all, I'd like to know how much, because—"

"Don't say any more, Alan. Don't say any more!"

Harry, arms folded, was still leaning against the building, shaking his head. Slowly Alan turned back to him, and asked: "Did you say Lil's been paying you to help her find me?"

Harry said: "She's paid me for her ticket to Maracanda. Neither of you owe me anything. As far as any incidental help I might have given her, well, I'm being amply rewarded for that."

"Oh?" Alan's eyes were vague.

Harry said: "Educationally, I mean. Looking for you has been a valuable experience. And finding you even more so."

Alan didn't quite know what to make of that. Clearly he would rather be talking about investments. Alan's trouble now was that he had no money of his own to invest. Or at least he thought that was his trouble.

After a bit, Harry straightened and stretched, getting ready to move on. "Well, shall I assume you two are going to be staying together from now on?" That was the polite thing to say, Harry judged, though at the moment the great reunion seemed a long way from a sure thing. "Lily, should I tell Kul you're moving out?"

"No," said Lily firmly. She had straightened up, standing against the wall almost as if awaiting the firing squad. "If Mr. Bulaboldo doesn't mind, I might not be moving out of his house just yet. I understand it's hard to find a place to stay in Tomb

Town." Standing with her hands clasped, almost as if in prayer, she kept staring uncertainly at her husband, as if trying to remember who he was.

The look that Alan gave her was uncertain, too. "That's right, housing is very hard to come by," he admitted. "Unless you're very well off. That's why I'm still sleeping in the Malakó men's dorm, still wearing this shirt. Women aren't allowed in there." He looked around suddenly, as if he thought someone might be watching. "It's also the reason I'm here in the square now. As long as you're living in the dorm, they expect you to kind of go through the motions, coming here and putting on a public show."

"You go on putting on your show, then, Alan." Lil turned to the man beside her. "Harry, take me back to where we're staying. I need to do some thinking, and I can't do it here."

The more Lily tried to come to grips with Alan's latest change of heart and mind, the angrier she grew. "I might have known it. He's done this before. If I face the facts, I can see he's done it over and over. Decided to devote his life to something, and then, in a few months or a year, quit it for something else. Well, now he's done it once too often."

Harry grunted something. He tried to give it a friendly and slightly upbeat tone.

Bulaboldo to all appearances was glad to see them both. Lily went off to rest in her room, with Kul's blessings, while he summoned Harry into an urgent conference.

It came out that Kul had his own ideas about the reason for Harry's attempted kidnapping. "And I'll wager, dear lad, that it had nothing to do with Dr. Kloskurb."

"No? You heard them use the name."

"Not sure I did, old fellow, and anyway I've got to take my idea more seriously. You see, the competition in my business becomes rather intense at times. I know why my rivals want to get their hands on you. I just wonder which of them it was."

Bulaboldo went on to say he could, without even trying very hard, think of at least three possibilities.

"Or it might even have been someone entirely new, just trying to break into the business. All masked, couldn't tell." The bulky one, looking distracted, chewed a thumbnail while he thought. "Except for the lad in the hospital, of course, and he was a total stranger to me. No knowledge to be gained there."

"You fought them," Harry said. "And maybe you saved my life. But there at the end you were sitting on me. Because you didn't want any of 'em caught."

"No, of course I didn't." Bulaboldo shook his head. "Best not to have the authorities come bumbling in, interfering with business matters. Under interrogation the question would be sure to come up—why do smugglers on Maracanda need a pilot?"

"I give up, why do they? You're getting paranoid. Those people weren't looking for a pilot. They thought I was someone else entirely. Doctor Kloskurb. I've seen him and talked to him, he looks like me."

Bulaboldo wasn't convinced. "So do a million other people, Harry. I think they knew just who you are."

"So your competitors want a pilot for the same mysterious reason you do. Am I right?"

"As always, dear man." The big man sighed, clapped both hands down hard on the arms of his chair, making a decision. "Very well. The time has come to show you, which means going out of the city, deep into breakdown zone. I'm changing clothes for the back country, and would suggest you do the same. Your closet should be well supplied, but let me know if there are any deficiencies."

Retiring to their respective rooms, the men met again on the main floor ten minutes later. Bulaboldo had now put on workman's or miner's clothes that made quite a change in his appearance. Harry had changed his spacefarer's garb for something that would attract less notice out in the back country: a different style of boots, rugged shirt and pants with lots of pockets, and a small indicator, strapped on the wrist, to tell whether he was currently in a breakdown zone.

They went into the large garage, high walled and roofed for privacy. Bulaboldo had thrown a few odd-looking lightweight tools, some kind of digging implements, into a pedicab's small cargo compartment. He opened a large chest nearby, and Harry saw that it held an assortment of clubs, knives, and swords.

"By the way, old thing, would you like to carry a weapon? You may need it for self-defense."

"What've you got? I've begun to appreciate that Maracanda is that kind of place."

Opening another drawer, Kul displayed a couple of modern handguns, butts curved to make handy bludgeons. "Useful in either kind of zone when trouble rears its ugly head."

"Expecting any?"

"Not specifically. I wasn't looking for it the other night in the caravanserai, either. One's business has grown extremely competitive in recent months."

"You're still convinced that fumble-fingered kidnapping had something to do with your business. This is where I ought to ask just what your business is these days. But I don't know if I will."

Bulaboldo nodded. "Not a secret. Not to you, old lad. But, as I say, easier to show than tell." He pointed at one of the long blades. "Know how to use one of these, old man?"

Gingerly Harry picked up the weapon by its short handle and gave it an intense look. "Not the fine points. The general idea seems clear enough." He essayed a few tentative motions, butchering the air, then decided he had probably better leave the sword where it was. Instead he pocketed one of the club-handled pistols.

 *   *   *

The vehicle in which Harry and Bulaboldo set out to examine Kul's mining claims was a pedicar, light in weight but ruggedly constructed, on a framework resembling a four-wheeled bicycle. Behind the forward-mounted motor, the reasonably comfortable cabin contained four seats, all enclosed by a light but sturdy shell. Plainly it wouldn't be this vehicle's first trip into the back country. Its lower surfaces, formed of some hard, off-world metal alloy, had acquired a smeary look, ingrained with particles impossible to clean away, that showed it had spent a large number of hours in contact with Maracandan dust and solid land.

After making sure there was food and water on board, they took their places in the two front seats, Bulaboldo with the steering lever in hand. You had to step up into the vehicle, which was built high for good ground clearance and off-road use. A small engine compartment held a hydrogen lamp or fuel cell, to drive the wheels in the free-zone stretches of road.

Harry was sitting back, trying to relax, letting Bulaboldo drive. "The question I ask myself is, what do your mining claims have to do with my getting my ship back? It doesn't take a lot of heavy thinking to get an answer, and the answer's getting clearer and clearer every second. But I'd like to hear the official version anyway."

"Very perceptive of you, Harry. There is a connection to be discovered."

"So tell me."

"Easier to show than tell—and much easier to show you if we're on the ground. All will presently be revealed."

They were heading away from the center of town, through moderate traffic. "What's that?" Harry's finger was pointing at a small, unlabeled indicator light, near the center of the dashboard.

"Shows where we are, old friend. Comes on only when the

vehicle's *not* in a breakdown zone, and therefore can be engine-driven. Otherwise one does not know when one has crossed the invisible border, and one might keep pedaling on and on, exhausting oneself unnecessarily."

Bulaboldo went on: "Trouble is, there are many stretches of road in this region where the bloody little light goes on and off every fifty meters or so. Not really worth the trouble to try to sit back and relax."

Harry wondered again, silently this time, why any Earth-descended humans wanted to live on this enchanted world at all. But no, in his heart he understood. The very oddities, the implicit dangers, the absolute cursedness of the place, drew certain people like powerful magnets.

Alan had heard Bulaboldo's name when Harry and Lily were talking in the square, and wasted no time in consulting a city directory and finding his way to Bulaboldo's house. He had discarded his Temple Malakó shirt and was plainly and cheaply clad when he arrived on the doorstep demanding to see his wife.

Lily, responding to a summons delivered to her room by one of the household robots, met her husband in the doorway—the robots had pointedly not invited him inside. She saw that he had somehow come up with enough money to hire a pedicab, though not a driver.

Alan was taut and earnest. "Come take a ride with me, Lil. We've got to talk things over."

Soon they were standing beside the pedicar, debating. Alan, trying to calm her down, promised he would do all the pedaling. "Take it easy, Lil—I was going to send for you, once I got myself established on this world. By the way, this is a pretty posh place, where you're staying."

"It's not mine, and it's not going to be. And if you're thinking of asking the proprietor to invest in your schemes, I'd think again. He has schemes of his own."

Alan displayed certain signs of jealousy, of Harry Silver's apparent role in Lily's life. If his wife had suddenly turned against him, it must be this interloper's fault. But even jealousy was hard to sustain, when all her husband could really think about was the possibility of going prospecting, and of investment, in land, in mineral rights.

"Lil, I can see how this would upset you. I've sometimes been undependable in the past. But this time it's going to be different. You'll see."

Before Lily could answer, another cab pulled up. For just a moment she thought the man getting out was actually Harry.

But it was Dr. Kloskurb, who bowed to her courteously. "Ms. Gunnlod. Is Harry Silver here? That attempted kidnapping has been preying on my mind, and I have some questions I'd like to ask him."

Harry and Kul were nearing the city's edge, on a different route than Harry had ever gone before. He asked: "Ever think of hiring someone to pedal for you?"

"Oh, that's easy enough to do, my boy. Lots of failed prospectors in town, available at modest wages. But that wouldn't do in this case, where particularly confidential matters are to be shown and discussed. Unless you're applying for the position . . ."

His voice trailed off as he studied the pedicar's small side mirror. "By the way, it would seem that we are being followed. Oh, not to take alarm, dear lad. I detect Ms. Lily Gunnlod, and two men I do not recognize. One of them looks a lot like you."

Harry turned in his seat and stared. The tailing driver was trying to be cagey, hanging back, but there did seem to be three people in the cab. One was almost certainly Lily, and the other two could very well be Alan and Dr. Kloskurb.

They were just at the edge of the settlement when the indicator light on the dash suddenly went out. Simultaneously the engine died, and they were coasting.

Bulaboldo reacted without surprise. "Time for the pedals. Ever ride a bicycle, old man? These work much the same. You'll notice that your seat is provided with a set as well."

Harry took the hint, and lifted his feet from the fixed rests where they had been idling.

With two men working their pedals, not trying very hard, the lightweight vehicle crept forward at the pace of a brisk walk.

For the next five or six kilometers, the road was fairly busy with similar traffic. But by the time they had taken a third branching, onto a smaller way so faintly marked as to be almost invisible, they were alone. The vehicle that had been following them was out of sight.

"This could get to be fun." Harry had increased his effort slightly. Maintaining the pace of a brisk trot was not too difficult, except when going uphill.

"For those of us addicted to exercise, dear lad." Bulaboldo puffed.

Road signs were scarce, but Bulaboldo had no problem finding his way, steering dexterously among the towering landforms, going around some ominous gaping holes in the landscape.

Harry said: "Looks like it could be easy to get lost in these hills."

"All too easy. Then one has to wait for approaching nightfall to get even a rough idea of one's directions—east and west."

Harry was determined to learn all he could. "What about a simple magnetic compass? I mean, if east and west have been more or less established, why not north and south?"

"It's been tried, old comrade. With mixed results. Too mixed, I fear, to inspire any confidence at all."

Harry spotted a stretch of flat ground broad enough to have done service as an athletic field, studded with chair-sized objects evidently meant as markers of some kind, all of foreign material, stone and wood and metal. Text of some kind was engraved on them, too far away to read.

He reached across the little cab to tap his companion's shoulder, and pointed. "What's that over there?"

Bulaboldo looked. "Cemetery. On this world, as on others, there are a lot of people who just don't go for cremation."

"I suppose being buried on Maracanda would not be dull, maybe not even peaceful."

"In that you are correct, dear coconspirator. The interment of dead bodies or anything else in Maracandan land is by no means as simple and straightforward an operation as you would expect. Making bridges is also a chancy undertaking."

Bulaboldo pedaled on a few more meters before he added: "Those who are looking for peace should be living somewhere else."

The territory declared open to prospecting encompassed many hundreds (maybe thousands; Bulaboldo said he wasn't sure) of square kilometers. There was a general fear that the Federation would change the rules, as soon as the undesirable nature of some of the minerals here became generally known.

The weird landscape of this portion of the Maracandan surface was honeycombed by a number of branching trails and roads, pocked and dotted by miners' adits and simple, amateurish holes. Here and there were also some big natural caves, mouths almost big enough to have accommodated Harry's ship—if any ship could have landed in this region.

Along the main roads, which were wide enough for vehicles to pass each other, signs, official postings, establishing claims, appeared every five hundred meters or so. Some of the signs had been all but effaced by the climbing, infiltrating landscape.

Harry and Bulaboldo passed several sites where people were in the act of prospecting for the legitimate ore, and another one or two where people were trying to dig it out. Unlike any other mining operation that Harry had ever witnessed, these were being conducted entirely without advanced machinery. Primitive, muscle-powered picks and shovels seemed to be the tools of choice.

People had set up camp inside a lightly fenced-off area. Tent walls provided privacy, shielding part of the works from observation, and in some cases made it impossible to tell with a glance whether any of the claim owners were actually on site or not.

But there were some indications of success. Enthusiastic men and women were digging energetically, grunting and sweating, their tools powered by no technology more advanced than the digger's own muscles. Greed was giving them grim strength and purpose.

The side road had degenerated to a mere trail when Bulaboldo stopped pedaling and put on the brakes. He had chosen a spot that to Harry looked pretty much like any other.

The big man got out and stretched, then made an expansive pointing gesture. "My land starts here. Runs back that way, far as that green outcropping, and over there." One hectare of land—as big a playing field as you were likely to see inside a real-world sports stadium.

"Been digging on it?"

"In a couple of places. Here, at what you might call the front, just a little bit, for show."

Wooden stakes had been tapped into the claylike surface as

property markers. Little ribbons tied to the stakes barely stirred in the faint breeze. Diggings had been started, then abandoned, at several spots across the hectare.

"Looks like a hard-luck claim," Harry observed.

"That's just how I want it to look." Grinning, the proprietor got one of the digging tools out of the pedicar's trunk, stuck one of the clubs in his belt ("Just in case. There've been claim jumpers around"), and indicated to Harry which way they should walk. "Did have hard luck for a while. But I don't think we'll give up on her just yet."

Harry looked at his companion for a moment, then picked up the other club, stuck it in the long, narrow pocket on the right thigh of his coveralls.

"Let me show you something." Bulaboldo closed the pedicar's doors, turned a key in the simple door lock, and led the way on foot.

There were a few tracks here, old random boot marks slowly turning into neat abstract patterns in the peculiar ground.

SIXTEEN

Bulaboldo, pacing a winding course among the small hills, obviously knew where he was going, though Harry could see no markings to indicate a path or trail. It would have to be a matter of memorizing small landmarks. The big man walked at a brisk and steady pace, except that now and then he looked around abruptly, as if checking to see whether they were still being followed.

In several places Harry took note of abandoned excavations, deep and wide enough for mass graves.

Harry's guide gestured toward one of these holes. "All dug by hand, Harry. There hasn't been prospecting and mining like this on any other world for centuries."

Harry doubted that any prospectors using primitive digging

implements would have made such neatly geometric holes, and said so.

Bulaboldo shook his head. "Whenever this land undergoes any artificial deformation, it starts to come back together by itself. It makes digging a mine shaft, or even a pit, a very interesting process. You have to think of this place in terms of geometry as well as geography."

A couple of the fresher ones still looked irregular. But it seemed that they were all changing with time, turning slowly into geometric designs. Some analogue of a healing process was under way.

Presently they stopped, in front of another digging, the start of a shaft or adit, driven into another low hillside. The hills here looked so much alike that Harry wondered if he would be able to find his way back to the vehicle without help.

Within fifty klicks or so of Minersville, almost the entire surface of the lifeless land, save for the strips reserved for roads, was divided into claims, of the same size as Bulaboldo's—one hectare, a square a hundred meters on a side.

Most of these had already been worked over and abandoned as nonproductive. Harry saw tracks, which Kul said were those of wild spheres, just roaming through.

Pegs with little pennants attached marked the corners of each claim and sketched the sides of each square of the standard size, all of this peculiar world that one individual was allowed to possess.

The standard claim, at a hundred meters square, afforded plenty of room to land a small ship, if anyone could fly a ship in here—maybe even enough room to conceal one, if the topography was sufficiently rugged, or you could somehow alter the shape of the land to make it so.

One hundred hectares—claims—in every square kilometer

of this land. In every thousand square kilometers, 100,000 possible mining claims.

Obviously claims located in free zones, where power machinery could be used, would be much easier to work—but a miner would have to pass through extensive breakdown zones to reach such isolated pockets. After the lucky prospector had hauled his power supply and digging equipment in by pedicab, he would be able to determine much more quickly that the mineral rights to his land were really worth nothing at all. Or in the minority of cases where they were, you could get right down to productive work.

Harry could well believe that a great many people had gone that route. But any claim in a free zone, whether rich in minerals or not, might be very valuable and useful as a place to set up processing and packing machinery. If any refining of the ore was necessary—probably it wouldn't be, at least in the case of the drug stuff.

"Here," said Bulaboldo, succinctly. "My claim."

Harry nodded. Part of his mind automatically took note of the fact that other hillocks blocked their line of sight to their car, and every part of the vestigial road.

"What now?" he asked. Maybe great Malakó or some other deity would see whatever happened here, back in among the little hills, but there'd be no other casual observers—no fear, here in a breakdown zone, that anyone with high-tech gadgetry was watching from afar. Spies would have to take a chance by coming close.

Bulaboldo squatted in front of the deepest part of the modest excavation. With a meaningful gesture he pulled a glove onto his right hand. Then, grunting as he bent over, he reached down with his gloved hand, pushed aside a layer of stuff that passed for topsoil, reached in, and pulled out a handful of what looked at first glance like unimpressive sand.

Without rising, he held it out for Harry's inspection.

Harry stooped for a closer look than any he had taken yet at the substance of Maracanda. He wasn't sure it would be right to call this material soil. It wasn't dirt, not of the kind you fought with soap, nor the type in which you planted flowers. It wasn't exactly sand or clay or gravel, nor like any kind of natural substance that Harry could remember encountering before. He knelt beside the hole and tried to scoop some up in his fingers, but the stuff resisted being handled. It felt bone dry, but it didn't want to behave like a powder. More like a cross between modeling clay and—and something else.

After looking around once more, Bulaboldo led the way behind a towering landform topped by a natural bulge in the shape of an onion dome. Here he used the digging tool to scrape away a few centimeters of the Maracandan version of topsoil.

Bulaboldo pulled out a piece of cloth, which he spread on his broad palm. Then he used the tool with great delicacy, to dig out a mere thimbleful of the underlying layer. Spreading this on the cloth, he held his flattened hand up for inspection.

Harry looked but didn't touch. He raised an eyebrow in silent query.

Bulaboldo said: "It's an honor and a privilege to show Harry Silver something he's never seen before."

Harry grunted, and looked closely. "This is, of course, not fairyground." For once the big man's voice was low. "The usual name for this is 'grit.' What this particular version is, old top, is unadulterated wealth. It'll be worth millions as soon as I can get it away from here and to the right distributors. Did I say millions? More millions than you'd be likely to believe."

Harry stared, fascinated despite his wariness. The stuff lying on Kul's palm was a mottled gray—but saying that didn't begin to describe the reality. Just looking at it brought on the beginnings of quirky sensation. For just a moment there was a hint, a flashing remembrance, of something he might have seen in the moment when the c-plus cannon fired.

Watching carefully, he didn't really see it crawl and creep, and keep infolding on itself, as if with a life of its own, but somehow it gave the impression of doing so. Harry didn't want to touch it, but even without doing so, he could understand how the stuff had got its name. He had an impression of small, hard particles, wrapped up in the flowing goo.

Bulaboldo was on the same wavelength. "If I were you, old man, I wouldn't let it touch my skin. Some individuals turn out to be very susceptible. But if you've got a pair of sensitive gloves with you, you can feel the grit."

Harry grunted. He had no gloves, and wouldn't have made the experiment if he had.

"No matter how finely you subdivide it, the parts behave in much the same way as the whole." With a faint sigh of reluctance, Bulaboldo let the sample sift back into the deposit in the ground. With careful movements he scraped the topsoil back in place.

Harry straightened, then stood back a half step, legs braced apart, arms folded. Now he had no doubt where this was heading.

Bulaboldo stood up, too, towering over him. He leaned closer, projecting emphasis. "It was just providential, old man, your dropping in on Maracanda when you did, and with your ship."

"Was it?"

Bulaboldo blinked. "What do you mean?"

"Never mind. Go ahead, wind up your sales pitch."

"Right. Now you've seen the product, and I can tell you that a considerable quantity has been mined, and put through the minimal refining process that is required. The problem is that all cargoes shipped out of Port City are examined carefully by badgers very difficult to bribe. But that difficulty can easily be got round by a fairly small and extremely agile spaceship, driven by an excellent pilot—"

"Ah. Aha."

"—and when I say excellent, I mean I don't know of any autopilot I'd trust to do the job. Not until the route is programmed into it. I mean one who can—when a pathway is charted for him—maneuver a deep-space-going ship in through all of these god-blasted veils and layers of crap making up this sky"—he gestured fiercely overhead—"and land it in the right spot. That spot is very near to where we're standing. The individual who pilots that ship is going to be stupefyingly wealthy. I guarantee it." And Bulaboldo leaned back, folding his arms, with the air of a geometry teacher concluding an important proof. "Wealthy enough to have a new ship designed and built. Or whatever other baubles your little heart desires."

"It seems to me I've heard this before. And not too long ago. About the great smuggling project, the urgent need for a small ship with a good pilot."

"Indeed?"

"Those two bastards were your partners, weren't they? You're the one who sent them out."

The big man drew himself up. For once he sounded cold. "Which two bastards have you in mind, dear boy? I know so many."

"You know the ones I mean. They called themselves Dietrich and Redpath."

Bulaboldo made a different kind of gesture, throwing something away with both hands, seemingly to say it was good riddance, whatever might have happened to them. Suddenly once more warm and friendly, he also looked pained.

"Dear fellow, not *partners*, no. Do show me a little respect. True, they were sent to Hong's World to acquire a ship, the means of doing so unfortunately left to their discretion. It seemed there ought to be plenty of vessels available there, with the evacuation going on, and a good bit of confusion to make things easier.

"But I never sent them with the idea of hijacking your beloved *Witch*, old chap! Impossible! Please give me credit for more intelligence than that. Had no idea you were going to be on the scene. Anyway, I can just see that pair, walking up to Harry Silver: 'By the way, old sport, we're taking over your ship.' I would've expected a bit of old-fashioned Darwinian selection at that point. Excising some defective material from the great gene pool of the species."

Harry nodded. "It came pretty close to that. How do you know so much about what happened out there?" He paused. "So Lily told you."

Bulaboldo seemed genuinely surprised. "Lily? No, not a bit of it. I had it yesterday from the men themselves. It is with mixed feelings, as you might imagine, that I acknowledge their return. I won't say I welcome them back."

"*Back*? Back here on Maracanda?" Harry could feel his jaw drop open.

Bulaboldo looked pained. "I was planning to break it to you gently, old fellow. Of course, the news of your attempted kidnapping got back to Port City by telegraph. And when our beloved Commandant Rovaki heard that someone had tried to kidnap Harry Silver, he took it to be only a skirmish in some war between gangs of smugglers. Rovaki has no high opinion of yours truly, either, and so he was not surprised to hear that the two of us had been seen together.

"You had told him that on your last flight you visited the Thisworld system, indeed that you had fought and recorded a berserker there. Somewhat to Rovaki's disappointment, spectroscopic studies of the images of background stars in your recording confirmed that that was indeed where the clash had taken place.

"I have met Commandant Rovaki a time or two, and I can

imagine how smugly proud of himself he must have been. In my imagination I can hear him saying: 'So I played a hunch, and sent a scoutship over to Thisworld to take a look. And guess what my crew found? Two men, very recently marooned on an abandoned research satellite.'

"Both of the lucky pair have criminal records, though neither is currently wanted anywhere, as far as anyone on Maracanda can determine."

"So what does Rovaki know about how they came to be marooned?"

"Nothing much, my sources tell me. Neither Dietrich nor Redpath was willing to give the Space Force an explanation—not one that anyone could believe. Told Rovaki they'd been given a ride by some mysterious character who picked them up at the busiest spaceport in the sector. Neither ever quite caught the fellow's name, and they have trouble remembering anything at all about his ship."

Harry was shaking his head. "Did this mysterious man look anything like Harry Silver?"

"Rovaki had no luck there, either. They could remember very clearly what the miscreant did *not* look like, and that was a perfect description of you, old friend."

"Sounds like you're better acquainted with that pair than I am. What do you think they'll do?"

"From now on, what I tell them, and nothing else. Unless they . . . What was that?"

Harry had heard it, too, a murmur of distant but familiar voices.

"Somehow they've found our trail." Kul moved a few paces back along the way they had come, putting some distance between himself and his secret cache. "One of them could have looked up the location of my claim. Matter of public record."

A moment later, Lily and Alan and Kloskurb came in sight, walking together around the squared-off corner of a tall landform.

"There you are, Silver." Kloskurb was apologetic, but said he had begun to worry about Harry's warning, and felt he had to talk to him again as soon as possible.

Alan was looking around avidly at the landscape, but not as if he knew what he was looking for. He totally ignored the scratchings in the dirt, beneath which part of Kul's illegal grit mine lay concealed. Bulaboldo studied him keenly, then seemed to dismiss him as a threat.

Lily ignored Kul. She said: "Hello, Harry."

"Hello yourself. Are we prospecting today?"

"Alan is. Rather, he's trying to learn how. I came along because he said he had to talk to me. So far, nothing he's told me has made much sense. Then he wanted to follow the people who he thinks know what they're doing—I guess that's you."

Alan had dragged Kloskurb away, wanting to consult him on some landforms in the middle distance, but Lily lingered with her two former traveling companions.

Harry said: "I've just heard that Dietrich and Redpath are back. Here on Maracanda."

Lily gave him a blank stare for a long moment. Then she shook her head. "That doesn't make any sense. They can't be here. Are you seeing ghosts?"

Harry said what should be done to ghosts. "Just saying what I heard. And if you turn around, you can see for yourself."

Dietrich and Redpath, dressed and equipped as prospectors, were standing at a little distance, in the mouth of another sharp-angled ravine. The pair were eyeing Bulaboldo warily, as if uncertain of their welcome. But now Redpath, his nervous tic no better than before, shifted his gaze to Harry.

"Hey, Silver. You don't have to worry about the Space Force. Rovaki kept pushing your name at us, but we never heard of you, never saw you or your friggin' ship, let alone rode in it. You're safe enough—for now. Business comes first."

Harry said nothing. He could see in their faces all the things that they would like to do to him, a heavy grudge. But there was lingering fear of him as well. And they did believe it, about the business coming first.

Seeing that Harry still had nothing to say, Kul assured his operatives they were obscenely lucky to be still alive. What had they been thinking of, trying to grab the *Witch*?

One reason for the attempt, they reluctantly admitted, was that they had gambled away half of the expense money Bulaboldo had given them to charter a ship. No, they hadn't known that Harry was anyone special, or a friend of their boss. They had chosen him because of his ship's size, and assumed they'd be able to intimidate him into driving just where they commanded.

Bulaboldo expressed his disapproval. "All right, dear vermin, let it go for now. When the time comes, in a couple of days, I'm going to need you to carry bags of grit, if for no other reason."

Dietrich was a little slow. "Carry them where, Boss?"

"Aboard the ship, simpleton. Aboard the ship." Kul dismissed the pair with a wave, and watched them turn and disappear back into the narrow ravine.

Alan had called to his wife, and she had gone to join him and Kloskurb at a little distance. Harry and Kul were alone again.

Harry said to Bulaboldo: "Now it's your turn to make pretty much the same offer that your dimwits did. Except maybe you won't tell me how much fun I'll have taking the drug myself."

"You're a hard sell, aren't you, Harry?" With an air of reluctance, that quickly vanished as his enthusiasm bloomed again, the pitchman said he had seen how well the stuff did in a small market and was sure it couldn't miss in a large one.

"How's it work as a drug?"

Matters of biology and medicine weren't really his department, Bulaboldo said. But when Harry insisted that he try, the big man explained. Introduced into the human body, through any orifice (the effects varied, depending which one was chosen), or simply by absorption through the skin, it produced a varied spectrum of sensations, frequently ecstatic but on rare occasions extremely unpleasant.

Harry made a slight pushing gesture, telling Bulaboldo he could put his sample away. "Let me guess. It could get bad enough to cost you some of your customers?"

Bulaboldo frowned slightly, and nodded, acknowledging the problem. "Not as many as you might think. It's still early in the game, of course. Hard to tell yet how many years the average user is likely to keep on buying."

Harry said: "I'm already fabulously wealthy. Hadn't you noticed?"

"Ah, when you say that, my friend, you imagine that you jest. But in sober fact you speak the truth. And my plan also provides something much closer to your heart (if I know you at all) than fabulous wealth—I mean the actual restoration of your ship. Come come, Harry, you must have noticed *that*. It gets you immediately back into a real, here-and-now spaceship, in fact, your very own dear *Witch*. Believe me, old man, I want to see that ship back in your hands as avidly as you do. Because not until it is, dear heart, will either you or your ship be of any use to me.

"Now. There is one more thing that I must show you, and then it will be time for you to start back to Port City. No slow caravan this time, but a private pedicar; the return journey will be substantially faster."

"What am I going back there for?"

"Why, dear lad, to pick up your ship."

"You mean the Space Force seals are off?"

"Probably not just yet, old fellow. But they will be, by the time you get there." Kul started to check his timepiece, realized the futility of such a gesture here in breakdown zone, and shook his head. "Very difficult to coordinate things properly on this world. But perhaps as early as this very hour, certainly by the time you are approaching the spaceport, the ship will be yours to drive, with the blessing of all authorities concerned."

"Including Rovaki?"

"Of course, old comrade."

"How in all the hells do you propose to manage that?"

Kul took a modest bow. "Simply by sending a certain person in Port City a certain word, old lad. A code word, of course, quite innocently transmissible by telegraph. But I thought it vital that you first have a good look at the ground over here, before you head back to the spaceport. It's essential, of course, that we are certain of our landing site. Now, for the one more thing that you must see. It's rather important. Please follow me."

Harry followed. "I would still like to know just what you're doing."

"There is a time for great cleverness, old douche bag, and a time for direct action. Right now is a time for simple bribery, the method much to be preferred on most occasions."

"I see. And where do you expect me to bring my beloved *Witch* down again? Assuming I'm allowed to get her off the ground."

"You will be." Bulaboldo rounded a hillock and came to a stop, gesturing at an approximate hectare of flat land just ahead. "Just now I spoke to my precious dimwits of loading a ship. That will be done right here, dear boy, right here."

"Here? In the middle of . . ." Harry let it die away. With his last step forward, his wrist indicator had suddenly glowed to life, showing that he had just entered a free zone.

From his side came the voice of Kul, puffing a bit from the short, brisk walk. "Thought that would get your attention, Harry."

"A landing site on Maracanda, as you may have noticed, is a priceless prize. And by good fortune there just happens to be *one* available, on another claim to which I have access."

"If almost anyone else was telling me this, I'd say that they were crazy. How the hell did you arrange that?"

"Not arrange, dear lad. There are limits on even my powers of arranging. 'Discover' is perhaps the correct word."

"You just happened to discover a free-zone landing site? On land you also just happen to own?"

"Tut tut. I fear you would find the details of all my arrangements and discoveries boring; or perhaps you would react even more strongly. Let it suffice to know that the way lies open. Also, it might be well for you to gain whatever knowledge you can about your final approach, by gazing up earnestly into the Maracandan sky."

Harry walked a bit, looked around. He squinted into the sky as if he might be able to see zone boundaries there. He did some thinking.

Meanwhile Kul had plunged for a moment into a niche between two cubic rocks, from which he emerged holding a small, strange-looking device. He described how he had already been doing some tests, with a little radio-controlled drone flyer, taking off here and scouting out the irregular shape of this particular live flight zone.

Harry was pressed to take the little drone in hand and look at it, wiggle its miniature ornithopter wings. The overall look was somewhere between that of a plastic mosquito and a metal hummingbird, but the size of a healthy chicken. A narrow, antenna-like loop of something projected from the front, and Kul said this was the probe used to detect the boundary.

"It's clear sailing up to about one hundred meters." Bulaboldo gestured up at the seeming overcast, which gave no indication as to whether a ship could fly through it or not. "At that altitude, a dome of breakdown field roofs it over. But at one side of the dome is a narrow channel of free-zone space leading out. Yes, all the way out, but through a somewhat labyrinthine passage. Hence the need for a pilot of more than common skill."

"How narrow?"

"Almost—yes, *almost* prohibitively so. I tell you frankly that many people, many respected pilots, would not want to take the risk. But the charts I have compiled show that there is certainly a path that a small ship can travel, just room for a vessel of the *Witch*'s size to squeeze through—though at the narrowest place with only this much clearance." And Kul held up two hands half a meter apart.

"How the hell do you know my ship's exact dimensions?"

"Not that hard to find out, old lad. Not compared to various other things I've dug up in my time. Been working on it since you came on world here. Shipyards and licensors and such like to keep records, you know, and records from many worlds tend to be accessible, even in backwaters like Maracanda."

Harry couldn't help being impressed by the scheme, though he wasn't tempted to sign on. It had the simplicity of all the best grand plans. The greatest physical risk would seem to be the pilot's, on his solo flight in here. But that was not why he was angry.

"What gives you the idea that I would use my ship to smuggle dope?"

"Well, to begin with, my lad, you'll be well compensated for a few hours' work—toil virtually risk free for a pilot as good as you are. No, 'well compensated' is too great an understatement. Your share of the total payoff will be vast indeed—far above and beyond the value of your ship, which we must agree is quite substantial in itself.

"Even including your c-plus cannon in the evaluation—oh,

don't look at me like that, dear heart. I would not want to hint at blackmail, and certainly would not dare. I am merely pointing out the advantages of close cooperation."

"How is it you just happen to own the claim with the open passage over it, as well as the one with the most valuable mineral deposits?"

"Industry is claimed to be a virtue, and heaven rewards the virtuous, dear lad, but I doubt that you really want to know how the intentions of providence were made manifest in this instance."

There were several other things that Harry also doubted, but he wasn't going to discuss them now.

Instead, he said to Bulaboldo: "Then you have no proof that any solution to this maze exists? You don't actually know there's an aerial free-zone route all the way from the field at Port City to your claim?"

"Let us say, old chap, that I am morally certain of the fact. My small scout has not made the whole trip, no. But I assure you that a lot of computer work has gone into my determination."

This scouting by proxy showed one of the charted passages to be clear for several kilometers, and to open at the end of that distance into a larger free-zone cavity, that in turn debouched into open space. From that locus there ought to be nothing but a free and easy flight of a few hundred klicks directly to the Port City landing field, and the unbounded universe beyond.

"No one else has ever looked for a clear passage to this end of the surface?"

"No one else seems to have got around to it just yet, dear lad. No doubt someone will, before long. Wouldn't do at all, old chap, to be messing about here, in these narrow, low-altitude passages, close above the surface, with a ship much bigger than yours. Almost certain to fail to get through, and any flight is likely to draw unwelcome attention. No, in and out is the game, one landing with a small ship and then away again. The product will be delivered and cash collected a good many parsecs from here."

Ahead of the little ridge where the two men were standing, the exotic desert, humped by a thousand little hills, stretched out for thousands of kilometers, toward what was literally the opposite edge of the world. He wondered how far the free zone sprawled out here at ground level.

Harry said: "Tell me one thing."

"Any number of them, old top."

"Just one, for now. Why should you trust me to keep my part of the bargain? What's keeping me from just driving my ship away, once I get back into her? Going on about my business, leaving you sitting here with your tons of grit?"

"I think I know you too well, Harry me lad, to believe you'd do a thing like . . ." Kul let his words die away.

Lily had rejoined them, and was displaying urgency. "Harry, there are some people over that way, acting rather strangely."

Looking in the other direction, Harry observed a small group, half a dozen men and women, about two hundred meters away. They seemed to be dragging something heavy along the ground, but he couldn't make out just what the object was.

"Why do you think they're acting especially strange?" Harry stopped. What the people were dragging was some kind of a machine. And he had seen one of those people somewhere before—yes, in Portal Square, arguing how nice it was going to be to die.

Kul was squinting in that direction, but he couldn't quite make out what the people were doing either. "What is it, Harry?"

He muttered: "Maybe Pike wasn't so crazy after all."

"Beg pardon?"

"Kul, turn around. Just walk with us. Lily, let's get out of here."

The three started moving. Looking over his shoulder, Harry saw the little group of goodlife hoisting an actual berserker android to its feet. There was no mistaking that silvery, steely, manlike shape; humans built no robots that looked anything like that. He grabbed Lily by an arm and started running in the other direction, towing her with him, heading for where he judged the nearest boundary of breakdown zone to be. Bulaboldo labored along beside them.

Looking back, Harry saw the machine just starting to move under its own power, making a few jerky stumbles, circuits coming back to life now that they were in a free zone.

Bullets from goodlife small arms began to fly around them. Dietrich and Redpath had reappeared from somewhere, holding pistols, and were shooting back. Harry was close enough to see the little hole suddenly pop into existence, right in the middle of Dietrich's forehead. Before the man's body had hit the ground, Harry was running past him.

Bulaboldo was in his element, fighting back at supposed claim jumpers or government spies. He took the opportunity, just before plunging into breakdown space, of firing his handgun at the enemy.

Moments later, the berserker responded, having completed its revival. There was a small, stuttering flash at the machine's right shoulder. Force packets shot at a target inside a breakdown zone evidently disintegrated on crossing the border, and the impact was tremendously diminished. Several meters deep in breakdown, not enough power was left to inflict more than a bruise upon a human body. Force became farce, and when Harry was shot in the side of the head the sensation was no worse than getting slapped in the face with a wet rag.

They were momentarily safe from the berserker, but half a dozen goodlife were coming on, yelling and brandishing a variety of weapons.

Harry ran, with Bulaboldo panting at his side, doing a surprisingly good job of keeping up. Not far ahead, Lily, Alan, and Dr. Kloskurb were scrambling together to get back to the nearest pedicar.

When Bulaboldo was about to turn off on a side trail, Harry collared him and yanked him to a stop. Looking back, he saw that the goodlife had given up their immediate pursuit. There was no longer any sign of the berserker. Its friends were probably getting ready to haul it through breakdown to some free zone where victims were available.

Harry demanded: "Have you got a telegraph of your own, hidden somewhere near here?"

"Telegraph? Not a bit of it. Why—?"

"We've got to call in an alert!" Harry was ferocious.

"But, old chap, a full alert's already been called. A fake, of course."

"*What?*"

"Already been sounded, I tell you." There was no mistaking Kul's fear, and his astonishment. His face had gone ashen, though his breath was gradually coming back. "I had to—make sure you'd somehow—be allowed to—lift off—didn't I? The code word already—sent out and acknowledged. Yes, of course, a fake. And now—turns out the bad machines are really here. Bit of irony in that. Perhaps I've saved the world. Without really trying."

"That thing that shot at us was real as they come. Except for this blessed breakdown business, we'd be toast. How'd you manage anything like that? A *fake?*"

Bulaboldo was smiling, in a ghastly way. "I swear, by all the profits I will ever make . . . It's just that one has—among one's acquaintances—those with extensive knowledge of the early warning system. And how it can be jiggled. All ships on the field will be not only allowed but compelled to get off the ground. Of course, your beloved *Witch* will still be there, waiting for your cunning hand at the controls."

"A fake." Harry was still having a problem believing that.

"Well, of course, old sponge." Kul showed injured dignity. "Even if one knew how to summon up actual berserkers, one certainly would not dabble in such matters. Accepting risk is one thing, committing suicide quite another."

"So, if an alert is already called—"

"Depend on it."

"—they'll know about it in Tomb Town and Minersville? They'll have got the word already, by telegraph."

"Private and public systems both, one would assume. But you're not thinking of going that way?"

Harry had thought of that. But he couldn't do it, wasn't going to delay his own effort to get himself back to Port City as rapidly as possible. "We're heading straight to the spaceport. I want my ship."

"That's the spirit. What about the caravanserai?"

"Don't intend to stop there unless we have to, and if we do, it won't be for long. I need my ship. Hell, this whole world needs it. There's not much else around in the way of fighting machinery. Very little Space Force, almost no Templar hardware."

"Good. Good, that's the ticket, old lad. Just don't be too eager to plunge into a space battle—one can always find those. But here, wait. Wouldn't do to forget this bit." And the smuggler handed over, in the form of another little message cube, the chart he had so painstakingly arranged for a pilot's guidance. "I'll be at the landing place, when you are. I'll look for you in about two days. I have a refuge nearby, where our product's stored. Solidly in breakdown zone, we ought to be able to hold out there for long enough. You will be quick as you can, won't you, old man?"

Harry ran on, catching up with Lily, Alan, and Kloskurb, who had been waiting for him uncertainly. "Explanations later. Run! All four get in one car—that way we can go faster."

"Can't believe—berserkers on Maracanda." That was Kloskurb, panting as he ran.

Harry said: "Better believe it. Whatever they're doing here, now that they know they've been spotted, they'll come out killing with everything they have."

Even as he ran, he cursed himself for a bumbling idiot, for not taking seriously a Templar general's warning. Even if Pike did tend to see berserkers and goodlife everywhere, the real ones that he discovered would be no less real.

Harry wished that he had some quick, direct means of communication with Robledo Pike. There were both public and private telegraph terminals in Tomb Town and Minersville, but there was no guarantee who would be in control of those cities.

So there was nothing to do but hurry on. The only help that he could truly depend on lay in the power and the optelectronic intelligence of his ship.

When the four of them reached the car, Harry jumped right into the driver's seat, and no one tried to dispute it with him; he was the expert pilot, even though he'd never driven one of these vehicles before. Lily, Alan, and Kloskurb jumped into the vehicle right after Harry. In moments, the pedicar was moving.

Hoping that the mental map he had been forming of the nearby terrain was accurate, Harry immediately turned away from the route they had followed coming out here, choosing instead a shortcut across country. Instinct suggested they might regain the main road a little faster going this way. Faint wheel tracks seemed to indicate a road, or at least a trail, ahead of them.

"Where does this lead?" Alan wondered aloud from the left rear seat.

"How the bloody hell should I know?"

Harry kept steering, and all four sets of pedals were turning briskly. Now they were deep in breakdown zone, and seemingly safe from immediate berserker attack. The idea of berserkers concocting an elaborate plan to attack Maracanda still made no more sense to Harry than it ever had. The vast breakdown zones of the habitable area were naturally protected against any invasion from space, more secure in that regard than almost any other world that Harry had ever seen. Well, sometimes berserkers did strange things, even counterproductive things, just for the sake of remaining unpredictable. At the moment, that seemed the only explanation.

Having been given a little time to think, Alan had a suggestion: "Maybe we should split up?"

Harry vetoed that at once. "No. If I understand this buggy we're riding, four active people can go faster, longer, in it than one or two or three people can. Pretty soon, if there's nothing chasing us, we'll ease up from this sprint. Two of us can pedal while the other two rest, then we'll change off. All four pedaling again if we need a burst of speed."

Kloskurb said, "Whatever you people saw back there, I missed it. I mean, apart from the humans shooting at us. Are you sure what you saw was a berserker?"

"I am," Harry answered at once. If the look of that machine the people were dragging hadn't totally convinced him, the looks on the faces of the people who did the dragging had. "But even if I wasn't, if all I had was a good suspicion, I'd be here pedaling."

Lily, sitting in the right front, made a small, throat-clearing sound. "Harry?"

"Yeah?"

"Maybe it *was* goodlife who tried to kidnap you, a couple of days ago, and not smugglers looking for a pilot."

Harry nodded. "I can believe that, though I still don't quite understand it. Goodlife, mistaking me for the good doctor here. Wanting to nab an expert astrogeologist, just like they took his colleague a couple of months ago. So now the question becomes why?"

Alan had been looking back, and reported. "There's another pedicar, coming after us."

"Chasing, or just running away like we are?"

"Can't tell. But I don't think we ought to let them catch up."

Harry saw no need to urge his companions to greater efforts. He did his best to look back through the small rearview mirror, along the curving, steadily vanishing line of telegraph poles. There was the other car, all right, but at the moment it did not seem to be gaining. If this was a pursuit, with goodlife pedaling the chase car, they might be slowed by the presence in their vehicle of an inert mass of metal. Would a berserker spring back into activity spontaneously on emerging from breakdown zone? Harry's imagination showed him that scene in painfully vivid detail. The instant the enemy vehicle rolled into a free zone, the berserker would slide out of the cab, in a motion as fluid as that of any living snake. Then, running on two legs or four, it would pull the cab and its load of goodlife with it. It was going to need them as soon as it hit a breakdown zone again.

Would a berserker machine's memories be adversely affected passing through a breakdown zone? Probably not the basic programming, he assumed. No such luck. But maybe the short-term memory? Imagination pictured a berserker forgetting just who and where it had been fighting before the curtain of breakdown descended to conk it out. Or which of the human forms in sight might be goodlife, and which bad.

The speeding cars were swaying on the turns—and the car with Harry steering was pulling slightly, slowly, into a greater lead.

Here came a couple of pedicars going in the other direction, narrowly missing a sideswipe on the constricted road. Harry shouted a warning without slowing down. "Berserkers!"

One approaching vehicle stopped as soon as the chorus of yells rang out, then began to turn in a tight circle, getting ready to retrace its path.

Another hesitated briefly, stopped at last, then after a few irresolute moments went on east. Harry wished them well.

"How did you know that they weren't goodlife, too?"

"Because they didn't steer into us head on."

Kloskurb was counting seconds, under his breath. An estimated minute passed, and then another, without a sighting of the car that might have carried pursuers. All in Harry's vehicle began to breathe a little easier.

"There are so many turns in this damned road, I can't see if they're still after us or not."

"At least they're not gaining."

Harry waited for what he judged was another minute, then took a chance. "All right, sprint is over. Front seats keep pedaling, rear seats rest. Alan, keep a sharp lookout to the rear."

"Right."

Kloskurb had a suggestion. "It seems to me we've got an alternative to simply running. We look for a good spot, and then loop around somewhere and ambush the bastards."

Alan said: "Here, in a breakdown zone?"

Harry said: "In breakdown would be the only place, if we were going to do it. Our guns won't work, but little popguns like these won't do us any good against a functioning berserker. But we're not setting any ambush. We're getting on as fast as we can to the spaceport, to my ship."

"Wish a man could bottle this breakdown stuff and take it into space for a defensive shield."

Alan brightened at that thought. He was only slightly discouraged when it occurred to him, as it soon did, that a couple of hundred other people must have already considered that idea and found it unworkable.

"Trouble is, the phenomenon doesn't seem to exist anywhere else in the universe, only on certain portions of the surface of Maracanda. Not even on any of the other half dozen azlarocean bodies."

Alan worked as hard at pedaling west as everyone else. But he wasn't going to allow shortness of breath to stop him from talking about the great opportunities this world offered, and his own unfortunate lack of investment capital.

At first, though he was talking to all his fellow riders in the car, his words seemed to be directed especially to Lily, telling her how tired he was of the business of praying at the Portal, and putting up a pretense of trying to make converts to Great Malakó.

After a minute or so his voice grew enthusiastic, as he proclaimed to all his companions how the truth, the real truth, had come to him in the form of sudden revelation. His own future—and Lily's, too, if she would only open her eyes to see it—depended not on anything in the Galactic Core, tens of thousands of light-years distant, but on the mineral wealth of Maracanda, right here beneath their feet.

There followed many kilometers of relative silence, with no one in the car having much to say to anyone else. A brief stop allowed people to stretch and change positions, but Harry kept the driver's seat.

"I'm sorry if you can't see it, Lil." Alan wasn't looking at her, but out through the window. As the terror of the first minutes of flight receded into the past, he came back relentlessly to his new enthusiasm. He sounded cool and remote, as if he and Lily had never been close.

At last she gave him a kind of answer. "I'm sorry for you, too, Alan." Her voice was tight. "You're right, I can no longer see any of the crazy things that you see. Not anymore."

Of course, the speedometer on the pedicar was not functioning here in breakdown, any more than their various timepieces were; but Harry, just by looking at the passing landscape, estimated that the four of them, pedaling determinedly two at a time, and relieving each other at frequent intervals, had so far been able to sustain a cruising speed of about thirty kilometers an hour. At that rate, ten hours should see them gone west as far as the caravanserai. By the time they got there, they were going to be in serious need of food.

Not that it was easy to tell time. When darkness fell, they lighted the pedicar's dim combustion lamps, smaller versions of those used on the caravan, and pressed on.

Currently, Harry and Dr. Kloskurb were laboring at the pedals, while Lily and Alan rested.

It seemed that husband and wife had less and less to say to each other, the more time they spent in each other's company. Lily had made a bitter comment or two about her husband. But then she quieted and concentrated on the job at hand.

Alan said something showing that he thought his wife and Harry were having an affair. But his chief reason in mentioning it seemed to be to show that he did not really care.

"On Maracanda, the only important resource is mineral wealth."

Harry said: "The only resource we have to worry about right now is breath. Let's not waste it."

Kloskurb tried to be a peacemaker. "Arguing can wait. But Harry's right. What we have to do is just keep breathing, and keep moving."

Silence reigned in the cab for a short time. But soon Alan was muttering again; it seemed impossible for him to keep silent on his latest means of salvation. Compared to the torment he felt at his lack of investment capital, the breakup of his marriage was only an annoyance.

Oh, they mustn't misunderstand him; he wasn't going to be selfish. He was generously willing to share his new treasure (as soon as he had it in hand) with his friends, and especially with Lily. But he now saw himself as having gone beyond Lily, advancing into realms of ideas and accomplishment where she could not follow.

There had been no further sightings of their theoretical pursuers, and Harry was beginning to think it likely they had given up the chase. Not that he could take that for granted. For all he knew, more of the berserker's playmates might be somewhere ahead, preparing an ambush of their own.

Whatever else might happen, he had to get back to his ship. He had to get back to his ship.

Weary from endless hours of pedaling, from many hours in the pedicar—they had no way, except the cycle of darkness and light, to tell how many—with only the briefest of stops, to stretch their weary legs and answer calls of nature, they at last rounded a turn between two hills and came in sight of the faint beacons of the caravanserai's oil lamps.

The dread that a metal shape might come bursting out to kill them was quickly laid to rest. The stationmaster, looking far more haggard than when Harry had seen him last, came to greet them at the main entrance. This time he had a pistol stuck in his belt. "You're from the east? What word?"

"No one's chasing us, as far as we know. And we need food." Harry remained slumped in his seat for long seconds, realizing that he was close to exhaustion.

The caravanserai was empty of guests at the moment, only

the stationmaster and a small handful of other employees remaining at their posts. There was the telegraph to be defended, the stationmaster explained, and the caravanserai's small central island of free zone.

The telegraph instrument, when Harry approached it, was sounding a steady clatter that gave an impression of urgency, even though he was unable to interpret the code.

The operator on duty interpreted. Serious fighting had broken out in Tomb Town and Minersville. Both settlements were under attack by a small force of berserkers. Where the machines had come from, how they had managed to materialize on the remote east side of Maracanda, no one knew. Casualties were substantial, but the battle was not hopeless. The enemy was few in number and seemed to lack any heavy weapons.

In the west, Port City and the spaceport had still seen no sign of the enemy, though of course both remained under full alert. The signals precipitating the alert, from the early warning units on the distant approaches to the system, had not been repeated.

It would take some time for the authorities to discover evidence that the original alert had been a hoax, but by then there would be even better evidence that the berserker presence on their world was all too real.

The recycler was still turning out enough food to feed a hungry caravan. Chewing on a crude sandwich that tasted like a gourmet treat—at the moment almost anything would have done so—Harry did his best to use the telegraph to get a message through to General Pike. He wanted to tell the Templars that Harry and Lily were on their way west and that nothing must delay Harry getting back into his ship.

Kloskurb, after waiting impatiently, had a message of his own to send: a private communication to his family, who were in Port City at the moment, and who must be wondering what had happened to him.

Alan, pacing restlessly in the common room, wistfully wished aloud that it might be possible to register land claims by wire.

The four travelers gobbled food and packed more in the pedicar. Sleep turned out to be another necessity, and Harry and his crew were soon stretched out, fully clothed, on four cots that had been pulled into the common room. This was where the stationmaster and his helpers also rested between tours of duty.

Acting on an inspiration, Lily ransacked the station's emergency medical kit and came up with some finely calibrated morsels of chemistry whose labels promised that they would put an adult man into two hours of deep and intensely restful sleep, followed by an indefinite period of high-energy wakefulness.

Just to make sure, Harry left instructions with the caravanserai worker currently on duty. "Wake me in two hours. No more than that."

A new day had dawned by the time Harry and his companions reboarded their car and pushed on west from the caravanserai.

When they reached and passed the place where spheres were kept in a corral, they knew they were on the very edge of free zone.

Moments later, the pedicar's engine purred into life, and four voices rose in a hearty cheer.

Harry still drove. The speed of powered movement was intensely gratifying. Kloskurb, to the surprise of all the others, announced that he was working on a poem, to be called "Ode to the Moving Chair."

Now and then Harry's thoughts strayed back to Bulaboldo and his cohort. It seemed very probable that the smuggler would be doing just what he'd said he'd do: keeping whatever people he still had with him under control, remaining hidden in the vicinity of his prize diggings, as long as berserkers prowled the land nearby. Guarding his treasure, and his available landing spot. Clinging to the hope, however forlorn it must appear at times, that Harry would soon be setting down his ship nearby. When that happened, Bulaboldo and his loyal people—if he still had any— would leap out of concealment, ready to load as much of his dirty stuff as he could aboard Harry's ship.

Well, they'd have a surprise coming, if matters ever actually got that far.

The talk in the pedicar kept coming around to legitimate minerals and claims for prospecting. Dr. Kloskurb said: "Don't worry, Gunnlod, berserkers aren't going to cave in all the mines."

Alan couldn't wait, berserkers or not, to take the first step toward filing the claims he meant to establish. He persisted in try- ing to pick the astrogeologist's brain for tips on where the valu- able minerals were to be found and how to get them out.

Kloskurb, irritated, at last grumbled that he expected to be paid for consultations.

Alan admitted that he was moneyless at the moment, having given practically everything he owned to the temple of Malakó. "But we can work out some other kind of arrangement, some share of the profits. After this berserker scare, some people will be dropping out, but money will be rolling in."

Lily said to her husband: "Too bad berserkers don't care about wealth. You could make a deal with them." Then she sud- denly looked wary, as if she thought she might have gone too far.

Alan took no offense; he was shaking his head, lost in some inner calculation. Harry was thinking that the only treasure that berserkers ever sought was life itself, just so they could kill it, to satisfy their programming. As fanatical as any human being who ever searched for gold.

Sometimes Harry wondered: supposing that the death machines could some day be sure they had succeeded, and all life had been expunged from the Galaxy, what would they do then? Spontaneously turn themselves off? Or possibly settle into an endless vigilance, ready to stamp out any recurrence of the disease? A third alternative might be to find some way to launch themselves successfully out into the intergalactic night, trying to go where no normal superluminal drive could ever carry them. Perhaps a couple of hundred thousand light-years to the Magellanic Clouds, or a couple of million to the spiral in Andromeda, looking for a new infection there.

Berserkers, of course, cared nothing for grit, or any other marketable treasure, in itself. But Harry wasn't so sure that they'd ignore the mines. They had learned the potential value of such stuff, as a resource useful in buying the services of certain marginal members of humanity. In the course of the long war there had been plenty of evidence that it was generally safe to depend upon human greed.

Cruising at several times the speed they had been able to make on the power of their own muscles, the refugees could take turns napping while one of them drove. Harry even relinquished the driver's position for a time. The endless passing of the road was insidiously hypnotic, even if the drug taken at the caravanserai had sharply boosted their reserves of ready energy.

There wasn't much in the way of other traffic, and almost none going in the other direction.

Now and then they passed a few frightened people walking west, some of whom tried to hitch a ride. Harry snarled that they were stopping for no one. He had to get back to his ship, and that was the only thing that counted.

When at last the outlying buildings of Port City appeared in the distance, Harry looked about sharply for a human presence, realizing that he might still stand in some danger of being arrested by the Space Force.

*   *   *

Sure enough, just outside the city they came to barricades across the road. These were ineffectual barriers that would hardly slow a berserker down, assembled from a mix of random materials, and defended by an irregular gathering of worried volunteers, armed with an odd assortment of weapons. Harry assumed the few professional military around would be busy in or with their ships.

The approaches to the city from the east looked practically defenseless, but the people present assured the new arrivals that so far it had not been attacked. They were beginning to allow themselves to hope that it never would be.

The haggard, irregularly armed people guarding the barricade were hungry for every scrap of news from the interior. They had heard wild rumors from other refugees who had come trickling in, and the new arrivals could confirm or deny some of them.

There were no Space Force people at the barricades, and none of the volunteers were going to try to arrest Harry, or even question him.

To match its second-rate early warning system, Maracanda probably had comparatively little in the way of man-made defenses. There were some robots in orbit, though here, as elsewhere, with the example of the berserkers constantly before them, Earth-descended humans refused to build fully automated fighting machines. There were also some ground defenses, all near Port City, sighted in on the main approaches.

Considering the wealth of natural peculiarities in the space surrounding this habitable body, and in the higher layers of what passed for this world's atmosphere, it would not be at all surprising that the local defense headquarters in Port City failed to keep a good watch on what ships might be maneuvering nearby.

The quartet of refugees were surrounded, at least for the time being, by science, sanity, and the illusion of safety.

"I'm getting off here. Coming, Lil?" It was as if all the talk of her leaving him had been forgotten, dismissed as some temporary aberration. "We'll take out a claim in your name, too. We can do that, can't we?"

"Legally?" Kloskurb was thinking it over slowly. It was as if his mind had to come back from some great distance before it could consider such a question. "Yes, I don't know why not," he said at last.

"Good." Alan was looking silently at his wife.

"I'm not coming with you, Alan."

"Oh." Alan looked from her to Harry and back again. "Well," he added finally.

"No, Alan, understand me. I'm not leaving you for Harry. It's because I've finally figured out what you are. You keep demonstrating it over and over, and at last I can't deny it any longer. And you're not going to change."

Alan stared at her a little longer, a man confronting a knotty problem. Then he turned his gaze worriedly to a nearby clock, checking the time.

One more try with another prospect. "Harry, you must have some money in your pockets. Can I interest you in a promising investment? I know I've asked you this before."

"Ask me just once more and see what happens."

Alan sighed. "I'll be seeing you around then, people." He gave his wife one last look. "I want to talk to you about this later, Lil." Then he turned and hurried away, still carrying his small collection of samples, in the direction of the Administration Building.

"Goodbye, Alan." Lily got in the last word, waiting until her husband was already too far away to hear.

EIGHTEEN

Even approaching the city from its eastern side, coming in from the direction opposite the space-port, Harry and his traveling companions would have had a good view of any liftoffs or landings that might have been taking place. But the open, sunless, starless imitation sky above the port was absolutely clear of traffic; doubtless every ship physically capable of getting off the ground had already done so in response to the alert.

There were definite signs of military activity along the city's streets and on its outskirts, and a notable lack of normal civilian presence. Harry's party was challenged again as it approached the spaceport, at another hastily constructed roadblock.

This time he saw to his relief that the barrier was manned by only a couple of lightly armed Templars. Harry immediately stopped the car, got out, identified himself, and demanded to be taken to General Pike.

Harry spoke confidently, but was a little unsure of what kind of welcome to expect from the general. He wondered what Pike had thought when he heard of the two rescued men from This-world, and the most improbable story Redpath and Dietrich had told in the Space Force office just downstairs from his.

Lily had got out of the car, too. She must have been thinking along the same lines, because she whispered in Harry's ear: "Maybe we ought to tell the general the entire truth?"

"We'll see."

Pike, who had been patrolling nearby streets and roads, was quickly summoned by radio, and in a few moments his command post came rolling up to the barricade, in the form of a sizable armored half-track, from whose turret projected the thick muzzle of an imposing cannon. Any berserker that happened to come this way was going to face some real opposition. Harry supposed this must be the most formidable surface weapon the Templars had on Maracanda.

The general had no staff or escort with him; Harry supposed he'd posted just about everyone available on guard duty at various places. Quickly he invited Harry and Lily into the vehicle's cabin to be debriefed.

Dr. Kloskurb hastily introduced himself to the general, then immediately made his excuses and took himself away as rapidly as he could, wishing Harry and Lily good luck in whatever they were going to do next. Now that they had rejoined civilization, Kloskurb wanted to get a message to whatever family or friends he had who had been worrying about him. "I've got to get to my family in Port City. They're going to be tearing their hair out."

Harry grunted. "And I've got to get to my ship."

Watching Kloskurb hike briskly away, Lily murmured

wistfully: "It must be really great to have someone who cares about you."

Once the three of them were inside the cramped cabin of the combat vehicle, Pike greeted Harry and Lily fervently, offered food and drink from his onboard supply of field rations, and eagerly demanded to be told everything they knew about the situation in the east. But a moment later he interrupted himself to briefly relate the story of Dietrich and Redpath, as he had heard it from his contacts in the Space Force office.

Harry interrupted briefly to assure the general that one of the men in question was dead.

"Hah. You knew them, then?"

"I wouldn't say that. Just met them very briefly, heard someone call him by that name." And Lily nodded in verification.

"Then you've probably heard the rest of their story."

The general went on to tell the version that he knew, while his audience heard him out in silence. Pike said his first impulse had been to suspect the unsavory pair of being goodlife, mostly because no one could believe their tale of a mysterious stranger who for no particular reason gave them a ride in his unidentifiable ship, and then marooned them.

In Pike's mind any peculiarity could be made to point in that direction. What had two men with criminal records really been doing on that abandoned satellite, anyway, in a system where a berserker had recently been sighted? Possibly they had been receiving instructions, or materials for terrorism, from one of the dark things of lifeless metal that served perverted goodlife as a god.

Pike did not give the impression of suspecting that the suspicious pair had anything to do with Harry. Far more likely they had been engaged in some forbidden commerce with the berserker that Harry's ship had struggled with. "I don't suppose you observed anything out there to suggest such contacts?"

"Believe us, general," said Lily, "we'd tell you if we did."

Glad to drop that subject, Harry got right to more important business, saying he was reasonably certain that none of the enemy was going to find their way this far west. It was good to be able to report that they had seen no sign of goodlife or berserkers on Maracanda since leaving the far east. They had experienced no serious pursuit. Quickly, Harry and Lily reported very nearly everything that had happened to them, leaving out only the fact that Bulaboldo and his crew were smugglers who had thought they were faking an alert when they arranged for one to be called.

Privately, Harry had been thinking over that coincidence: but no, it *couldn't* be coincidence that the real attack had come along just when the phony alert was called. No; instead, the news of the alert must have flushed out a goodlife crew and their malignant hardware who were already in place on Maracanda, prodded them into the open before they could accomplish whatever secret nastiness they had been planning.

Harry was beginning to think it could be worth an arm and maybe a leg to know just what that was.

"Everything I see and hear, general, convinces me that we're really facing only a small force. If the people in the field say they're facing no more than a dozen machines, I see no reason to doubt that. Not a routine invasion, only a small party, here for some special purpose. Aided and abetted by not more than a handful of goodlife, and it seems most of those bastards have already been disposed of. Maybe one or two will be available for questioning."

"Ever try to question one of those?" The general let it drop, and went on to describe the overall military situation. According to Pike's latest information, this was little different from what the telegraph had been reporting at the caravanserai. The lines were still open to that midpoint, and on to Tomb Town and Minersville, where fighting still raged, and casualties on the human side had mounted into the thousands. Active goodlife, fighting fanatically, had reportedly been well-nigh exterminated by now, but of course the machines were much tougher to defeat, especially given the humans' shortage of effective heavy weapons. One small berserker on the edge of Tomb Town had been rammed by a kamikaze pedicar and knocked into a breakdown zone, where it was probably going to lie inert till doomsday.

The most recent telegraph reports were mildly optimistic, despite the heavy casualties. A majority of the population had fled Minersville and Tomb Town into breakdown territory, where berserkers could not follow.

Of course, if the enemy got control of a telegraph line at any point, they could be sending false, deceptive messages, spreading disinformation at a great rate, just to create panic or to get our military looking in the wrong place.

Even without such interference, the authorities in the west had only a hazy picture of what must be going on in the east. No more than an occasional telegram and the trickle of refugees could tell them.

If Pike could find some way to transport his armored vehicle across hundreds of kilometers of breakdown zone to Minersville, the people who were there fighting for their lives would certainly bid him welcome. The general announced his intention of getting started on that effort as soon as possible, entrusting the half-track to a junior officer who would drive it east as far as free zone stretched, then work with the caravan people to come up with some way to hitch the massive weapon to a doubled team of rollers for transit through the long stretches of breakdown zone. Pike had delayed this redeployment until now, thinking that the peculiar small attack in the east was only meant as a feint, a distraction, and that the main assault was soon to come down out of space on the spaceport in the west.

The general went on to say: "A berserker attack on Maracanda seems an odd choice, to pick a place where their operations will be restricted to a few small areas of free zone."

Harry said: "But this is the battlefield they've chosen, and you're absolutely right, general. I don't get it either. Of all the possible targets in the Galaxy, why should they organize an attack on the back country of this world? It doesn't seem to make any sense from their point of view . . . and berserkers are not stupid. Whatever else they may be, never that."

The general growled, deep in his throat, making the sound of an unsatisfied predator. "You're saying their real objective on this world must be something other than the lives to be harvested in those two small towns."

"That's it." Harry slammed down a fist on the arm of his chair, meant to be occupied by some crew member who must be busy elsewhere. "Something, but we don't know what. All we can be sure of is that it will somehow add up to killing a lot more people."

Lily said: "There are other forms of life, and berserkers want to kill them all."

"Sure, other kinds of life, but in berserker calculations, we're always the kind of breathing thing that really counts. As an old book says, one human is worth many sparrows . . . and God knows how many blades of grass. Because once the thinking part of life is disposed of, and that is us, then all the rest, all the orchids and insects and elephants, will be an easy harvest."

Pike said: "The presence of machines in the east implies their use of a secret landing place in that region, perhaps somewhere outside the habitable area. How can they have any kind of force in place near Tomb Town if there's no place to land? And how come, after that first alert, days ago, the early warning system robots haven't picked up a trace of any incursion?"

"General, I'm not absolutely sure there's no place to land on the east side of the habitable zone. In fact, I'm got some evidence in my pocket right now, suggesting that there is. As soon as I can get my ship off the ground, I'm going to check it out."

"Evidence?"

Digging out the message cube that had been given him by Bulaboldo, Harry displayed it on his palm. "This is said to contain a chart, showing a route to be followed, a narrow channel of free space extending all the way through breakdown space, to a spot where a small ship might be able to land. It's only a few kilometers from Tomb Town and Minersville."

Pike was incredulous. "How in the Galaxy did you get hold of a chart like that? Any reason to think it might be accurate?"

"Well, you sent us over there as secret agents—and yes, I think there is a reason. But please, don't push me yet on where and how I got this. Let's see if it works. If I can get the *Witch* safely on the ground over there, I ought to be able to do our side some good."

"Well. In any case I'm going to make a copy of that, before you dash away with it again. Just in case." The general snatched the cube from Harry's hand and snapped it into a slot on the side of the half-track's communicator. Moments later it reappeared, a duplicate beside it.

Harry nodded. "Right. Just in case. But let that go for a moment. I've got what may be a better idea about where the berserkers landed. It may have been right here at the spaceport."

When others looked at him, Harry explained: "I think it would be fairly easy for people to smuggle in any kind of hardware they wanted here. Outgoing cargo is rigorously inspected at this port, because of the problem with illegal drugs. But I don't think many incoming containers ever get looked at. And even if you opened one, an inspector couldn't necessarily tell berserker components from lawn mowers at a glance. What do they look like? Just machinery.

"Goodlife could package berserker components somewhere else, ship them in here, then on east by freight caravan, along with tons and tons of other gear brought in by miners and builders. Berserkers come in a variety of shapes and sizes, and possibly there are kits for more goodlife at this end to put it back together. You know, 'some assembly required.'"

Harry was just getting up to leave the half-track when Pike called him back. "Oh yes, Silver, I almost forgot. You've got some mail." And he handed over another tiny cube.

When Harry squeezed the little object lightly, a neat, small readout popped into the air above it, showing that the message had originated on the planet Esmerelda, some sixty light-years distant. Also listed in fine print were the various relay stations through which the message had been forwarded, between the stars, by the regular robot courier service. Sometimes personal messages were forwarded in multiple copies, by regular interstellar couriers, the service sometimes duplicating and reduplicating the message without reading it, and sending copies on to different places, as often happened when the exact location of the addressee was unknown. Harry's eyes lit up on seeing the point of origination, and he accepted the little cube with what seemed like reverent care.

Lily was staring at him curiously. She asked: "Not going to read your mail?"

He juggled the messenger indecisively for just a moment, then muttered: "It can wait." A moment later it had been stuffed away in a deep pocket of his suit.

Once a red alert had been called, standing orders and regulations forbade anyone, including Space Force officers, from trying to keep any ship on the ground. Even Rovaki would not dare detain a capable pilot like Harry on mere suspicion, certainly not when it was a question of getting a ship up and into space. Instead, they would be working hard to get every vessel and its crew off world, where they could either fight the enemy or try to get away.

General Pike was as eager as Harry to get into action. He was now recalling his single scoutship to the spaceport, so he could get aboard and lift off.

Just as Harry was about to leave the half-track, a message came in, relayed to the mobile vehicle through Templar headquarters. It was from Commandant Rovaki, who was out in space himself.

Rovaki's original query was some routine question about how the patrol duties in space were going to be shared—the Space Force had more ships available than Pike. But when he was informed that the *Witch* would soon be lifting off, the commandant made it clear that he was still very suspicious of Harry Silver. He informed General Pike that his agents had discovered some evidence suggesting that the original alert had been a fake, and Rovaki hoped to connect that fake with some elaborate smuggling scheme. Of course, there was no question now, with fighting actually in progress, of aborting the alert. But there was also some criminal plan afoot, and the commandant had no doubt that Harry Silver would be found deeply involved in anything of that kind taking place on Maracanda.

General Pike seemed momentarily stuck for a reply. Harry leaned forward a little in his chair, letting Rovaki get a look at him. "I'm shocked to hear it," Harry said. "Deeply shocked. That man is a friend of mine."

On discovering Harry's presence in the vehicle, Rovaki glared at him. "I'm not through with you, Silver. As soon as this is over, I'll want to see you in my office."

"Not as much as I'll want to see you."

The image on the small screen blinked beneath its silvery eyebrows. "What?"

"Rovaki, we're berserker-scuffling now. You don't know how deliriously happy I'll be, when this is over, if I can still see anything."

As soon as Harry got the chance, he wolfed down a few more mouthfuls of Pike's field rations, thanked the general for effectively keeping the other authorities off his back, and announced that he had to be on his way.

Pike gave Harry and Lily his blessing.

When Harry climbed out of the half-track, thinking yearningly of how good a real drink would taste right now, he discovered a pair of suited figures waiting for him, two people carrying carbines and clad in heavy Templar armor.

Harry stared with disapproval at the hulking pair. For a moment the suspicion flashed across his mind that Pike was about to have him arrested after all. "What's this?"

The general's head protruded from the half-track hatch. "A couple of men I'm sending with you, laddie. They just arrived on world shortly before the alert and have no battle stations assigned as yet. Wish I could go with you myself, but that's out of the question."

The pair of newcomers, having saluted the general, were leaning forward slightly, obviously ready, or thought they were, for whatever test the enemy might be about to throw at them.

In a moment Pike had performed introductions, accomplishing the whole job in about a dozen words.

Corporal Teagarden looked a couple of years older than his subordinate; the younger man, Private Zhong, gave the impression of being even more gung-ho than his partner. His clear blue eyes were flashing with excitement.

Harry asked: "Have either of you been at this kind of thing very long?"

Private Zhong was ready to answer that one. "We just finished Tactical Training, mister. We're ready. All you have to do is get us there."

"I'll do my best."

The ride to the field, in one of the general's groundcars, was swiftly accomplished. Sitting beside Lily in the car, Harry told her: "Last chance to back out of this, kid. Once you plunk your bottom down in that copilot's chair, you're signed on for this next mission."

"When I want to back out, Harry, I'll let you know." She was smiling at him, a little. She looked ready.

"Good." He found her hand and gripped it briefly. "Another pilot will definitely be good to have, because I don't know what we're getting into. But I wanted to make sure you had the chance."

A very few minutes later, Harry, with Lily still at his side and the two armored Templars almost treading on their heels, was striding up the ramp leading to the *Witch*'s main hatch.

He was telling her: "Soon as we're aboard, you put on some coveralls and then a spacesuit, while the *Witch* and I run a checklist and get us moving. I'll be getting my suit on later. That'll be a bit of a special project."

Pointing to the sealed hatch, Harry issued another order: "Corporal, you've got some hands on. Get that bubble gum off my ship."

The seal was made in jarring colors, like a plague warning, and was almost a full meter square. At the first touch of Teagarden's armored fingers, a recorded warning coded in its substance shouted out a stern command to desist. At the first real tear in the gooey inner material, there burst forth a loud discordant squawk of official outrage, followed by threats of retribution. Their volume faded swiftly as the corporal flung the fragments away into the night. Zhong and Teagarden exchanged faint smiles, quietly appreciating this defiance of the rival authority.

An ugly stain persisted on the hull where Rovaki's chemicals had been, and the sight of the blemish made Harry use foul language.

Harry was weary already, in a way that went deeper than pills were likely to help. He thought what he needed was a good fight, just to get some of the anger out of his system, and then about a day of sleep. Just looking at the pair of Templars as they marched aboard his ship, to stand expectantly in the control room, made him feel worse. They seemed to radiate an innocent enthusiasm that could wear him out as fast as gamma radiation.

The corporal in turn was looking appraisingly at Harry. "Any combat experience, Mr. Silver?" The question seemed to be asked in perfect innocence.

Lily uttered a small noise, as if suppressing a sneeze.

Harry grunted, a kind of wavering sound. By all the gods, the pair in their fancy armor appeared younger every time he looked at them.

He couldn't come up with any response that seemed appropriate. But at last he got out: "Let's just say I'm a tired old man. But I'm also the captain of this ship. So don't irritate me."

The young faces inside the helmets both looked faintly disappointed.

N I N E T E E N

Moments later, having success-
fully invoked the secret entrance code, Harry was back in his
familiar control room, snug in his combat chair, his helmet on and
melding with his thoughtware, powering up equipment of all
kinds, and running through a series of checklists.

He asked the *Witch* if the Space Force had done anything
else to her in his absence and got a negative reply.

The ship assured him in its imperturbable voice that no one
else had entered while he was gone. She remarked that there had
been eleven unsuccessful attempts to uncode the software downlocks.

"I missed you, too, baby," he said to his dear ship, patting an
arm of his familiar chair. He didn't expect any answer to that kind

of remark, and he didn't get one—at least not from his ship. Certainly the *Witch* had not missed him.

Lily had no comment to make, but one of the Templars did. "Think she was faithful to you, captain?"

Harry only grunted. He was wishing he could get out his mail and read it, but the chances seemed hopeless at this point.

Curtly, Harry assigned combat stations, installing Lily in the chair immediately to his right. Two other chairs, these lacking any controls, he awarded to the pair of Templars. Whether he was officially under military authority or not, while his ship was under way he was going to be its captain.

Maybe now, Harry thought, would be the best time to dump the damned useless cargo of machinery that he had already hauled, to no purpose, over so many light-years. Six big crates of some kind of food-processing gear. But no, he could do that anytime, and there were people watching, the Space Force in particular, who might decide the action was suspicious. Rovaki might even manage to use it as an excuse for inflicting further delay.

The two Templars exchanged some banter between themselves, on the surface confident but naturally nervous underneath. What they said confirmed Harry's impression that they were both new to Maracanda, too, maybe even newer than he was.

"Going to find us a place to land and look around on the east side, captain?" Corporal Teagarden sounded cheerful.

Harry nodded. "That's the plan."

Even in the midst of his flight preparations, running the checklists as rapidly as possible, he was pondering privately whether he should take time out to unpack his one suit of heavy combat armor from its special locker and put it on. He had little doubt that it would soon be needed, provided he was able to land at Bulaboldo's claim.

Despite his satisfaction on having Lily aboard, he wasn't

anxious to leave the controls to her, not until he had seen her work, or conditions forced him to it.

But about three seconds' thought convinced him that getting on his own armor could wait till after he had seen whether Bulaboldo's maze chart was any good or not. Right now he couldn't spare the couple of minutes he would need to get into his meeting-with-berserkers outfit, and run the checklist on it and his carbine. But he decided it would be wise to allot a few seconds just to take a look at it.

When he did see the suit, calling up a video view of the compartment where it was kept, he was jarred by getting a look at the scars from the last time it had seen action. That had been several standard months ago—no, almost a year—on Hyperborea. Harry stared unhappily at the ugly marks. He could clearly remember the time, not that many more years in the past, when the suit was new. Now it looked like it might be time for a replacement, another expensive undertaking.

He hadn't realized that he was muttering aloud, but Lily had a question: "Will you get a new one?"

"Good suits cost a lot."

"I would think that bad, worn-out ones cost even more. Yours has evidently seen some use."

"You're right about that."

The cuirass of Harry's heavy-duty armor had once displayed a painted motto, long since totally obliterated. There had been an image also, but only the outline of a winged shape was faintly visible. The symbols once so clear had been so drastically defaced by fire and impact that no one could read them anymore. Next time he had a design, a decoration, put on anything—if he survived long enough for there to be a next time—he was going to keep it simple.

He could tell that Lily in her nearby chair was looking at the display. But she made no comment.

Harry said; "I once had some high-flying ideas."

"And now you don't?"

Harry grunted. "Can't afford 'em."

Lily said: "I think high-flying ideas are like good suits."

Harry didn't answer that. His hand strayed, as if unconsciously, to the coveralls pocket where he had stowed away the message from Esmerelda. But right now there was no time to spare for interruptions.

One of the gung-ho young Templars had turned his chair around and was looking curiously at the small display. "I never saw armor like that."

"Count yourself lucky," Harry grunted.

Turning off the image of the suit, he buried himself in an intense concentration on his current task of astrogation. For the first time in days Harry felt at home. He was at home, and just being there put him a long step closer to feeling that all might yet be made right with the world.

But the process of making things right had a long way to go. There was no time to waste.

There was a big question that hadn't been answered yet: Just what big idea did the berserkers have in their warped optelectronic brains when a nasty knot of them went swarming to the far end of Maracanda? Their presence couldn't, it absolutely couldn't, be just a casual intrusion. However they had got there, it must have cost them and their sick-brained human helpers a considerable effort, and a lot of planning. They wouldn't have run such an elaborate operation just to pot a few small towns.

Harry got out the message cube holding his copy of the pilot's chart that Bulaboldo had so thoughtfully provided. By concentrating on printed matter, while he and the ship were sharing the right thoughtware mode, he could transfer the content directly to the *Witch*'s own data banks.

Harry needed only a few more moments to get the *Witch*'s bottom up and off from the Port City field, where not a single ship now remained. Lifting off, he noted how odd the broad expanse appeared when it was absolutely empty.

The *Witch* had not broken any speed records getting off the ground, but gauges showed that the breathable atmosphere had fallen away below the ship with what seemed unnatural suddenness, compared to the slow thinning that normally occurred when you lifted off from a planet.

Up into space, on a comparatively short arc, only a few hundred klicks, the shape of the orbital curve being very close to that of one end of an ellipse. Then back down, approaching the strange mottled sky from above, it looked almost like a layer of normal cloudy overcast, aiming more or less by instinct and estimate at where he supposed Tomb Town and its environs to be.

Now to find the unmarked and practically invisible entrance to the free-zone passage he required.

The approach system bombarded him with insistent warnings to stay away. He ordered the *Witch* to suppress that kind of message until further notice.

Getting his ship quickly up into space, at an altitude of about five hundred kilometers, he found himself well clear of the habitable body's more obvious peculiarities. By comparison, the local pulsar, and even the flame-fringed ebony of hurtling Ixpuztec, the black hole, looked refreshingly normal. More to the point, none of the *Witch*'s probing senses, generally keen at this kind of work, could detect any sign of any enemy presence within ten million klicks or so.

Both Ixpuztec and Avalon, the neutron star, were visibly in

motion. Each body was tracing out a curving passage, in a movement that looked stately and slow. It was hard to escape the illusion that both were no more than a few kilometers away, moving at no more than a few kilometers per hour.

Scattered here and there throughout the inner system were elements, including General Pike's scoutship, of the modest defense force that had got off the ground.

Pike came on the communicator, the light-speed signal delayed by less than a minute, to tell Harry that the system's early warning apparatus, a largely automated setup, was still reporting no intrusion.

Rovaki had perhaps been listening in, for now a message came in from the Space Force commander, ordering Harry and the *Witch* to take over patrol duties in a certain region, in expectation of a strong berserker attack from space.

"Do you copy, *Witch of Endor*?"

"I seem to be having some trouble reading your transmissions" was Harry's answer.

The two Templars in his control room smiled faintly at seeing the rival authority thwarted. They trustingly had taken their helmets off, and for a moment Harry toyed with the idea of gassing them to sleep, just to get them out of his hair for a few minutes. Put them to sleep, then out the airlock with them. He'd put their helmets back on before throwing them out, being the nice guy that he was. Someone with a portable air supply might survive being thrown out into that strange sky, if tossed at slow speed and low altitude, bouncing from pseudocloud to pseudocloud, eventually down to the surface.

Lily's voice interrupted his ruminations. "I have the feeling you'd like to get all these authorities out of your hair, and just deal with berserkers in your own way." It seemed that she could almost tell what he was thinking, and there weren't many who could do that.

Harry shook his head. "The idea's tempting, but I'm not sure I'm big enough to handle them all by myself."

"The authorities?"

"No, I meant the berserkers."

"At least you don't have them right here on your ship."

"The berserkers?"

"No, I meant the authorities."

Looking at each other, they shared an almost silent chuckle. Then on impulse Harry said: "If your husband was still here, I might gas him."

Lily wasn't sure just how to answer that. But she wanted to laugh, and finally gave in. "Should I lie down on the deck, captain? Save myself a fall?"

"This time, kid, you'll get the nose spray first."

The pair of Templars, hearing only the laugh, looked suitably mystified.

Then for a time Harry had to forget everything else, and, with the help of Bulaboldo's patented Smuggler's Guide, concentrate on weaving a tricky course through the topmost layer of the spectacular Maracandan "sky," gradually working the *Witch* closer to the ground. From this altitude, the habitable area was still optically invisible, hidden beneath the mounded grayish matter of the sky.

What could be seen of the uninhabitable regions looked every bit as inhospitable as it truly was, while even the overall shape of Maracanda seemed to change, depending heavily on the observer's distance.

Instruments told a somewhat different story, and there Harry saw some indications that the ground defenses, such as they were, were tuning up for action.

Seen from this altitude and position, Maracanda was like something from an evolving dream, a dream that might sometime develop into beauty, and not necessarily evil. There seemed to be no pinning it down, as to what was really there. Not only the colors and contours, but the very size of the habitable body varied, moved, and shifted, even while Harry watched. He could no longer be sure which end of this turning object humanity called east and which end west. He had to trust that somewhere in the *Witch*'s vast opt-electronic brain were circuits somehow capable of keeping track.

It was Harry's job to guide his ship away from the designated and approved flight paths, while trying not to provoke any nervous reaction by the ground defenses. While an alert was on, special rules might be in effect—or some routine rules might be relaxed.

Harry's next task, even more difficult, was to nurse the *Witch* through the nearly impossible passage back to the vicinity of Tomb Town. To simply grope his way along, without the guidance of Bulaboldo's plan, would have been hopeless. He was going to have to trust the chart worked out by the insatiable curiosity of little flying robots.

Maracanda seen from this distance in space was not as flat as the habitable region below the clouds. Instead, the whole body was rather football-shaped. He couldn't see the expanse of habitable surface, which seemed so flat when he was on it, nor could he guess just where it might lie.

Harry would have liked to send a little flying probe, like the one Bulaboldo had used to chart the passage, ahead of the *Witch* to mark her way. But he had nothing of the kind available.

Under these strange conditions, a flight of a thousand or two thousand kilometers, only a few minutes' quick cruise in ordinary atmosphere, might keep a pilot busy for an hour or more.

Maneuvering his ship through the small apertures in the various atmospheric layers had to be done with excruciating care, even if Bulaboldo had somehow managed to provide him with a kind of guide.

There were places where the ship's movement had to be accomplished in centimeters rather than meters. Once Harry made a wrong choice, and had to back the *Witch* very slowly out of a tight spot, feeling his way like an elephant performing on a high wire. Once the ship's flank just brushed the sharply defined, invisible boundary between zones. Through the pilot's thought-ware, Harry sensed the tremor of irresponsibility go shivering through programming and hardware alike. Half a meter more in the wrong direction, and the *Witch* could have gone plunging down, systems cascading into failure, her engines as well as her optelectronic brain totally disabled.

Minutes passed, the time elapsed since leaving the space-port dragged out to an hour. How many more people could ten or twenty berserkers kill in an hour?

But meter by meter, minute by minute, the real habitable surface was creeping closer. The lowest layer of the sky was breached, and the eerie landscape where humans worked and fought came into view at last.

Harry swore a heartfelt oath. "Got it. Got it at last." And Lily said: "All *right*!"

Through cleared ports Harry could watch a broad expanse of the peculiar hills, bathed in the strange light that was only natural on Maracanda, but never did look quite natural to an Earth-descended human. It was almost impossible to judge by sight the distance of the alien landscape. First the hills were a little bit below, then they came gently up on all sides as the *Witch*, on autopilot, straightened out her slow descent to come down precisely on her tail.

Looking out through cleared statglass ports, Harry could see the stripes Bulaboldo had drawn on the ground to mark the landing spot for him.

···········

TWENTY

···········

"**R**eassuring," said Lily at Harry's side. "I mean that Kul's taken the trouble to mark the spot for us."

"Yeah. But I wish he hadn't made it look so much like a bull's-eye."

The free-hand stripes of paint had not been much affected yet by the creeping neatness and regularity of the Maracandan landscape, so Harry guessed they were probably less than a day old.

Lily burst out with a question. "Are you getting into Bulaboldo's business, Harry?" A moment later she tried to call it back. "None of my business if you do."

Harry, his mind busy with half a dozen other things, didn't answer. He watched as the painted pattern neatly disappeared under the ship's hull. A moment later the precise voice of the autopilot reported that the *Witch* was safely down, and all onboard equipment was functioning.

Harry nodded at the two Templars, who had been staring at him earnestly, constrained by their own officer's orders to wait for a go signal from the ship's captain. In another second Teagarden and Zhong were both up and out of their chairs.

Now the *Witch* was reporting in her unemotional voice that conditions outside the hull seemed nominal for unshielded human activity.

"That's what you think," Harry murmured. He was still in his seat.

"Comment not understood." That was about as close as the *Witch* could ever come to reprimanding her boss.

"Let it pass."

Teagarden and Zhong, gripping their carbines in what Harry supposed was the position currently approved in combat training, and obviously keyed up to hurl themselves into battle, were already standing in front of the hatchway leading to the main air-lock. They were practically crouching in their armor, like sprinters on the mark. Now that they were out of the way, Harry climbed out of his combat chair, motioning for Lily to remain in hers.

"You two," he told the Templars on radio, "don't go out till I can join you. First I have to get my armor on. It'll take one minute."

The corporal looked back at Harry and away again, and that was all the response the captain got. The ship was on the ground again, and what its pilot might want no longer counted. The Templars were intent on their own businesslike preparations, and it seemed they might not have heard him.

Standing beside his chair, Harry turned up the volume of his voice. "Hey! You two know anything about breakdown zones?"

His shout got Corporal Teagarden to turn his head. "Just open the hatch for us, Harry, and you stay on the ship. We've been on Maracanda as long as you have." The corporal was crisply giving orders. No more Mr. Silver. No more "captain," now that the ship had landed. The corporal's voice was stern, and sounded ready for an argument.

Lily was shaking her head, but wisely kept her mouth shut. Harry sighed. There was no time for this. Sometimes he wished he had a diplomatic nature. He said to the Templars: "All right. It'll open for you when you give the word. But wait for me before you get aggressive with anything out there."

He thought maybe Private Zhong gave him a slight nod of agreement. They were busy mumbling ritual to each other, running through some final checklist, or engaged in some last, futile effort to communicate with their officers on the other side of the world; Harry wasn't even sure they heard what he was saying to them.

Taking one more look around the control room, he had a word with the *Witch*, and then stepped down through a hatch in the deck that opened accommodatingly for him just as his foot reached it.

Over his shoulder he told Lily she had better run the checklist once more on the suit she had put on at the beginning of the flight and make sure her helmet was patched in to the copilot's controls. She acknowledged briskly.

Now he was standing, alone, in the small, well-lighted chamber that he thought of as the armory. The *Witch* had the special suit unpacked and waiting for him, laid out in segments, and in a moment Harry was getting a good start on putting it on over his flight coveralls.

Twenty additional seconds had passed when Harry's ship told him that the Templars were on their way out the main hatch, which the ship tidily remembered to close behind them. At the same time she showed him what was happening on the armory's small wallscreen.

The *Witch*'s smooth voice said: "The Templars have ordered

me to pass on to you certain instructions from them. Do you wish to hear these words?"

"Instructions. Telling me what I'm supposed to do." His hands kept working, fastening, sealing seams and joints.

"Affirmative. You are instructed to hold the ship in readiness for—"

"Never mind. Can it. When I catch up with 'em, I'll tell them what they can do with their—What was that?" Harry struggled to his feet, half clad in heavy armor.

It had sounded like the impact of a single round, some kind of small arms fire, whanging off the forcefield shielding of the outer hull.

Harry demanded: "Let me hear outside noises, *Witch*. Did that one do any damage?"

"Negative." The *Witch* seemed to take a moment's thought. Then she advised imperturbably: "But there is good evidence of combat in the immediate vicinity." For another moment the out-of-doors in the immediate vicinity seemed quiet, in the usual spooky Maracanda fashion. Then there were a couple more shots, but nothing hit the ship. Whoever was shooting, that one had probably been a stray, intended for some other target.

One ineffective round did not indicate an actual berserker attack, Harry told himself, hurrying to get the remaining components of his suit in place. Harmless sniping with light weapons was not that enemy's stock in trade—unless they were doing it as a trick, which was entirely possible.

More likely, he thought, some goodlife who were truly in love with death had taken a shot at the two combat infantrymen as soon as their suited figures appeared at the top of the landing ramp. But Harry wasn't going to sweat the details, not as long as no one he was concerned about got hurt.

Bulaboldo and his people, Harry thought, would be too smart to try anything like that with armored soldiers, but then, thinking over the recent behavior of Dietrich and Redpath, he was not so sure.

"*Witch*, can you patch me into the Templars' radio?"

Probably the ship had been anticipating that order, for accomplishing it took only a moment. But when Harry tried to talk to the pair of warriors, the only response was an answering yell, sternly admonishing him in effect to be a good civilian and hold the ship in readiness for their return.

When he tried to repeat a warning, he realized they had tuned him out.

"Shall I attempt to force a communication?" Harry's ship asked him. If Zhong and Teagarden were somewhere near the ship, the *Witch* could probably make their helmets vibrate.

"No, let it go."

He hated to think what kind of a mess was probably developing out there. But Harry wasn't going to stick his nose outside the airlock until he was as buttoned into his armor as he could get.

Getting the suit on and checked out had probably taken him less than a full minute. He wasn't sure, but he thought he might have set some kind of personal record.

The moment the last fastening of his heavy suit had sealed itself shut, Harry scrambled back up into the control room, moving lightly and swiftly on fully powered limbs.

"Sounds like the shooting's started up again," Lily remarked. Her knuckles were white, gripping the arms of the copilot's chair, but she didn't sound anywhere near terrified, and that was good.

"Doesn't sound like the kind we have to worry about," Harry assured her. "Must be only a few crazy people." Even as he moved he was checking out his alphatrigger carbine. The weapon was in satisfactory condition, fully charged from the fusion lamps of the *Witch*'s main drive. Harry kept it loaded for berserker, and one force packet from its muzzle ought to hit hard enough to stop a runaway groundcar in its treadmarks.

With the *Witch* obediently bringing in outside sounds, Harry could hear some yells, then a staccato burst of gunfire.

"Ship, see if you can get me some kind of connection with Bulaboldo. You know who I mean?"

"Order understood."

It took only another moment, but the connection turned out poor, audio only, with quite a bit of static. No doubt the smugglers had been concentrating on hiding even their electronic presence from the berserkers.

Harry said: "I'm back! Anybody home? Are you people all right?"

In reply he got one shadowy glimpse of Bulaboldo's face, and a vaguely reassuring answer. A couple of words, sounding choked with some kind of emotion.

Crossing the control room in half-adjusted armor, Harry tried once more to force through a radio signal, a last caution, a plea to wait, to his two temporary shipmates.

All he got in return was a few curt words about avoiding unnecessary radio activity. That was followed by terse orders directing him to stay on the ship and hold it ready for liftoff.

"Have you got that, Silver?" Teagarden must have been practicing his command presence since he made corporal.

Harry didn't bother to reply.

He made the last few adjustments on his way back to the main hatch, during one stretch hopping on one foot for a few steps.

He detoured by two steps, to stop just beside the copilot's seat, where he rested the fingers of one armored gauntlet gently on Lily's arm. "You going to be all right? Yeah, sure you are."

Her eyes were luminous inside her statglass helmet. There was fear in them, of course, but along with the fear was something else, something personal, that Harry didn't want to see just now, let alone think about.

Lily said: "I could come out with you." She made it sound like something she really wanted to do.

"Definitely not. What I need you to do is stay here and run the ship—if and when something needs to be done. The autopilot recorded our route in here, and it'll be the only route to get the ship out. So rely on the *Witch* if and when the time comes for a retreat."

"Not without you!"

"I hope not. But if more machines than you can handle turn up from somewhere, I don't think that's likely."

"They'd better not. Dammit all to hell, Harry, you take care of yourself! Let the Templars do all the brave deeds. That's what they get paid for."

Once more Lily sounded as if she really meant what she was saying, and the tone of her voice made Harry turn back just as he was starting away. He asked: "You know how to use the thought-ware to hook yourself into the ship's armament?"

Lily shook her helmeted head. "Told you once before, no gunnery training."

"Hook yourself in, anyway, as best you can. It's simple enough, and maybe not too dangerous. Then, if berserkers come in sight, use everything the *Witch* has got."

"Well, I won't be digging out your secret weapon. We used up the last c-plus round a while back, as I recall."

"So we did." Harry put a finger very gently under her chin, lifted slightly, trying for emphasis. "Whatever else happens, don't let them take the ship!"

"Order understood."

Approaching the inner airlock door, Harry reminded himself that he would have to be particularly careful when he got outside. The bad machines were not the only danger here; anyone who strayed into a breakdown zone with heavy armor on would be a dead duck. With all its powered components paralyzed, the suit would turn very quickly into a death trap. Just moving the heavy limbs would be next to impossible for the occupant, but he wouldn't have long to worry about that, as his breathing would be cut off, too.

The *Witch* was able to pirate signals for him during his fast passage through the airlock. Communication between the two Templars was meant to be scrambled, but thanks to his own ship's efforts, Harry heard scraps clearly.

"One tin man in sight," the private was barking to the corporal.

Tin man, by all the howling gods! They'd made real contact with the enemy. Harry felt his throat start to constrict. He wanted to bark orders at the two kids, but then he thought it was too late for that, they wouldn't listen anyway, and he'd better not distract them.

As soon as the lock's outer door sighed open, Harry spotted first one dead human body and then another, both unarmored and now lying unattended, within a few meters of the ship. They had been two young men. Light weapons lay beside them.

There was some satisfaction in the fact that Harry could recognize the nearest corpse as one of the goodlife who'd been shooting at him before his flight to the west. *Enthusiastic goodlife, come face to face at last with the god they worshiped.*

More Templar chirpings came through on radio. The enthusiastic tone of their voices frightened Harry. Having blown away a couple of stupid fanatic humans, no great trick for armored infantry, the newly minted soldiers doubtless felt themselves world-beating conquerors.

Tin man in sight. Gods of all space.

If giving the Templars orders wasn't going to work, if that would only start an argument, then maybe, Harry thought, he should try asking. That was what the reasonable people that he knew often recommended.

As Harry moved quickly down the landing ramp, he got his ship to hook him into Templar radio, and tried. "Will you people wait for me? I want to be on hand when you get killed." Even as he spoke, he knew that wasn't exactly the right way to put it. He also knew their berserker opponent might well be listening in, but that could not be helped.

Almost before Harry could set foot on Maracandan soil, another oversized figure came practically leaping out at him, darting around the bulk of the ship from its far side. It was a shape that Harry had been more or less expecting to encounter, but even so he came near blasting it.

Bulaboldo was encased in his own version of heavy armor and evidently beside himself with joy, because the vessel that he thought of as his ship had actually come in. Kul had a carbine slung on his back, but both arms were full of something else, a sack so heavy that it made the big man wobble as he ran, despite his powered suit. In passing Harry noted that Kul's armor seemed to be of excellent quality. The smuggler's suit, of a practical camouflage coloring that changed subtly as you looked at it, showed no visible signs of wear or damage.

Harry got the impression that the bulky one had almost given up hope, though Bulaboldo wasn't going to admit it. In his excitement he could barely restrain himself from pounding Harry on his armored back.

Kul's voice came smoothly through the open communication beam as he wrestled his bag of grit into a handier position and started for the ship's entry ramp. "I knew you could do it, old sod! I had no doubt at all—but time for felicitations later. We must begin our loading."

Harry glared at him. "Take shelter aboard if you like, but

leave that bag of shit outside. And don't even think of trying to touch any controls on board. My copilot's in command."

"Of course, dear lad! Whatever you say." Instantly Bulaboldo turned away from the ramp, and the bag slid from his shoulder to hit the ground.

The smuggler had yielded with suspicious willingness, but there wasn't time to fret about that now. Harry demanded: "Which way did the Templars go?"

Kul raised a heavy arm to point in the direction where he had once told Harry a cave lay hidden. "Your two saints in suits have followed that path, whether to death or glory I'm not sure. Likely both. Either way, they're out of sight. Listen, Harry, if you could only consider allowing us to load at least a few samples, we could decide later—"

Lil's voice reached him from inside the ship. "Harry, can I give you any support from in here?"

"Not yet. But keep your eyes open."

Kul's eyebrows had gone up behind his faceplate. "Ah, there is in truth a copilot. So, the lady came back with you! Must say I wasn't expecting her. And the husband?"

Harry was staring down the path the Templars must have followed. There would be no use trying to move his ship in that direction; the chart had clearly shown the ground-hugging channels of free zone were too narrow. Harry pointed that way, toward the small, steep-sided hills standing north of Bulaboldo's claim. "Where's that cave you were talking about? Just over there?"

"Yes, dear lad. And I believe one berserker also, a nasty sentry type. But you should leave the dirty work to the Templars, old darling. They *enjoy* such things. That's what they're *for!*"

"What else is over that way? What've you seen?"

Kul went on to hurriedly explain that on his earlier scouting expeditions he had gone just far enough in that direction to catch a glimpse of the cave entrance and spot some traces of human presence on the ground. After that, all the smugglers had stayed prudently away. Someone was working over there, and whether their project was legitimate or illegitimate, it was certain that they would not welcome visitors.

The smuggler seemed to be thinking that as soon as Harry got what he considered his duty out of his system, the sooner they could lift off. And Harry's absence would allow time for some loading.

In the meantime, Bulaboldo must have given some kind of signal, for several of his remaining helpers, daring to appear without special armor, came into view, staggering as they walked, bearing sacks of grit. At Kul's crisp orders they dropped their burdens on the ground, where they could be quickly loaded on the ship as soon as Harry gave approval.

But Harry wasn't listening. Stubby carbine cradled in his right arm, he was loping away from the smugglers, hoping to catch up with the two gung-ho Templar training graduates before they met disaster. At the moment Teagarden and Zhong were not having much to say, not even to each other.

Despite the heavy armor's bulk, a man could run a lot faster with its help than without it. The path took Harry around the corner of a sharply geometric cliff, out of sight of the ship. Lily would not be able to offer him any support, even if he trusted her to work the weapons.

TWENTY-ONE

Before he had taken a dozen more strides, what sounded like a real firefight burst out not far ahead, gunblasts blurring briefly into a continuous roar.

Harry ran faster, the power in the suit's legs giving him gazelle-like speed. He kept reminding himself that he should be in no immediate danger of running into a breakdown zone, not just here. Because the Templars had made it this far, and a little farther on, Private Zhong's tin man was walking.

Crouching, Harry rounded a corner of sharply angled Maracandan rock and came in sight of the cave entrance Bulaboldo had mentioned, a dark, broad hole. Harry was just in time for the end of the fight the two Templars had been making, though he couldn't see it clearly. The echoing racket of heavy shoulder weapons had died away, the dust of the latest chain of explosions still hung in the mild air, over the sides of a couple of steep, almost pillarlike Maracandan hills, just forcibly remodeled.

Another burst of gunfire rang, and suddenly Harry's helmet radio was squawking, with a desperate call for help. He couldn't tell whether the voice was Teagarden's or Zhong's.

Harry kept his answer short, in the tone of a cautious reprimand: "My orders are to remain on the ship." Maybe the damned thing would hear that, maybe it would even believe it.

The Templar's words broke off in screams, and the screams trailed off, then came back, at lower volume . . . only to fade again.

Harry eased his way along until he could see the entire cave mouth, a roughly triangular opening quite big enough to drive a freight hauler into. Not that there were any vehicles in sight at the moment.

He still had not seen a berserker, but abruptly enemy fire was being directed at him, and he jumped for better shelter. The outer layer of weird Maracandan designer rocks on the steep hillside above Harry's head dissolved in a roaring rain of chunks and powder, head-sized lumps cascading down on his heavy armor. The slide of debris would have pulped an unprotected man, but only nudged his suited body slightly off balance as he moved.

Peering round another rocky edge, Harry caught got one quick glimpse of a moving object fifty meters or so away, the leg and foot of a berserker, definitely of anthropomorphic shape, darting across a gap between large rocks, just outside the cave. Very fast, as always when they wanted to move fast. Still, he thought there had been something jerky in this one's movements, a hint of awkwardness. Just one glimpse and it was gone, behind a rock. The sight sent a brief electric jolt down Harry's spine. It was the same feeling he had had out on the edge of the Thisworld system, when the little red dot came on the holostage.

Adjusting his position carefully, a step at a time, exercising patience, Harry eased up to another corner, and presently was able to get a somewhat better look at his opponent. He saw the two-legged shiny body with bulging shoulder turrets above its arms appear momentarily at about the same range as before, then quickly vanish again between two small hills.

This time Harry was sure there had been something a little odd, a little off balance, about the way it moved. The thing looked a trifle awkward—for a berserker. So, one of the Templars must have hit it, Harry thought. Hit it once, at least. If it hadn't been damaged already, it might still be too fast for Harry to even get a look at it.

There was no longer any radio signal from the Templars at all. Not even noise. Harry was afraid to discover just what had happened to his two allies and all their top-notch equipment. But it was essential that he know.

Slowly and cautiously Harry continued to advance. Soon he could see the exposed area where one of the Templars, Teagarden he thought, was lying, his armored suit all crumpled in a little heap. It took Harry a little longer to make out what was left of Zhong. The private was clearly dead, sprawled amid a messy rearrangement of his own internal organs, with fragments of his equipment scattered around him, in the middle of the flat open space immediately before the entrance to the cave. Obviously whatever version of Space Force gear these lads had been issued had not been heavy enough. Not at close range and against the real enemy.

Corporal Teagarden was suddenly back on radio, sounding as if he must be on his last gasp. He reported that the berserker machine was definitely damaged.

Harry muttered something back, while his eyes kept probing for the enemy.

"Silver, is that you? Silver, I hit it once." The poor wretch sounded proud.

"Great. You can relax, corporal. Take it easy now, you've put in a good day's work." Harry thought that was probably halfway true, and he was trying to be nice. Damn it, why couldn't he say anything that sounded right?

"Zhong? Where's Zhong?" The corporal's voice seemed to be failing steadily.

"Private Zhong's discharge came through. He's cleared the base already."

Teagarden still had something else he wanted talk about, between gurgles, but Harry didn't suppose that hearing it would do him any good. He had to consider the geometry of the situation. Harry himself and the two Templars were all within thirty or forty meters of each other, with their single opponent a slightly greater distance away, closer to the entrance to the cave.

Scattered around among the little geometric hills there were a lot of geometric rocks, many of them big enough for man or machine to hide behind, which made the tactical problem interesting. Harry, edging his way slowly round the side of a sheltering rock, got the muzzle of the carbine up in place and then took his time looking things over.

Neither Templars nor berserker were going anywhere in the immediate future. Not unless the berserker, which could still move faster than a man, even a man in armor, decided to retreat back into the cave. But retreating did not appear to be what it was programmed for.

Teagarden was back on radio, doing what he could to pass on information. The dying Templar was insisting that he and his comrade had seen only one berserker here.

"There's only one of them, Silver. Only one."

"Yes, that's good, corporal. Over and out."

"Be careful, Silver. Be careful. Oh God."

"Yeah, I will be. Thanks."

There was no way of knowing how many machines the two novices might have missed. As far as Harry could tell from his own observation, there was still only one guarding the cave mouth, and it didn't appear to have any weapons heavier than Harry's. So far it was winning against the human competition, but that could be put down to speed and skill.

Harry confirmed this when he caught another glimpse of the berserker, as it darted into what it must have computed as a better position. It might strongly suspect that there was now only one human opposing it, but it couldn't know that for sure. That thought gave Harry the beginnings of an idea.

In the course of its last movement, Harry had got his best look at the thing yet. He could see that the left side of its torso had been blasted open, right where the lower ribs would have been on a human. The metal leg on that side appeared to be dragging slightly.

He slammed the carbine's stock against the automatic clamp on the right shoulder of his suit. What he needed now was reliable speed, not firing-range safety. He switched to alphatriggering mode and clipped the sighting mechanism on the side of his helmet. From that position the gunsight would track a reflection of Harry's pupils and aim faithfully along his line of vision, ninety-nine times out of a hundred hitting the exact spot of anything that he was looking at. Now he would be able to aim and fire almost instantaneously while keeping both hands free.

A sudden movement between rocks, and the alphatriggered carbine stuttered and flared, spitting armor-piercing packets of force. But the thing must have seen Harry at practically the same time, for it was elsewhere when his fire arrived, safe by a handful of milliseconds. And shooting back. One blasting roar after another. More shattered rock, more fragments flying at bullet speeds. Some of the gravel was taking long seconds to fall back to the ground, making a prolonged pattering.

Behind the spot where the berserker had been standing yawned the broad, dark entrance to the goodlife cave. What in all the hells had the machines and their playmates been doing in there? Why was it guarded now? But questions would have to wait.

When the dust from the latest barrage had settled, Harry could see that the cave entrance was marginally wider than it had been a few seconds ago. The inside was still a great void of darkness, except now he could see that the darkness was spotted in the middle distance by some kind of electric lights. The sight reminded him that he didn't want to be still engaged in this fight when whatever strange powers ruled on Maracanda decided it was time for darkness to fall again.

His thought kept coming back to the question of what could possibly be inside the cave. There had to be something that the enemy thought it necessary to guard. The whole berserker presence on Maracanda was obviously quite limited. Yet one very capable fighting machine, instead of being sent out ravening to slaughter whatever life it could find, had been kept here solely to defend this spot. Evidently the guardian of the cave had not even located Bulaboldo's hideout nearby, and that could only be because it had not gone looking. It must be constrained to remain right here, on sentry duty, just on the chance that some intruder might come by.

So the enemy must have a lot invested, in one way or another, in whatever the sentry had been detailed to guard.

Harry murmured a curse at the unpleasant way the universe in general kept turning out to be organized. The curse was followed immediately by a muttered blessing on the two Templar idiots, one of whom still breathed and groaned. If Teagarden and Zhong hadn't insisted on launching their all-out attack before Harry came to help, he would now be facing an undamaged fighting machine with lots of charge left in its power pack. He would also be enjoying the benefit of two live and energetic idiots as allies, certain to be shouting orders at him and getting in his way. They might very easily have got him killed along with themselves.

But never mind what might have been. Concentrate on the job at hand.

Peering slowly round an edge of rock, wishing he could somehow have equipped his suit with a little periscope to use at times like this, Harry studied the situation.

At unpredictable, irregular intervals the berserker would dart from one rocky place of shelter to another, methodically maneuvering to find the best position from which to kill him. It was armed with a carbine-type weapon, not much different from Harry's, except the machine's would be built right into it, in the form of a small turret on each shoulder. There were two arms and hands, all of an anthropomorphic model, to facilitate the operation of human-made tools and ships and weapons, if and when the thing got a chance to do that.

Experience also made Harry wonder if the berserker could be keeping something in reserve, maybe some kind of a grenade to launch with one of its almost human-looking arms.

Of course it could.

Harry fired again at the silver shape as it went flashing between rocks, and had no better success than before.

What was it going to do?

If it ran out of ammo, of charge-power for its weapon, it might play dead and try to draw him near. It wasn't going to come charging out of the cave even if it calculated it could kill him that way.

Without putting itself in Harry's view, the berserker fired several rounds close to the Templar who still breathed, but missed the killing shot deliberately. Harry thought, What was the point of that? All he could imagine was that the machine was probably trying to bring its human opponent running out of cover in response to the renewed screams of the dying man.

Yeah, that was the kind of altruistic thing that humans might sometimes do. But Harry wasn't having any.

Looking at the other mangled Templar body, the dead man in the open space, Harry caught himself listening for the buzz of flies. But there were no insects on Maracanda—he wondered if there were even any germs. Berserkers might find a lot to love about Maracanda. There wasn't going to be a germ left in the whole Galaxy if the machines had their way.

Harry thought he would rather have germs get him than the damned machines.

The berserker had gone silent and immobile for almost a full minute. He thought he knew just where it was, but he could be wrong. They could be as patient as rocks, once they computed that was the best tactic to employ.

Harry knew his enemy's sight and hearing were at least as keen as his own when he was using all the help his suit could give him. And the berserker's reflexes were faster.

Gunfighting a berserker, one that knew at least approximately where you were trying to stay hidden, was not the surest way to make a long-term contribution. Harry thought that maybe the smart thing for him to do would be to get back to his ship, if he could manage to traverse that path without getting killed, and try to find some new way to help the cause. But he wasn't going to do that—the reason seemed to have something to do with Zhong and Teagarden.

All right, then, he was going to fight it out here, one of him against one of it. About all Harry really had going for him was the big hole in the machine's side. The hole was as wide as the span of a man's hand, but he thought probably not very deep. Most of what had been torn and blasted away was armor. But that wound wasn't going to kill it, not unless he could put another packet right in there.

Still silence, immobility. Had it decided to play dead and try to fake him into approaching it?

Harry had to assume that by now the enemy was doing its best to try to listen to his radio. Of course, if it came to a duel of optelectronic communications, the *Witch* ought to be able to prevail over one machine of only this berserker's size.

Unless her master told her otherwise.

Casually Harry got on the communicator. "Lily. Got a message for the ship." After her terse acknowledgment, Harry spoke three words in a different language, and a moment later the *Witch* confirmed that the coded signal had been received. The idea was to allow the enemy to listen in on Harry's next communication.

After letting a few seconds pass, Harry called again, and when Lily answered, told her where to direct the reinforcements when they came. There was a clever woman for you. She caught on quickly and didn't ask just who he thought he might be expecting.

Now it was Harry's turn to begin to play the silent, waiting game. He was going to see if he could do it better than a machine. If the berserker had really heard him that last time. If it would allow itself to be convinced that human help was probably on the way. If it should compute its best chance of defending the cave lay in emerging from its shelter to try to kill its current opponent before he was reinforced.

Once more the enemy shuttled between rocks, too fast for Harry to react.

Then it made another dash, doubtless trying to provoke him into moving also. His eyes picked out the dark wound disfiguring the darting target's flank. Harry willed destruction. His carbine's gunsight read the pinpoint target of his gaze, the weapon aimed itself, the almost weightless packets streamed out of the muzzle faster than bullets.

Fractionally slowed down as it was, the berserker could not dodge this time. Impacts pounded home, the first blast on metal, tearing armor, staggering the enemy, the second freezing it momentarily in place. Then a third, deep into the old wound. The flare of a secondary explosion splashed light across the jagged landscape. The metal body, torn nearly in half, was flung away from the cave entrance, tumbling in the open, somewhere between the two men it had killed.

Harry stepped out into the clear before the flying shape came down. Standing where he had a clear line of fire, he pumped packet after packet singly into the lifeless metal, one impact hurling the maimed puppet back into the air, another smashing it against the broken geometry of the cliffside. A third and a fourth tore it to pieces before it could fall back to Maracandan soil.

There was little left of the berserker machine but tumbling fragments, sparks dying in the dusty atmosphere. Nothing anywhere but burning wreckage, no piece bigger than a human hand or foot.

"Harry?" Lily's voice came from the ship. "*Harry?*" At last she sounded like she might be cracking with the strain.

"I'm all right. Just shut up a minute."

He had heard something else, something that made him stand and listen. Turning up his airmikes' sensitivity, he waited for his own breathing to quiet, and listened very carefully.

Cautiously he moved to a new position, still keeping a barricade of rock between himself and the cave entrance. There might, after all, be one more bandit somewhere in there. Then, with his carbine ready, he moved closer to the cave's mouth.

His airmikes told him there were faint sounds coming from inside, faint sounds as of another pair of human lungs.

TWENTY TWO

Keeping a sharp eye out, Harry advanced step by step to the very threshold of the cave. Deep inside, thirty or forty meters ahead, the discreet lights that he had noticed earlier still burned, making modest pools of illumination in front of and around mysterious equipment whose purpose the intruder could not yet guess. The moaning sounds were coming from somewhere in the same vicinity.

Harry's view of the area was partially blocked by squarish intervening objects, and he saw that he was facing the back of a row of high crates and cabinets that formed a rough partition across most of the width of the cave.

The pummeling Harry's armor had absorbed from falling rocks and glancing shots had started up some stray vibrations in his suit so that the arms and legs were taking turns in palsied quiverings. Inside his helmet and its forcefield pads, his ears still rang. He hoped and expected that, given a little time, his gear could readjust itself to deal with these several problems. Meanwhile, he could still see and hear and walk. He could fire the carbine again if he had to. He only hoped he could still hit something.

It was almost as if his quivering suit had suddenly turned coward on him. Before turning his back on what was left of the berserker, Harry instinctively gave the ruin one more careful look, just making sure the bits and pieces were now harmless. In the past he had seen the damned berserkers do too many wonderful and horrible things to ever feel safe in the presence of one of them, even when it had been torn apart. Maybe after the remains had been thoroughly gone over by human experts and their tools, and then mounted in a museum for about a year. And even then Harry thought he would be cautious.

Before advancing any farther, he also glanced once more at each of the fallen Templars. No, there wasn't any doubt. They were both as dead as the berserker.

Having got in a few meters under the cave's roof, Harry paused, aware that he needed a breathing space, just to pull himself together. Automatically he ran a checklist on his suit and weapon and felt reasonably satisfied with the result. The vibrations were slowly damping down. He didn't need to take a fresh look at himself to know that the surface of his armor must be freshly scorched and scarred, and he thought it might be still glowing red in one place on his back. His helmet's small statglass faceplate, in nearly pristine condition when this little skirmish started, was going to need replacement before it took another shot.

But he had to give the lights and the equipment in the cave at least one quick look before he took time out for maintenance. One look, and then get right back to the *Witch.*

*   *   *

Meanwhile the sounds of breathing still kept on, indicating that someone else was still alive. Unless they were being made by some kind of recording, and that seemed stupid. If there was some living victim who could be rescued, that would be fine. But something more than that was driving Harry now, pushing him deeper into the cave: the nagging thought that if one of the berserkers' fighting machines had been programmed to do nothing but guard this place, then its contents must be of great importance to the enemy, might offer some means by which the death machines could be seriously hurt.

Very rarely would the damned machines keep anyone. alive. They always needed some especially bad reason for doing so. But the human whose lungs now labored up ahead was someone the berserkers wanted to keep breathing. Or, alternatively, it was only some wounded goodlife, whose metal masters had not yet got around to finishing off their faithful but worn-out servant.

Or there could be a third scenario: the sentry machine had been unable to leave its post for even a few seconds, the time it would have taken to go deeper into the cave and kill the stubborn breather off.

All three possibilities were interesting. Maybe, Harry thought, if a berserker's directing unit awarded it points for every death achieved, not many would be handed out for terminating a life that was almost over anyway.

Harry was moving again, stepping slowly and carefully, looking out in all directions for possible booby traps. He was well aware that there could also be some lurking berserker auxiliary machine, designed for something other than direct combat, but still ready to take a whack at any creature that moved and breathed and happened to come in range. Or there might be yet another goodlife here, one who wasn't dead or dying. Yes, there were all sorts of interesting possibilities.

Harry had reached the crude partition of crates and cabinets, and was passing through a gap in the uneven barrier. A standard, plain, plastic-paneled cabinet, doubtless housing a small hydrogen power lamp, stood against one of the cave's side walls. Just a piece of furniture you might see almost anywhere, in a mine or a home or a simple office. Just an ordinary power source keeping various kinds of equipment going, including a few modest electric lights that it seemed no one had bothered to turn off.

Having come this far, Harry could see that the illuminated portion of the cavern went back a long way, much farther than he would have guessed, maybe a hundred meters or even more. The surface of the rock in the remoter sections had a raw, shaved look, as if someone or something had worked on it intensively, sculpting what had begun as a natural fissure of some kind into a secret tunnel.

Already the land had begun the process of natural smoothing, almost healing, that seemed to follow any artificial deformation on this world. The final result was a tunnel of uniform diameter, wide enough to accommodate something even bigger than a pedicar, maybe half the diameter of Harry's *Witch*. Harry had to assume that the whole length of the tunnel lay in a free zone, for heavy, modern mining machinery must have been at work. Whoever or whatever had done the digging must have moved tons and tons of the fabric of Maracanda. Doubtless they had dumped the debris down a crevice somewhere, as there hadn't been any huge pile outside the cave.

Harry's sensitive airmikes were now beginning to pick up, along with the breathing and the moans, the words of someone weakly calling for help. He thought it sounded like a woman or a child, but he could not be sure.

Such of his suit's sensors as were still working informed him that, besides a human heart and lungs, several high-tech devices were still operating inside the cave. Subtle things, emitting their delicate purrs and whines. Listening carefully, Harry didn't think that any of them were actual berserkers. If another fighting machine was waiting to ambush him, he would probably never hear a thing.

He kept expecting the worst. But what he actually discovered, one after another, was a series of empty shipping containers, irregularly strewn about. He could see that a couple of them had been labeled in several places as MINING MACHINERY.

It seemed that other, similar crates had been broken up to make crude furniture. Even goodlife, Harry supposed, had to sleep somewhere, and had some use for chairs and tables.

Standing beside the electric lamp placed farthest from the entrance, he could see that at this point the new tunnel diverged from the natural cave, which here bent itself, in abrupt Maracandan fashion, diving sharply downward, beginning a precipitous descent to unknown depths. Probably, Harry thought, the material excavated from the new tunnel had been dumped down there. From here the new passageway still drove almost straight ahead, descending only on a much gentler slope. The last electric light threw its fading radiance along the straight tunnel that went on endlessly into darkness, starting to curve down more as it went deeper and farther. Neither the fixed lamp nor Harry's suit's headlamp, which fortunately had survived the fight, could show him what lay at the end.

Harry turned his head. For just a moment he thought he heard faint, mechanical sounds, coming from somewhere down the tunnel.

The sound was not repeated. Anyway, he had an investigation near at hand that might be more important. The sound of ragged human breathing, mixed with an occasional moan for help, had been growing nearer as Harry advanced. His sensitive airmikes enabled him to close in on the sounds, and now their source must be almost within reach.

Moving warily around a machine that might have been some kind of berserker device, but demonstrated its innocence by not attempting to mangle him as he stepped past, he could see what looked like a cell, part of some primitive jail, except that it seemed too small. Actually it was only a kind of cage, fashioned in a very low-tech way from another of the surplus shipping crates. An improvised door was fastened shut with a simple lock.

Harry peered in through the slats that served as bars. Inside the small crude cell, a ragged shape stirred, a head lifted from a simple pallet on the cave floor inside the cage.

A woman's voice croaked out: "I heard the shooting. Oh, thank God, thank God. You're . . . human."

"Last time I checked," said Harry with his airspeaker, thinking that a lot of people, seeing him in his suit, would probably have taken him for something else. "And as badlife as they come."

"Me, too." The woman turned painfully from her side to her back, holding up her right hand as if it might be hurt. Her long hair was matted, colorless with neglect and grime; her prospector's work clothes were dirty shreds. Sunken, fearful eyes looked out of a pasty face. Her voice sounded rusty, as if from lack of use. "Are they gone?" Then: "Are you alone?"

Harry was giving the cage a quick inspection for booby traps. "They're gone, for the time being anyway. And I'm not alone now, I'm with you. Might your first name be Emily?"

The woman nodded. It was hard to even guess her age. Tears were streaking her face. "My name is Kochi. Emily Kochi."

Harry nodded. "Dr. Kochi, people have been looking for you for several months."

The cage having passed its swift inspection, Harry took hold of the slats that made the door, and broke it open, an easy task for servo-powered arms.

"Don't touch my hand!" she warned him, holding it up carefully. He could see something wrong with a couple of the fingers, a bad bending and discoloring.

"I won't." Leaning into the cage to help the prisoner out, he cautioned: "And you be careful of my armor. The outer surface may still be very hot in places."

Fortunately, the waves of stray vibrations in the limbs of Harry's suit had run their course. By the time he had extracted Dr. Kochi from her cage, he could once again move his arms, and walk, without looking like a drunk or a case of some ancient nerve disease.

Dr. Kochi, the astrogeologist, had to crawl out of the cell to give herself room enough to stand. The victim was able to stand up, but only barely. Then she stumbled and had to lean on things. Harry gave her a drink of water after she pointed out where the supply was kept.

Presently Harry had got her moving back toward the exit from the cave, on the way to medical care. Fortunately it turned out that the front of his armor had cooled enough to touch human skin without scorching.

Meanwhile, the words, the revelations, once started came pouring out. Dr. Kochi was eager to start telling someone things she deemed of great, of terrible importance.

In her haste and confusion, the revelations came out only gradually, in the form of disconnected details. Slowly Harry was getting the picture, of some murderous plot created by the berserkers and their goodlife helpers.

Turning back toward the glow of daylight from the cave's mouth, taking what seemed a more direct route past the barrier of crates and boxes, Harry's attention was caught by a kind of mockup or simulation of the infernal device the bad machines were trying to create.

Not wanting to delay by even a few seconds, Harry paused only momentarily to look at the holostage model. Clearly it was a representation of Maracanda itself, revolving slowly in space.

The woman's voice was soft and weak. "This was for the goodlife to watch, you see. To inspire them. So the machine could show them what they were working toward, they could understand what the berserkers were trying to accomplish. One of those—those people—wanted to broadcast it somehow to all the people on Maracanda, once it was too late. So the people on Maracanda could understand, before they died, how many billions of others were going to die with them."

The images on the holostage abruptly shifted. Now the presentation was of another model, this one obviously representing the tripartite Maracandan system. One spot of ebony, backlighted with a flickering glow, plainly symbolized the black hole Ixpuztec, and a metallic-looking sphere, fringed with infalling radiance, was standing in for Avalon, the neutron star.

The trouble was that at first Harry couldn't make much sense out of it. Something about a great explosion.

The woman's vast relief at finding herself still alive, at being rescued, was turning into a new panic. The next thing she said was: "Somebody's got to do something. Interfere somehow and stop them."

"Slow down. Take it easy. It'll be all right now. What're you talking about? Where? Stop them from doing what?"

"Blowing up the world. This whole solar system." She paused a moment to take a breath, and then hit Harry with a stunner. "But that's only the start. Turning the pulsar into a hypernova. Within a hundred light-years there are a hundred inhabited systems, and they'll all be fried."

Harry stopped dead, thinking about that statement. He could only hope it was delirium. In a moment he had picked up Dr. Kochi, gently, and was carrying her at a brisk walk. "Come along. I'm going to get you back to my ship." He shifted her slightly in his arms, giving himself room to use the carbine if he had to.

"No, listen to me! I'm not crazy, I'm not!" She beat with her good hand on his armored chest. "I don't know if it'll work, this thing they're trying to do. But I'm afraid it might."

More words poured out, most of them making sense. She had been kidnapped while working alone out in the field, trying to discover the properties, fathom the nature, of breakdown zones, with a view to ultimately being able to do away with them. Or re-create them, in free space, as weapons and shields.

The people who kidnapped her had shown themselves to be strange, crazy villains, and when she had realized that they were goodlife, she had realized there would be no ransom, had given up hope of ever getting away from them alive. They served a machine, a terrible machine with a squeaking voice, that dwelt in this cave, and had asked her questions. The fact that it was not of human shape had only made it worse somehow.

But that was not exactly the kind of work the berserkers had wanted her to do for them.

Harry was jarred back into giving her his full attention. He had been fixated on what a neat weapon a breakdown zone would make if you could only throw it at your enemy. Find some way to get a berserker entangled in one.

"Then what?" he demanded.

"They wanted to know everything . . . about the interior of Maracanda. All about the subsurface layers of this world. Not the really deep ones. Maybe a hundred meters down. Before the dimensions really start to—go crazy. Oh, can I have more water, please?"

A pause for a swallow. "What they really focused on . . . There are deposits of antimatter down there. Ten, twenty metric tons sometimes, in one lump. Maybe even more. Shielded in magnetic pockets. Objects that just can't exist in our universe anywhere but here."

"Go on."

"They wanted to know how to excavate a lump of antimatter, bring it out intact, without inducing a landfall or an explosion. You might only have a half second's warning—without upsetting the balance of forces, and being crushed by ten thousand gravities. Above all, how it might be possible to dig one of those lumps out."

Meanwhile, Dr. Kochi kept on trying to explain things to Harry, elaborating on what she knew of the berserker plan. She was probably garbling some of it, and there was more that Harry couldn't have grasped even sitting in a classroom. But enough, more than enough, was coming through. The woman hadn't spoken half a dozen more sentences before Harry began to run, sweating anew inside his armor. Maybe this woman was crazy, but on the other hand maybe she was not. He had to get back to his ship.

Dr. Kochi was weeping in his arms. "I talked, I told them everything they wanted to hear. Gave them the right numbers, told them what computations to run on their computers. I couldn't help myself." As she neared the end of her story, the woman raised a quivering, grayish hand, to show Harry where the berserker, using irresistible strength and great delicacy of touch, had slowly torn out two of her fingernails.

"That's all over now. No one's blaming you for anything you told them." Harry certainly wasn't. He had seen what the bad machines could do to people, in their businesslike uncaring way, when they wanted information.

The berserker had conducted its own interrogation, ruthlessly and without wasting words. Skills gained in centuries of experience with human prisoners, knowledge passed on from one machine to another over the centuries, were efficiently brought to bear on this one.

"How come they left you still alive?"

"They told me there was only one reason. They still thought they might have to ask me more questions. One of the goodlife spelled that out for me. If their project didn't work on the first try. And there were things they were going to do to me, if it turned out I had been lying to them." The woman sobbed, and her voice changed. "But I didn't lie to them, I couldn't, I didn't have the guts. It told me that—that if I didn't tell—it would do something that would be much worse."

"That's all right, never mind that now. Meanwhile, we're on our way out of here. Before any of them come back."

"If their plan is working, they won't be coming back. But hurry, hurry anyway!"

Urgently Harry demanded of Dr. Kochi: "How much time do we have to stop them?"

"I don't know."

"How long ago did the berserkers leave you?"

But the prisoner couldn't say, with any accuracy. Her best guess was that it had probably been a couple of days ago. The machines and their helpers expected that the work of extracting the antimatter bundle from its natural site deep underground, and getting it out into space, would take at least a couple of days.

She was obviously in pain, faint and drifting in and out of consciousness, and Harry thought she might be feverish from an infection. There was no way she could tell the actual time when the enemy team of machines and humans had left the cave, taking their newly constructed space vessel with them. She had seen them pushing it along into the new tunnel, on some kind of improvised rails.

Her weak voice whispered on. "One of the goodlife wanted to go with it, ride it out into space, and right into the neutron star. But the machine said that wasn't going to be allowed."

"Yeah, yeah. Listen, Dr. Kochi—so it's possible that they could be launching this thing right now?"

The woman rolled her head from side to side. "That's what I'm trying to tell you. I'm afraid they are."

Harry was trying to be comforting. "Even if the radius of destruction from the supernova extended out for a hundred light-years, people would have years of warning. Decades of time to evacuate most of those planets—"

The woman drew in her breath sharply. "No. No, you don't understand. You don't know what a hypernova means."

Harry was calling ahead to his ship, telling Lily and the *Witch* to get the medirobot ready.

TWENTY THREE

"Are you wounded, Harry?"

"It's not for me." He explained in a few words, and Lily crisply acknowledged. The *Witch*'s own soft voice came on, promising to have the medirobot ready.

Emerging from the cave, carrying the rescued prisoner in his suit's tireless arms, he could think of no real alternative to bringing her aboard the *Witch*. The only other choice would be to leave her with Bulaboldo's smugglers. Harry's ship at least had a medirobot aboard, and it would afford the victim reasonable care. As soon as the *Witch* was back in space, in contact with the world, Harry meant to put the scientist on radio, to transmit her message of warning directly to the Space Force and Templars, and whatever scientific experts might be available to listen from Port City.

Harry was hoping that the patient would not pass out entirely until he had learned more. "Tell me about it as we go," he urged her. He was walking quickly past the casualties, human and otherwise, of the recent skirmish. The burden of one thin woman scarcely slowed down the armored suit at all. He said: "Tell me more about this plan of theirs that's going to destroy about half the Galaxy."

The woman's face looked horrible in the flat, overcast Maracandan daylight. She lay limp in the embrace of Harry's metallic arms, but her eyes were still open and she was shaking her head slowly from side to side. "No joke. I'm not crazy. You still don't understand. They mean to dig out a mass of several tons of antimatter, lift it into space, and drop it into the pulsar. If they can do that, the result will be worse than a simple supernova, much worse."

"How can it be much worse than destroying a whole solar system?"

"It can—it is." Dr. Kochi broke off, choking in her eagerness to speak.

"More? What more? There are no other habitable bodies in this system."

A shake of the head. "Worse . . . worse . . . much worse . . . everything within a hundred light-years. Almost a thousand solar systems."

Harry took his next few strides in stunned silence. He could hope that the goodlife had made it up, just trying to drive her crazy, and succeeding.

She told him: "I'm no astrogator, I'm not sure how many populated worlds lie within that volume. But the goodlife seemed to think there could be as many as a hundred. They named some of them, gloating, and for all I know they were right." Dr. Kochi went on to repeat some of the names that she had heard. "They told me about Meade, and Nisur, and Esmerelda. And—"

"What was that last one?"

"Esmerelda."

Harry walked faster.

Dr. Kochi was still talking, murmuring at least, but Harry wasn't really listening. He was thinking that Twinkler's world-blasting detonation, the stellar explosion that had indirectly caused him to be here, had been a small show indeed compared to what this lady was describing.

He found one hope to cling to. Maybe the goodlife and the bad machines, and their ghastly display inside the cave, had only been describing something they would like to do, not a project actually under way.

But then why had they kept her alive?

Dr. Kochi, ill and exhausted as she was, struggled on with her explanation. "The idea is to carry this mass of antimatter somehow out into space, somehow keeping it intact—carry it, or project it, until it strikes the surface of the pulsar. In that gravity, the velocity of a falling mass will be thousands of kilometers per second . . ."

Her voice was running down, like a tired recording. Some kind of reaction was overtaking her, and she sounded faint. "You've got to . . . tell people . . ."

"Tell them to do what? How can we stop this?"

"I watched them build a kind of vehicle in the cave—really a small spacecraft. They mean to launch it into space from the other side of Maracanda—then propel it into the pulsar somehow.

"And one berserker, a kind of commensal machine, will go with the launch device out into space. Not one of the anthropo-morphic models. Multiple limbs. It can withstand a lot of gravi-ties, manipulate small objects and controls, effect simple repairs. Provide redundancy, in case some of the other systems fail, or are damaged. When they got word of the alert, they had to hurry."

The scientist went on to describe how, as soon as the infernal machine had started down the tunnel on its mission of destruction, the goodlife and the remaining machines had gone out of the cave at the ground-level entrance, headed on a sortie into the nearest town, where they meant to kill and die. At that point, the machine that had tortured her, and all the other berserkers, had totally ignored their prisoner, while the goodlife had hurled their last bitter taunts at her.

"They told me they were going to Tomb Town and Minersville, people and machines alike. The machines just to kill, the goodlife to fight and die, and make sure the badlife all knew what was about to happen. That's what they said. That's what they said."

That outburst had ended on a questioning note, and Harry answered. "That's just what they did. But that's not our problem now."

"Except eventually I realized that they had left one machine to stand guard. Looking out from one side of my cage, I could just see a slice of the cave mouth in the distance—and twice I saw a berserker walk past.

"I thought perhaps that it was running on some timed program, and that after their scheduled time of launch had passed, when there could be no more possible need to question me again— that their sentry would come back into the cave and kill me."

"But it didn't. Now you're safe."

"None of us are safe."

"So, you think it's possible that the time of launch, from this supposed deep cave, has not yet passed."

"Possible, yes. But I fear—"

"Sounds utterly crazy," Harry told the woman hopefully.

Her sunken eyes glittered at him. "I would love to believe you're right, but I know you're not."

"Tell me again. How are they going to get this huge lump of antimatter up into space, from the surface of Maracanda? They can't, we can't, lift off any kind of vehicle through a breakdown zone."

Feebly the woman was shaking her head. "Don't have to. You don't lift off from the habitable surface. Instead you avoid hitting breakdown by burrowing all the way through Maracanda and coming out the other side. In effect, this world's much thinner than any habitable planet."

Harry kept coming up with objections, scrambling for reasons to hope that this was all a fever dream. "That would mean burrowing through hundreds of kilometers of solid rock, wouldn't it?"

She nodded weakly. "In normally dimensioned space, yes. Inside an azlarocean body, there are almost certainly drastic shortcuts. I think they looked for one and found it. They spent months digging."

Until, at a depth of perhaps no more than a hundred meters or so, they had encountered a layer of substance, of the land, that would be very dangerous to penetrate.

The rescued scientist told Harry: "If you go any deeper than that, conditions will swiftly become—well, uninhabitable. The researchers I know who've tried couldn't find any way to protect themselves. Our field generators won't work down there, at least not well enough to compensate for the transverse surges in gravity waves. If we powered the generators up enough to compensate— well, something would have to give way. Our whole little almost-Earth-like zone up at this level would probably evaporate pretty quickly."

Even before he got back to his ship, Harry made an effort to bring his copilot up to speed on what was going on. Lily seemed to take the bad news calmly enough. Harry figured that probably she just didn't quite understand it yet.

It was no longer possible to doubt that Dr. Kochi's nightmare vision was the truth, no longer possible to hope that she was simply deluded in her fear and pain. Harry's first impulse was to find a way to use his ship, to reach the cave with the *Witch*'s weapons, blasting everything inside it. But an impenetrable wall of breakdown zone protected that target from the approach of ship-sized objects.

If the *Witch* was going to play any active role at all in coming events, it would have to be out in space.

Getting her back through the labyrinth, up and out into free space near Port City, must be his first priority. Once there, he could begin to do his best to overtake the berserker vehicle, assuming it had already been launched but had not yet dropped its cargo. If humanity was lucky and the killer device had not been launched, Harry would try to pot it as soon as it appeared. Whether his own ship would survive the comparatively nearby blast of several tons of antimatter, combining with an equal mass of ordinary matter in the form of the berserker vehicle, was something he would find out when it happened.

Harry was thinking that it must have taken the enemy considerable time, probably several years, to get a useful number of reliable goodlife in place on this world where they were wanted. Many of the warped people who chose that road were tried and found wanting, judged to be disastrously undependable and kept on the outer fringes of the group, knowing nothing of its serious projects and inner secrets.

As Harry had more or less expected, he encountered two or three smugglers, lightly armed but suitless, at the foot of his ship's landing ramp. Behind them, the pile of dark bags of grit had grown as tall as a man. At least it was good that no one seemed to be trying to load. This time Bulaboldo was not in sight. Harry vowed that if the fat one was aboard his ship, he would not be there long.

Bulaboldo's people took one look at Harry as he approached and stepped back slightly. They had nothing to say as he carried the former captive up the ramp and through a doorway that opened with perfect timing to receive him.

Lily raised her helmeted head and waved to him from the copilot's chair. When she saw the condition of the woman in Harry's arms, she put the ship on autopilot and jumped up to help.

Meanwhile, the *Witch* acknowledged her master's homecoming with a repeated verse, spoken as usual in tones of elegance:

> *When shall the stars be blown about the sky,*
> *Like the sparks blown out of a smithy, and die?*
> *Surely thine hour has come, thy great wind blows,*
> *Far-off, most secret, and inviolate Rose?*

After a momentary pause, with a sound like modest throat clearing, came the announcement of attribution: "William Butler Yeats, 'The Secret Rose.'"

"Can it," Harry commanded. "Not now." Some day, if he lived long enough, he was going to have to find out what a smithy was.

"Order acknowledged."

As Harry had ordered, the medirobot, a coffinlike receptacle with a glassy lid, had been brought out and installed in the control room, while a couple of chairs had been put away. Lily was quick and gentle, and Emily Kochi seemed to appreciate the presence and touch of another woman as she was being helped immediately into the medirobot. As soon as she was flat on her back, probes like thin snakes appeared and began to seek out several places on her anatomy.

When they had done all they could for Dr. Kochi for the moment, Harry said to his new crew member: "Now may be your last chance to get off the ship; I doubt that I'll be landing at the spaceport. Of course, the way things are, I don't know that you'll be any safer on the ground."

Lily was already back in her copilot's chair. "If you're staying aboard, Harry, then so am I."

Harry said: "Try to make sense. How the hell could I not be staying aboard?" He started to add something to that, but then he broke it off and said: "Right. Put her on autopilot and get her up. Let's see how you work." He was in his own chair, holding his helmet in his lap.

Watching Lily and the *Witch* run the brief checklist, Harry remembered a conversation he'd had with a stranger back in Portal Square at the center of Tomb Town. Looking back at the incident now, he realized he had been talking to an authentic specimen of goodlife.

The goodlife had expressed a feeling of great reverence toward black holes—seeing in them a welcome negation of light and life.

Berserkers and goodlife were both servants of an Infinite Emptiness.

Harry recalled some of that conversation. "Is there a black hole at the heart of everything?"

"At the end of the Galaxy, it will claim everything—everything."

As the *Witch* worked her way back through the smugglers' ingenious maze, a process occupying several minutes, Harry and Lily had time to talk and think.

Now that Emily Kochi was in the medirobot, the pain of her hand already blocked, and food and medicines and fluids already flowing into her bloodstream, she was able to tell them more.

*　　*　　*

Once the berserkers got their super weapon out into space, they would need to exercise great care not to send it accidentally into the path of swiftly moving Ixpuztec. Their work would be wasted then, because any black hole of that class could swallow almost anything. Even a few tons of antimatter would disappear into that maw without provoking so much as a hiccup or belch.

To make sure the packet reached its intended destination, the berserkers would have to work their trick at exactly the right moment in the three-body orbital dance. But probably the right moment repeated every few hours.

Harry had about given up all hope that the woman was totally deluded about the berserkers' plan, flat out of her mind after what she had been through, but he could see no evidence at all to support that comparatively happy conclusion.

And if the berserkers were successful in accomplishing their task today, they were going to wipe out, at the very least, this entire solar system, together with all the ships in nearby space.

That would mean half a million dead, or thereabouts; but that would be only the beginning.

During her months of captivity, Dr. Kochi had heard enough conversation between goodlife and berserkers to understand some of the details of the enemy plan.

She told Harry: "When their vehicle emerges into free space, it'll be on the other side of Maracanda. Believe it or not."

He sighed. "At this point, you can tell me just about anything about this place and I'll believe it."

Goodlife scouts must have carried out the first reconnaissance on Maracanda. Then, playing the part of prospectors and miners, they had claimed land and established the necessary base for digging.

Whether human or machine had been first to realize the possibilities of destruction inherent in the Maracandan system, it was impossible to say. For the killer computers to verify the opportunities available, and then to devise a plan to set the disaster in motion, it had been necessary for a few of the machines to land on the surface and operate clandestinely. The entire project, from early planning to finishing touches, was far too difficult and delicate to be entrusted to mere goodlife, who frequently proved unreliable, sometimes downright treacherous.

So much mining and processing machinery was being brought on world by so many people, that no one took any particular notice of the imports required to dig the necessary tunnel.

Each time Dr. Kochi explained another detail of the enemy's plan, Harry's reaction had been to say, "But that can't possibly work. Can it?"

And each time he got essentially the same response. "I'm afraid it's all too likely that it will. Even if they are compelled to launch before making their final tests, before the precise alignment of the three bodies comes about."

"How come they didn't finish you off before they left?"

"I can only think of one reason . . . because they thought they might have to come back and ask me more questions."

"So what happened when the alert was called? How'd they find out about it? There must have been people in the back country who didn't get the word right away."

Emily Kochi had no reason to suspect that the alert had originally been a fake. She reported that the alarm had actually posed a great threat to the enemy's plans—a pair of goodlife sent on a routine trip to Minersville for supplies came back early, greatly upset and babbling of the news. Confirmation was soon provided by an official messenger, a Paul Revere sent out from Minersville or Tomb Town, pedaling his way through the back country at top speed, alerting all he met.

Some of the goodlife had argued that it was probably only a false alarm, or had been called for practice. But the berserker machine in command of the operation had quickly overruled these optimists, announcing that the operation must go forward at once. All truly essential preparations had been completed.

The berserkers had been concerned that some badlife warship, patrolling through the inner system on alert, would sight their machine and shoot it out of space before it could deliver its deadly cargo to the surface of the neutron star. But conditions in the inner system were such as to make any space combat, in the normal sense, extremely difficult.

Harry had another question. "What does this packet of antimatter, wrapped up in magnetic force, look like? Are we going to know it when we see it?"

"Very difficult to say. Indistinguishable from normal matter, perhaps rock . . . but you won't see it, only the shielding. Otherwise, on the least contact with normal matter, a great explosion . . ."

Dr. Kochi thought it probable that besides the berserkers themselves, only the goodlife, who were willing to take any risk with their own lives and the population of Maracanda, had so far been able to get close enough in the deep mine to look at the antimatter capsules.

It would seem that releasing the packet, separating it from the launch device, would be unnecessary, and also a less reliable delivery method. The plan should work just as well if the launcher, still carrying its awesome burden, simply plunged right into the maelstrom of infalling matter surrounding the pulsar.

Dr. Kochi babbled that several goodlife had volunteered to ride with the burden of destruction on its final trip. What a way to go, knowing you were carrying death to billions of human beings! But the machine had rejected all their pleas. The vehicle lacked any artificial gravity, so the first time a serious acceleration was required, the goodlife would be crushed to pulp or flung off into space, their presence having contributed nothing to the cause. She said: "Most of their digging went on a long way from the cave you saw. But the tunnel between was all in free zone, and I could watch on holostage."

The berserker flyer, mounting a standard drive unit of the type generally used in normal space, probably carried the lump of antimatter in an aft compartment, to minimize the chance of its contacting normal matter and prematurely detonating. It would be necessary to pass at high speed through a thin haze of normal particles when approaching the neutron star. The commensal machine stood by, helping somehow to maintain the necessary shielding.

All of the berserkers that had not gone into space were quickly mobilized for fighting. These were mostly digging machines; Emily thought there were no more than three or four devices designed primarily for fighting, one of these having been detailed to guard the prisoner remaining in the cave.

Harry could picture in his mind's eye what would have happened then: machines concealing themselves in pedicabs, or on freight wagons drawn up to the entrance to the cave. The band of perhaps two dozen goodlife throwing their minds and bodies into the task of secretly hauling berserkers through the intervening kilometers of breakdown zone to the very gates of the nearby towns.

Harry nodded. Except, he thought, for one pedicar load that had scared the smugglers back to their hideout and then had tried unsuccessfully to catch up with Harry and his party.

Reanimated on coming out of breakdown at the gates of Minersville and Tomb Town, the machines had deployed themselves in an all-out attack, intent on the methodical destruction of all life that came within their reach. Whether or not their great space project succeeded, at least some killing would be accomplished.

The goodlife who had served this project faithfully for months were all truly dedicated. Certain that death by hypernova must overtake them in only a few hours, they plunged joyfully into a state of murderous frenzy.

Harry had his own helmet on and was monitoring Lily's work. With the ship running on full autopilot, she kept a close eye on progress, as the *Witch*'s own optelectronic intelligence eased her up and through the mazy free-zone channels that wound their way through breakdown zone. The retreat from east to west followed in precise reverse the charted course that had brought her safely to a landing. With human hesitancy removed from the equation, the return journey was going considerably faster.

TWENTY-FOUR

The *Witch* had clawed herself up into clear space, kilometers away from the highest lobes and tendrils of the invisible breakdown zone. Harry drew a deep breath, rejoicing in the sensation of freedom from all the strangeness that was Maracanda. He was back in a normal, honest world, with the prospect of starting what might be an honest fight, with weapons that could be expected to do their job. He had to call on all his skills, maximize his close relationship with the computers that made up the *Witch*'s crafty and elegant brain. He had to determine at what speed and in which direction he wanted his ship to move. If the murderous berserker device had already been launched, it ought to be somewhere along an orbital curve between Maracanda and the pulsar Avalon.

Half a minute was enough to cure him of the illusion that he and his ship were free of strangeness. Stranger quirks of space-time than any his ship had traveled lay ahead, between the *Witch* and the swiftly moving neutron star.

Maracanda's automated system of robot guides and piloting advice, which generally guided local traffic, had shut down when the alert was called. But Harry's ship's data banks had incorporated an astrogational chart of the entire Maracanda system. That chart now began to blare stern warnings about the course he had just chosen, until Harry commanded the *Witch* to shut down the noise. He didn't doubt the close vicinity of Avalon was a dangerous place to be, but he wanted to get there as quickly as he could.

He and his ship engaged in a brisk and silent thoughtware dialogue, setting the ship on a course that would carry them quickly into the dangerous proximity of the pulsar. Contrary to what Harry would have expected in a normal system, almost continuous corrections were necessary.

Ever since the early stages of the alert, several Space Force ships, along with the Templars' single scout, had been deployed defensively around the habitable body, trying to keep themselves between its people and the expected onslaught from deep space. Harry now hastened to reestablish radio contact with those ships and with the ground facilities at Port City. The *Witch* had emerged from the maze at a spot where it had the broad expanse of the spaceport's cloud cover distantly in sight.

He also ordered an intensive search for any object in-system that could conceivably be a berserker vehicle recently launched from Maracanda.

In a few moments his ship's voice reported that nothing of the kind was visible.

"Keep trying!"

The communications gear had quickly become jammed with incoming messages, the holostage displaying the names and locations of half a dozen senders, all clamoring for a response. Before replying to anyone, Harry passed on an urgent warning to them all, based on what he had seen in the cave and heard from Dr. Kochi.

All of Harry's listeners rejoiced that he and his ship were back among them. As soon as they heard of the surprising rescue he had been able to accomplish, most offered congratulations. But the warning that the pulsar could soon be triggered into going hypernova was less readily accepted.

In a few moments Harry was deep in conversation with General Pike, cruising round Maracanda in a comparatively low orbit. Since shortly after his last talk with Harry, Pike had been hovering in space in his scoutship, more than half expecting that he and his small crew were soon going to die, opposing an overwhelming berserker attack that would come sweeping in from the system's outer reaches.

He and his scoutship crew, like their Space Force counterparts, kept looking outward, into deep space, for an attack that never came.

His first question was "Are my two men there? Teagarden and Zhong?"

"You can get a couple of medals ready, general, but they'll have to be posthumous. They met one real berserker on the ground."

Pike naturally wanted the details, but Harry insisted on first making sure his warning was understood.

Joining them on radio was Dr. Emil Kloskurb, now standing by in Templar headquarters in Port City. Hastily, Harry reported the circumstances of the hidden cave. Then he put Dr. Kochi on line. Speaking from the medirobot, she told her story, delivered her warning, and began to answer questions.

The general expressed suspicions about the way the alert had originally been called. "The first signal came from our distant early warning units, and yet the only place the enemy has actually been seen is on the ground. Does anyone have an explanation for that?"

(And Lily muttered, for her captain's ears alone: "Well, general, you have to remember that this is not a planet.")

All doubt that the alert was justified had vanished long ago; but it still seemed impossible to understand why, following that first ambiguous signal, no enemy machines had been detected in this system's space.

"We're standing guard, of course, and we'll do what we can. But anyone who tries to fight a space battle in the inner portions of this system is going to have the devil's own time doing it."

"How's that?" Harry demanded sharply.

"We run into the difficulty every time we try to conduct maneuvers. Space and time in-system here are never quite what you expect them to be, however much research you do—and not what your gunlaying system expects, either, whatever type you have. To put it simply, you are not likely to hit anything you aim at."

"Are you saying the berserkers won't be able to hit the pulsar when they drop their package?"

"Oh, I've little doubt that they could manage that. But their machine will have to get very close to its target, and there may be some lengthy maneuvering involved."

By now Dr. Kloskurb had spent several hours in Port City, convincing the local authorities that he generally knew what he was talking about. They were listening intently to the scientist as he admitted that he saw no reason why the threat reported by Dr. Kochi and Harry Silver could not be true.

"In calculating the gravitational interactions between Maracanda and other bodies, you can treat it mathematically as if it were a sphere. But when you're working problems on the much smaller scale of ships and launch vehicles, of human bodies if it comes to that, things get much more complicated."

Kloskurb went on to say, "The devastation would go far beyond that caused by any ordinary nova, beyond what happens in the ordinary supernova types. It would reach hypernova status."

Someone else put in: "I thought that hypernovas were only a theory."

"They have been, until now. I don't claim cosmology's really my field, but—"

"Then let's talk to someone who does."

Experts in celestial mechanics were quickly located and brought into the discussion. When they had heard Dr. Kochi's report and warning, none of them were inclined to say that it was fantastic and should be disregarded.

One expressed the consensus: "In theory it would seem impossible to produce a more violent explosion, from any objects of equivalent mass."

No way had ever been found to send electromagnetic signals through flightspace to convey information any faster than solid vessels, ships, or robotic couriers could move in that exotic domain.

When natural disaster threatened on an interstellar scale, as in the case of Twinkler, humanity might enjoy the luxury of decades or even centuries in which to dodge destruction. Death by supernova could move to engulf its victims no faster than light itself. The strain on human time and resources would be enormous, and ragged fleets of refugee ships would provide good hunting for the berserker enemy, but still worlds and systems could be evacuated, whole populations resettled somewhere else. Not all life forms could be carried to safety, and in that the death machines could claim at least partial victory. Ultimately the berserkers' programming committed them to the destruction of all the lower forms of life, just as surely as to the obliteration of humanity.

"But that's not how they usually go about their job. They definitely assign priorities."

"They sure do. If they tend to concentrate their efforts on fighting us, it's because we're about the only life form in the Galaxy who can fight back. We keep interfering with what would otherwise be the neat and efficient pattern of their work. They must compute that once we're out of the way, the rest of the task should be clear sailing."

The most horrific possibility, which about half the assembled experts were ready to accept, was that an explosion of the type now threatened could actually propagate through flightspace. The evacuation time available, even for distant planets, would be reduced to only days, and the possibility of getting out a timely warning to them would be all but eliminated.

While the experts tried to digest the news and come up with a prediction, Harry and Lily were able to listen to reports, relayed through Port City, about the ground fighting still in progress in the east.

In the early stages of the alert, both Pike and Rovaki had successfully dispatched robot interstellar couriers from their respective facilities at the spaceport. The nearest bases of both Templars and Space Force, each only about a day away at c-plus velocities, were informed of the attack and asked for reinforcements. But several days must pass before any help could be expected.

Additional couriers were dispatched at intervals to carry news of the latest developments and updated estimates of enemy strength. The latest of those had been guardedly optimistic. It was even possible to predict an eventual human victory without reinforcement, given the small size of the enemy force and the fact that it included no large fighting machines.

There was no reason to doubt that berserkers could have devised a plan as intricate and cunning as that described by Dr.

Kochi. Some warped goodlife scientist might have been the origi-
nator, or the bad machines might have discovered it indepen-
dently. Berserker computers were certainly capable of organizing
and building complex engineering projects, and even engaging in
scientific research, exercising their indefatigable patience. Their
command units, like the greatest of human generals, were relentless in the pursuit of knowledge of any kind that would help them
to destroy their opposition.

But history suggested that the champions of the cause of
death, like other computer brains, tended to be no better than
second-rate when engaged in pure research. They were all but
incapable of truly insightful discoveries, unable to make the
imaginative leaps that were so important in the thought processes
of human investigators.

In every Maracandan settlement there were some who
believed at first that the alert was only a false alarm. These
scoffers were quickly converted when the machines showed up at
the gates of Minersville.

The great majority of Galactic citizens had never laid eyes
on a real berserker. The number of humans who had seen the real
thing and lived to tell about it was astonishingly small. Even
among combat veterans, very few had sighted the enemy except
as red dots on a holostage. During those periods when people
believed that the alert was genuine, they generally reacted in one
of two ways. A majority of capable adults took up arms, while
others ran screaming into the wilderness.

Despite warnings to the contrary, a good part of the population of Port City, including a number of families with children,
was soon showing up at Maracanda's only spaceport, demanding
to be evacuated. When the attackers were already on the ground,
interplanetary space seemed like the safest place to be. It was hard
to convince these people that all civilian traffic in and out of the

system had been halted for the duration of the emergency—any normal shipping arriving in the early warning area was being warned and shuttled away to other ports.

The mere killing of the local population on this peculiar world had always been only a secondary goal for the berserkers. All their work and planning was intended to get their project of mass destruction launched. They would be more intent on defending their work site than attacking the town.

So far, the most intense fighting was concentrated in and around Minersville. Volunteers from Tomb Town had armed themselves and rushed to Minersville to join the fight.

The Space Force office in Port City announced: "We're sending what help we can by caravan, but it'll take days to get there."

Those who elected to stay and fight dug weapons out of storage or tried to improvise them from tools of mining and construction. They set up roadblocks and other kinds of defensive barricades to block the enemy's entrance to the settlements.

The machines that came against them, a few hours later, rolling out of goodlife pedicars and wagons, went quickly through the barriers or around them. The attack was every bit as fierce as an old warrior might have expected, though carried out by only a handful of machines.

The berserker digging machines, pressed into service as combat units, were powerfully destructive, though comparatively slow in both movement and computation. They were also highly resistant to the small arms fire directed against them by the citizens of Tomb Town.

The main thrust of the berserker advance was directed against the power stations and the recycling plants providing local humanity with food and atmosphere. Their destruction would bring on accumulating disaster in a matter of days. So far, volunteers armed with improvised mines and rockets had succeeded in keeping the enemy from those targets.

Almost all Space Force and Templar weapons on the ground had been concentrated, like their people, in and around Port City. The process of reinforcing the eastern settlements had begun, but would take days to complete, with much of the movement restricted to caravan speeds.

The most intrepid badlife among the citizens of Tomb Town had gallantly gone out against the enemy with inferior weapons, and were already dead. A few looters were playing hide-and-seek with death among the mostly deserted and partially ruined buildings of the town.

So far the enemy had found and uprooted all but one of the eastern telegraph terminals. When the last one went, all direct communication east of the caravanserai would be effectively cut off.

The early reports sent west by the humans under attack had understandably exaggerated the numbers of enemy machines, and of the goodlife auxiliaries, too.

People terrified by the berserkers' immediate presence, or just by rumors of their approach, and running for shelter, at least those who had their wits about them, would seek refuge in the deepest breakdown zone they could find.

Some realized that to survive for a matter of days in breakdown, they would have to bring with them substantial supplies of food and water. Others didn't have that much sense.

People who had access to pedicabs, bicycles, tricycles, or similar vehicles, used them to get out of town, and into breakdown sanctuary. But there weren't enough vehicles available to accommodate the entire population. A few were stolen, a few more hijacked.

*   *   *

The flagship of Commandant Rovaki's miniature fleet was a Space Force craft very similar to General Pike's Templar scoutship. But Pike's colleague and sometime rival was thinking along somewhat different lines.

Rovaki was slow to join in the general radio discussion. When he did, his comments were terse, his questions suspicious. He was still ready to be convinced that somehow Harry Silver was at the bottom of the trouble.

As Pike kept getting garbled reports of events on the surface, he grumbled that the civilians on Maracanda, despite laws and regulations requiring them to do so, had never made any meaningful preparation against a possible berserker attack.

But it was beginning to seem possible that the enemy plan, for anything beyond small-scale assaults on local settlements, had already failed. There was no berserker launch vehicle yet in sight.

Pike had been considering landing his lonely ship again, just long enough to put himself back on the ground, where all the real fighting had been so far. He would delegate command of Templar space operations, such as they were, to a subordinate.

Before doing so he meant to take a close look at the place where, if Silver's and Kochi's warning had any validity, the enemy launch vehicle was scheduled to appear. He would drive his scoutship, at as low an altitude as he could safely manage, over the eastern part of the habitable zone—or over the place where his instruments indicated that zone must be located. But there was nothing to be seen, except the rugose upper surface of the Maracandan "sky," which seemed to offer nothing but destruction to any ship that tried to pass through it; there was nothing to be done, no way to interact directly with the people and events down there on the ground.

At last, sending an electric jolt through all badlife nervous systems, the dreaded enemy did appear.

When the berserker launch vehicle came shooting up out of that peculiar background, it flew past his scoutship before either he or his autopilot could react effectively, coming so close, within a few kilometers, that Pike instinctively recoiled, as from an imminent collision.

"There it is!"

For the moment, Harry thought it wasn't going to be hard to get a good look at the speeding enemy; in this relatively clear space, the berserker had nothing to hide behind. In ominous accordance with Dr. Kochi's warning, it seemed to have lifted off from the middle of Maracanda's uninhabitable region, and was accelerating fiercely out of an environment where even a berserker ought to find survival difficult.

"That's it, our bandit, the gadget Dr. Kochi's been predicting. What else can it be?"

"There's no doubt it's the berserker launcher. And we have to assume it's carrying several tons of antimatter."

"We must stop it, at all costs, before it gets near Avalon."

Everybody knew that already. But it was easier said than done.

Harry quickly realized that it was going to be hard just to get a good look at the thing. The oddities of intervening space imposed an optical distortion that the onboard computers could not seem to filter out. When Harry managed at last to get the *Witch*'s telescopes zeroed in, he noted that everything in this berserker's construction had a crude and awkward look, which was not surprising, since this particular model was not expected to ever make a soft landing anywhere. He enjoyed a brief interval of clear vision in which it was possible to see that it was skeletal. The exposed innards included a small standard drive unit, good for propulsion and maneuver in normal space, but lacking any transluminal capability. Also lacking, in accordance with what Dr.

Kochi had reported, was anything like a cabin or enclosed space for prisoners or goodlife. And no artificial gravity generator. Any fanatic who had managed to get aboard had doubtless already been thrown free or crushed by relentless acceleration.

Where was the antimatter? Somewhere aboard the hurtling vehicle there must be a package the size of a groundcar. At first Harry thought the berserker was carrying its deadly burden forward, supported ahead of it on two skeletal arms. Then, getting a momentarily clearer look, he spotted a massive, boxlike segment, carried in the rear, where it would be shielded from the ceaseless, high-velocity wind of intrasystem particles by the slender shape of the berserker machine itself.

Harry tried to magnify the image of the package, striving for a better look. "That has to be it. It must be carrying the antimatter inside there."

The voice of Dr. Kochi, soothed and drugged as she now was in the medirobot, had a gentle and mellow sound as she confirmed Harry's conclusion. At her request, the *Witch* was giving her as good a view as possible of everything that happened.

Hit that compact package with any kind of weapon, Harry was thinking, and it ought to rupture. Swift interaction with the normal matter of the berserker machine itself ought to cause an explosion that might easily wipe out every spacecraft in the system, but save the human lives on Maracanda by preventing the incalculably greater blast the enemy was trying to achieve.

But hitting the package, or even coming close to the berserker itself, proved to be practically impossible. And if there was no way to get close, there clearly was no way to ram.

Lily's eyes were growing frightened. Off radio, she told Harry; "If you only had one more slug for the c-plus, we might be able to do something."

"If your aunt had a mustache, she might be your uncle."

A cycle of commands and exhortations was now making the

rounds on badlife radio, all of it to little purpose, as far as Harry could see. The crew of every ship in the system could see what had to be done, but doing it was quite a different story.

Rovaki's ship had somehow fallen behind the others in the chase, and presently he was on radio, wondering aloud if this sortie by the enemy with only a single spacecraft was only some kind of a diversion. Rovaki was already almost a radio-minute behind the *Witch*, and Harry didn't bother answering.

The warheads of Space Force and Templar missiles aimed at the berserker were going off like fireworks, nuclear and exotic-matter blasts in a random rapid scattering. So far, none of them had come close enough to have any chance of stopping it. Harry had nothing more to contribute to the barrage. The *Witch* had now entirely used up her modest complement of legal, normal missiles, as well as all the secret c-plus slugs.

A missile from one of the other ships, aimed at the fleeing berserker, came near hitting the *Witch* instead.

After a minute's delay, Pike's voice came crackling back. "We're trying, Silver. But you've got a better start at heading it off than we have. If you can't hit it with a weapon, we don't have much chance. If it comes down to trying something else, that'll be up to you."

"Naturally." Harry didn't feel in the least bit heroic. The way things were working out, they were all going to be dead in the next few minutes anyway. It wouldn't cost anyone in this system anything to try to save a few billion other people.

"What else is there to try?" Lily asked him, speaking privately.

"I suppose he's talking about ramming it. But if we can't even get close enough to hit it with a beam . . ."

The berserker was not going to be doing any c-plus jumping, a tactic almost certainly suicidal here near the heart of this crazy system. Nor were the ships now in pursuit. No computer check was needed to confirm that any ship or machine that tried that trick, out of desperation, would be swiftly eliminated without doing its enemies any harm.

Harry was talking to himself—and to Lily, and to the *Witch*, if either of them cared to listen in. "We don't have to shoot it. We don't have to ram it, in the normal sense. Just touching it, with something, anything, made out of normal matter, ought to be enough."

Avalon was growing larger, in the scope images, and in the cleared ports, too. The stepwise series of concentric orbital shells was actually visible in some wavelengths.

Harry went on radio again. "What am I looking at now? Like rings?"

Someone familiar with the mechanics of the system, most likely Dr. Kochi, watching the proceedings from her berth in the medirobot, explained to Harry that objects in space near this particular pulsar were restricted as to the orbits they were allowed to occupy—almost like electrons orbiting the nucleus of an atom. "It's a form of the Pauli exclusion principle."

"In celestial mechanics? That's crazy."

"I know. But that's how it's going to be when you get very near the star."

TWENTY-FIVE

If the berserker were to release its deadly cargo now, no computer on either side would find it possible to predict just what trajectory the bundle of antimatter might follow. But the enemy would be taking a great risk that all its work and planning would go for nothing.

One definite possibility was that the packet would simply fall back on Maracanda. That would certainly cause catastrophic local destruction, and heavy casualties, but nothing like what the berserkers were trying to achieve. From the purely human, badlife point of view, the best possible outcome, not a very likely one, seemed to be that the deadly bundle would go plunging harmlessly into the black hole.

Harry still had General Pike's lone Templar ship in sight, as well as the several Space Force vessels. All of them were aware of the enemy and doing their best to close with it. Trouble was that all the other human crews, starting from greater distances, were having even less success than Harry.

As soon as the *Witch* had settled into her course, which because of local spacetime distortion turned out to need a correction every few seconds, Harry unlocked his weapon systems. The range was not long by usual gunnery standards, but he was suddenly not confident that he was going to be able to shoot the berserker out of space.

Not only was the *Witch*'s modest magazine out of missiles, after his previous berserker skirmish, but this space was even trickier than it looked, for purposes of gunnery. Harry quickly found that accurate aiming of a beam weapon was impossible. Sighting the target was deceptively easy, but hitting it was another matter.

The berserker craft seemed to be carrying no armament at all, except for its deadly bundle. Maybe the enemy had already computed the uselessness of conventional weapons in this odd space and decided not to bother.

Chasing it, even gaining on it, seemed simple enough, too, but distortion slowed everything down, and Harry was beginning to realize that catching up with his quarry might be as hard as hitting it with a beam or missile.

Harry wondered if the enemy had calculated in advance what size of machine they could optimally use to deliver their payload. Damn them, they had had months, maybe even years, to work out the technical details. Harry and whatever help he could enlist on the spot had only a few minutes.

The berserker craft was now hauling its murderous cargo into the very dangerous zone of spacetime distortion that encompassed both the neutron star and the black hole. So far, it was only on the subtle threshold of that zone. If it were to release its cargo now, the packet of antimatter might take an unacceptably long time to fall into the neutron star—indeed it might miss the intended target altogether, and be swept up, harmlessly, by the grim bulk of advancing Ixpuztec.

As far as Harry could tell, Lily was doing a good job keeping up with everything.

She asked him: "Are we still gaining on it, captain? I can't tell."

"Yeah, but only a kilometer at a time. Not good enough."

The *Witch* would have to get a lot closer to the berserker than she was, if he was going to have any possibility of shooting it out of the sky. And Harry now doubted there would be any chance worth mentioning of doing that, even at point-blank range.

Looking out now through a cleared control-room port, adjusting the window's built-in magnification, Harry had a good view of the black hole coming on, tracing the great invisible figure eight of orbital track it shared with the pulsar Avalon and the brooding mystery called Maracanda. In half a standard hour, allowing as nearly as he could for some elements of local time distortion, Ixpuztec ought to be out of the way, Avalon would have come round the far curve, and the berserker could release its burden with every expectation of hitting the onrushing neutron star.

At last the *Witch* had managed to clear some kind of signal path through all this noise, and a human voice, crackling and delayed, came in on Harry's radio. Pike or Rovaki (the voice was too distorted for Harry to identify) was asking: "Where are all the bandits?"

Harry did his best to transmit a response. "Still only the one bandit. But we've got to stop it."

If the berserker vehicle, still continuously accelerating, could be said to be in orbit around anything, it was none of the system's three principal bodies, but the center of the invisible figure eight, at the moment unoccupied by any of them.

A somewhat garbled voice was coming in on radio from another ship, objecting. "It doesn't look like it's going for the neutron star." The radio signal was distorted; it seemed a wonder that the equipment could bring through the words at all.

Harry was quick to reply. "It may not look that way to you, through the distortion. But I'm closer, and I can see that's what it's doing, no question."

Harry briefly allowed his autopilot to try on its own to maximize the efficiency of the pursuit. But after about thirty seconds, when his instincts told him that wasn't working, he'd turned the pilot completely off, and wasted another half minute before he could be sure that he was doing an even worse job.

At last he'd set the autopilot up in one of its auxiliary modes. Now Harry could intervene in the autopilot's work when he saw fit, while remaining subject to the *Witch*'s own intervention when she saw disaster looming a few seconds away if he kept on with his plan.

He said to Lily: "What we need to get us through this mess is a celestial mechanic—with a big bag of tools."

He was beginning to fear that clearing his viewports, confronting this mad world face to face, might have been a mistake. His pilot's instincts were practically useless in this degree of distortion, and he had to rely on the computers anyway.

They had no good news to impart. To have any chance of success, the *Witch* would have to pass frighteningly close to Ixpuztec, skim in dangerous proximity to the rim of the pit, barely avoiding the point where her engines would no longer be able to pull free of the black hole's monstrous field of influence.

The berserker vehicle seemed to be taking a similar chance. Well then, Harry could do it, too.

When Harry lifted his eyes from the holostage, he saw that Lily was gazing at him.

He asked: "Did you understand what the *Witch* was telling me just now?"

Her chin lifted. "About skimming close to Ixpuztec? It was not good news."

"No, it wasn't. If you're still in a mood for prayer, you might give that a shot."

"If I do pray, it won't be to great Malakó." And the copilot concentrated on her thoughtware again.

Contending with this maelstrom of hard streaks and swirls of dust and gas and radiation, of matter moving at incredible and unreasonable speeds, of actual space warps and mind-bending gravity, Harry thought it would be impossible in any kind of ship simply to set a direct course to the position you wanted to reach, relative to the system's major bodies. The same difficulties that delayed the pursuit were holding the berserker back from accomplishing its deadly plan.

Meanwhile, the Space Force and Templar ships continued their sporadic firing at the berserker with an assortment of weapons. But as far as the instruments on Harry's ship could tell, no part of the barrage was even coming close to the target. Beams slewed sideways unpredictably, like water from a hose, and missiles misfired or simply vanished, God knew where, snatched away like the props of some conjurer on a stage. Had the *Witch* been hit instead of the enemy, it would have been no great surprise to Harry.

In the random intervals when useful radio contact was possible, his allies kept assuring him they were doing all they could, but reminded him that the outcome of the struggle might be up to him. They were all even farther than the *Witch* was from getting into a position where they could hope to somehow come to grips with the enemy.

As for Harry and his ship, the moment of truth was upon them. He said to Lily: "Here we go. Nothing to be done at this point, just enjoy the ride."

The *Witch* was skimming at its closest to the black hole. If it grabbed them, only the instruments would know for the first few minutes. The world around them would still seem relatively sane and normal, the engines would appear to be working with their usual effectiveness.

With the ship in the middle of the close passage, the black hole was hurtling by, the invisible singularity at its heart clutching with tidal gravity at every atom of ship and human body, beginning to shred spacetime itself down to its raw components. The ebony bulk of Ixpuztec was magnified by intervening distortion until it filled half of the insane sky.

"Harry!"

"Yeah, I know. I know, kid. I've got my eyelids clamped tight shut. Close your eyes and hang on."

"I'm afraid to close my eyes."

Now the ship was passing on warnings of threatened power failure, warnings that Harry had no choice but to disregard. For the second and a fraction of time comprising their closest passage to the black hole, almost all the power available from the *Witch*'s engines had to go to keeping spacetime normal inside the hull, battling the tidal effects that would otherwise have already killed everyone aboard.

Lily cried out. Harry had to look. A moment later, he shut his eyes again, to keep out the impression that the flaring flames from ebony Ixpuztec's rim of fire had burned their way into his control room.

And the injured Emily Kochi was screaming, from her berth in the *Witch*'s medirobot. Lily was saying something to her, trying to be reassuring.

Harry forced himself to count slowly to ten, then opened his eyes again. All of his cabin furniture was still in place, despite his instinctive sense of recent havoc. He had lost sight of the enemy, but the *Witch* had not. There on the holostage rode the berserker craft's neat image, still carrying its world-ending burden.

*   *   *

Lily, the terror in her voice gamely reined in, was talking to him again from the copilot's chair, offering to do whatever she could, even wearing the gunner's helmet, but Harry had decided that in the circumstances, that was only a useless distraction.

"We haven't got anything else to throw . . . Wait a minute."

Now inspiration came. Or maybe it was only the kind of thing that could pass for inspiration when your brain had just been stretched by tidal forces.

Harry said, as much to himself as to his copilot: "I do still have six crates of cargo—all unpaid for. If we jettison them one container at a time, they may move faster than this ship can move, here in this space."

It was worth a try. At this point, anything was worth a try. A string of quick orders to the *Witch*, and the process was under way.

Harry was counting. "There they go . . . three . . . four . . . five . . ."

Together, he and Lily watched the procession of boxes exit the cargo bay, hoping that one of these improvised missiles would hit the magnetic packaging and spill antimatter prematurely all over the middle of the Maracanda system.

It proved to be a forlorn and futile effort. The crates moved on ahead of the *Witch* just as Harry had hoped, but then went sailing wide of their intended target, vanishing with the same finality as the missiles had.

Anyway, dumping out the cargo would at least lighten ship. Harry could draw faint comfort from the fact that his jettisoned cargo might appear to the berserker as some new form of weapon, and it could serve as such, if gravitational anomalies were sending the crates hurtling toward the enemy at many kilometers per second.

But the unaimed missiles were no more effective than any

of the sophisticated ones that were supposed to be precisely guided.

Immediately after the sixth crate left the ship, Harry took note of the fact that one more object, totally unexpected, also came flying out of the cargo bay.

"What in all the glorious hells was *that*?"

Lily said, "It looked like a—a bag of something. Didn't it?"

Harry pounded a fist on a chair arm. To the *Witch* he snarled, "You didn't tell me we had that crap on board!"

His ship's voice was as unperturbed as ever. "That is correct. It seemed to me that other matters took priority, and that distractions of any kind ought to be minimized."

When he faced Lily with the same question in his gaze, her nerves throbbed, and it was almost like he was charging her with murder. She shrieked: "I didn't know! Bulaboldo and one of his people came on board while you were gone. I heard you give them permission to do that. Kul came in here and talked to me. I must have lost track of the other man, what he was doing."

The bag of stuff was gone now, as utterly out of sight and useless as everything else they had unloaded. But they had gained a little more ground on the enemy. Harry could get a slightly better look at the berserker. Nothing that he could see offered any encouragement.

From the haggard look Lily was wearing, he thought she might be just beginning to understand that they were going to die. But all she said was "Harry. I'm sorry I let you down."

For a moment he didn't remember. "What?"

"About the grit. Letting them bring it on board."

"Never mind that now. It doesn't matter."

"Can I do anything?"

"I'll let you know, kid. It seems we can't shoot the thing, so I'll have to try something else."

The *Witch* kept incrementally gaining ground, gaining space.

Both objects were in comparatively tight orbits round the neutron star, but Harry's ship was one turn higher, in the unique stepwise system of Pauli orbits. The best measurement Harry could make, somewhat unreliable, assured him they were less than a hundred kilometers from the berserker, and somehow locked in step with it, even though their orbits were at different altitudes above the star. But the distance might as well have been a hundred light-years.

He said again, "If we can't get close enough to shoot it, we certainly aren't going to get close enough to ram."

But . . .

The boxes and the bag of stuff had moved ahead, like dropped bombs in front of an airplane. Working quickly with his thoughtware again, he soon confirmed that the problem of speed in this strange space was mainly one of size.

The *Witch*, built on a somewhat larger scale than the berserker, was too bulky to go directly from one turn of the spiral to another, to catch up with her enemy directly. When Harry began an attempt to force his ship across the gap between turns he was quickly compelled to abort the maneuver, seeing and feeling his vessel about to be hurled into a helpless spin that might either propel it free of the system altogether, smash it back like a meteor into the strangeness of Maracanda, or fling it right into the unbreakable grip of Ixpuztec.

A moment later, Harry was telling his copilot: "A smaller ship, a smaller shape, might do it. In fact, that's the only way. I'm going to try to shoot the gap in the lifeboat."

"What can I do?" Lily asked again.

"Just what you're doing. The *Witch* is going to need help. Any competent human pilot is better than none, at this stage, as long as you don't go crazy."

"I've had a lot of practice in not going crazy." She paused. "Does your lifeboat have any weapons?"

"Whatever I can manage to carry aboard." Harry went on:
"Hold the helm, let the autopilot keep working on centimetering
us closer. Once I'm out in the lifeboat, keep an eye open for the
boat, just in case I do manage to get back—and the other eye on
the berserker, just in case."

"You'll keep radio contact?"

"I'll try."

All he could think of at the moment was to try to ram the
enemy with the lifeboat. But no one could tell what might happen
in this crazy place, and he intended to bring his carbine with him.
Suppose the boat also turned out to be too big, as the *Witch*
implied might very well be the case? What would be his next step
after that?

For the second stage, a man in a spacesuit might be adequately small.

"Oh, Harry." As if she could be somehow reading his mind.

He said to Lily: "You've got the helm now. Do the best you
can. No, don't look at me like that. Playing hero has nothing to do
with it. It's just that if someone doesn't stop that thing in the next
twenty minutes, about a billion of us are all dead anyway."

TWENTY-SIX

"**Y**eah. Yeah!" It was a cry of joy.

Harry, at the controls of the *Witch*'s compact single lifeboat, had just ejected from his ship, and could already see plain confirmation that the smaller shape was going to make a great deal of difference. In less than a minute he had got notably nearer to the berserker, even though the lifeboat's little engine was no powerhouse. Yes, he was gaining ground—more accurately, cutting through distorted space, where the orbits of objects round a star came to resemble those of electrons round an atomic nucleus.

Very soon he would have moved a whole orbital ring inward, approximately halving the distance to his target. Things were going very well. Except that some of the local distortion seemed to have invaded the small boat's tiny cabin.

Space distortion hell, no, this was something worse. He mouthed murderous profanity.

Lily's voice, anxious, said: "What is it, Harry?"

"More of Bulaboldo's shit! He or his people got into this boat somehow!"

It was plain what had happened. When the smugglers had boarded the ship in Harry's absence, they had used the lifeboat as a hiding place for more bags of the cargo Harry had refused to carry. Some of the damned stuff had spilled, and some got on Harry's suit. Again he had an impression of small, hard particles, wrapped up in flowing goo.

As long as he was in his suit, he could breathe in safety, the drug wasn't going to be an immediate problem. In another minute he had worked his way close enough to the berserker vehicle, reducing the range to only about ten kilometers, to see it clearly with only modest optical help.

He had gained on his enemy by one full ring, in this crazy system of quantified orbits. But there was still one more ring to go, he thought. Suddenly there came an extra flash of light from up ahead, and Harry had the impression that the berserker craft was firing some kind of weapon at him. He couldn't be sure, with all the natural flaring and fireworks that grew up in this strange space like weeds. But probably the flashing was more distant; it came again, followed swiftly by effects sounding like nearby missile detonations, hammering wavefronts of radiation against his little hull. Anyway, Dr. Kochi had said the enemy mounted no weapons. And even if it did, berserker gunnery shouldn't have any better success here than the kind where human thought waves pulled the trigger.

Only one more orbital notch to descend, one kilometer of effective distance to be gained; but his gauges were no longer showing any progress. In frustration Harry pounded an armored fist on the controls of the lifeboat's feeble drive. That didn't help.

The lifeboat had taken him as far and as fast as it could, and now he would have to find another way. Somehow, he felt no surprise, but only a sense of the inevitable.

For this outing Harry had of course chosen to wear his heavy armor, with a miniature fusion lamp in its backpack to give him power, and small jets for maneuvering in space. The suit was also equipped with a compact system for recycling air. This would not be the first time he had relied on it to keep him alive in space.

It only made sense to keep his fellow human beings informed, as best he could, of what was going on.

"Lily, I'm leaving the boat here, going out in my suit. That's the only card I've got left to play."

"I read you." Lily's voice showed a quaver, but obviously she'd been expecting to hear something of the kind. "I'll pass on your message when I can."

A minute later, Harry had left the boat. Carbine clamped on his suit's right shoulder, he went headfirst out the little hatchway half expecting to be swept away, caught up in the great wind from that crazy poem, the blast that blew the stars around like sparks from a smithy, which he kept visualizing as some kind of primitive communal fire.

But there was no great wind, not yet, only the insane displays that might not drive him crazy as long as he stuck to business and refused to look at them. He was flying alone in the maelstrom, and he wanted very much, even more than when he had been in the control room, to close his eyes. But the job he had to do would not allow that.

Quickly he discovered he could indeed make headway with his suit's little maneuvering jets. Power did not count for much in this environment, but smallness evidently did. He was swiftly sinking to the next lowest orbital ring—how many there might be altogether he could not guess—catching up with the murderous machine. Harry could see the berserker much more clearly now, a long, thin cylinder that was mostly open framework. If it was of a size to snugly fit that tunnel in the cave, then he must have closed to within about a hundred meters of it.

Minute by minute, that distance shrank.

He was certain, somehow, that the enemy must be able to see him coming, though he had no evidence that the launch vehicle, built under strange conditions to do one simple and straightforward job, was equipped with sensors that could pick up a sneaking human. But there was the communal machine that Dr. Kochi had described, which had sounded like a kind of combination guard and maintenance robot. A thing like that would certainly be equipped with senses, with powerful limbs and small but nasty grippers, maybe with other devices that could serve as weapons. It would see him coming, and then it would do its best to shoot him, or melt him down, to crush him to a pulp, armor and all, or shred him into little fragments, like the tidal grip of Ixpuztec.

Now Harry was so close to the berserker, he estimated only about ten meters, that the last trivial veil of distortion seemed to have fallen away, and he could see it clearly. Hope leaped up again. He reminded himself that this was a stripped-down, specialized model, constructed out of kit parts, by crazed goodlife in a cave. The prisoner might have been wrong about the robot riding with it. So it might well have no way of dealing with such an audacious invasion.

One ominous aspect coming into clear view was a huge gripper device, mounted forward. That was something Dr. Kochi had somehow neglected to mention. Probably it was what the thing had used to drag itself through the tunnel.

And there at the rear, where it had been vaguely visible from a distance, was the solid box that must enclose the magnetic wrapping, which in turn was required to sheath the antimatter from all contact with the normal world.

Letting his gaze slide forward along the framework, Harry knew a sudden chilling, an inner emptiness. Emily Kochi had been right after all. Halfway along the big berserker's length, motionless as a crouching spider but plain to see—there was really no place for it to hide—was the extra machine that she had warned him of. It looked to be about the size of a man, but of a very different shape, with limbs enough to wrestle an octopus on equal terms.

Harry had no doubt at all that it saw him coming and was standing by to repel boarders.

Fiddling with his suit's little maneuvering jets, Harry slightly altered course, heading first toward the enemy's prow. When the small machine scrambled quickly to intercept him there, he waited until it was almost at the prow, then sent his suited body as quickly as possible back toward the stern.

Moving with unnerving speed, the metal spider reversed its progress, too, clambering swiftly back along the framework to anticipate his landing.

Hoping at least to avoid running right into it, Harry tried another swerve at the last moment, a dodge that brought him in contact with the framework of heavy metal about amidships, with the spider still far aft. Setting the carbine in alphatrigger mode, just as he had during the duel before the cave, Harry fired blast after blast against the payload box, with no visible effect. Meanwhile the spider, evidently lacking any projectile weapons of its own, had moved to the far side of the long framework, where it came scuttling toward him.

Quickly Harry switched his aim, letting go another small barrage. Inevitably, most of his force packets spent themselves, in vain, against the heavy framework of the long machine. But one passed through the interstices between girders and deprived the spider monster of a leg. Another tore off a chunk of its midsection. Still moving with deadly speed, the thing came leaping at Harry from one side, and grabbed his carbine by the stubby muzzle. The weapon was still clamped to his helmet, and momentarily he had the feeling that his helmet was going to be wrenched off, with his head inside. Instinctively he grabbed with both hands for the berserker's arm. The servo power of his suit allowed him to almost match its strength, and after a timeless moment of straining struggle, he was able to slide away.

Clinging to a framework girder with one hand, he felt with the other for his carbine. The weapon was a ruin now, the barrel sharply bent. Harry released the clamp and shoved the useless junk out of his way.

Where had the wounded spider gone? He quickly decided that about the only place it could be hiding was aft, behind the heavily armored box. Doubtless it had retreated there, because defending that would be its top priority. It must be lurking, watching, saving itself to leap at him at the last moment, if he should come up with some new weapon.

The spider evidently didn't realize that it had totally stripped him of his armament, deprived him of his last hope of getting at the antimatter. And Harry knew that one more bout of wrestling with the spider would be likely to finish him off.

But the enemy was not so confident, and it needed to take no more chances. The spider didn't have to kill him, to win the game. All it had to do was keep him motionless as the final minutes and seconds ticked down toward the end.

He couldn't reach the antimatter. But there might be one more chance.

Turning around, Harry clambered forward, making sure he had a tight grip with every move. Any little twitch of the launch vehicle would probably shake him loose, treat him to a slow death in a long orbit, even if something went wrong with its main plan and he survived the coming blast. The berserker vehicle could have rid itself of him by that means at any time since his arrival. But, short of absolute compulsion, it wasn't going to twitch. Because it was now tracking through the last minutes, maybe the last seconds, of the run to the precisely calculated point where it would drop its bomb.

Feeling nakedly disarmed, and knowing full well that the spider might, after all, be creeping up behind him, Harry kept moving forward along the framework of girders. Somewhere up here must be the drive, and also the guidance mechanism. Conceivably there was a weak point where he could get at one or the other.

Two-thirds of the way toward the nose of the machine, he came to a flat surface, dark even in the glare of Avalon. Built into the surface was a large niche, and inside the niche seemed a very likely place to search. He would be looking for some kind of structure, housing a vital part. Maybe he could even find something recognizable as an access panel.

Harry's groping arm and peering eyes found nothing of the kind. There was only a strangely familiar rounded shape that made the saboteur recoil momentarily. Then he saw that it was a spacesuit, wedged and strapped into the recess.

Harry hung there for a few seconds, celestial glories blurring overhead and underfoot, before he understood just what he had discovered. He was looking at the dead body of some ultrafanatical goodlife, one who wore a spacesuit of an older model, much inferior to Harry's. Strapped on outside the suit was a crude belt pouch. A lightweight pistol, as useless to Harry in his present situation as it had been to the goodlife, was holstered at the figure's side.

Somehow he (or she—though the glare of Avalon shone in through the faceplate during one segment of the vehicle's slow axial rotation, it was no longer possible to tell) had defied the metal master in the cave and contrived to come along, seeking death in this way as a special honor, disregarding such niceties as life-support systems and artificial gravity. The inevitable result had been that tidal forces or acceleration had already crushed the organs and broken the bones of the living body inside the suit. Undoubtedly the berserker would like to do the same to Harry. But just completing the bombing run would efficiently take care of him, and maybe a billion others.

Harry hesitated, his thoughts racing. Did the spider even sense that this corpse was here? Probably it knew, and was simply ignoring the object's presence, knowing that the pistol at its belt was too feeble a weapon to do a berserker damage.

The belt pouch. What else would a fanatic goodlife be likely to be carrying on his or her last sortie against the universe?

Thrusting an armored hand into the old-style ammo pouch, Harry found two solid, fist-sized lumps. A couple of grenades— old-style drillbombs, obsolescent and crude by the latest ordnance standards, but still effective. In the hands of a goodlife such weapons would be contraband; berserkers never wanted to trust their helpers with anything that could be turned against the machines themselves. But these were special circumstances; and this particular helper would not have dreamed of any such rebellion.

Unconsciously shifting to a private mode of speech, and cutting off his radio, Harry put his helmet close to the other one, and whispered to the shapeless mass inside: "Thanks, pal. I'll never let anyone tell me that fanatics do no good."

Then he drew a deep breath and moved.

Backing out of the recess, Harry turned and headed aft again. When he had scrambled a few meters, and judged his distance, he hurled one drillbomb ahead of him, with all the strength and velocity that a skilled user could get from a servo arm. He aimed straight for the middle of the flat surface of the armored antimatter box. The missile was only a fraction of a second from impact, when the crippled berserker spider jumped out of conceal-ment to get its own body in front of it. A moment later, grenade and spider had vanished together in a spray of metal fragments.

One grenade was left, one chance, and Harry wasn't going to gamble with it against the fortified box that the packets from his carbine hadn't even scratched. Working his way forward, the single remaining drillbomb in hand, Harry twice had to dodge the huge gripper that the berserker launch device wielded. It looked immensely powerful, but, fortunately, it was just a little slow.

A moment later, moving forward again along the girdered skeleton, pushing recklessly in among machinery that would probably be trying to electrocute him, or administer a lethal dose of radiation, Harry located a bulging, shielded unit centered in the cage of framework. To Harry his discovery looked more like a housing for the guidance mechanism than for the drive, but he would settle for either one. It was protected with a tough cover, yes, but he could gamble that this one would not be tough enough.

With a brief and confused thought of saying goodbye to everything, he slapped the drillbomb home.

The fury of the controlled explosion, focused into a molten, armor-piercing jet, was channeled in the direction of the slapping impact, away from Harry's impelling, suited hand.

But he felt the result right through the soles of his armored boots, braced as they were against a beam. In the next moment the whole berserker vehicle lurched violently, twisting itself out of its planned orbit. It went shooting upward, away from Avalon, and in moments it had lost an entire orbital lap, fallen hopelessly off course in its pursuit of the exactly proper launching position. Now the berserker would need more time to regain the exact position that it wanted.

If it had any chance of doing that at all.

The lurching acceleration did not exactly take Harry unawares, but there was nothing he could do about it. The sudden change of direction exerted only a few gravities of force, but those were easily enough to whiplash him away from the convulsing metal.

The large berserker was seriously disoriented, but not dead. Even as Harry's body flew free, the swinging gripper struck at him. It was not quite fast enough to clamp him in its jaws as he flew by. His suited body continued hurtling through space at a fantastic orbital speed, while at the same time drifting slowly outward, upward, away from blazing Avalon, on a rising curve that would soon carry him back and through the level where he had left the lifeboat.

The whole launch vehicle, dislodged from its inner orbit, was rising, as was Harry, like a giant cork in water, gaining speed. He'd hit it hard and hurt it seriously, in its guidance system or its memory. But whether the machine was still following a plan, or only homing on a target of opportunity, it was coming after the one human being it had in sight. And it was starting to catch up.

Deprived of a billion lives or more, a berserker will methodically and unemotionally accept the next best opportunity, and take whatever number it can get. In this case, one.

Harry's lifeboat must have been somehow tracking him, too, keeping itself as near to him as possible, and now it came hurtling toward him, falling like some damned demon from the upper reaches of this impossible space. The boat flashed near him and away again at bullet-speed, as Harry shot helplessly past, climbing slightly out of the grip of Avalon, rising toward the next higher orbital ring, the one in which the *Witch* herself still traveled.

Looking round, he discovered to his horror that the launch vehicle was still with him, bearing down on him at tens of meters per second, giant gripper poised to grab and crunch him at its leisure.

*   *   *

The neutron star had suddenly lurched away, with the speed of a stage illusion. Some trick, Harry supposed, of that crazy Pauli exclusion business, sharply altering his orbit, and the berserker's, too. In place of Avalon here came Ixpuztec, speeding toward their common perihelion, the point where the two extravagantly massive bodies passed closest to each other.

And in the same moment, Lily's radio voice came through: *Harry, I'm coming. Goodbye Harry.*

Under what might have been a thousand gravities of acceleration, the *Witch*, with Lily still at the controls, was only a streak. But the crash of Harry's ship into his pursuing enemy was spectacular, destruction dancing in pure silence in the depths of space.

Harry got one clear look at the magnetic package of antimatter, still unruptured, flying free from its broken box. A moment later it had melded into the rest of the debris, forming one bright streak. A streak that moved as fast as the darting curve of some graphics line drawn on a holostage, headed, not for the pulsar, but in the direction of the swiftly approaching black hole.

Tons of antimatter, and many tons of normal matter in the *Witch* . . . the joining of matter and antimatter must have produced a mindbending explosion. But that sprang into life only at a safe distance, far enough down the gravitational well that its results were all drawn into the maelstrom.

The ship was gone, her voice still there, faintly echoing, ringing in the void: *Goodbye, Harry.*

Avalon rolled on, its surface untouched, as serene as that of a hungry pulsar could ever be.

Much nearer, berserker and ship had utterly evaporated, blurred into one bright smear. The detonation of a bomb that might have killed a billion humans, but in fact took with it only one berserker and one ship. Harry's *Witch*, along with every living thing aboard, humans and bacteria all melded together in the bright streak of the blast. Matter and antimatter squeezed into one bundle, never mind if they should be compelled to explode. The blur would be moving at the speed of light when it went through the black hole's event horizon. Once caught in the full grip of Ixpuztec, even the unadulterated fury of an antimatter explosion was crushed and quenched, frozen like a bug in amber, embedded in the soon-to-be-infinite distortion of spacetime that went swirling away, perpetually vanishing into the guts of the ultimate abyss.

Goodbye, Harry. Only a technical echoing, but it sounded as if Lily could still be saying it again, even out of the pure hell of the great blast, as she went down. No human being in the history of the Galaxy had ever gone down farther, faster, than she was falling now.

Her last cry, as she neared the event horizon, would never stop sounding—in the perception of an outside observer, time down there on the rind of Ixpuztec appeared to die entirely. But each iteration of the signal would be fainter, and of longer wavelength. In only a minute or two of Harry's time the frequency would have dropped out of his radio's range, and the volume diminished to the point where no instrument would ever be able to pick it up.

But Harry Silver knew that he would never cease to hear that sound.

Goodbye, Harry.

TWENTY-SEVEN

Harry was looking around.

Ixpuztec had rushed on its way, taking with it a trivial amount of recently ingested mass.

But the pulsar was once more comparatively close. A long way below the suited man, at the center of whatever convoluted orbital path his body was now following, Avalon still rolled on about its business, gobbling megatons of infalling dust and gas, not in the least perturbed by whatever nearby antics some microscopic beings and machines might be up to.

When Harry's suit's faceplate adjusted itself to filter out most of the glare from the hungry neutron star, he could just make out a tiny object moving uphill against the distant streaks of glory, and the more distant stars beyond—here came his lifeboat, still on autopilot, clawing itself up out of the well after him. Tracking down suited human bodies in strange spaces was one of the jobs at which lifeboats had been designed to excel.

Still Harry kept looking around. After a time it dawned on him that he must be still trying to spot his ship—some part of his mind was unwilling to concede that the *Witch* was gone, taking with her Dr. Kochi and the medirobot.

And Lily, too.

And Lily.

He hung there in his orbit numbly, watching the lifeboat slow down as it approached him, not thinking much, not trying to move. His body seemed to have come through this last fight virtually unharmed, though for some reason his ears were ringing. At some point he became aware that his little suit communicator was overhearing a radio conversation, among people who were sure that he was dead. People in other ships, friends and foes, who were now ready to swear, quite accurately, that they had seen his ship destroyed.

The little thrustors on Harry's suit still worked—one of them did, anyway, and that was enough to get him going. With a little practice, he found that he could even get himself moving in the right direction, toward his approaching boat. He thought a little time might pass before someone on some other ship noticed the cruising lifeboat, and started to untangle its automatic distress signal from the howling background noise.

Harry drifted, watching the boat get closer, and pondering how strange it was that he was still alive. What an infinite gift someone had given him. Even as he thought things over, and almost without realizing it, he was working the little technical routine that allowed him to bring one of his arms in from its spacesuit arm, and reach into a pocket of his inner coveralls. Extracting a small object, he worked another little trick that let him pass it out through his spacesuit, where his gloved hand waited carefully to receive it.

By now people on and near Maracanda were beginning to realize the dimensions of the disaster that their world had just escaped. Their first comments were coming through on radio. Some of the scientists down on the habitable surface were awed at even the best-case scenario, had the antimatter gone where the berserkers wanted it: a gamma ray burster that over the next hundred standard years or so would have sterilized a thousand systems scattered over hundreds of cubic light-years—not a major event in the Galaxy's existence, affecting not much more than one millionth of its volume. But of supreme importance to certain living things. Experts on the ground in Port City, refining their calculations, had come up with some chilling scenarios, speculating on the creation of dark antimatter, and the creation of an antineutron star, had the berserkers had their way.

But Harry was no longer listening. Holding the little message cube in armored fingers, he turned it on.

Floating in space beside him there appeared the holographic ghost image of a narrow-shouldered young woman. She was sitting up in a bed, her body supported and half covered by large hospital pillows, holding a baby to her breast. The diapered infant was very small, and still had that unfinished newborn look. Its head was fringed with dark hair, disorganized and short.

Some aspect of the recent turmoil in space must have affected the message cube's presentation of its image, so when Becky materialized, she was upside down from Harry's point of view. But he wasn't going to complain.

Her partially revealed body looked frail, as it so often did, making Harry marvel that sometimes it could be so tough. If you looked at her dispassionately—not that Harry could—Becky had never been a tremendous beauty. And childbirth, in the very-nearly natural mode, was not the finest beauty treatment.

But no woman had ever looked better to Harry than this one did right now.

He had to fiddle briefly with his suit's communicator before he could hear what she was saying, drifting out there in the cold vacuum just about an arm's length away. But then her soft, familiar, and beloved voice came through.

". . . gods and spirits, Harry . . ."

Becky paused, running the fingers of one hand through her hair, a familiar gesture. The hair was indeed a different color, and curlier, than Harry remembered from a few months ago. That was one thing about his girl that she was always changing.

"Hi, Harry—Hi, *Daddy*, I should say. Gee, we can call you Daddy now. See who's here with me?" She slightly jiggled the tiny bundle in her arms. "Look at him, just look at him, the little . . .

"Everything went well, the doctors were right, it was best in our case not to go with the artificial womb.

"Little Ethan's fine and healthy. Oh, look, see the way he waves his hand? He's waving to his Daddy, aren't you, sweetheart? And I'm fine, too, just kind of sore. Look at him nurse. We're both so anxious for you to finish peddling your machines and get home from your silly business trip. We don't care whether it makes you rich or not. We just want you home, so you can be with us. Right, Ethan? Tell Daddy you want him back on Esmerelda."

Ethan was intent on his own business.

The robotic lifeboat had kept homing in on Harry steadily, and it was getting very close. Harry had to fold up the woman and her baby and put them back in his pocket, so that he could concentrate on the next task.

In another minute Harry was settled in the lifeboat, ordering its expert autopilot to cruise him back to Maracanda's one and only spaceport. The trip would take a good many hours, unless someone came in a real ship and picked him up, which he supposed was likely. He wanted to take off his heavy helmet, but if he did, he would have to breathe lifeboat air, sniffing Bulaboldo's spilled drugs. He should probably flush the cabin air out thoroughly, before his rescuers arrived.

It seemed that he had slept, or passed out, for a short time. The keep-you-going stuff that he had dosed himself with back in Port City must be starting to wear off. What woke him was the next voice coming on the boat's radio. A gauge told Harry he was less than a light-minute from Maracanda now.

The voice was indeed Bulaboldo's, who seemed to be bearing up well under the impact of his secret financial losses: After offering effusive congratulations, he reminded Harry obliquely that there was a little bonus benefit associated with the loss of his ship.

"Well, as you know, old sock, there are all the problems that old ships accumulate. At least you'll now be free of those."

"The what? Oh, yeah." Bulaboldo of course was sending a hint of felicitations on Harry's being rid of the c-plus cannon and its associated problems.

"Did you know, old thing, that at first you were reported missing, and then you were presumed dead?"

Harry reacted quickly. "Well, squash that! At least keep it in system. Don't let it get out on the interstellar news. No use scaring anybody."

"Of course, old chap. I'll see what I can do. And by the way, things have also worked out rather well for yours truly."

"Oh?"

"May I quote from a very recent dispatch? It names me as 'a prominent Maracandan miner and philanthropist,' and goes on to credit your humble servant with great cleverness in discovering the berserker presence and finding a way to trigger an alarm—certain details are being withheld for security reasons—thereby alerting Port City to the berserker presence on this world."

"So. You probably wrote that yourself."

"Of course I wouldn't want to claim more credit than I'm due . . ." Bulaboldo's voice went on. He was enjoying this.

With no trace left of any of Harry's ship, or its cargo either, he saw no point in reporting to anyone the fact that someone had stuffed a few containers of grit into the *Witch*'s hold.

Kul went on to inform his listener that the first elements of relief forces were now in system. Strong ground forces would soon be landed, and the berserkers still active in the eastern section of the habitable zone would be hunted down and destroyed.

At first the reports of the number of willing, active goodlife were greatly exaggerated; when it came to an actual body count, no more than twenty-two had so far been tallied. And it seemed that there had never been any more than about a dozen machines, a majority of them still active.

And then, without warning, Alan Gunnlod was suddenly on the communicator.

"I hear you did a great job up there, Silver. All we're getting down here is garbled reports from distant observers, but it sounds like you performed some real heroics." The prospective prospector sounded elated. "I took a chance, when things looked iffy and other people were getting scared about Maracandan property values. I was able to sign a great land contract. But I'm still going to need capital. Is Lily all right?"

Harry thought a moment. Then he reached for a manual switch and severed the radio connection.

"She's great," he told the silent equipment, after contact had been broken. "She's absolutely great."

At that moment Harry discovered in himself an urgent need to think of something else. He was having some kind of reaction that left his vision blurred, and to deal with the problem he reached into his pocket, groping for a message that he couldn't wait to see and hear again.